Under the Summer Moon

Praise for *Desert Fire, Mountian Rain*

"Another excellent book by Amy Schisler. Well researched, gripping story. Anxiously await the next book in the Buffalo Springs series."

Amazon Reviewer

"This book did not disappoint. I love how Amy writes, so heartfelt, twists and turns to keep people real and engaging, short chapters that allow me to read a little, even for 5 minutes, and a great story that makes me want more. Great characters that work together to make a small town better for all."

Rose E, Guyther, Amazon Reviewer

Praise for Award-Winning, *Island of Miracles*

"A beautiful account of the love and healing support of community!"

Chandi Owen, Author

"I can already see the Hallmark Channel movie!"

Anne, Goodreads

Praise for Award-Winning, *Island of Promise*

"[Amy] draws you in to the lives of her characters…she paints the picture so eloquently it's almost like you are there."

Cindy, Amazon

"I love Amy Schisler's books. I cried tears of both sadness and joy while reading this. I read this book in a day!"

Mitzi Mead, Goodreads

Praise for Award-Winning, *Whispering Vines*

"The heartbreaking, endearing, charming, and romantic scenes will surely inveigle you to keep reading."

Serious Reading Book Review

"Schisler's writing is a verbal masterpiece of art."

Alexa Jacobs, Author & President of Maryland Romance Writers

Also Available by Amy Schisler

Novels

A Place to Call Home

Picture Me

Summer's Squall

The Devil's Fortune

Whispering Vines and sequel *The Good Wine*

Buffalo Springs

Desert Fire, Mountain Rain

Under the Summer Moon

Chincoteague Island Trilogy

Island of Miracles

Island of Promise

Island of Hope

Buffalo Springs Stories

Desert Fire, Mountain Rain

Children's Books

Crabbing With Granddad

The Greatest Gift

Spiritual Books

Stations of the Cross Meditations for Moms (with Anne Kennedy, Susan Anthony, Chandi Owen, and Wendy Clark)

A Devotional Alphabet

Under the Summer Moon

By Amy Schisler

Chesapeake Sunrise Publishing
Bozman, Maryland

Chesapeake Sunrise Publishing

ISBN-13: 978-1-7346907-8-1

Published by:
Chesapeake Sunrise Publishing
Amy Schisler
Bozman, MD
2020

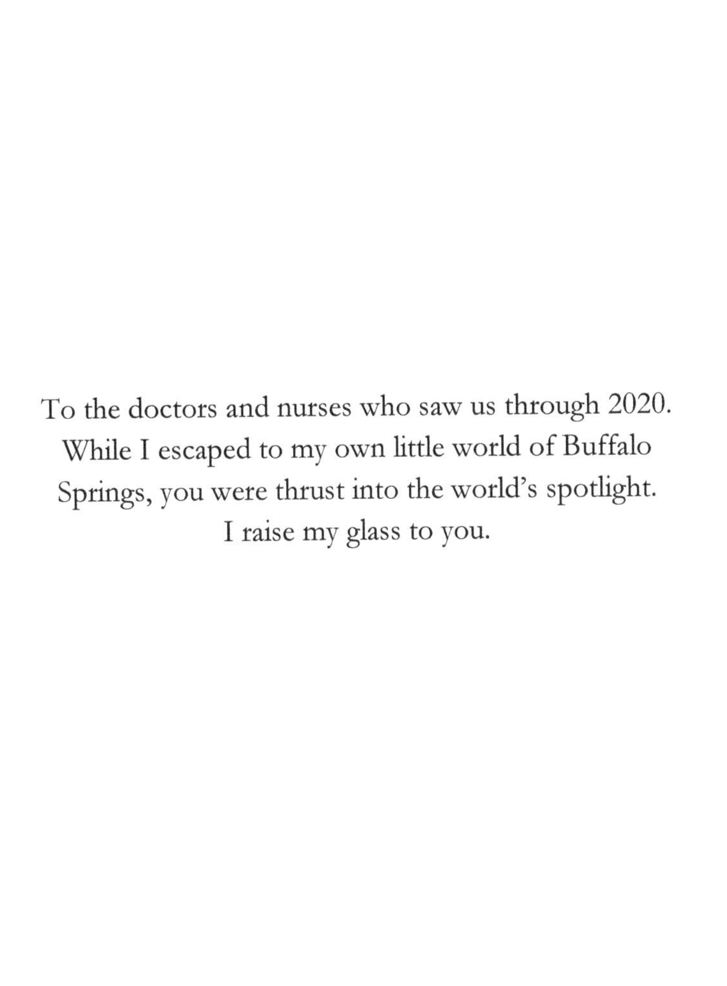

To the doctors and nurses who saw us through 2020.
While I escaped to my own little world of Buffalo
Springs, you were thrust into the world's spotlight.
I raise my glass to you.

One

The smell of flowers filled the library. A beautiful bouquet sat on the circulation counter—courtesy of Helena's mother, Grace—and the scent of hydrangea and lavender perfumed the air. Helena had always admired her mother's garden and knew that warmer days and sunshine were ahead as soon as Grace began filling vases with the bounty of her spring bulbs. Though Helena liked to think of the library as a cheerful place all year, she loved the extra bit of happiness that her mother's plants brought to the space. If only the cheerfulness extended to Helena's heart and mind.

It had been five months since the local police and mayor, with the help of the Feds, ended the reign of a drug operation that nearly destroyed the town. New businesses were opening right and left. Helena's sister, Andi, was planning a fall wedding, and their brother was talking about returning to college full time to finish the last semester of his senior year now that their father was once again gainfully employed. Helena should be on top of the world, and she was irritated with herself for not being happy.

Oh, she was happy for her family—especially her sister—her neighbors, and her friends, but she felt at loose ends with her own life. She loved being a librarian, and she enjoyed seeing the many faces that graced the converted turn-of-the-century house with their presence, but she was restless and longed for something more. What that something was, she didn't know. The town was bursting with opportunity, and Helena longed to harness some of the energy and excitement and turn them into…what?

"Good morning, Ms. Nelson."

Helena was brought out of her thoughts by the sunny greeting of Suzy Mackenzie. The little girl looked up at Helena with bright green eyes framed by the whitest hair which made her the spitting image of her mother, Ruth. The hair color always reminded Helena of her own hair color at that age. Over time, however, Helena's hair had darkened to a dirty blonde, though it maintained its natural curl, the envy of all of her peers and the bane of her existence. Among the curly strands were natural light blonde highlights that couldn't be found in a bottle, but Helena still missed that bleachy tone of her childhood locks.

"Suzy, shouldn't you be in school?"

"Not today, ma'am. Mama had another doctor's appointment, and then she and Daddy are taking us out to lunch. They said I could come pick out a book while they talk to Dr. Blake."

Suzy's smile was so sweet and innocent, so full of hope, but alarms blared in Helena's mind.

"Your mama isn't feeling well again?"

"No, but it's okay. I'm sure she'll be better soon, just like before when she got better after her operation. Daddy says she just needs some sunshine, and we've got plenty of that today."

Helena watched the child bounce across the room without a care in the world, and her own heart ached. Ruth Mackenzie had been sick for some time. She was just beginning to rebound from the months of chemo, and her hair was coming back in, but she looked weak and pale. She told Helena's sister, Andi, that Dr. Blake had been telling her for weeks that she needed to slow down and let her body heal. Was this family lunch a celebration or…? Helena didn't want to think about the alternative.

She walked to the other side of the library and glanced out the window. The chief of police's car was parked outside the clinic, located on the side street behind the library. Dale had only been in the position since November, when he replaced the former chief who had prior knowledge of the drug operation. What a difficult decision that had to have been, to take on the demanding job while his wife was battling cancer, but that was the kind of man Dale was. He never shied away from taking responsibility and doing what he could to help others.

Dale and Ruth were the perfect couple, together since high school, parents of Suzy and her brother, Jamie, active in their church, and all-around good people. Jamie sat on the sidewalk outside the clinic, staring at his phone, no doubt engaged in battle on some other planet or building a virtual brick-walled fortress. Poor kid, she thought, shaking her head. Helena went back to the desk and watched Suzy run her fingers along the bookshelf. Helena closed her eyes and said a silent prayer for the family.

Upon hearing the creaking of the front door, she opened her eyes and smiled at Imogene Baker, the town's retired mayor and beloved matriarch. Helena took a deep breath, ran her hands through her short curls and shook all sad and bewildering thoughts from her head. She had patrons who counted on her help, her knowledge, and her smile. She would give them what they wanted and save her own restlessness and melancholy thoughts for another time.

***

Joe rested his head in his hands, his elbows on his desk. He had gotten to know the Mackenzies very well over the past couple months, and his morning meeting with them cast a pall over the rest of his day. As soon as he saw the sonogram, he was certain the cancer had returned. He tried to remain optimistic while they waited for the test results, and he had dreaded having to share the confirmation of his fears. After lunch with their children, the family would drive to the big hospital in Fayetteville where Joe had already arranged for Ruth to be admitted, probably for the last time.

Days like these were the only times when Joe disliked his profession. As an ER doctor in Houston, he had seen many death sentences, but he had rarely known the patients on a personal level. Getting to know Dale and Ruth and their kids, following Ruth's case and consulting with her specialists, and seeing them at Mass on Sundays had made Joe keenly aware that being a doctor in a small-town clinic was going to be much harder than the hectic pace, all-nighters, and frantic buzz of a Houston hospital.

"Excuse me, Doctor. Shelley is here for her checkup."

"I'll be right in, Dotty. Thank you."

The nurse—a grey-haired, perky, always smiling sexagenarian—nodded, and Joe took a deep breath before pushing himself up from his chair. Shelley's pregnancy was going well, and Joe was grateful that she was his next patient. Her bright smile and enthusiasm were just what he needed. He glanced out the window just as little Suzy Mackenzie ran down the sidewalk, proudly displaying the book she had just gotten from the library. Thinking about the director of the library around the corner usually put a smile on Joe's face, but today, all he saw outside his window was a family whose life was about to be shattered, forever altered into tiny pieces that could never fully be put back together. Joe knew that from experience. He forced a smile as he headed to the exam room, reminding himself that even when one life was ending, a new life was always a reason to celebrate.

***

"What's wrong?" Helena asked when Andi came through the door that night. Her sister's eyes were red and puffy, and she looked like she carried the weight of the world on her shoulders. Helena had a dreadful feeling that she knew what her sister was going to say.

"It's Ruth." Andi sniffed back her tears, the former Naval officer taking over, keeping her emotions in check.

"Oh, sugar, I'm so sorry. I know how close you've grown to her and Dale these past few months." Helena went to her sister and welcomed her with open arms.

Andi melted into her sister and sniffed a few times before pulling back. "Thanks. I don't know what Dale and the kids are going to do."

"It's that bad?"

Andi nodded, pressing her lips so tightly they turned white. "Her oncologist admitted her to the hospital today. Dale told Wade that they don't expect her to come ba—" Andi choked back her words, and her eyes filled with tears.

"Oh, Andi." Helena felt her own tears slip down her cheeks as she blinked hard, trying to be strong for her big sister who had always been the strong one in the family. "Little Suzy came into the library today to borrow a book. She said they were having a family lunch after her mama's appointment. I had hoped it might be a celebratory lunch."

Andi shook her head and walked toward the kitchen. Helena followed.

"Just the opposite. Dale called Wade once Ruth was settled into her room. She started having pains last night, and by this morning, she was so weak, it was all she could do to get out of bed. Dale said he knew then that she needed to go to the hospital, but she insisted on going to her scheduled appointment with Joe instead. She told him it was a stomach bug, but Dale said they both knew it was more." Andi gave Helena a wry smile. "Dale told Wade that Joe had already done an ultrasound and ordered tests recommended by her oncologist. They were just waiting for the results. They all knew it was going to be bad, but you know Ruth. She was never one to stop believing in happy endings."

Andi reached into the cabinet for a glass, and Helena instinctively opened the refrigerator and took out a small can of diet ginger ale which she popped open and handed to her sister. Andi didn't need the diet drink, but Helena would have only diet drinks in the house. She was perpetually trying to shed those last ten pounds.

She watched as Andi poured a healthy amount of Irish whiskey into the soda, and she waited for Andi to continue speaking, surprised her sister hadn't simply tipped back the bottle straight into her mouth. Andi had other friends in town, but she and Ruth had rekindled their friendship from their days on the high school track team, and now they were closer than they ever had been growing up.

Andi took a sip of her drink and turned toward Helena. "They decided to take the kids to lunch before heading to Washington Regional because Ruth wanted to tell them on her own terms, and she wants them all with her while she can still…" Andi looked away.

Helena felt helpless. She put her hand on her sister's back and rubbed it back and forth as Andi took another sip.

"How long?" Helena asked.

"Not long. A couple days to a week."

Helena felt the chill that ran through her sister. "Is there anything we can do?"

"Pray?" Andi said uncertainly. "If not for a miracle, then for mercy. And for comfort for Dale and the kids."

"I can do that. What about food? They're going to need help for a while. House cleaning, childcare? Name it, and I'll arrange it." Helena's natural instincts to help and to organize kicked in, and her mind filled with images of charts, checklists, and phone trees.

"Those are all good ideas. I'll check with Dale's mom. She's going to bring the kids back and take them to her house for the next few days." Andi inhaled and exhaled a long, slow breath. "You thrive on this, you know? Organizing, planning, helping where needed. Our town is lucky to have you. And it feels so good to be back in a community that pulls together in times of need."

"Because that's what you thrive on," Helena told Andi. "I don't think you loved the Navy half as much as you loved the camaraderie of your team."

Andi smiled. "You're right. I didn't think I'd ever get that feeling back, but it's here, all around us. I don't know why I never felt it before. I had to go around the world to figure it out."

"Because sometimes we can't see what's right in front of us. We search far and wide, seeking what we need everywhere it's not, until God leads us right back to where we started. It's his way of reminding us just how good we had it all along."

"How did you get to be so smart?"

"I'm a librarian, remember?"

They both laughed, and without thinking, settled into their familiar evening routine. When Wade called Andi to say goodnight to his fiancé, Helena excused herself for bed.

After she brushed her teeth and went through her normal bedtime routine, Helena stared at her reflection in the mirror. She would be twenty-nine in a couple months. She talked a big game, but she'd never been around the world. She'd gone as far as the University of Missouri to get her master's degree, and then she returned home just in time for the previous librarian to retire. She never felt the need to go searching anywhere else. Until now. Why was she feeling so discontented? She loved her job. She still had her parents. Her sister was back home for good. What was she longing for?

Or was the question, what was she waiting for?

Maybe it was time for her to spread her wings, to travel, to see the world. Maybe she could find a young graduate student who was looking for some place just like Buffalo Springs to get her feet wet. There was a whole world out there just waiting for her to discover it, and Helena was ready to explore. Maybe Ruth was her inspiration. Helena was alive, and she wanted to do more than just live.

***

"I've made a decision," Helena announced at the Nelson family dinner on Sunday. She made sure she had everyone's rapt attention before proceeding. "I'm leaving town for a while."

"What?" Grace asked, voicing the surprise in everyone else's expressions. "Where in heaven's name are you going?"

"I'm still working on that, Mama, but Europe for sure." Helena tried to keep her voice steady, but she felt a tremor in her hand when she picked up the salad tongs and refilled her bowl. She did her best to act nonchalant, but she was nervous, both about telling her family and about taking this huge leap of faith.

"Where in Europe?" Wade asked.

"Well, Greece for one. I've read all the Greek classics—*Jason and the Golden Fleece*, Euripides' plays, *The Iliad* and *The Odyssey,* Plato's *Republic,* and *Antigone*—but I've never seen the Acropolis or walked along the Mediterranean or visited Corinth."

"Where else?" Jackson asked, clearly picking up on his sister's plan to see more than just one country.

"To Rome to see the Vatican and Florence to visit the Uffizi and the Academia. Probably Venice while I'm at it. And then on to France to see where Quasimodo rang the bells of Notre Dame and experience the city that inspired *Les Misérables* and The *Three Musketeers*. Maybe go on a pilgrimage to Lourdes while I'm over there. Then I'd like to see London. I want to see one of Shakespeare's plays at the Globe Theater and sit on London Bridge where T.S. Eliot wrote 'I sat upon the shore fishing, with the arid plain behind me'." She sighed at the thought and closed her eyes as she pictured the scene.

When Helena opened her eyes and looked around, she found her family and Wade staring at her, dumbfounded by her words.

"What?"

"I'm not sure what to say," Grace said. "When are you going, and for how long?"

"Well…" This was the part that made her a bit nervous. "I contacted the library school and inquired about any grad students willing to take over the library for the summer." She held her lip in her teeth. "The whole summer. I would leave in late May." She turned to Andi. "But I'll be back before the end of August, plenty of time to give you a shower and help with the wedding. Oh, and don't worry about the farmer's market. They can still use the library parking lot in the mornings."

Silence engulfed the kitchen as if a roaring train had blocked out all sounds such that even a blood-curdling scream would be drowned in the thunderous noise. After a moment, Andi raised her glass of iced tea.

"A toast to my traveling sister, Helena. May you see the world and come back even more armed with knowledge than you already are."

"That's a scary thought," Jackson murmured, raising his glass.

Slowly, Grace picked up her glass of iced tea, followed by Wade and Helena's father, Joshua. As her family toasted her announcement, Helena suppressed the urge to cry. Though she would embark on the trip she'd always dreamed of, she knew she would be leaving her heart in Buffalo Springs in more ways than one.

***

"Anything good available?" Joe smiled at Helena.

The light blonde highlights against the darker strands of hair shone in the sunlight that streamed through the window, and her blue eyes, the same color as her sister's, sparkled with delight as she gazed up at him from behind the circulation counter. Normally, Joe preferred long hair on women, but Helena's short curls, twinkling eyes, and pale skin gave her the delightful appearance of a pixie and often made Joe recall the class he suffered through as an undergrad in which his eccentric professor made the students memorize Cornish poetry about the childlike, bubbly creatures. He saw Helena as both childlike and bubbly in the most complimentary way.

Helena's bright blue dress, a favorite color of pixies, added to the imagery while her white cardigan made her appear both modest and beautiful. Joe admired how nice she looked with little makeup and only a small pair of sparkling, blue studs in her ears. Yes, she was exactly what he pictured a pixie to look like.

"I have the new Harlan Coben. I hid it back here just for you." Helena gave him a radiant smile as she reached under the counter and pulled out the book. "Library card, please?" Her smile was wider than normal, and there was an added gleam in her eyes. Joe had to work hard to push aside thoughts of medieval folklore.

"What's got you in such a good mood this afternoon?" he asked as he removed his card from his wallet and handed it across the counter. The smell of the flowers on the counter was so intense, it instantly clogged his sinuses, and he held back a sneeze.

"I've been making plans for the summer."

Joe watched her scan his card and then scan the barcode on the back of the book with more than her usual flare. "What kind of plans?"

"I'm going abroad, as they say." She beamed at him, and her smile caught him off guard as it always did.

A sworn bachelor since… since that day he didn't like to think about, Joe typically didn't have any trouble ignoring a woman's looks or charm or responsiveness. He could love them and leave them without a second thought, and he had, often. Not anymore. Now, he had no desire to be with any woman at all. He was content to be a bachelor until his dying day, but… there was something about Helena's smile that set off some kind of internal alarm, like the faint wail of a distant emergency siren—you hear the sound and recognize that something is amiss, but the thought that the emergency might have a personal consequence never even crosses the mind.

"Well, good for you. Where are you going?" he asked casually, wondering why he cared and why his mind had automatically wondered, how soon, for how long, and with whom?

"Greece, Italy, France, England. That's as far as I've gotten, but I haven't ruled out Amsterdam, Germany, maybe Belgium or Spain."

Joe nodded and continued to smile. He couldn't care less about her travels, but something about her had him entranced, and he couldn't find the will to walk away. "Well, that sounds like quite the adventure. I've never been to Greece, but the other places are wonderful to visit. You'll have to take lots of pictures. Are you, uh, going with Andi?"

"Oh, no, Andi has much too much going on with the bakery and her September wedding. I'm flying solo."

"Really?" he asked, wondering what had gotten into him. He was unable to stop himself from prodding for more information. "What brought on this elaborate plan to head across the pond?"

"Well, I'm not getting any younger, you know, and I've spent my whole life here in this building, long before I ever became a librarian. I would check out piles and piles of books, not just fiction, but atlases and history books and even cookbooks from around the world. Movies, too. I adore movies of all kinds. The library and my collegiate studies took me to so many places, but never did I actually leave this town. Other than college and grad school of course."

"Of course." He nodded as if he had known all of this all along. "So, now you're going to go see all the places you've read about."

"Well, some of them. I mean, I'll probably never stroll the same streets as Tolstoy or explore the world of Kipling, but three months should give me plenty of time to see a good deal of Europe, and I'll be able to see so much of the art and architecture I studied."

"Three months!" Joe blinked in surprise. "That's quite some trip. What about the library?"

"I'm hiring a library school graduate for the summer. She can run things and get some on-the-job experience before heading off to a larger, busier library."

"You certainly seem to have it all figured out, don't you?"

"Not yet, but I will by the time I leave."

The door opened, and Joe turned to say hello to Helena's good friend, Allie Michaels. After inquiring about Allie's health—she had a rather bad stomach flu a couple weeks back—he turned back to Helena, happy that Allie had broken the spell Helena had on him.

"Well, I hope to see you before you leave."

"Joe, it's only April. I'm not leaving for another month."

He nodded and gestured to the book and library card she was still holding. "Right. Well, I'd better get back to work. Dotty will send the cavalry for me if I'm late for my first afternoon appointment. It will get us off track from the start."

"Far be it from me to hold you up." She held out the book, the card clasped tightly between the cover and her long, graceful finger, and Joe took them, careful not to let his hand brush against hers.

"I'll see you around, Helena." He turned to go but stopped short as he suddenly thought of his brother. Jeremy and Andi had been in love before a helicopter crash took his brother's life and prompted Andi to give up her career with the Navy SEALs. Neither Andi nor Jeremy had ever told him they were in love, but he knew it as sure as he knew his own name. He wondered about the regret he knew Andi carried with her despite her upcoming marriage to Wade Montgomery. What that had to do with Helena, he had no idea, but he found himself swinging back around to face her. She and Allie were just beginning an animated conversation, and he hesitated before blurting out words that seemed to come from nowhere.

"Helena, I meant what I said. I'd love to get together before you leave. Before then even. I mean…" What was he doing? He'd already taken her out once, and it ended in a friendly goodbye at her door. She was obviously not interested in anything casual, and he wasn't either, anymore.

Before he knew what he was saying, he asked, "How would you like to go to dinner Friday night and tell me all about the plans for your grand adventure?"

Helena looked back at Allie and then turned and stared at Joe, blinking a few times as if she didn't quite understand the language he was speaking. Her perfect mouth opened slightly then slowly closed before opening again to speak.

"We haven't gone to dinner in a while, have we?" she said with a smile. She looked uneasy, and he regretted asking her, especially with her friend, eyes agog, joining Helena in staring at him.

"I thought I could give you some travel suggestions for the places I've been. If you want them."

She bit her bottom lip, and he watched as her gaze shifted once more from him to Allie and back to him again.

"Um, okay," she said hesitantly. "That sounds nice. I'd love to get your advice."

"Great. I'll call you later in the week."

Joe turned to leave, catching Allie's eye as he headed toward the door. Her stare was icy, and it occurred to him that she did not approve of her best friend going out with him even to discuss travel tips. What had Helena told her about their one and only date? It had been Valentine's Day, and they enjoyed a nice dinner at the Smoke Pit, the only restaurant in town at the time, before the revitalization began in full.

He thought about the night as he walked toward the clinic. The food was good, the conversation was light, and Joe was happy to be spending the evening with a member of the opposite sex instead of a book and a glass of gin, his usual evening companions since moving to Buffalo Springs. They talked about so much yet so little, carefully keeping to topics about family, the happenings in the town, and their favorite pastimes. Joe liked Helena, and she was great company, but he wasn't interested in dating or marriage or anything even remotely permanent. He hadn't asked her out again, afraid she'd get the wrong idea.

Besides the fact that Joe was a confirmed bachelor, he was married to his work. His hours were much better here than they had been in Houston, but he still didn't have time to entertain any ideas of romance, nor did he have the desire to. It was one thing to work in a hospital. It was another thing entirely to run the whole operation. Middle-of-the-night emergencies, spur-of-the-moment childbirths, and minor accidents were not things that followed a set time schedule. All of which suited him fine. The only thing he missed was the ability to destress with a pretty young intern or nurse, but that was in the past. He was a changed man, no longer the casual 'Dr. Casanova' Joe knew he'd been called behind his back.

His minor aches and pains reminded him that he wasn't getting any younger either, and he was a doctor, after all, who knew that casual, while fun, was not healthy. Nobody back home would ever believe that 'Dr. Casanova' spent most of his nights falling asleep with a book in his hands. For the first time in his life, Joe was okay with that. No matter how enthralled he might feel when he was around the beguiling Helena Nelson, he was not in the market for romance or anything even resembling it.

Two

The next day was a busy one in the clinic, and Joe used the quiet calm after his last patient to catch up on paperwork. He looked up when he heard a knock on the office door.

"Dr. Joe," Dotty opened the door, her voice uncharacteristically despondent. "Dale just called."

Joe saw the tears in Dotty's eyes. Unable to answer, he nodded his head to let her know that he understood.

"Should I lock up for the day? Everything's tidy and ready for tomorrow."

"That's fine, Dotty. Thank you. Have a nice evening." Joe watched her leave and then allowed himself a moment of grief for the patient he lost and for this new-found emotion he hadn't yet figured out how to handle.

When Joe left Houston, he thought it would be for the best. He thought he would be making a fresh start. He wanted a new life away from his brother's ghost and away from the reputation he had made for himself. What Joe hadn't counted on was falling in love.

He had fallen in love with Buffalo Springs, with the Ozarks, and with the community that came together to save a dying town and build a future for their children. He had fallen in love with taking care of people's most basic needs, of stitching the arms and legs of little boys who fell from trees, of showing first-time parents the ultrasound image of their growing baby, of doing well checkups and ear, nose, and throat exams. He had fallen in love with being a doctor again.

And then there were days like this.

Joe stood and walked to the window. He thought about Dale and Jamie and little Suzy. He wondered how they were doing and how they were going to cope with their loss. Joe knew what it was like to lose a brother, but he was blessed to still have both of his parents and his sister, and he had never lost a spouse. How does one go on?

As he stared out at the flowers beginning to show their colors in the garden that flanked the library, he thought about Helena. He'd been thinking about her a lot since she told him about her trip. He was going to miss her when she was gone, but he didn't know why. He'd walked her to her car several times before the annual hourly shift in time that reverted dusk back to daylight. He'd taken her out to dinner once, and that was the extent of their relationship. So, why did he feel this way? Helena was nice, beautiful, intelligent, well-read, and well-spoken, but he simply was not interested in her or anyone else for that matter.

He snorted in frustration. He had work to do, and he didn't have the spare time to spend on thoughts of any woman, especially one who was leaving town in a month. Once she was out in the world, she might decide never to come back. And that suited Joe just fine. His impetuous invitation to dinner only proved that she was no good for him. She made him do things he regretted, and he was through letting women, or his feelings for them, manipulate him. He stopped looking for love about six years ago, and he was through using women and letting them use him. It was for the best that Helena would be gone all summer. Thinking about her was a distraction Joe couldn't afford.

***

"I can't believe you've had this all these years." Andi held up her sister's passport, absent a single stamp.

"I always knew there would come a day when I'd be able to use it." Helena pulled a dress from the closet. "What about this one?"

Andi looked up and wrinkled her nose. She gave her head a shake. "No way. Little sister, you need to go on a shopping spree. Europe is where fashion was born. You can't traipse around the Champs-Élysées wearing a sundress you bought in eleventh grade."

"I just bought this for Rose Ellen's wedding."

"Didn't Rose Ellen get married two years ago?"

"That's not that long ago," Helena insisted.

Andi stood and walked to the closet and fingered the meager selection. Helena watched as she began pulling out one thing after another then hastily put them back. Helena didn't have a big wardrobe, but she liked her clothes. They were comfortable and covered those problem areas Helena was always telling herself she was going to work on.

"I'm telling you, you've got to buy new clothes."

"With what? I'm on a strict budget right now so that I have enough for the trip. Do you know how much a plane ticket to Greece costs?"

"Do you know what the economy is like in Greece right now? Why not pack a few essentials and buy the rest when you get there? You'll be at the height of fashion and save some money at the same time."

"You really think so?" Helena scrunched her face and looked at Andi. She didn't know much about shopping in Europe, but she had to believe it wasn't cheap.

"I know so. Italy is different. You want to buy leather there, maybe a bag or shoes, and a few scarves to add some flare, but you can buy great clothes in Greece for almost nothing."

"How do you know? You never spent time in Europe. Weren't you pretty much confined to the Middle East?"

"I was, but Monica was with the Sixth Fleet. She was based in Naples, Italy."

"I remember her. You graduated together."

"We did, and she's an authority on Europe. She spent her entire time of service there. Whenever she had leave, she explored everywhere she could get to by ferry or train, which in Europe is just about anywhere."

"Do you think she could give me some tips?" Helena asked, realizing how little she knew about world travel.

"I'm sure she could." Andi looked down at her smart watch and frowned.

"What is it?" Helena asked, seeing a look of concern cross Andi's face.

"It's Wade. He's supposed to be at a town council meeting. Let me see why he's calling." She pulled her phone from her pocket and answered.

Helena continued surveying her wardrobe as she listened to her sister's one-sided conversation.

"Oh, no. When?... How's Dale?... Poor guy… Okay, thanks for letting me know… Love you, too. Bye."

"Ruth?" Helena asked.

Andi nodded with a pained expression.

"I'm so sorry, Andi." Helena went to her sister and held her while the tough, former Naval officer cried.

***

The church was standing room only. There wasn't a person in town who didn't know and love Ruth Mackenzie. Many had known her since birth. There were classmates, from kindergarten through high school, and families of her children's classmates. There were the parents of her own class, grade three at Buffalo Springs Elementary, and parents of past students, children in tow. There were church members and fellow soup kitchen volunteers and coaches and team parents. There was a whole host of others who knew the warm smile and big green eyes of the woman who no longer stood in front of a classroom or gave Communion at church or ladled soup into bowls or cheered from the sideline.

After the graveside burial service in Our Lady of Perpetual Help Cemetery, Helena helped serve food in the church hall. It almost felt like all the other church dinners she had organized with town folk catching up and children chasing each other around the room. If she looked past the black dresses and the slideshow prepared by Ruth's siblings, Helena could pretend that they weren't there to say goodbye to a beloved teacher, mother, wife, and friend.

"The service was nice, wasn't it?"

Helena looked up into the caring blue eyes of the town doctor. "Hi, Joe. The service was nice, but I reckon Ruth would've been as embarrassed as all get out at hearing all those things people said about her. She was the humblest person I've ever known."

"I didn't know her for long, but I'd have to agree. Do you know that she used her chemo sessions to tutor adults, the ones who were there with her and couldn't read? Who does that?"

"Ruth Mackenzie, that's who." Helena's misty-eyed gaze wandered to little Suzy, giggling in the corner with two girlfriends. "Suzy looks just like her. And she's got her mama's heart."

"She's a sweet girl," Joe agreed.

"Hi, Helena." Stan, a local carpenter and friend of Andi and Wade's, smiled bashfully at Helena. She felt herself blushing. She was pretty sure Stan had had a crush on her since she moved back home after grad school. He was a regular in the library though Wade teased him that he had never opened a book back in high school.

"Hi, Stan. How's your sister holding up? I can't remember a time when she and Ruth weren't together."

"They were best friends. Ruth was like a sister to me."

"I'm sorry, Stan. This must be hard on your whole family." She laid her hand on his arm and thought of his sister, sobbing throughout the funeral Mass.

Joe stood silently by, and Helena felt his gaze on her.

"It is, but I have to believe she's home with the Lord now and at rest."

"She is, Stan. I'm certain of it."

Stan glanced between Joe and Helena. "Dr. Blake." Stan acknowledged Joe with an outstretched hand. "Thanks for coming."

"You're welcome, Stan. Please tell your sister how sorry I am for her loss. Ruth was one of a kind."

Stan nodded. "She was." He looked back at Helena. "I guess Andi's pretty broken up, too, huh? She and Ruth got pretty close over the winter."

"Yeah, she's taking it hard, but maybe she and Alicia will be able to console each other."

"That'd be nice. Alicia could use an understanding friend right now."

"I'll mention it to Andi," Helena promised.

"Thanks, Helena. See you around?"

"Of course, Stan. Nice seeing you." She turned back to Joe. "Poor guy. His sister is heartbroken. I can't imagine losing your lifelong best friend so tragically." At Joe's wince, she gasped. "Oh, Joe. I'm sorry."

"It's fine." Joe looked away, and an awkward silence filled the already stuffy air around them until Joe pulled his phone from his pocket and frowned.

"Everything okay?" Helena asked.

He nodded and shoved the phone back into the recesses of his jacket pocket. "Blasted telemarketers won't leave me alone."

"I hear ya. They can be a pain. Did you get enough to eat?" She opened her arms and gestured toward the spread—four folding tables stretched across the room without so much as a quarter inch of space between dishes. "We have plenty of food. Dale won't have to worry about cooking until July."

"I think I've had my fill, but thanks. I only closed for the morning, so I've got to head back to the clinic. I just wanted to see if we're still on for tonight. You've been working non-stop the past few days, organizing this luncheon, and under the circumstances, I'd understand if you didn't want to go out."

"Why, Joe Blake, are you trying to get out of buying me dinner?"

Joe laughed, and Helena felt a stir in her belly that she hadn't felt before, not around Joe anyway.

"On the contrary. I'm giving you an out in case you'd rather not spend the evening with me."

"To be honest, Joe," Helena said quietly. "Between organizing this, trying to get the altar schedule for the whole summer completed before I leave, training someone to run the soup kitchen while I'm away, making sure everyone knows what's to be done for Memorial Day and the Fourth of July, and planning my travel, I could use a night out."

"Then a night out you shall have. Dress casually. Those heels must be killing you. I'll pick you up at seven."

"I'll be ready." Helena smiled and watched Joe walk away. He really was nice to look at with those sky-blue eyes and kind smile.

"Earth to Helena." Andi prodded her sister in the ribs.

"Oh, stop that."

"What was that about?"

"Nothing. Just firming up plans for dinner."

"Dinner? Tonight? You didn't tell me you and Joe were going on a date tonight."

Helena narrowed her gaze at Andi. "Who says it's a date?"

"Did he ask you to go out to dinner?"

"Yes," Helena replied testily.

"Is he picking you up?"

"Ye-es." She dragged out the word.

"And he's paying?"

"I assume so." Helena didn't know Joe well, but she was certain he would never let a lady pay for her own meal.

"Yeah, it's a date." Andi's smug reply stirred something in Helena that she couldn't quite put a finger on.

"It's a dinner out," Helena snapped. "That's all. Joe's going to give me some tips about some of the cities I'll be visiting this summer." She picked up two platters and took them into the kitchen.

Andi followed with another platter and a bowl of something that resembled a casserole but was mysterious enough to have gone untouched. "I thought you liked him."

Helena pulled the commercial sized plastic wrap from a shelf and started transferring small sandwiches from a platter to a sheet of plastic. "I do like him. He's a nice man who's doing a lot of good for this town."

"That's not what I meant, and you know it."

Helena stopped and glared at her sister. "I like Joe. I do not *like* Joe. We are friends. He has his practice, and I'm getting ready to go away for months. And every single woman in Buffalo Springs is in love with him, and half the married ones, too. By the time I get back, he'll probably have dated half the town."

Andi stared at her sister, and Helena stared right back, challenging her to object. Finally, Andi shook her head.

"Suit yourself, but don't be surprised if he *is* off the market by the time you get back. Attractive, successful men like Joe don't stay single for long."

"Hmph," Helena scoffed. "Men like Joe are always single."

"You don't believe that, do you?" Andi raised her brow in question.

"I do. Joe Blake is married to his clinic. And he likes to flirt. He's not looking for anything more than a quiet night out, maybe followed by a wild night in." She looked through the doorway and watched the doctor as he told Dale goodbye and wondered if that was really true. Was he the love 'em and leave 'em kind of guy?

As if reading her mind, Andi gasped. "Helena, you haven't—"

"Hush your mouth. You know I haven't, but I know his type. He's fun to go out with, but he's the last person you'd want to fall in love with." Of that, Helena was certain. But based on the way her body had reacted to him a few minutes before, the end of May and her three-month sojourn couldn't come fast enough.

***

Helena's idea of casual was a pair of tight jeans over her slightly rounded hips—hips just the right size for a man to hold onto—a blue silk top that matched her eyes, and a pair of cowboy boots. She wore a single gold chain with a crucifix pendant and gold hoop earrings. Joe stood on her front porch, transfixed by how beautiful casual could be. It affirmed his suspicions that Helena was a magical creature indeed who was beginning to cast a charm over him.

"Joe? You ready?" Helena asked with a chuckle.

"Yes, of course." His mind strayed to places it shouldn't, places it hadn't gone since he left Houston and swore off his previous lifestyle. He cleared his throat, hoping to clear his thoughts. "We should get going. We have a lot to talk about before you leave. About your trip, I mean. About the things you should do. On the trip."

Joe opened the car door, waited for Helena to get settled, then closed the door. As he walked around to the driver's side, he took a deep breath and shook off the visions in his head, visions that undoubtedly would make Helena not only blush but go running as far from him as she could get.

Joe closed the door and started the engine. "I hope Italian sounds good. The Russos are opening the restaurant tonight. I'm sure it will be packed, but I asked them to save us a table in a quiet corner."

"Oh, special treatment, huh? What did you do to deserve that?"

"Doctor-patient confidentiality, Helena. I could tell you, but then I'd be barred from practicing medicine in the state of Arkansas ever again."

Helena laughed. "Then you should go to your grave with the information, Dr. Blake."

"I will do just that, Ms. Nelson." Joe felt more at ease, the pictures gone from his mind. Their flirting and playful banter reminded him why he enjoyed her company and affirmed that they were nothing more than friends who liked to tease and laugh with each other. Feeling relaxed, he pulled into the parking lot and grinned at Helena as he escorted her into the restaurant where the scents of garlic, oregano, and marinara sauce clung to the air.

The evening went well. As he knew she would, Helena made Joe laugh, and he appreciated her sense of humor. He liked the sound of her voice and the way her eyes sparkled when she talked about books and movies and the worlds they opened up for her. He loved to hear her talk about her many volunteer activities, and it made him question his lack of involvement in the community. He was reminded how much he enjoyed her company, how he missed those walks to her car when the winter evenings were dark and menacing.

As they ate their pasta, Joe gave Helena advice on traveling in Europe and suggested some places for her to visit. He told her to visit Bruges rather than Brussels and to see Windsor Castle rather than Kensington.

"Have you traveled a lot?" Helena asked.

"Not in a while, but yes. My father was stationed in Germany for most of my childhood."

"Oh! You've never told me that. Was he Navy like, uh, your brother?"

Jeremy was a touchy subject that he and Helena danced around. Andi blamed herself for his death for a long time, but Joe never held her accountable, and neither did the Navy.

"No, my father was in the Army. Jeremy always wanted to be a SEAL, and Daddy was okay with that."

"So, you did all your traveling as a child?"

"Most of it. I spent a semester in London as an undergrad, so I did some exploring then, weekend trips and such."

He refilled his wine and topped off Helena's as well. He tried to gauge what she was thinking as he took a sip of the robust Italian wine. This was typically the time of night when he began to make his move, and most of the women he dated expected it. He had no intentions of even trying with Helena.

"Do you like the wine?"

"Very much. I don't know a lot about wine, but I know that this is really good."

"It's from a region of Italy outside of Verona. I went there once with a group during my semester abroad. We were studying Shakespeare and took a weekend trip to Verona. I loved the area so much, I planned a trip there for our…" He stopped himself just before the words tumbled from his lips. He shook his head and reached for his wine, taking a long drink as he thought about what to say, mentally chastising himself for taking the discussion in that direction.

"I ended up going back there by myself a few years ago. Anyway, I went on a tour of this vineyard named, Belle Uve. The Amarone was remarkable." Joe chuckled. "I remember being amazed by this little family-run business. It was owned by a husband and wife, not much older than I was at time. She was an American, by the way, and she dealt with the marketing end of the business, including scheduling the tours. The husband, born and raised on the vineyard, oversaw the growing of the grapes and the wine production. Other family members—cousins, I think?—took care of the other business aspects like bookkeeping, hiring migrant workers for the harvest, and the like. I was really fascinated by the vineyard's story and how it went from a struggling little winery to one of the top wine producers in the country." He shook his head. "I'm sorry. I'm probably boring you."

"Not at all," Helena protested. "You must have spent a lot of time there to get to know them so well."

Joe shook his head. "Not really. Just an afternoon. But the pride that this couple had in their business, their grapes, and their wine was so remarkable, I found myself trying to find out more about them. I Googled them and was really impressed with everything I learned. I still order wine from them regularly." He picked up the wine bottle and inspected the label. "This Amarone isn't nearly as good, but it's not bad. Not bad at all. Shall I top you off?"

"No thanks." She shook her head. "I can't even imagine being able to travel like that." She sipped the wine and then placed the glass toward the center of the table as if to move it out of her own reach. "Should I go there? To Verona?"

Joe shrugged and sat back in his chair. He was in uncharted territory with Helena. She truly seemed more interested in travel tips than in enjoying the buzz of an expensive, full-bodied wine. Was she truly impervious to his charms? Joe forced himself to turn from that line of thought and searched his mind to recall her question.

"It depends upon how much time you have in Italy. It's a lovely city, but you should spend most of your time in Florence."

"You've been there, too, I suppose."

Joe thought he detected something in her voice, which confirmed that neither the wine nor his charm was having an effect on her. "I have, but it's been many years." Joe bent forward, pushed his plate farther up on the table, and leaned on his elbows. He had the overwhelming desire to be honest with her, something he rarely felt when out with a beautiful woman. "You know, the military life isn't as glamorous as it sounds. We got to travel around Europe, but our home life was pretty normal. And the truth is, I've never really been anywhere here in the States. I'd love to visit the Northeast, walk the Freedom Trail in Boston, or go west to wine country in Napa someday." He saw her relax a bit.

"Other than college in Missouri, the only place I've ever been is to Annapolis for Andi's graduation. We drove down to the ocean for the weekend before she shipped out, and that's the only time I've even been on a beach."

"Well, look here. A night out, Dr. Blake?" Imogene Baker stood next to the table. She surveyed the expensive bottle of wine and cast a glance from Helena to Joe. "Are you enjoying your dinner at this fine establishment?"

"We most certainly are, Madam Mayor," Helena answered.

Imogene looked around. "It looks like half the town is here." She turned back to Helena. "That future brother-in-law of yours is doing a fine job as mayor. You can tell him I said so."

"I will," Helena said.

"Enjoy your evening," the former mayor said before walking toward the restroom.

Helena's eyes sparkled, and her smile was a tad impish as she watched Imogene walk away. Joe adored that smile and had to force himself to stop staring at her. He could have sat there all night staring into those sparkling blue Mediterranean pools of hers, but a familiar buzz caught his attention, and he reached for his phone, silently praying it wasn't an emergency.

"Uh oh," Helena said. "Does somebody need help?"

Joe shook his head and put the phone away. "Just an anonymous call," he said. "I've been getting them a lot lately."

"You should sign up on that Do Not Call list."

"I did. A lotta good it did." He watched her eat a forkful of pasta, trying not to slurp in a stray noodle, and he smiled. "I'm curious about something. You mentioned the other day that you studied art and architecture. Don't you have to have a degree in library science to be a librarian?"

"Yes, that was my graduate study. I earned a bachelor's degree in history as well as art history. I really wanted to be a museum curator, but then I moved back home, and the library was in such sad disarray. I knew I needed to save it, so I went to library school."

"And you don't regret not following your dream?"

"Dreams change," she said wistfully. "I really love what I do, and now I can't imagine working in a stuffy office and not interacting with the public. Mama always says that God's plan may not be the same as our plan, but he will show us the way."

Joe thought about this. God certainly had revealed his plans for Joe in mysterious ways, including ending up in Buffalo Springs.

Joe raised his glass. "Well, then, let's have a toast. To God's plan in our lives, and to all the places you're about to see that you've only been able to dream about."

Helena smiled, and Joe found it hard to look away. "To God's plan and my European adventure," Helena said, glass raised.

Without moving the glasses to their lips, they both sat still, wine gently lapping back and forth, eyes locked. Joe felt as though time had stopped. After a moment that felt like a day, Joe tipped the liquid to his lips and took a sip, his eyes still holding hers. He watched her do the same and reminded himself to take it easy. This was a friendly dinner and nothing more.

***

Helena sipped her wine, a very good wine indeed. She enjoyed the conversation, more than enjoyed it. Joe was fascinating, attentive, and humble despite his worldliness. He was well-read and laughed easily. She knew his age—thirty-five—because Andi had told her.

He and Jeremy were twins. She was only twenty-eight, making her feel young and inexperienced compared to him, but he didn't seem to notice. If he did, he didn't seem to care.

Helena did her best to keep things light and casual. She was, after all, leaving town for three months, and she didn't want anything holding her back. She wouldn't let this handsome, intriguing man distract her from her plans. Besides, she believed what she said to Andi, Joe was not the kind of man to settle down. She needed to be careful, or she would end up with a broken heart.

After they paid the check, the evening air greeted them like an old friend.

"Spring is certainly here," Helena remarked.

"It is," Joe agreed. "I don't remember the last time it was this pleasant so late in the evening."

"You're going to love springtime in the Ozarks. It's magnificent."

"I'm looking forward to it." He turned to her. "I hate to waste such a beautiful night. Would you care to take a walk around town for a bit, perhaps stop somewhere for a drink?"

Here it was. He was subtly letting her know what he had in mind for dessert. Though she expected this, she was disappointed. She really had hoped she was wrong about him. She weighed her doubts against her desires. She wasn't ready for the night to end, but she wasn't going to play his game.

"How 'bout this? I don't live very far. If you don't mind walking back by yourself, why don't you just walk me home? We can have a nice, long stroll and chat a little more without staying out too late. I have some things to do before going into work tomorrow, so I still need to be up early." She wanted to convey to him that she had no intention of inviting him in but wouldn't mind getting to know him a little more. Would he accept, or was he only interested in getting her in bed?

To Helena's surprise, Joe looped his arm around hers. "That's a great idea. I'd be honored to walk you home."

As they walked in the direction of her house, they talked about the transformation the town had undergone in the past several months and the changes that were still taking place. Helena had seen a marked decline in the number of people attending the monthly soup kitchen, and visitors were beginning to wander into the library as they strolled through the town, a sign that their first summer as a reinvented tourist town should be successful.

When Joe and Helena turned the corner onto her street, it occurred to Helena that their heights were perfectly suited for each other. If she wanted, she could lean into Joe, and her head would rest comfortably below his shoulder, nestled into his chest. She shooed the thought away as they neared her walkway. Clearly, he was not the nestling type, unless it was post-coital and nonbinding.

Andi had left the porch light on, but they hardly needed it. The light of the full moon illuminated the evening as if it were day. How she loved being outside in the light of the moon. The smell of violets rose from the flower beds, always the first spring bloomers in the area. Their perfume, the moonlight, and the robust wine gave her a heady feeling, or was it the feeling of her arm in Joe's?

When they reached the front door, Joe let his arm fall to the small of her back, turning her toward him. Helena's heart raced, and she felt as if she were fifteen again. She looked into his blue eyes and smiled, her stomach aflutter with nerves. While she hoped he understood her message about not continuing their evening beyond the walk home, she couldn't help but wonder what his kisses were like.

"I had a wonderful evening, Joe. Thank you." She was careful not to sound too inviting or to let her gaze fall to his lips though the urge was fierce.

"I'd like to do this again before you leave if that's okay with you."

Her stomach did a small flip, and she nervously swallowed before answering. Did he like spending time with her, or was he determined to take her to bed?

"I'm going to be really busy over the next few weeks, but we can try to fit something in." She really wanted to go out with him again, but she was worried. She didn't do one-night stands. She didn't even do multi-night stands.

Joe looked at her for a moment, and she saw clouds in his eyes, a look of uncertainty and indecision. He didn't know how to respond, and Helena wasn't sure what to think.

"How 'bout you give me a call?" she said. "We can find a day and time that works."

Joe gave a quick nod. "I'll do that." He let her go and backed up a step. "Have a nice night, Helena."

"You, too, Joe." She opened the door and went partway inside, listening to his footsteps as he walked back down the steps to the sidewalk. She refrained from turning back to watch him go.

When she closed the door behind her, she leaned back against the smooth wood with her eyes closed. Confusion mingled with excitement, sending her brain into a state of panic.

"That good or that bad?"

Helena jumped and thumped her fist on her beating heart. "I declare, Andi! You scared the daylights out of me. I thought you were with Wade."

"I was. I just got home a few minutes ago. How was your date?"

Helena hung her purse on the hook by the door and kicked off her boots. She saw Andi glance at the footwear, and she knew her sister was wondering how long they'd lay there until Helena decided to put them away. She left them there anyway and made her way to the kitchen where she filled a glass with water.

"It was nice. Joe had a really cool childhood. I guess you know he lived on a base in Germany until he was twelve."

"I didn't know that," Andi said quietly.

"Their dad was in the Army. They traveled around Europe a lot as a family." She took a long drink, eyeing her sister over the rim of the glass. "Jeremy didn't talk about his childhood?"

"Not really. He was a quiet, private kind of guy." A strange look passed over Andi's face before she gave a small smile. "So, tell me more about Joe."

"He grew up in Germany and moved to San Antonio, Texas, in middle school, where his daddy commanded Camp Bullis Army Base. It's a medical unit training base, and that's where Joe fell in love with medicine. When his daddy retired, his parents moved to Galveston, and Joe joined the hospital staff in Houston."

"Wow," Andi said, her eyes open wide. "You learned more about Joe in one evening than I knew about Jeremy after all the years we served together."

Helena wondered what on earth Andi and Jeremy talked about and decided life as part of a SEAL team must be much different than anything she could imagine.

"Joe's easy to talk to and easy to listen to." She put the glass in the sink and knew her sister was wiling her to take the extra step and put it in the dishwasher, so she picked it up and did as she was mentally told. "He's just, um, a little too old for me, I think."

"Too old? What's that mean?"

Helena stared into the dishwasher as she spoke. "I think he wants more from me than I'm willing to give."

Helena felt Andi's eyes on her back, but she didn't turn around. Instead, she rearranged a few of the glasses in the top basket.

"Helena?" Helena felt Andi move closer to her. "Did he—"

She shook her head. "He was a perfect gentleman. It's just..." She squeezed her eyes shut and gave her head a quick shake before turning toward Andi. "I told you before. I have this gut instinct about him. He's much more a Rhett Butler than an Ashley Wilkes."

"You always thought Ashley was a wimp."

"And you always thought Rhett was a scoundrel."

Andi laughed. "A scoundrel? I'm sure I never used that word."

"Maybe not, but you know what I mean."

"I do, but Rhett's love for Scarlett was undeniable."

Helena scoffed. "Yet he still broke her heart and stormed off into the night, not giving a damn."

"I always thought Mama made us watch that movie one too many times, but now I'm thinking you didn't watch it enough."

"Meaning what?" Helena asked indignantly.

"Rhett was the one with the broken heart. Scarlett broke it when she married Charles Hamilton and then continued to break it over and over again."

"Well, I doubt Dr. Blake has ever had a broken heart. Just the opposite, I'm sure. I bet he's left a sea of broken hearts in his wake."

Andi studied her sister for a moment. "Well, all right then," she eventually said. "I guess that's that. I'm going to bed if you don't mind. Wade and I are going hiking tomorrow. You're welcome to come."

"Oh darn, I have to work." Helena feigned disappointment. "Thanks for asking though. You two have fun." She closed the dishwasher, picked up a sponge, and began wiping down the counter, turning her back to Andi.

When she heard the door to Andi's room close, she tossed the sponge in the sink and headed to bed, not giving a thought to the boots that she'd left in the middle of the foyer.

As she lay in the dark, she thought about the dinner and what a gentleman Joe was despite his casual mention of going out for a nightcap. He didn't actually try to make a move on her, and he seemed to be interested in her as a person. At least, she thought he was.

She rolled over, away from the moonlight that slipped around the edges of the window shade, and closed her eyes. Before drifting off to sleep, she said her evening prayers, including a prayer that she wasn't losing her innate ability to read people. Was Joe a scoundrel? If so, her departure couldn't come fast enough.

Three

Helena arrived at the library early enough to peruse the farmer's market. It was only the second weekend, and already, shoppers were crowding the parking lot to see what goodies the townspeople had to offer. Helena took a deep breath as she walked past the flower stand, laden with heaping pots of Purple Coneflower, Asters, and several varieties of Lilies. She gazed at some of the local artwork, sighing with pleasure at the vibrant mountain landscapes and the glow of the rising sun over the Buffalo River Valley.

Something unique caught her eye, and she stopped to look at Jess Swanson's blown glass creations.

"Good morning, Helena," Jess called, making her way over from a table laden with handmade soaps and candles. "I was just catching up with Nora. Have you smelled her candles? I wish I could afford to buy one of each! I need them to help me keep my sanity with my houseful of kids." Jess suddenly blushed and looked away as though having many children was an embarrassment. Helena knew that money was tight for the Swansons and having so many mouths to feed must have made it even harder, but Jess was a wonderful mother, and Helena could tell she loved each of her children abundantly.

Jess, as she insisted on being called rather than Mrs. Swanson, was somewhere between Helena and her mother, Grace, in age. Her six children ranged in ages from middle school to toddler. Helena sometimes babysat for the oldest Swanson kids when they were younger.

"Good morning, Jess. These are exquisite." She leaned closer to a hummingbird alight on a columbine. She wanted so badly to touch it but was afraid she would knock it down and break it.

"Thank you. I used to keep a few pieces in a shop in Eureka Springs, but that was years ago. Andi talked me into making some more and trying to sell them here. Your sister has done a remarkable thing for our town, for all of us."

A sense of pride swelled in Helena. "She sure has. We're all so happy she's home and that she and Wade were able to turn things around with the town."

"I still can't believe Ted Mitchem wanted to run the whole town into the ground. And for a drug business, no less. What is this world coming to?"

"Well, we don't have to worry about him anymore." She moved her gaze over the many tables crowding the lot and the dozens of people carrying bags and handing over dollars. "What a beautiful sight this is, to see everyone coming together to support the town and each other."

"It sure is," Jess agreed.

"What do we have here?"

Helena turned to see Joe eying a magnificent glass vase streaked with blues, greens, yellows, and oranges.

"This would be stunning in my kitchen."

"Really?" Helena said with a raised brow. The thought of Joe buying an exquisite vase for his kitchen intrigued her. "Why is that?"

"My kitchen has a Tuscan theme. These colors would blend in perfectly."

"Of course, it does. I'd forgotten how fond you are of Italy."

"You just wait. You'll love it as much as I do." He looked at Jess. "You know, we might be able to work something out."

Helena saw them exchange looks and wondered what was going on, but she didn't ask.

"Dr. Joe. This couldn't possibly cover the—"

"Oh, it's worth much more than you think, Mrs. Swanson. I'll let Dotty know that she'll be hearing from you."

There were tears in Jess's eyes as she nodded and said, "Thank you, Dr. Joe. I'll give your office a call on Monday."

"No rush, Jess. Tell Kevin I said hi." He turned to Helena. "Can I walk you to work?"

Helena grinned. "This is my work." She gestured toward the library as she wondered what had just transpired between him and Jess.

Joe let out a much-exaggerated sigh and winked at Jess. "Lost my chance, I guess. I'll see you later Helena.

Goodbye, Jess." He gave a quick wave and headed toward the clinic.

"That is one amazing man," Jess said.

Helena watched him walk away, thinking, Dr. Blake might be even more interesting than she already thought.

***

"You were a cheerleader?" Joe wiped his face with the thick napkin and took a swig of beer.

"I was. All through high school and college actually." Helena laughed and licked barbecue sauce off her fingers. She couldn't believe she had agreed to another date—or whatever this was—but here she sat, across the table from Joe. "I know, I've gained a few curves since then." She felt herself blush. Why had she said that?

"And no professional sports team swooped in and grabbed you for their team?" His eyes sparkled with amusement rather than judgment. To his credit, Joe ignored her comment, and Helena put a check in her mental *pros* column. She hated when people tried to point out her good traits or tell her how 'healthy' she looked.

She shook her head and felt her springy locks of curls bounce as she reached for her beer. "I wasn't interested in that life at all. I have friends who went into the business, and they love it, but it wasn't for me."

"You have friends who cheer professionally?" Joe sat up and looked at her like she had said she had friends who lived on Mars.

"It's a job just like any other. The employees just happen to be glamorous, physically fit, top models." She eyed him suspiciously. "Come on, you've surely treated someone from the Houston Texans cheer squad."

"Can't say that I have. Not that I know of anyway." Joe took a long drink and signaled the waitress for another. "Did you ever do any modeling?"

"Some. In college. Just for a few extra bucks now and then." She thought back to those days and the crazy schedule she kept—conditioning every morning at sunrise, classes throughout the day, practice every afternoon, homework and modeling shoots, a social life in the evenings, and doing community service on weekends there were no football games. At times, she wondered how she survived it all. It had certainly kept her skinny, but too skinny at times. She'd had a brief battle with an eating disorder, but thankfully, her coach recognized the signs and got her help before it was too late. Still, those evil thoughts penetrated her mind every time she looked in the mirror, and she had a love-hate relationship with food. She told herself that it was okay to enjoy life, and that included food, but sometimes her thoughts went to the dark side—

"Helena?"

She realized she had completely spaced out for a moment and blinked Joe back into focus.

"A penny for your thoughts." He reached into his pocket and used a thumb to flick a penny in her direction.

Helena caught it in mid-air and laughed.

"That was pretty good!" Joe remarked.

"I'm a trained athlete, remember? It's all about the hand-eye coordination." She observed the copper coin that sat in her palm. "I'm just amazed you had a penny in your pocket. Who carries change anymore?"

"Call me old fashioned, I guess. I like the sound of a jingle in my pocket." He sat back and looked at her. "So? What were you thinking about just then?"

She blushed and shook her head. "Nothing special. Just how hectic those days were and how quickly they went by. But I have no desire to go back and be young again." She forced a laugh, trying to make her tone sound lighter than her thoughts had been.

Joe laughed. "You are young. What are you? Twenty-nine?"

Helena squirmed a bit, wondering if he was trying to play it safe by throwing out the proverbial 'twenty-nine' or if he actually knew her age. Had he looked up her medical information? Was that legal since she wasn't a patient of his? Did he have some kind of fetish for young women?

"Almost," she said slowly. "I'll celebrate my twenty-ninth birthday in Greece. Or that's the plan anyway."

Joe raised an eyebrow, and she wondered if confirmation of her age surprised him. Or was she right that he had a thing for younger women?

"Were you hoping for younger or older?" she asked, looking him in the eye, trying to portray maturity and confidence.

"Neither. Your age suits me perfectly. You're young enough to be carefree and old enough to know what you want in life."

Really? Because right now I have no idea what I want.

"Well, in any case, there isn't anything I can do about it, is there? We're born when we're born, and we die when we die. I like to think it's what we do between those two dates that defines who we are."

"I couldn't agree more, Helena." He raised his bottle and offered a mock toast before taking a drink.

Helena took a sip of beer and placed her bottle on the table. Her curiosity had gotten the better of her. "What were you referring to the other morning with Jess?"

"It was nothing, really. Just a financial thing." Joe waved it off, but the gesture didn't feel secretive or evasive, and Helena recognized that he was trying to maintain confidentiality.

She didn't ask any more questions about the matter, but Joe must have seen that she was pondering the situation. He smiled and said, "Just suffice it to say, small town doctors sometimes have to compromise a little more than their big city counterparts."

Understanding dawned, and she smiled, lifting her bottle to offer her own mock toast. "Well, then here's to small town doctors."

He picked up his own drink and made the same gesture, taking a sip through his grin. "What do you say we pay the check and try out that new mini golf course that just opened?"

Now that was an offer that intrigued her. "Oh, I'd love to! I was so excited when I heard that Davy and Betty Jean were adding mini golf to their Christmas tree farm. What a clever way to keep the business going all summer."

Joe motioned for the check and reached for his wallet. "I hear they're opening a Christmas themed shop that will sell ornaments and decorations all year."

"They are. Betty Jean quit her job at the grocery store to open the shop. She and Davy were able to hire a whole crew to help with the farm and work with Betty Jean in the shop. Apparently, their investors were really pleased with their ideas and loaned them all the money they needed to get things up and running." As she spoke, the waitress ran Joe's card and tore the receipt from the handheld card scanner.

"So I heard." He signed the receipt and put his wallet away. "Your brother and sister must feel really good about all the changes they helped create in town."

Joe stood and gestured for Helena to lead them outside.

"They are. Jackson's going back to school in the fall but plans to keep tabs on everything here, and we're all so happy Andi came back to town. She's really happy here, and she and Wade are just perfect for each other." Helena's breath caught in her throat. "Oh! I'm so sorry, Joe. I didn't meant to imply that—"

Joe stopped abruptly and faced her. "Helena, there's no need to apologize. My brother is gone, and to be honest, I'm not sure there ever was anything concrete between him and Andi. Even if there was, Andi and Wade are obviously happy together, and Jeremy would want it that way."

Helena thought about that for a moment as they stood by Joe's car. Though Andi had certainly loved Jeremy, she knew so little about him. "You know, I think you're right. They were very much in the wrong place at the wrong time. They could never be together and stay in the same platoon, and neither of them would've given that up. I think all they ever really wanted was for the other to be happy."

Joe started toward his car, and Helena matched his pace.

"You know, I always suspected Jeremy had feelings for Andi, but he never mentioned anything that led me to believe they were a couple."

"It never got that far. And now he's gone, and Andi's with Wade. I'm glad you're okay with that."

"As far as my brother being gone, there's nothing to be okay with. It is what it is. Nothing can change that. As far as Andi being with Wade, it's all good. I guess things turned out the way they were meant to be."

Joe opened the door for Helena. As she got inside the car, it occurred to her that she was having a really nice evening. Perhaps her suspicions about Joe were off base after all.

***

"Woo-hoo!" Helena shouted. "A hole in one!" She beamed at Joe, and he felt his stomach clench. What was it about her that did that to him?

"You're killing me," Joe said with a laugh. "I must be a lot rustier than I thought."

Helena picked up her ball and headed toward the next hole. "I thought all doctors graduated from medical school with a certification in golf. Isn't that a requirement for the job?"

Joe set his ball at the next hole and lined up his shot. He pulled back on the club ever so slightly and tapped the ball, sending it around the bend, past the frozen pond and through the legs of the reindeer. It bounced off the back bumper and came to a stop a few inches from the hole.

"Nice shot."

"Thanks. To be honest, I'm not much of a golfer. I played football in high school, like all good Texas boys, but I didn't have time to do athletics of any kind beyond that."

He watched her place her ball, size up her trajectory, and hit the ball. His gaze followed the ball's path around the bend, watched as it just skirted past the pond, and blinked in disbelief as it rolled right through the middle of the deer's legs and into the hole. He shook his head.

"You're amazing."

When he looked up at her, she was wearing the most peculiar look on her face, a blend of coyness and disbelief, and his breath caught in his throat. Magic. This pixie charmed him with her magic. What the heck was wrong with him?

"Beginner's luck?" The tone of her voice had him shaking his head again, and the way she bit her bottom lip with her front, left incisor… Endearing was too innocent a word for what it did to his pulse rate. It was that childlike quality that made her so appealing and completely beguiled him.

"Somehow, I don't think you're a beginner."

She flashed a guilty smile. "My friends and I might have played a game or two up in Branson during the off-season."

He scoffed as he readied his club to tap the ball into the hole. "A game or two might be an understatement." He tapped the ball and watched as it rolled into the hole, circled around the rim, and popped back out again. "Argh." He threw his head back in frustration.

When he looked back at Helena, she was trying to suppress a grin.

"Oh, you think that's funny?"

She slowly shook her head back and forth. "Of course not. I, um, I…"

"Yeah, yeah, yeah. Go ahead. Laugh at me. I'm a big boy. I can take it."

"I would never laugh at you, Joe. I'm just enjoying myself."

He shot an annoyed look at her before gently tapping the ball into the hole. He reached in and retrieved it. "I'll bet you are. Next time we go out, we're finding a place to play darts."

"Oh, really? Next time? Who says there will be a next time?"

Joe stopped and stared at her back as she walked to toward the gingerbread house at hole fifteen. Did she mean that, or was she teasing him? He felt as though the tables had turned, and he had no idea how to respond. As if reading his mind, she turned back and gave him a broad grin.

"If you're going to recover your dignity, I guess we'd better make Rick's Place our destination for next weekend. There's a dart board on the other side of the pool tables."

With his heart beating wildly and his whole body reacting to the way she was smiling at him, Joe was beginning to wonder if another date was a good idea. Things were getting complicated. Still, he heard himself responding, "Then it's a date. Or is it a rematch?"

Helena dropped her ball onto the artificial grass and looked at him with twinkling eyes. "Call it what you want, Dr. Blake. I'll be there."

Saved by the bell, or the buzz, Joe thought as he reached into his jeans pocket. He looked at the screen and shook his head before pocketing the phone.

"You really should start blocking those calls," Helena said.

"I wish I could. I tried, but the number's blocked, so it won't work."

Helena's perky nose scrunched up, and she tilted her head to look at him with dismay. "All of them?"

"Yeah. It's getting pretty annoying."

“That’s really strange.”

“You’re telling me.” He gestured toward her golf club. “Nothing to worry about at the moment. Let’s see how you handle this hole.”

Helena shot Joe that impish grin, and he felt his insides curl into a knot. He never took his eyes off her as she teed up and sent the ball through the front door of the gingerbread house. He knew without looking that it would land right in the hole on the other side. Even a meaningless game of mini golf proved what he was beginning to realize more and more.

Everything about her was magical. Now, what was he going to do about it?

***

They sat on a bench in the park, licking ice cream from freshly made sugar cones. The night was clear, and the sky was full of stars.

Helena asked, “Do you ever think about the moon?”

Joe looked up. “The moon? Not much. Why do you ask?”

“I love looking at the moon. It holds so much mystery. Only a handful of people have been there, so we have very little knowledge of what’s up there on that white surface waiting to be discovered.” Joe glanced up but quickly looked back at her, transfixed by her countenance. “There’s something magical about the moon, the way it controls the tides and the way it changes night after night but in such a predictable way that it can always be counted on."

"I guess I never thought about it before." He watched her face as she gazed up into the night sky.

"What fascinates me the most about it is how it's held in place simply by the gravitational pull of the earth, and it doesn't actually produce its own light. It only reflects the sun's light." She turned to him. "It reminds me of people and the way we're dependent upon others whether we want to be or not. And we're dependent upon God, and we should be reflections of God's light. Like Jesus said, we should reflect him and his light and treat others the way we want to be treated."

Joe wasn't sure if she was just sharing with him what was on her mind or trying to tell him something. He didn't know how to respond. His date night conversations typically didn't run very deep. He looked up at the sky. He needed to change the subject to something within his control.

"I've never given a lot of thought to the moon, but the stars… Now there's something I could go on and on about." He pointed to a cluster of stars. "See those two really bright stars and the smaller ones with them?"

"Cygnus the swan?"

"You know it?" He was surprised though he didn't know why. She seemed to be an endless source of knowledge on a variety of subjects even though she seemed to think of herself as not very worldly.

"Andi and I used to watch out our bedroom window at night, trying to see which one of us could find it first."

"Did you know that the shape to its right, with the bright star, Vega, is Lyra the Harp? And below it is Aquilia the Eagle. It's bright star is Altair."

"Wow. You might not pay much attention to the moon, but you know your stars."

Joe laughed and proceeded to name all the constellations they could see. They sat and talked until long after their ice cream was gone. He wasn't sure if it was her magic or the magic of the night that kept him talking about the stars and the sky. The more he talked, the more he realized how hard it was going to be to tell her goodbye.

***

"How was the date?" Andi was walking out of the bathroom when Helena arrived at home.

"It was nice. What are you doing home already?" She hung her purse on the hook by the door and kicked off her shoes, aware that her sister was cringing at the thought that, as always, the shoes would still be there in the morning.

"Already? It's almost midnight."

"It is?" Helena looked at her watch for the first time all evening. "I had no idea it was so late?"

"Oh, really? And what did the good doctor, or should I say, what did the scoundrel do to erase the past several hours from your memory?"

Helena made a face of reproach and tossed her cardigan onto the back of a chair then collapsed onto the couch. "We went to dinner, and despite my earlier assumptions about his gun-running, bootlegging ways, he made no inappropriate passes at me but instead, took me out to Betty Jean's." She grinned at the memory of her easy victory. "Have you been to the mini golf course yet? It's awesome."

Andi sat next to her sister. "Wade and I went last week. I told you that. But your head has been way up in the clouds lately." Before Helena could protest, Andi went on. "What else? You couldn't have played mini golf for the past three hours."

"We played a round and then went to the new candy shop and got ice cream cones, and then we walked to the park and looked at the stars while we ate our ice cream. The evening was so warm, and the night sky was so beautiful." Helena let out a long sigh, unsure of her own feelings. Was she letting her guard down too soon? "Did you know that Joe is an expert on the constellations? He says you can't really see the stars in Houston, but his family has a cabin in Colorado. He and Jeremy spent hours looking at the stars on their family vacations." Helena glanced at her sister and asked quietly, "Does it bother you?"

"Does what bother me?"

"When I mention Jeremy?"

Andi smiled. "Not at all. I like hearing about Jeremy from Joe's perspective. He's a whole different person than the Jeremy I knew."

Helena thought about the things Andi didn't know, and something clicked for her. "'I guess that makes sense. It's a whole different world on a military mission in the Middle East as compared to a family vacation in the Rockies."

"You like him." Andi said, her gaze boring into her sister as she swung the subject back around to Joe. "I mean, you really *like* him."

Helena blew another long breath out through her pursed lips. "I do." She looked at Andi. "What the heck am I going to do? I know he's no good."

"You don't know that."

"I do." She sat up straight and looked pointedly at Andi. "I just have this sense that he's not all that he seems. I'm sure he was trying to get me to go home with him the other night…" She stopped as a thought occurred to her. "Then again, he's never even tried to kiss me, so maybe I'm wrong." She blew out an upwards breath that sent her curly bangs aflutter. "He came across as Prince Charming tonight, but I still have this feeling he's just a cad, and it's so confusing."

"So what? You're leaving soon. Enjoy your time with him now, and then go have the trip of a lifetime. If you're right, he'll move on to the next Southern belle before your plane hits the ground in Athens. If he does, then you were right, and you've lost nothing. If he doesn't, then maybe you've got something good to come home to."

Helena bit her bottom lip, a habit she'd had for as long as she'd had teeth. "Do you really think so?"

"Helena, look, you're still young. You're allowed to go out with a man without worrying about your future.

You can enjoy yourself without wondering where it's going to go, or if it's even going anywhere. It's okay to just be in the moment. Once you're gone, you can relax and enjoy your trip without any strings attached. If Joe is the rogue you think he is, that's too bad, but he will have lost the best thing that ever could've happened to him."

Helena felt her heart tug. "Thanks, Andi." She reached for Andi's hand and gave it a squeeze. "I appreciate that."

Andi squeezed back. "You're welcome." She pulled her hand away and stood up. "I was on my way to bed when you walked in. I'll see you in the morning, okay?"

"Okay. Hey, how was your evening?"

Andi's smile lit the room. "As good as yours baby sister. Every bit as good as yours."

"I'm glad," Helena said. She watched her sister retreat into her room and close the door. "I guess it can't hurt to have some fun before I leave," she said to herself. "Who knows? Maybe I'll find my own Leonardo di Caprio in Europe or a Joe Alwyn, like Taylor Swift did, and forget all about Dr. Joe Blake."

She stood, made sure the front door was locked, turned off the lights, and headed to her room, but she was certain it would not be Leonardo's face she would see in her sleep.

Four

A week went by, and Joe and Helena barely spoke. When he met Helena at her door on Sunday night, he had an ominous feeling working its way up his spine. Was it guilt or confirmation that the evening was going to go badly? He'd already cancelled their date on Friday and then had to postpone on Saturday. The weekend had ended up being a whirlwind of accidents, injuries, and fever spikes. He'd been busy for sure, but it wasn't just the emergencies that had caused him to cancel. Joe knew that Helena was a nice girl, the kind of gal a guy would be thrilled to introduce to the parents, which Joe was never going to do. He'd been there. Once. And never again.

Despite his misgivings, though, Joe found himself standing on Helena's front porch. He had decided that this was it. Over dinner, he was going to tell Helena that he was too busy to date and that he hoped she'd have a great trip. At least he wasn't going to tell her with a text message. He'd still buy her dinner and act like a gentleman. Maybe by the time she returned from her trip, he would've gotten her out of his system.

That was the plan, yet standing on her front porch, all he could think of was that she looked amazing. She wore cropped pink pants, a flowered t-shirt, and a jean jacket. Pink flamingo earrings, the exact color of her pants, dangled from her ears, and her blue eyes sparkled. The more he saw her, the more Joe loved her style—cute, sexy, and fun, just like her—and the more those sirens in his mind blared. He was nearing the danger zone, and he knew it. Tonight was it. It had to be.

"Are you ready to engage in a true competition?" he asked casually, holding his arm out for her. She looped her arm around his and smiled widely.

"Are *you* ready?" Sparks flew from her eyes.

Joe froze and looked at the devilish look on her face before shaking his head. Sirens blasted throughout his consciousness, but he ignored them and put on his familiar 'Dr. Casanova' mask to hide his true feelings, as much from her as himself. "You grew up with a dartboard hanging on your living wall, didn't you?"

"I wouldn't go that far," Helena said with a mischievous grin.

"I guess I'll just have to do my best to live up to my macho bragging, huh?"

"Show me what you've got, Dr. Blake. I'm quite the competitive gal, but I might let you get a point or two."

Joe threw his head back and laughed. "You make me laugh, Helena Nelson. In a good way, I mean. How 'bout we get some dinner and then see who the competitive one is."

"Sounds like a plan."

They walked arm-in-arm down to the middle of town. Rick's Place was in the dead center of Main Street, directly in front of the dry, broken fountain and across from Town Hall. It was where Joe and Andi first met and talked about him opening up the clinic. The food was good, and the atmosphere was what one would expect of a good, southern saloon. Tiffany-style lamps hung over pool tables, and a long mirror lined the wall behind the bar where dozens of liquor varieties stood, ready to be imbibed. The tap was ice cold, and the fries were red hot.

They grabbed a table in the back, near the dartboard, and perused the menu while they waited for the waitress to appear.

"I don't know why I bother looking at the menu," Helena said. "It hasn't changed in my whole life."

"So, what's your favorite meal here?" Joe asked, already certain that Helena wasn't going to choose a salad or plain chicken with a healthy side.

"The bacon mushroom burger with sweet potato fries and coleslaw. Oh! And an extra pickle on the side."

Joe laughed. Helena never shied away from eating a good, hearty meal like so many of his dates had over the course of the past several years. She had made an offhand comment or two about her weight, but he thought she looked perfect, and she obviously didn't let any insecurities she had about her appearance get in the way of enjoying life. He liked that about her. Just another reason he should walk away now. She was different, and he knew it. Pushing aside the voice in his head telling him to just end things this moment, he looked down at her selection on the menu.

"Ah, the Bogart Burger, I see. How about the Captain Renault? Is that good?"

"A well-done burger topped with bleu cheese and caramelized onion on a brioche roll with a side of French fries. My dad's favorite, though not what I'd expect from a doctor."

"I may be a doctor, but I still like good food, just not always good for me food." He had always felt the same about women, he reminded himself. And Helena was absolutely not good for him though in a different way than the others. She confused him and made him think about a life he had deliberately shunned. No, he would not go there. He would allow her to have her burger, and then he was going to end things once and for all even if it meant backing out of their darts duel.

They ordered their burgers along with a pitcher of beer and spent a few minutes watching a group play pool. They kept their conversation light, and Joe couldn't help but feel that Helena, too, was holding back. She was friendly and flirty, but something was missing. He tried to read her, but she was a mystery to him. The pixie continued to work her magic on him.

Just as their meals arrived, Joe felt his phone buzz. He excused himself and reached into his pocket, figuring it was another blocked caller, but this time, it was a local number with a frantic voice on the other end.

"Dr. Blake." He listened and felt the familiar rush of adrenaline mingled with an unfamiliar feeling of annoyance. Typically, any emergency call sent his heart pumping and his mind racing. It was what he'd always lived for—the chance to use his skills to help another person, perhaps even save a life. At the moment, though, all he felt was irritation mingled with relief at not having to face Helena when he told her it was over—whatever 'it' was.

"Meet me at the clinic. I'll be right there." He put away his phone and stood, frowning at Helena. "I'm sorry. I hate to run, but—"

"Joe, you're needed. I understand."

He pointed to the burger. "Take this to your dad. I'm sure he'll appreciate it."

Helena shook her head. "I'll have Arlene pack it up for you. I'll drop it by the clinic later. If you're still busy, I'll just leave it on Dotty's desk."

"You're the best. Thank you." He hesitated for just a moment, but then he leaned forward and kissed her on the cheek. It was an impulsive move but one he felt he had to make. As he turned to go, their eyes met, and he felt certain that she knew, just as he did, that it was the first and last kiss he was ever going to give her.

***

The bed was piled high with clothes, and shoes littered the floor. The open suitcase sat empty next to the clothes, a yawning reminder of the tedious task.

"I told you not to worry about packing. You're in desperate need of a European makeover." Andi lifted a light blue blouse from the top of the pile and held it out in front of her. "I think you were wearing this the day I left for Annapolis, and I was in the Navy for twelve years."

Helena laughed and snatched the blouse from her sister's fingertips. "That's not true." She held the blouse up by the shoulders and inspected it. "I bought this for Jackson's high school graduation."

"Helena," Andi said with a sigh. "He has one semester left of college, and he's behind at that."

"And it still looks nice."

"And boring." Andi put her hands on her hips, and Helena detected a lecture coming. "Helena, you're going to Greece. Do you know what they wear on the beach in Greece? Nothing!"

"Well, I hardly think I'm going to lie on the beach wearing nothing." She pictured the boring, red and blue flowered one-piece suit hidden somewhere in the pile and tried to remember the last time she had even worn a bikini. Not in recent years, that was for sure. Those old insecurities began to resurface like a looming shadow growing taller in the moonlight.

"That's not the point. You want to fit in, not look like a tourist."

"But I will be a tourist." Helena threw the blouse back onto the pile.

"Look, you don't leave for a few more days. We'll go shopping tomorrow for a few basic items. The bakery is closed on Tuesdays, so I'm free."

"What about the library?"

"Don't you have that student, Sarah? Can't she be left alone for a few hours?"

Helena thought for a moment. Sarah really was quite intelligent, and she'd been working at the college library since she was an undergrad and in Buffalo Springs for almost a week now. "Well, I suppose she could manage for a little while."

"Good. We'll run up to Harrison. All the summer clothes have been out since Valentine's Day. We'll be able to get whatever you need."

"I thought you said I shouldn't take too much."

"You shouldn't. You just need some essentials to get you through the first few days. Then you can pick up an outfit here or there on your travels. You'll come back looking like a European fashion icon."

Helena laughed at her sister. "I don't know about that, but maybe I could find some fun things to bring home."

"Bring home some sexy things. That should make Joe remember what he was missing while you were gone."

Helena pushed her sister away. "Come on. Joe isn't gonna miss me. He's so busy with the clinic, we barely see each other as it is. He's already putting distance between us. I can feel it." As she said the words, she thought about the kiss. Though anyone else might've taken it as a sign that he had growing feelings for her, Helena saw the look in Joe's eyes when he turned to leave. The kiss wasn't a promise or an invitation. It was a goodbye.

***

Joe was exhausted. He'd almost slept through his alarm on Monday, and he was barely able to focus on his patients. He'd been up half the night tending to his patient—a local farmer who accidentally shot himself in the hand while putting a hog down for butchering.

He spent most of the day seeing patients, and in between, he squeezed in time to review applications from other doctors, a task he had planned to do over the weekend but never got to. He knew that operating a clinic would be time consuming, but he had no idea it would be life consuming. On top of that, Joe was becoming much more than a general practitioner; he was a dentist, an eye doctor, a general surgeon, an OB-GYN, and almost every other doctor one might need.

With the closest hospital over an hour away and no other doctor's offices nearby, the clinic was more than just a physician's office where people went for sore throats and routine stitches. Joe was learning that he needed every bit of training he learned in medical school, and then some. When someone called to report a possible heart attack, how could he say no? They could be dead before they reached an emergency room. He quickly learned that, no matter the injury, nobody could be turned away. There simply weren't any alternatives nearby, and when a bad snowstorm hit, like it had in early March, there were no alternatives, period. That was why Joe sent letters to colleagues for donations for equipment such as the X-ray machine and the ultrasound, much of which was paid for out of his own pocket, as were many of the medical supplies he used every day. He was able to get a friend back in Houston to donate an EKG machine, and he was searching for optometry instruments. Many of his patients had never had an eye exam. Common injuries ranged from farming accidents to horseback riding falls. In the short time Joe had been in Buffalo Springs, he had seen just about every ailment one could imagine in the rural south and many that would never cross the mind. What he needed most was another doctor to help relieve some of his workload and offer medical advice about things Joe had never encountered before.

When the shadows in his office started to grow longer, Joe removed his glasses, rubbed his eyes, and wiped his hand down his face. He let out a long, exhausted breath. He had narrowed his choices down to one woman and one man, both highly qualified, both seeking to leave the city for a slower pace. Boy, were they going to be surprised. Joe's days were sometimes far busier in the little Buffalo Springs Jeremy Blake Medical Clinic than they had been in the hectic Houston ER.

Joe shut down the computer, switched off the desk lamp and stood, stretching his back to the sounds of pops and cracks. His thoughts drifted to Helena, and he admonished himself for the kiss, as chaste as it was. He should've just ended things from the start, right on her porch, and not gone to dinner at all.

Throughout the marathon of his busy days, the many people he encountered, the stories he heard, and the diagnoses he made, thoughts of Helena peppered everything, and Joe was bothered by it. He wanted to share with her a funny anecdote he'd heard from his patient, Mr. Daniels. He wondered if she would like the chocolate cake offered as payment from Mrs. McCoy. His sandwich from the new cafe made him remember how much she loves ham and cheese croissants, a fact she shared with him over dinner when he told her about the croque monsieur sandwiches she must try in France.

As he finished turning off lights and closing up the clinic, he pushed thoughts of her aside. By this time next week, she would be gone, and he was going to make an effort to forget her. Despite his vow to leave 'Dr. Casanova' in Houston, he was afraid that his own Mr. Hyde might be the only way for Dr. Jekyl to forget about Helena Nelson.

***

Exhaustion was pushed aside by excitement as Helena stood by the carousel and waited for her luggage to drop. She had slept in mere fragments of time on the transatlantic flight, occupying herself with two movies and the latest Sheryl Woods ebook. The iPad she read on was an early birthday present from Andi who pre-loaded it with the most recent offerings from many of Helena's favorite authors.

The birthday gathering the day before she left had included her parents, Andi and Wade, Jackson, her best friend, Allie, and, to her surprise, Dr. Joe Blake. She couldn't help but wonder if that had been Andi's doing despite Helena's insistence that she did not want a relationship with him, but Andi's narrowed gaze and subtle shake of her head told Helena that her sister was not playing matchmaker and shared her chagrin at his presence. As it turned out, it was Grace Nelson who invited the good doctor on the spur of a moment when she ran into him at the grocery store.

"The man had oatmeal, frozen dinners, and a bag of apples in his cart. I knew it was a sign that he needed a good, homecooked meal."

Helena laughed at her mother's account, partly because she felt better that Joe's presence was not a set up and partly because Joe had remarked to Helena several times that he loved to cook but never has the time. He seemed to enjoy himself, though he kept his distance from Helena and didn't act at all like a man she'd now been on several dates with.

Grace and Joshua gave Helena a new suitcase, something she desperately needed but hadn't wanted to spend the money on. Jackson's gift was a set of noise-canceling headphones for the plane, which Helena appreciated but found quite uncomfortable for sleeping. In addition to the iPad, Andi and Wade gave her a beautiful, leather travel purse—small, lightweight, and with RFD blocking technology to protect her credit cards and phone from being hacked.

Allie's gift was practical, thoughtful, and a way to stay in touch with everyone back home. At first, when Helena opened the birthday card and saw the odd-looking gift card inside, she wasn't sure what it was.

"It's a European SIM card. I ordered it online and hoped it would arrive in time," Allie told her.

Helena unconsciously bit into her bottom lip as she turned the card over in her hand. "A SIM card?"

"It's for your phone. So you can stay in touch with…" She hesitated, glanced at Joe and then quickly looked away. "Well, with all of us back home."

Darn that Allie. She knew how Helena felt, but whether she intended to or not, by her glance, she had included Joe in 'all of us.' Helena wished they were still sitting at the kitchen table rather than the living room so that she could discreetly kick her best friend in the shin. Instead, she avoided looking at Joe and turned her attention to the gift.

"How does it work?"

"Honestly, I'm not sure," Allie admitted with a chuckle. "You're Miss Technology. I figured you'd know."

"I can show you," Joe spoke up, forcing Helena to look his way. "I attended a medical conference in Copenhagen not long ago, and we all used them."

"Oh. Thanks, Joe. I'd appreciate that." She smiled, and he smiled back, but she noticed that his smile did not reach his eyes. What was going on with him? Was he pulling back because she was leaving or because he simply lost interest in her? If so, why had he come to the party at all?

After she thanked everyone for the gifts, Joe took the time to show her how to remove her phone's SIM card and replace it with the new one. He made sure she knew what to do and then carefully put her old card back in place.

"Just switch them before you land and activate it once you're on the ground."

"Will I know how?"

"I'll write down detailed instructions for you. You shouldn't have any problem."

Helena had been a librarian long enough to understand technology, and she was the go-to person in the family for all things technical, *Miss Technology*, as Allie had put it. Even Andi had asked for her help with her business software a time or two, and Andi was no stranger to modern technology and computer usage.

"It looks easy enough." She looked at him and smiled. "Thank you, Joe." She turned toward Allie. "And thank you. I'm going to miss you."

She went to Allie and wrapped her arms around her. No matter how often they annoyed or upset each other over the past twenty-four years, they would always be best friends.

Allie wiped away a tear. "I expect to hear from you, you know. I want all the details about your travels. Nothing is going to be the same around here while you're gone. You'd better text me every day."

"Her phone number will be different," Joe told them, "but she can text everyone once it's set up and let us know that she arrived."

Helena cast a sidelong glance at Joe. Did he mean that? Was he really expecting her to text him while she was away?

Standing in the strange airport now, the memory made her heart flip, and Helena wondered if it was because she was in Athens or because Joe might be waiting to hear from her. She opted for the former.

She spotted her new turquoise suitcase when it fell to the conveyor belt and watched it make its way toward her. She grabbed the handle and hefted it off the belt and onto the ground. With both nerves and excitement flowing through her like the electric pulse she'd once been treated with by a chiropractor when still cheering, Helena made her way out into the hot sunlight and hailed a taxi. Once in the car and on the way to downtown Athens, she pulled out her phone and turned it on. While still on the plane, she had carefully repeated the steps Joe showed her to replace the SIM card. In the taxi, she referred to his instructions and activated the phone, holding her breath as she waited for it to connect. She breathed a sigh of relief when suddenly a message popped up on the screen welcoming her to Greece. Messages from the carrier began flooding the screen. She let them finish before she sent a quick note to the family group chat to let them know she'd arrived. She sent a similar text to Allie, once again thanking her for the SIM card, and a brief 'Arrived' to Joe. She then sent a message to her host.

The Airbnb was a good forty-five-minute ride from the airport, and Helena fought to keep her eyes open, but every now and then, her head jerked back as she was jolted from sleep. She didn't want to miss a minute of her trip and took several deep breaths and blinked her eyes, willing herself to stay alert and look around.

"Is hard to stay awake after long flight, yes?"

Helena met the driver's eyes in the rearview mirror. "Yes, very hard." She smiled at his friendly brown eyes. "You speak very good English."

"I attended university in America."

"Oh? What did you study?"

"Engineering."

Her jaw dropped. "Really? Why are you…" She stopped herself, not wanting to be rude.

"Why I drive taxi? America says it does not need foreign engineers, only American, so I come home, but there are no jobs in Greece."

"You have a degree in engineering, and you can't get a job?"

He shrugged. "Yes, is too bad. I have wife and baby, so we live in small apartment, and I drive taxi."

She had no idea what to say to that. She hoped this job was enough to sustain them. "Is Athens very crowded right now? I mean, do you pick up a lot of tourists?"

"No, not yet. It will be more crowded in another month. You came at good time."

"It's not as hot as I thought it would be."

"That will be another month, too. How long will you stay?"

"I'm in Athens for four days, then to some of the islands for a week, and back to Athens overnight before flying to Rome."

"Not much time to see it all. There are many beautiful places to visit in Greece. Your first time?"

"Yes, my first time away from the States. There's so much I want to see." Her last few words were almost a whisper as the sight of the Acropolis overtook her thoughts. It was massive, high atop a hill overlooking the city. She gasped as they drew closer.

"You picked good place to stay. You are very close to Acropolis," the driver said as he pulled up to the curb in front of an apartment building.

Helena thanked the driver, gave him a hefty tip, and watched him pull away. She stood with her bags at her feet and marveled at the ancient ruins, looming above the buildings.

"Are you Helena?"

She turned to see a handsome young man standing on the steps to the building. He wore casual white pants and a flowing shirt. He had deep blue eyes and dark wavy hair, and Helena blushed as she thought about her day-old clothes and unwashed hair.

"Yes. Anastasios?

"Yes, welcome. I will show you to studio."

He led her inside and to a small elevator with an iron gate. He opened the gate and then opened a second door before gesturing for her to go in. He glanced at her bags and smiled at her. "There is not much room in lift. I will take stairs with your luggage. The floor is number three. Be sure to always close gate before you close door, or lift will not operate."

Helena nodded and took her smaller carry-on from him, then watched as he closed the gate. She shut the door and pressed the number three on the panel. There were five floors. When the elevator stopped, Helena pushed open the door to find Anastasios opening the gate for her. She followed him to the apartment.

Once Anastasios had given her a tour of the one-bedroom apartment, he showed her the air conditioner remote, the WIFI password, and the few amenities he had provided—Greek yogurt, biscuits, and dates for breakfast as well as a chilled bottle of wine, some cheese, and a bowl of grapes. He told her which keys were for which door and bid her "Ya," which she knew meant goodbye, and left her on her own.

Helena went straight to the sliding glass door of the balcony and pulled open the drape. She was almost parallel to the Parthenon, and the site took her breath away. She hurried to the table where she had left her phone and rushed back to the window as if the view might disappear before she had a chance to really appreciate it. She snapped a photo and sent it to her family. She hesitated a moment before sending it to Joe, hoping he meant it when he had told her to text often and send pictures.

Five

Joe smiled as he looked at the view from Helena's balcony. It was nice that she had sent him the photo although… He frowned as the thought crossed his mind that she might be reading too much into their dates. He had hoped she would pick up on his cues that they were just casual. The only kiss they shared was his hasty peck on her cheek, and he'd made a point of not calling her after that. Maybe it was a mistake to go to the birthday party, but he didn't want to offend the rest of the family. In hindsight, it seemed that nobody else knew he'd been invited, so he could have declined without worry.

He thought for a moment before his fingers began typing a message.

Beautiful. Enjoy your trip.

He read the short message over and over, wondering if he should say more, but hit send before he changed his mind about answering at all. It was short, to the point, and didn't invite an answer back. That was what he wanted…wasn't it?

Dotty knocked on the door and opened it a crack, sticking her head inside and pushing Helena from his thoughts. "Dale's here. Suzy stepped on a piece of glass. Looks like she may need stitches."

Joe stood. "Thanks, Dotty. I'll be right in." As he pocketed his phone, he felt a vibration and pulled the device back out, holding it out to see the screen.

You should see it, Joe. It's just like I imagined. I'm going to tour it tomorrow. I can't wait. I'll send pics then. Heading out to find food now.

Another, more insistent buzz from his phone caused Joe's frown to grow deeper. The caller ID was blocked. It was the third call Joe had received from a blocked number in the past twenty-four hours. Should he answer?

"Darn telemarketers," he said, hitting the decline button and sliding the phone into the pocket of his lab coat.

He headed to the exam room, an uneasy feeling in the pit of his stomach. How was he going to handle the situation if Helena kept texting him? He brushed off the thought and headed into the exam room where Melanie, his recently hired nurse, was taking Suzy's blood pressure.

"Well, if it isn't my favorite patient. What brings you to see me today, Miss Suzy?" He looked at the blood-soaked gauze wrapped around her foot. "I hear you've been dancing on glass."

"I wasn't dancing," Suzy said with a sniffle, doing her best to put up a brave front as tears threatened.

"Then what were you doing?" He gently began to unwrap the bandage.

"I was trying to get a drink, but the cabinet was too high. I fell off the chair and dropped the glass. I wanted to be good and clean it up for Daddy, but when I tried to get the broom, I stepped on a, on a…" She looked up at Dale. "What was it, Daddy?"

"A shard, honey, a shard of glass."

She nodded and looked back at Joe. "I stepped on a shard."

Joe put on gloves and gently prodded the cut. "Melanie, can you please shine a light on this for me?"

"Yes, Doctor." She held the light so that Joe could see inside the cut.

"Thank you. No pieces of glass in the foot." He took some pieces of gauze from the nearby counter and held it tightly against the cut. "Melanie is going to use a needle to put some medicine in your foot so that you can't feel it. It will be kind of like when your foot falls asleep. Do you know what that feels like?"

Suzy nodded.

"Once your foot feels like it's totally asleep, I'm going to sew it back together so that it won't bleed anymore. You might feel me sewing, but it won't hurt, okay?"

"I pricked my finger with one of Mommy's sewing needles once. It hurt, and it bled." Her eyes were wide with fear.

Joe gestured for Melanie to take over applying pressure. She took another few pieces of gauze and added them to the existing gauze as Joe slipped off his bloody gloves and placed a hand reassuringly on Suzy's shoulder.

"Sewing needles can hurt a lot and can make you bleed a little bit, but these needles are different. They stop the bleeding. I promise, you won't feel any pain."

Suzy looked from Joe to her father. "Daddy, will you hold my hand?"

Dale smiled at his daughter. "Oh course I will, Suzy Q. You can squeeze my hand as hard as you want."

Suzy nodded and turned back to Joe. "Okay. I'm ready."

"Let's get the medicine on it first." He put on new gloves and took over for Melanie who removed her gloves before leaving the room. "Melanie is going to get the medicine and all the things I need to sew up your foot."

"Is it still bleeding?" Suzy asked, stretching forward to get a better look.

"Hopefully not, but I don't want to peek. The more we look at it, the longer it will take for the bleeding to stop. I'm going to keep holding the gauze on it real tight until Melanie gets back."

When Melanie returned, she placed a plastic-covered tray on the counter and put on new gloves. Suzy watched intently as Joe removed the gauze, and Melanie prepared the shot. She let out a small gasp when Melanie squirted a tiny bit of the liquid from the syringe. Suzy quickly looked away and inspected her foot.

"The bleeding stopped," Suzy said, her voice tinged with awe.

"It did, but don't try to move your foot," Joe advised. "Or it might start back up again."

Suzy nodded and bit her lips tightly together as she stared at her foot, and she closed her eyes tightly when Melanie stuck her with the needle.

While they waited for the foot to numb, Joe asked Dale how he was doing.

"We're okay. Still trying to figure things out, you know?"

"I understand," Joe said. "It's not easy losing someone you love and trying to figure out what you're supposed to do with your life after that."

Dale looked at Joe with sadness in his eyes and nodded. "Luckily, my parents and my brother, Coop, are here for us. I don't know what I'd do without them. I felt bad that Cooper moved back here to help out, but he's been a lifesaver." He looked at Melanie. "I hear Wade's mama isn't doing well. Have you heard anything?"

Joe had snatched Melanie up as soon as she received her ASN though she was still going to school for her BSN. She'd previously worked for the mayor while attending nursing school, taking care of his mother until Blanche's dementia got bad enough that she needed to be placed in a nursing facility, and Wade highly recommended her for the job at the clinic.

Melanie blinked away a tear before she answered. "Andi told me she's not able to talk anymore. She eats very little. It's only a matter of time."

"That's a real shame," Dale said. "I always loved Miss Blanche."

"Everyone did," Melanie said with a sad smile. "Taking care of her was one of my greatest pleasures in life."

"I hear your new boss is a real slave driver," Joe said, hoping to lighten the mood.

"He's not bad," Melanie said with a grin. "He lets me study for my classes when we don't have patients." She looked at Suzy. "How does your foot feel?"

"I can't feel it at all," Suzy said in wonder.

"Then let's get to work," Joe said.

Joe expertly stitched Suzy's foot while she gripped her daddy's hand. In no time at all, it was done, and Joe was waving goodbye to his current favorite patient. Joe smiled as he entered the next room and greeted the former Mayor Baker.

"Well, if it isn't my favorite patient," he said as he closed the door.

***

In just one evening, Helena browsed the shops along the Apostolou Pavlou and Ermou Street, drank a glass of wine in the shadow of the Acropolis, and wandered through Plaka where she found a sidewalk restaurant on Andrianou that indulged her with more food and wine than one person could consume. She sat back in her chair and sipped her wine while watching other tourists stroll by. She saw a few families, an obvious mother and young adult daughter, and many couples, holding hands, stealing kisses, and slowly walking to the gently swaying rhythm only the music of love can orchestrate. She thought of Joe and wondered who he was going out with that evening.

As the sun sank behind the ancient ruins atop the hill, Helena made her way back to the apartment. Sleep was beckoning, and she was more than ready to give in to its siren call. It was mid-afternoon back home but nearly ten o'clock in Greece, and the shower she took earlier in the evening gave her just enough of a boost to make it to a normal Athens bedtime. Other than the short naps on the plane, she had now been awake for over thirty-six hours. When she finally crawled between the sheets on the bed, the air conditioner above the door blowing a steady stream of cool air into the room, Helena sighed and closed her eyes. Her thoughts produced just the first two words of her evening prayers before her mind went blank and her breathing slowed to a light caress of air against her pillow.

***

Joe frowned as he looked at the screen on his phone. At least he could see and recognize the number this time. The amount of calls with blocked numbers he was getting had become more than a nuisance. It was beginning to cause him to lose focus. What call list had gotten his number, and how could he get off of it?

He debated answering the familiar number, but he found himself unable to resist. He slid the button across his phone and accepted the incoming video call.

"Good morning. It's mighty early over there." He watched Helena's face came into focus and, for just a moment, he felt a slight tug in his gut. He ignored it as he asked, "Is everything okay?"

"It is, and I hope it's okay that I called so late. I won't keep you. I just wanted to thank you again for the advice and for showing me how to switch the SIM cards."

He sat back in his chair and held the phone out in front of him. It was close to eleven, and the waning moon cast only the thinnest sheen of light in the night sky, but he could see the glow of the early morning sun on Helena's face.

"You're welcome. I'm actually still working, but that's okay. Is there something you need? Are you all right?" Though he tried to sound casual, he felt a wave of alarm.

"You're still working at this hour?" She sounded okay, not panicked or in trouble.

"Until I hire another doctor, and a bookkeeper, my hours are going to keep increasing, but that's to be expected. Tell me about your trip."

"It's wonderful, though I've only seen a small part of it. I took your advice and tried to take in as much as I could yesterday, and I pushed myself to keep moving. I think I did pretty well. I went to bed around ten which is why I'm now awake at six." Her eyes twinkled as she smiled, and Joe felt an unexpected jolt in his chest. "And that's why I'm calling. Thank you so much for all the advice. I feel so confident being here by myself, and I'm not sure I would feel this way if not for your guidance and encouragement."

Joe was happy that she felt the information he gave her was helpful, he truly was, but a voice in the back of his head told him he shouldn't encourage her to keep calling.

Rather than tell her he was busy, though, he found himself asking, "And the Acropolis? Is it spectacular?"

"From what I can see. I'm gonna be at the entrance before it opens, like the guidebook suggested."

"Good. I look forward to seeing pictures." Where had that come from? His intention was to stop her from calling and sending pictures, not have her continue.

She hesitated. "I'll be sure to do that." Her smile faltered, and he wondered if she, too, wasn't sure that was a good idea. "Well, I guess I should let you finish your work so you can go home."

"Yeah, I should get going, but thanks for calling." He tried to keep his tone casual and his message clear. He did not want her calling him throughout her trip, but if that was true, why was he disappointed that she was saying goodbye?

"You're welcome, Joe. Have a nice night."

"Thanks, Helena. I hope you have a really nice day."

"Thanks. I'll talk to you soon." She hung up before he could tell her not to worry about calling him, to just enjoy the trip, and a part of him actually felt glad that he hadn't brushed her off or discouraged her from calling again.

The room darkened as a storm cloud covered the sliver of moon that hung in the sky, and Joe couldn't help but think about what Helena said about the moon the night they sat looking at the stars. He wasn't much of a reflection of light and good. In fact, he'd been living in shadows for several years now, and it was where he was comfortable, or so he thought. The face he showed the world was one of confidence and self-reliance. He kept his distance from others, kept his love life short and simple, and held back in his personal life. Or he had, until he found himself opening up to Helena. He was grateful she would be gone all summer. He needed to get her out of his system. For almost seven years, Joe had kept everyone at a safe distance, even his parents. It was easier than getting hurt again. With Jeremy gone, the only person who knew all his secrets was his best friend, Darrin, his and Jeremy's sidekick since they moved back to the States in the sixth grade.

Joe had come close to confiding in Andi once or twice when he'd first come to town. He knew they shared heartache, but he quickly figured out that Andi was more adept than he at moving past her pain. He'd opened up more to Helena than he had to anyone in years, but he hadn't told her about…

The rumble of thunder shook him from thoughts of his painful past. He looked around the dimly lit office and wondered if this was all he'd ever have in life—his job, his patients, and his loneliness.

The rain dimpled the window, and Joe breathed a long sigh, reminding himself for the thousandth time that the job was enough. It filled him and made him feel good about himself in ways that another person never could. And it would never leave him standing at the altar, with Jeremy and Darrin by his side, trying to figure out where everything had gone so terribly wrong.

***

The woman smiled as she handed Helena back her phone after snapping a photo.

"Thank you," Helena said, taking the phone and shielding her eyes from the late morning sun. "Have a great trip."

She watched the family walk away and felt a small pang of envy. It would've been so nice to share this adventure with someone. She sighed and shook her head as she turned to gaze at the Parthenon. No regrets, she told herself. This was going to be the trip of a lifetime no matter what.

She brought the photo up on her phone and scrutinized the image. She posed with hands in the air, channeling the cheerleader she once was, with the Parthenon behind her. A few puffy clouds hung in the perfect blue sky. She wore a lacy top with cap sleeves and coral-colored embroidered flowers that she picked up in one of the shops the previous afternoon and her favorite long, white shorts. The sun glinted off her hair, and she looked like a different person. In fact, she looked good, really good. The bit of weight she'd put on in her twenties perfectly filled out the shorts and top, and she looked much healthier than she'd ever looked in college.

Helena bit her lip and tilted her head. She pinched the screen and spread her fingers to zoom in on her face. It was the face of a girl she hadn't seen since high school. The face of someone with no worries, no stress, and no fears. It was the face of someone who still believed in love, still believed in finding a soulmate, still believed that all her dreams would come true, and still believed she'd see the world someday. Where had this girl been for the past ten years?

"Excuse me, miss?" A voice with a beautiful British accent startled her, and she looked up to see a young couple standing before her. "Would you mind taking our picture?" The man asked.

Happy to oblige, Helena answered, "Sure," and accepted the man's phone with a smile.

"We're on honeymoon," the pretty blonde said, turning toward her new husband with a look of pure love and admiration.

"Congratulations." Helena raised the phone to take the shot. She snapped a few pictures then handed the phone back. "I hope you have a nice trip and a lifetime of happiness."

As she watched the couple stroll hand-in-hand through the ruins, she couldn't help but wonder, is there still such a thing as true love, soulmates, and dreams coming true? She thought of her sister and how happy she and Wade were. After devastating tragedies, they had found each other just when they needed each other the most. An image of Joe entered her mind, and Helena frowned. He was nice, and she enjoyed being with and talking to him, but she was certain he was not the type of guy who believed in soulmates. She had no doubt that he was pushing her away before she left.

Helena had a sudden realization. She would be twenty-nine in a few days and was still single. The realization being that she no longer cared about either. She spent every minute of both high school and college on the arm of some boy. She never stayed home on a Friday or Saturday night, and she was practically engaged to Bret her last two years at Missouri State. Since then, she'd gotten her Masters, taken over and rejuvenated the town library, ran countless organizations, and discovered that God was more than a notion; he was a very real part of her everyday life and had been since her flirtation with bulimia. She had dated here and there but nothing serious since Bret, and she was okay with that. She was happy, more than content with her life. The only thing she hadn't done was travel, and here she was on the adventure of a lifetime. She was in Greece, for heaven's sake. Who needed romance when they had paradise at their fingertips?

Feeling a confidence she had never felt before, Helena lifted her phone and took a wide-grinned selfie with the Temple of Athena behind her. She took dozens of photos as she roamed the ancient site, taking the time to read each historical stone tablet and every modern tourist sign. She wandered in and out of the ruins that were accessible to visitors and photographed the incredible view of Athens from the pinnacle of the Acropolis. She followed the footpath around the back of the site that took her down to another part of the city.

It was warm but not hot, and a light breeze caressed the back of her neck below her short crop of curls. She pulled out her phone and checked off 'Acropolis' on her list. She had more to see before the temperature reached its peak, and she didn't want to miss a thing.

***

A parade and festival were planned for Memorial Day Weekend, and somehow Joe found himself sitting on the planning committee.

"We're just three days away," Helena's friend, Paige, told the group. "I assured Helena that everything would go smoothly in her absence, so please tell me that nobody has run into any glitches."

"Everything is all set for the parade." Dotty stood and looked at Paige. "Dr. Blake has agreed to be one of our judges." She smiled at her boss and Joe fought the urge to roll his eyes. *No town this small needs judges for its parade. How many floats could there be—five? That's probably pushing it.* "We also have Mayor Montgomery." She grinned at Wade who looked as excited as Joe felt. "And Father Michael who isn't on the committee but said he was willing to judge." Dotty sat down with a smug look on her face.

"Thank you, Dotty. How many floats do we have?"

Dotty stood back up and flashed a triumphant smile. "Twenty-seven." She flounced back down and held her head up high as if she had just won first place in the watermelon seed spitting contest, which Joe had learned was an actual thing.

"Twenty-seven!" Andi sounded surprised, and Joe blinked in amazement. "Where did you find enough groups to get twenty-seven floats?"

"We've got two Girl Scout Troops, three Boy Scout Troops, both schools, the saloon—"

"The saloon?" Paige asked, her eyes wide.

"Yes, and most of the other businesses as well—the theater troupe, the Italian place, the toy store, the Baptist Church. Oh!" She looked up from the list on her phone. "Father Michael says he won't hold that against them. That they're Baptist, I mean."

Paige just nodded, but Joe found himself grinning at the thought of Dotty holding her priest accountable in the judging of a parade.

"Anyway, we have three antique cars, the American Legion Ladies Auxiliary, the Ozark Mountaineers horseback riding club—who will clean up after themselves—and ten emergency vehicles from here and other nearby towns. You know, fire trucks, ambulances, and the like. And, of course, we have all the town's veterans walking in the parade as well. They will lead the parade and will then be given seats of honor next to the judging platform."

"Wow," Paige said. "That's great, Dotty. Thank you for all your work getting participants."

"You're welcome." Dotty sat down, her smile even bigger than normal.

Joe listened to the other details—the three-legged race, egg toss, and of course the watermelon seed spitting contest. There was some discussion about the booths being rented out to local artisans and restaurants and the afternoon bingo game that would wrap up the day's events. Joe tuned out a bit when the talk turned to whether the horseback riding club was going to clean up during or after the parade, but Dotty had that under control as well. The thought struck Joe that perhaps he needed to give Dotty more to do around the clinic, but then again, she had boundless energy and could multi-task better than a monkey eating a banana while swinging from the trees. The proceeds from the booth rentals were going toward redoing the garden around the war memorial outside City Hall and to build a new playground and spruce up the existing town park. If all was successful, the July Fourth festivities should pay for the repairs to the cracked fountain in the center of town.

"Dr. Blake?"

"Joe?"

Joe was jarred from his drowsy thoughts. With blinking eyes, he focused on Andi.

"Yes?" he said, feeling his face flush.

"Paige asked if you have everything you need for the First Aid tent?"

"Oh, yes. I'm supplying the First Aid kits, and the EMTs are going to run the tent."

"Very good. I think that's it." Paige answered a few questions and then dismissed the group.

Before he had a chance to stand, Andi asked Joe to hang back for a minute. She looked worried about something.

"What's up, Andi?" he asked, hoping that neither she nor Wade was having any health problems.

"Joe, have you heard from Helena?"

"Me? No, not since Monday. She was up early and Facetimed me to thank me for the advice. She promised to send pictures, but I haven't gotten any since her visit to the Acropolis." Why did he feel the need to justify her call; moreover, why did Andi assume that he had heard from her sister? He wasn't her keeper, and he certainly wasn't her boyfriend, though, when he let his guard down, he did picture her lying on the beach at sunset with the likes of Orestis Karnezis of the Greek National Football Team, and he wasn't happy with the image. Snapping back to his senses, Joe peered at Andi. "Is Helena okay?"

Andi shook her head dismissively. "I guess so. She's sent me some pictures and a few short texts, but she seems so…distant."

Joe smiled. "Andi," he said soothingly. "She is distant. She's in Greece."

Andi huffed. "I know that, Joe." He saw her clench her jaw in frustration or perhaps annoyance. "She's not being her usual chatty self. It's strange. I would think she'd have so much to tell me that she'd be bursting to talk, but I can't even get her to call me."

Joe nodded, picturing Orestis Karnezis again but pushed the image aside. "Maybe she's just keeping herself busy. You know how hectic vacations can be. Has Allie heard from her?"

"Not much." She chewed on her lip. "Really, how hectic can it be?" Her frustration was made more obvious by her narrowing eyes and jutted-out jaw. "She's by herself for heaven's sake!"

"Andi," Wade called from the doorway. "Leave Joe alone. I'm sure Helena is just fine. How often did you call home when you were overseas?"

Andi flinched, and Joe knew that Wade had struck a nerve. His family never heard from Jeremy when he was on assignment.

"That was different," she said, but there was defeat in her voice. She looked penitently at Joe. "I'm sorry. I just miss her."

"I understand, Andi, but I wouldn't worry about it. I'm sure she's fine."

Joe walked away, his mind a jumble of thoughts. Helena was an adult. She could take care of herself. And he was *not* her keeper. Still, Andi's words echoed in his head, *I just miss her*, she had said, and though his mind protested, a little voice inside his heart said, *So do I.*

Joe left the building and walked toward his car. The light from the full moon was brighter than the streetlight. He felt his phone vibrate and huffed a breath of annoyance. The calls were totally out of hand. Maybe if he answered, he could get them to take him off their list. He'd already contacted the Do Not Call Registry to no avail. The calls continued.

"Hello," he said angrily. "Who is this?"

He heard a gasp on the other end, and the call abruptly ended. He took the phone away from his ear and stared at it, watching as it changed from his lock screen to a black screen reflecting the moon above. A sudden chill came over him.

He shoved the phone back into his pocket and paused with his hand on the door handle while the car automatically unlocked. He cursed as he slid into the driver's seat, trying to shake the eerie feeling that was creeping up the back of his neck. It was only a gasp, barely audible, not at all distinguishable, but still, something about it had turned his blood to ice.

Six

Helena stretched out in the beach chair, soaking up the sun and listening to the lapping waves. An island breeze kicked up sand, threatening the smooth polish on her freshly painted toenails. She had stepped out of her comfort zone that morning and tried out the fish foot massage that she passed along one of the touristy streets on the island. Far less crowded than Athens, the paved streets curled around through the town of white stone buildings which flowed into each other like a cavernous maze decorated with blue doors and buckets of bright pink blossoms.

The massage had consisted of dozens of tiny fish let loose inside the fish tank to go to work on her dangling feet, scavenging for the skin on her heels and toes. She resisted the urge to giggle as the fish did their job, massaging and smoothing the rough edges. Helena wondered how many native Greeks actually did this and decided it was a total tourist trap, but she sat back and let herself enjoy it anyway. After, she agreed to let the spa technician give her a pedicure.

Wearing a new bikini, the first she'd owned since college, Helena and her shiny toes were thoroughly enjoying the lure of the Mediterranean. She reached for her daiquiri and took a sip of the frosty concoction. Her sunglasses shielded her eyes as she gazed out across the white sand and turquoise water.

Helena let out a long, contented sigh and tried to remember the last time she felt this relaxed, this at ease with her body, this content with her life. Just as she began pondering her life of leisure, her phone buzzed on the table beside her. Reluctantly, she reached for it and held her hand over the screen to block the sun's glare as she read the text from Andi.

Happy birthday! Miss you. Hope you're having fun. Send Pics.

A tinge of guilt entered her mind as her finger hesitated over the keyboard. She hadn't exactly been avoiding everyone, but she hadn't kept in touch like she promised. It wasn't that she didn't miss them; in fact, the opposite was true—she missed them terribly, especially today.

Helena was so happy for the first few days—enjoying her solitude, people watching, strolling through the streets of Athens and the small islands—but now, on her birthday, she just wanted to have Andi there with her, or Allie, or… No, she wasn't going to say or even think it. She did not need Joe or any other man with her to make her vacation complete. However, she did wish she had someone to talk to at night, take photos with, share a bottle of wine with over dinner, or plan the day together.

Rather than stay in touch with everyone back home, Helena found it easier to push them away. She could imagine them going about their lives, not giving her a thought, and it made her feel better about not thinking about them. But she knew how her family would worry if she didn't let them know she was okay, and it made her feel loved that the still remembered her birthday when she was so far away.

Thanks! Having a blast. Here's my view today.

She held up the phone, took a picture of the Mediterranean with her polished toes at the bottom of the screen, and hit send. She followed up the text with the message, Sending my love, and a kissing emoji.

Helena hit send on the second message but didn't lay down her phone. She stared at the list of messages where Joe Blake's name seemed to jump off the screen. What could it hurt to send him a picture? After all, he had been terribly kind, and sending a photo didn't mean that they were entering a relationship. She would still be a single woman, roaming the world, defining her own path and destiny.

Her finger tapped lightly on his name, and a new message block appeared. Helena brought up the photo gallery and scrolled through until she found one she liked from the isle of Naxos. Taken from the stone walkway heading back from the ruins of Apollo's Temple, the photo showed a white moon suspended above pink clouds in the early evening sky. At the other end of the walkway, behind Helena, the white buildings circled the hill in ascending layers, resembling a windowed pyramid jutting up from the beach. Helena's blue shirt perfectly matched the hue of the sea and made a stunning contrast to the pink clouds and white stone architecture. Her radiant smile rivaled the glow of the moon.

Helena selected the photo and typed, *Naxos at sunset*, but she hesitated. Was she sending the wrong message? Would he think that she was pining away for him? She stared at the photo. It portrayed exactly the mood she wanted it to. It was beautiful, and admittedly, so was she. Her tanned skin glowed, and the highlights in her hair gave off a sun-kissed luminescence that made her facial features seem ethereal. More importantly, she didn't look like a naïve young woman exploring a strange place. She looked like a seasoned traveler, confident in herself and her abilities to navigate the world.

No, it was just the right message. It said, *See, I'm having the time of my life, better than ever, and I don't need approval or guidance or advice from anyone.*

She hit send and put down her phone. When she heard the vibration a few minutes later, she smiled but continued lying still on the chair with her eyes closed, inhaling the scents of salt and sand and the prawns being fried at the seaside bar-restaurant not far down the beach.

Whether it was Andi or Joe or another well-wisher on her birthday, they could wait. For the first time in her life, Helena found herself enjoying her solitude, awash with the knowledge that she was finally doing exactly what she wanted to be doing—no time commitments, no committee to answer to, no patrons asking for help. Her life was an open sea, and she was not only sailing her own ship but navigating its course with clear skies and gentle waves surrounding her.

***

Joe gave his best friend, Darrin Ewing, credit. The man sat on Joe's leather couch and good-naturedly listened to his friend lament about the maddening calls he'd been receiving.

"But they haven't called back since you answered, right?"

"Right, but that makes it even stranger. Why call incessantly for weeks only to hang up as soon as I answer?"

"Maybe they heard your voice and realized they'd been calling the wrong number."

"Maybe. I don't know. There was something about that last call…" Joe absent-mindedly swiped the phone's screen as he thought about the calls. His thumb hit the photo app, accidentally opening a picture of Helena.

Darrin grabbed the phone and whistled at the photograph. "You've been holding out on me. Is this the librarian? She's quite the looker."

Joe snatched the phone away from Darrin and pressed a button, turning the screen black. He tossed the phone onto the recently delivered coffee table in front of his brown leather sofa. "You don't need to whistle at her like she's a street walker passing a construction site."

Darrin waved his hands in the air. "Whoa, hold on. I didn't mean anything by it. She's nice looking, that's all."

Joe took a sip of his beer and slowly swallowed before turning back to his oldest friend. "Sorry, Dare. I was still thinking about the calls." Darrin knew him better than anyone, so there was no use lying. "Helena's beautiful. I'll give her that."

"You like her."

"Everybody likes her. She's the nicest, most caring, most genuine woman I've ever known."

Darrin raised one brow and looked skeptically at Joe. "So, what exactly is the problem here?"

Joe focused on his feet as if they would give him the answer he was looking for.

He felt Darrin's stare, and when he finally turned toward his friend, he saw Darrin's lips curl into a sly smile. "You've got it bad, brother."

Joe's head snapped up. "Don't be ridiculous." He tipped the bottle back and let the rest of the beer run down his throat. He put the bottle on the table and sat back on the couch. "We're just friends."

Darrin laughed. "You may be friends, but that doesn't mean that you don't have the hots for her." He crossed his arms and surveyed Joe. "In fact, from what I can tell, you've more than got the hots for her. You're falling for this woman." Darrin cocked his jaw to the side. Joe watched as his mouth widened to a self-assured grin. "Joe Blake, eternal heartbreaker, is finally in love."

Joe rolled his eyes and tried to ignore the drop he felt in his gut at his friend's words. "Not a chance. I've made it this far without getting suckered in. I've got a great, upgraded historical house, a rewarding job, lots of new friends, and a full life. I have no need to complicate things with a woman."

"I hear your words, but I also see the look in your eyes. It's not so bad, you know. That complicated life you're working so hard to avoid. There's something to be said for having someone to go home to at night, someone to talk to about everything, someone in your corner who always wants what's best for you and would do anything in the world to make you happy."

Joe shook his head. "Fairy tales. That's all that is. A giant fairy tale."

"Look, Joe, I know Lindsay did a number on you. She crushed you. But, man, that was years ago. It's time to get over it."

Joe sat back against the smooth, leather cushion and pondered his friend's words. What did he know? Darrin married the only girl he ever dated. They were friends as kids, got together in high school, made it past four years at different colleges, and were now married with three kids. Darrin's whole life was nothing but a fairy tale. Not everyone got that lucky. Some people never made it to the 'I dos.'

"Hey, Joe." Darrin bumped his friend with his elbow. "I didn't mean to hit a nerve. It's just that…I hate to see you blow the greatest chance at happiness you've had in a long time."

"Oh, really? And what makes you an expert on my happiness?"

"Joe, I've known you since we were twelve. I remember what you were like back when you thought you and Lindsay were going to be together forever. She was all you could talk about, her and your future together. You used every penny you earned as a resident to buy her that ring. When she left you at the altar, it more than broke your heart. I wasn't sure you'd ever get over that, but I see you now, the look in your eyes when you talk about this Helena woman and the way you look at her photo, a photo you saved to your phone by the way. That right there means you're starting to think about the possibilities. You talk about the people you've met, about Andi and Wade and the man whose wife died, but none of them make you light up the way you do when you talk about Helena. The same woman you took on a few dates and *didn't* sleep with. Sex aside, when's the last time you took out a woman more than one time, not to mention had dinner with her family and took over her spot on a town planning committee? Admit it, Joe, this woman is special."

Joe sat, staring at Darrin, and sighed. "I'm not that bad, you know. I've dated plenty of women without having sex with them."

Darrin gave Joe a half-grin. "Sure, you have."

Joe ignored the dig. "Okay, I admit it, she's special." He held his hands up before Darrin could respond. "But she's young, just turning twenty-nine this week, and she has dreams of travel and—"

"Stop," Darrin commanded. "Just stop. I don't want to hear excuses. Stop trying to push away any and every chance you have at loving and being loved. You've been doing that for what? Seven years? And it only got worse after Jeremy died. Just give this a chance. See what happens. I promise you, if she's the one, you won't regret it."

"Easy for you to say. You and Cheryl were destined to be together from birth."

"And how do you know you and Helena weren't? Just because it took you thirty-five years to meet her doesn't mean you weren't destined to be together. You're back to being a church-going man. Don't you think God could've put you here, in this struggling little town, because he knew you needed each other? You and her? Would you really want to walk away from something that is his plan for you?"

Joe chuckled. "What's Cheryl done to you? I haven't heard you talk about God since you tried to talk your way out of Confirmation back in the eighth grade." He tried to act nonchalant, but Darrin's words brought to mind Joe's conversation with Helena. What was God's plan for him?

"Maybe Sister Mary Ellen was onto something. After all, it was at that very Mass that Cheryl and I sat next to each other and something sparked."

Joe groaned. "Okay, okay. Enough. Don't remind me about Sister Mary Ellen this close to bedtime. I may have nightmares."

Darrin looked at his watch. "Speaking of which, I'd better hit the hay. It's been a long day, and I know you're going to have me up before dawn."

"You bet I am. The fish won't be biting much after the sun comes up."

The men tossed their bottles into the recycling bin and said goodnight before Joe headed to his bedroom and Darrin to the guest room.

Fifteen minutes later, Joe laid in bed, staring at the ceiling as the faint glow of moonlight was caught by the whirling fan overhead. Was Darrin right? Was Helena the real reason he was in this town? Was meeting her part of God's plan? Joe moved there the previous year because he found out that his brother's former… Former what? Friend? Girlfriend? Lover? It didn't matter. He moved because he found out that Andi was fighting to rebuild the town, and he needed to get away from Houston and all the memories of his dead brother. He figured she could use a doctor to help bolster the town, and he was right.

But maybe there was more to it than that. Maybe he was supposed to be here, just like Darrin said. Maybe he was supposed to meet Helena and discover his destiny, God's plan for him.

Joe scoffed. It sounded ridiculous. Besides, if Helena was his destiny, why was she spending the whole summer halfway around the world?

He reached for his phone on the nightstand and punched in the passcode. He brought up the photo he'd saved and considered what might happen if he gave it a try. Maybe her being on the other side of the world was a good thing. Maybe they could get to know each other in some kind of old-fashioned, letter writing exchange.

He brought up his email and searched for her name in his contacts. She'd emailed him about the Memorial Day festivities before she left, and he'd saved her address.

He thought for a moment about what to put as the subject and settled on, Your Trip.

Joe spent a few minutes constructing a friendly, but not too-friendly, message. He asked how she was and how the trip was going. He let her know that everyone missed her but hoped she was having good time. He gave her a few tidbits about goings-on in the town, made sure he wished her a happy birthday, and typed his name.

He read it over twice and then thought about his ending. Should he put more than just his name? How could he sign off casually but in a way that would elicit her to answer?

He erased his name and simply typed, Miss you.

Before he could change his mind, he hit send. He immediately felt a wave of regret wash over him. He put the phone back and groaned as he rolled the other way, as if not seeing the phone would erase what he had done and said. It was too late now. Maybe Helena would read it, smile, and hit delete. That would be best for both of them.

***

Dear Joe…

Helena's fingers hesitated over the keyboard on her iPhone. She hit the delete button several times and started over. She had already waited two days to answer Joe's email, and she still wasn't sure what to say.

Hi there, Joe!

She sighed and bit her bottom lip.

"Would you like another drink, despoinída?"

Helena tilted her head to look at the waiter from beneath the brim of her big floppy white hat she found in a shop on the island. Her typically pale skin was glowing with color, but the freckles on her cheeks were emerging like ants on a picnic blanket.

"Naí," she told him. "The same, please."

Helena had learned that cocktails were a recent discovery by Greek bartenders, and every bar and restaurant had their own specialties. She decided she had a certain fondness for the Greek mojito, heavy on the watermelon and light on the mint. She finished the little bit that was left in her glass and cast her gaze onto the sea. She heaved a frustrated sigh before turning her attention back to her task at hand. She frowned at the largely blank screen and started over for the tenth time.

Dear Joe,

Thanks for the update from home. This is my last day on Milos and my last full day in Greece. Milos is interesting. It's made up of several small towns, ranging from a bustling mini metropolis to teeny tiny fishing villages. I rented a car and drove around the island yesterday. I found the most amazing village where the little houses along the water are all painted different colors, and the fishermen in their tiny boats brought their catch to the shore to sell it to people waiting for them to come in. It was a step back in time, and I found myself wanting to just sit in the little seaside café and watch them fish all morning. My Airbnb is an actual windmill. Isn't that amazing? It's on a little farm, and the rabbits, chickens, and cats—so many cats!—have the run of the farm. The couple that owns it are so nice, but they don't speak a word of English.

Tomorrow morning, I fly back to Athens and then straight to Rome. I will so miss the beaches and the sparkling blue water. It's like nothing I've ever seen. And the food! Oh, it's so good! You must come here someday.

As much as I love Greece, I can't wait to see the Vatican, and stroll through the Coliseum, and toss coins in the Trevi Fountain. I've dreamed of doing those things my entire life, and it feels almost surreal that by tomorrow evening, I'll be sipping a glass of Italian wine while watching the sun set over St. Peter's. Does the sun set over St. Peter's? I assume it must when viewed from the correct angle. I'll let you know! Speaking of the setting sun, you know what? The moon looks the same here as it does at home. Tonight, when you look up and see the moon, know that a few hours earlier, I was looking at the same moon, in the same shape, appearing in the same sky. I think that's pretty amazing.

Anyway, I'm enjoying this. This world, so far away from our own, is everything I imagined it would be. Don't worry, though, I promise to come home.

She stopped and read the last line again. Did he worry that she wouldn't return? Had he already moved on to someone else? She hoped not. Sure, she was an independent woman, traveling the world on her own, but she was also a human being, and the longer she was away, the more he crept into her thoughts. She deleted the last sentence.

Please write back soon. I look forward to hearing from you.

Again, she paused. Did it sound like she was begging? Was 'I look forward to hearing from you' too formal?

She leaned her head back. Why was this so hard?

"A beautiful drink for a beautiful woman," the waiter said, setting down the full glass and picking up the empty one. "May I get you anything else?"

"Advice?"

"Naí, anything for ómorfi kyría." He smiled broadly, and Helena blushed at the compliment. Did he really think she was beautiful? Did Joe?

"If I wanted someone to reply to my letter, I mean, if I was hoping to hear back—"

"Ah, love advice." His smile widened. "Let your heart speak. A cat with gloves never catches mice."

Helena laughed. "What?"

"It is Greek proverb. It means, do not be too careful, or you will lose what you want to catch. Write what your heart says."

"Okay, then. I'll try that. Thank you."

The waiter bowed and began to turn before leaning down toward Helena. "In Greek, we do not say, 'I miss you.' We say something that means, 'You are missing from me.' Let him know this."

Amidst the rapid beating of her heart, Helena smiled as she quickly erased the last few sentences and typed a new ending. She finished the letter and added a photo to the bottom. She hit send before she could change her mind.

***

Today, I learned that the Greeks don't say I miss you. They say, You are missing from me. I like this a lot, and it makes me think of you.
I'd love to hear from you again.
Helena

Joe read the email again and then again, surprised that she had replied. When two days passed without a word, he assumed she was no longer interested, if she ever really was.

He looked at the photo of Helena standing atop a cliff where a white stone village behind her was cascading into the blue water below. Glowing blonde highlights reflected the sunlight on her hair, which had gotten lighter in the past ten days, and her blue eyes mirrored the glint of the sun on the blue sea. She wore a flowing white lace top with a bright green tank top underneath. The image, like the one she sent from the

Temple of Apollo, cemented his prior association of her with the pixies of British and Celtic lore.

Joe glanced at his watch. His first patient was due in fifteen minutes. After that, Kevin Swanson would be in to get his cast removed, and the day would just get busier from there. Turning his attention to his screen, he hit Reply.

Dear Helena,
Thank you for the email. It was the perfect way to begin what is sure to be a hectic day. With the arrival of summer comes the nearly constant flow of injuries—bike accidents, falls from trees, bare feet stepping on glass, and all manner of cuts and breaks. I'm getting to know the community faster and better than ever! I've hired another doctor who will begin in next week. I'll be glad to have the extra set of hands.
The Memorial Day festival was a grand success, thanks to all your pre-planning. You wouldn't believe how many floats there were in the parade! You'll be happy to know that the winning float belonged to the Girl Scout Troop the library sponsors. The float was a tribute to the library and all the books that promote the Girl Scout ideals of courage, confidence, and character in girls and young women. You would have been proud.
The town is coming to life in the way that towns typically do this time of year. Flowers are in bloom everywhere, but nowhere as beautiful as in your mother's gardens of course. The first tourists of the season have found their way to Buffalo Springs. The tourist center Andi and Wade set up looks to be busy at all times. Somebody finally took up Andi on her idea to turn the old jail into an escape room. The town is buzzing with excitement, and everyone is looking forward to giving it a try when it opens.

I'm happy to wait until you're back, and we can tackle it together, if you want to.
Dotty just stuck her head in to tell me that my first patient has arrived. Have a safe trip to Rome. Arrivederci!
You are missing from me, and tonight, I'll be looking at the moon.
Joe

Without hesitation, Joe hit Send and listened to the whooshing sound of the email being sent across the ocean. He stood, left his office, and greeted his first patient with a goofy grin on his face. Not until he looked up from the chart on the iPad in his hand did he realize he was in trouble. His heart seized in his chest, and his knees threatened to buckle.

"Hello, Joey. Long time, no see."

Lindsay Johnson sat on the exam table, her legs swinging to and fro, looking the same as she had looked seven years earlier. She grinned mischievously, and Joe swallowed hard as he took in her low-cut blouse and dark red lipstick.

"Lindsay," he managed to croak out before he cleared his throat.

"Miss me?"

Joe thought of the words he had just written to Helena. Until Helena came into his life and abruptly headed across the ocean, there was only one woman he had ever truly missed, and here she was, sitting in front of him. What was she doing here, and what did it mean for him?

***

Helena wiped a tear from her cheek as she knelt in front of the tomb of Saint John Paul the Great. All of St. Peter's Basilica overwhelmed her, and she found herself unable to control her emotions. After praying for safe travels and mentioning the intentions of her loved ones back home, Helena crossed herself and sat down in a pew, taking a moment to marvel at the beloved Pope's beautiful marble tomb beneath Domenichino's masterful painting of the martyrdom of St. Sebastian.

It was still very early, just half past seven, and the basilica was nearly empty. Relying on advice she found on a traveler's blog, Helena was at the church when the magnificent, bronze Jubilee doors opened at seven o'clock. She had time to wander around the interior, gazing at the paintings and statues, before most people were even awake. The blog also advised not standing in the long line to go up into the dome. According to the author, once the dome opens at nine, the line will disappear until close to eleven when the crowds descend upon the church. As Helena watched the line grow, she hoped the advice was good and that she wasn't making a mistake. Her tour of the Vatican Museums was to start at noon, and she didn't want to be late.

Sure enough, by quarter to ten, the line had dissipated, and Helena was able to walk right to the elevator without any wait at all. She debated walking all 551 steps to the top, but she opted for the elevator, which still left 320 steps but seemed more manageable for someone who hadn't done much exercise since the days of college cheerleading.

After a quick stop on the flat roof of the basilica to look out over the city, Helena made her way to the dome. Huffing and puffing her way through the last fifty or so steps, Helena emerged from the dark, winding staircase into the brilliance of the sun's rays that beamed through the stained-glass windows above the main altar. The magnificence of the basilica once again overwhelmed her, and she grabbed onto the railing as she gazed down at the golden rays surrounding the depiction of the Holy Spirit rising above the Chair of St. Peter.

Nothing in her life could have prepared her for the emotions she felt throughout that day. From the view of Rome behind the twenty-foot-high statues of Jesus and the Apostles on the rooftop of St. Peter's to the grandeur of the ancient marble sculptures and the majesty of masterpieces by Caravaggio and Rafaella in the museum to the breath-taking depiction of The Creation on the ceiling of the Sistine Chapel, Helena was in awe. The only thing she regretted was that Joe was not there to share this experience with her.

Thoughts of him were beginning to consume her. Every new experience made her long for his presence. She wanted to share her excitement and wonder with him despite the claims to her family that she was more than happy to be traveling on her own. Only Andi saw through her and encouraged her to make note of her favorite places so that she could return someday with a traveling partner. Neither of them named Joe as the possible companion, but Andi often mentioned seeing him around town and loyally reported that he had not been spotted on any dates with anyone else in Helena's absence. He had even told her that he missed her.

So, why hadn't she heard back from him? His response to her initial email was long and detailed and ended with the same Greek ending she had sent him. She answered back almost immediately, sending him pictures and telling him how beautiful everything was and how much fun she was having. Had she been too enthusiastic about her trip? Had he thought that she was having so much fun that she didn't miss him at all despite her saying she did? She tried not to read too much into his silence, but it was hard.

The other news she was receiving from home was equally good even if there was no mention of Joe. The town, on the verge of total collapse just nine months ago, was experiencing a true renaissance. Stores were open, the hotel was filled, and interested business owners were inquiring about the vacant buildings. Jackson was back at work at the local Tractor Supply for the summer and looking forward to his last semester of school in the fall. Allie had helped their friend, Paige, a graphic designer, kickstart a t-shirt shop; and Paige's fun collection of custom-designed shirts, hats, water bottles, and other items adorned with local lore were selling as quickly as they could produce them. Part of Helena was a bit envious that she wasn't there to witness the town's first summer as an Ozark tourist attraction, but she knew there would be other summers.

As she wandered through the Piazza Navona that evening, eating gelato, listening to violin music, and watching peddlers attempt to lure passersby with their trinkets and knock-off handbags, she reminded herself that she was lucky to be experiencing the world. She'd waited her entire life to stand in this square beside Giacomo's Fountain of Neptune. She gazed fondly at the seahorses, dolphins, sea nymphs, and cherubs as she circled the fountain and stopped in front of Neptune slaying a giant octopus. The fountain was so different from the one in the center of Main Street in Buffalo Springs which was just the standard small-town fountain with three ascending basins spurting water into a pool below, except there was no water. The fountain hadn't worked in years—ten at least. Joe had said that the Memorial Day festival was a success, so she hoped that the next festival would bring in enough to fix the fountain. Maybe she should check in with Andi, see if they had raised enough money for the courtyard grounds and playground, and make sure the Fourth of July plans were shaping up.

Helena reached for her phone but stopped herself. For once in her life, she needed to let someone else be in charge. She had handed over the town's fundraising activities to several capable hands, including Andi. There was no reason to interfere or to make them think she didn't believe they could handle things. Memorial Day seemed to go off without a hitch, so there was no reason to worry about the Fourth.

Helena licked the melting gelato off the back of her hand and continued her stroll back toward her hotel. She inhaled the smell of garlic and marinara sauce and smiled at the waiters imploring her to have a seat in the outdoor restaurants. She didn't want to forget a single thing she saw or heard or even smelled. She forced melancholy thoughts from her mind as she passed through the Eternal City, alone, and refused to look up into the sky where the full moon, suspended among the stars, reminded her of someone back home.

Seven

Sweat ran down Joe's back, and his breathing was labored, but he was determined to keep up with Wade and Dale.

"How ya doing back there?" Wade called from several feet ahead on the trail.

"Just fine." Joe managed to keep his voice steady, but he was certain the other men weren't fooled. Though they promised to keep their first run together to a measly two miles, Joe knew they would run three times that distance had he not been with them. According to Wade, he hadn't run much in the ten plus years since graduating from college, but meeting Andi had changed that. An avid runner, she had gotten Wade back into a routine, and Wade had then convinced Dale to take up the practice. Without Ruth, Dale was a lost soul, and the men were constantly trying to think of ways to cheer him up and help him live without his soulmate. While Joe had agreed with Wade that they needed to keep Dale busy, he wasn't too keen on being persuaded to join their daily run.

"We're almost there," Dale said, slowing to Joe's pace. "You're doing well for your first time out."

"Thanks," Joe grumbled. "Sorry to hold y'all back."

"Are you kidding? Wade nearly kills me on these runs. I'm happier than a pig in mud to go at an easier pace. I'm not my brother. He's in better shape than Wade or Andi."

"It's as hot as all get out," Joe said, using his arm to wipe the sweat from his face. "Maybe we should've started earlier."

"I would've, but Mama couldn't watch the kids until a little after nine on account of she had to run by the bank first, and Coop's working."

Joe winced. "Sorry, Dale. I guess I wasn't thinking about where the kids are while we're out here."

"No worries, Joe."

They came to a stop beside the Buffalo River. A hawk cried out overhead, and all three men turned toward it and watched it soar into the trees.

"I never knew this place was so big," Joe said. "I've seen the signs for the state park, but I've never ventured in before now." He watched as Dale stretched out on the ground, lowered his head toward the river, and splashed water on his face. He turned to Wade. "Back a ways, I saw a sign that said something about zinc mining. What's that about?"

"Used to be a zinc mine there. Nothing left now except the little building built into the rock that served as the opening to the shaft. Several years ago, I was in high school at the time, a group of local boys wandered in with their dog, thinking they'd find gold. A few minutes in, the ground shifted, and the dirt ceiling collapsed on them. They were trapped in a pocket, and a mud wall formed from the collapsed ceiling, about a hundred feet high, blocking the entrance. They were lost, about two-hundred feet underground, for two days. Thank heaven they were found and rescued, unhurt, but scared and starving. After that, the mine was sealed off."

"Wow. I can't imagine how frightened they must've been. And their parents."

Wade nodded. "It must've been awful."

"Why keep the building? Isn't that just begging for someone else to get trapped?"

"Nah. It's completely sealed off from the mine now, and I'm pretty sure it's always locked up tight. Andi and I come here a lot, and we've run past it. I've never seen anyone near it. I'm not sure what it's used for, if anything." Wade took a long drink from his water bottle and blew out a breath.

"Maintenance shed," Dale added from where he sat on the ground. "The rangers have keys to it."

A movement in the woods behind Wade caught Joe's eye, and he squinted to get a better look.

Wade turned. "What?"

Joe shook his head. "I thought I saw something, someone maybe. I guess I'm just seeing things. Forget it." Despite his words, he wasn't so sure he hadn't seen someone. He had the strangest feeling they were being watched. Was someone hiding in the woods, listening to their conversation? He dismissed the thought. Why would anyone follow them or care about what they had to say? Unless… No, Lindsay was many things, but a stalker?

Wade broke into his thoughts. "Andi loves it here. She likes to hike and run out here whenever she can instead of in town. Says it served as her safe spot all her life before she left for the Academy."

Dale stood and looked at Wade. "What's it like dating a Navy Seal?" He shook his head, and water droplets flew from his curly hair, still short but obviously not cut since Ruth passed. Joe knew without a doubt that the kids' needs came first.

Wade shrugged. "No different than dating anyone else. Andi's all girl, just like her sister, but when she wants to, she can flatten a man faster than a coon dog on a jackrabbit."

Dale laughed loudly. "And you know this how?"

Shrugging again, Wade took another long sip of water. "None of your business." Wade winked at his childhood best friend. "Speaking of Andi's sister…" He turned toward Joe. "I hear Helena is having the time of her life in Europe. Have you heard from her lately?"

At the sound of her name, something inside Joe's stomach flipped. He tried to picture Helena, but the only image his mind conjured was Lindsay. "Got an email from her the other night. She's in Rome. She said she was going to visit the Vatican yesterday and the Coliseum today. It sounded like she's having the time of her life." He tried to sound casual, but he kept thinking about his *appointment* with Lindsay.

Wade watched Joe, and Joe wondered if Wade could see through his nonchalant response. "Andi says Helena is having a good time. Although…" Wade slid the water bottle back into his small, lightweight backpack and zippered the pack before pulling it back over his shoulders. "She gets the feeling that Helena is feeling a bit homesick."

"Oh, really?" He thought about the tone of Helena's emails in which he, too, recognized a bit of melancholy amid the cheery descriptions of her day. "What makes Andi say that?"

Wade frowned. "Not sure. She just thinks Helena might be regretting doing this trip alone."

"Anyone in particular she wishes was with her?" Joe asked, not looking at Wade as he took a long sip from his own water bottle.

"I think the name Stan came up once or twice."

"Your friend, the carpenter?" Joe nearly choked on his water, his voice sounding higher than he intended.

Wade burst into laughter. "I'm kidding, man. I have no idea who Helena talks about to Andi, but if I had to guess, I'd have to say it's the new town doctor."

Joe wished the words would make him feel better, but he only felt guilty. "Oh. I mean, there's nothing wrong with Stan, I guess. If she's interested in him, that's her business."

Wade clapped Joe on the back. "No worries, Joe. I won't tell anyone that you have a thing against carpenters."

"Not carpenters in general. Just tall, muscular ones who look at Helena the way Stan does." *Ones who don't have an ex-fiancé lurking around town.*

Wade raised his brow. "Oh, really? So, you noticed that, too."

Joe nodded. "Hard to miss."

"Well, I may not know too much about Helena or her fondness for carpenters," Wade said, "but I sure do know how her eyes light up every time you walk into the room."

Before he had a chance to find any solace in Wade's words, Joe noticed Dale standing off to the side, quietly staring up at the sky, a look of sadness on his face. Joe motioned with his head, and Wade nodded.

"And I know that if you're going to compete with the likes of Stan, we'd better whip you into shape. What do you say, Dale? Should we race the good doctor back to the car?"

Dale turned back to the men with a forced smile. "Last one back buys six packs for the other two." Before the men could register what he said, Dale took off down the trail.

Joe held onto his water bottle as he followed the other men through the park, his borrowed backpack flapping behind him. With the knowledge that Wade thought Helena had feelings for him, Joe should feel like he was running on air. Instead, he felt like he was mired in quicksand and sinking fast.

***

Helena carefully folded her clothes and laid them in her suitcase. She'd had another full day, but she knew she'd barely scratched the surface. What had she been thinking? Three months to do most of Europe? She'd been here for three weeks already, and she knew she would never have enough time to see everything. Rome felt like a whirlwind, and she'd only seen the highlights—the Vatican and St. Peter's, the Coliseum and the Roman Forum, the Spanish Steps and Trevi Fountain, as well as the Pantheon and a few of the best-known basilicas. There was so much more she wanted to see, but she had to move on if she was going to be in Florence for the festival of St. John the Baptist, the equivalent of the American Fourth of July.

Once she felt that she was ready for her early morning departure, she brushed her teeth and climbed into bed, reaching for her iPad. She frowned, her anticipation met with nothing but junk mail and a few photos of Josie, the new puppy Allie was training. Why she needed a puppy while trying to kickstart a new business at the beginning of the tourist season was beyond Helena, but she couldn't help smiling at the pictures. Josie was darn cute!

Helena sent a quick reply and closed the tablet. She rolled over and said her prayers but lay awake for what felt like an eternity. What had she done or said to make Joe stop writing to her? Had she read too much into his email? Was he not at all interested in staying in touch or in seeing her when she returned?

Another thought crept into her mind, but she squeezed her eyes shut, hoping to squelch the image. It was no use, though. She drifted off to sleep with a vision of Joe walking down Main Street with his arm around someone else.

***

Joe read the text and wondered what she wanted now. He liked it better when she was blocking her number from view. Now, every time he saw her name on his phone, a sick feeling overcame him. He thought about their encounter in the clinic three days before.

Lindsay sat on the exam table, looking at him in the same way that Captain Ahab had gazed at the great white whale. Her red lips were pressed in a tight, seductive smile, her eyes peeped through lashes heavy with mascara, and her cheekbones were darkened and prominent. It was classic Lindsay, and he wondered how that look ever cast a spell over him when they were a couple. Now, he saw it for what it was—the same tantalizing and provocative stance that allowed a fly to be lured into the spider's web. As the thought crossed his mind, an image of Helena appeared, and he knew that the pixie's magic was much stronger than the black widow's poison he'd once been subjected to.

"Lindsay, what in the name of the devil are you doing here?" He'd quickly shut the door but stayed across the room, unwilling to expose himself to her venom. She'd always had a way of entangling him in her web, and he refused to give her the chance to do it again.

Her smile widened, and she batted her lashes at him as she purred, "Joey, baby, I missed you. I heard that you had moved here, and I couldn't stay away. I never could, you know." She leaned back on the table and uncrossed her legs, smiling seductively. "Remember when I used to visit you when you were a resident?" She ran her hand across the paper sheet.

"Lindsay, I don't have time for games. What is it you want?" He kept his feet planted firmly on the ground and warned himself not to get closer.

"Oh, Joey, don't be mad at me. I know it's been a long time, but you remember how good we were together."

"I remember how good I *thought* we were together. You, on the other hand, obviously had other thoughts." He crossed his arms over his chest and felt his jaw clench.

Lindsay sat up, her smile fading. "I always thought we were good together. It was you and me against the world, remember? We had so many plans and dreams."

"We did. Until you decided to ditch me on our wedding day. Do you remember that? Or did that memory somehow slip your mind?"

Oh, how he'd loved her, or thought he loved her. His friends couldn't stand her, but he saw things they couldn't see, or so he thought. What he saw was a loving, caring woman who stood by him through medical school, busy internships, and long hours of residency.

He saw a woman who was willing to give up anything and everything to move wherever his career might take him. He saw someone who wanted to share his highs and lows, who supported his dream of becoming a doctor, who shared his passion for helping others. He never saw the woman they warned him about, the one who was only interested in marrying a doctor, who pretended to support him but had her own agenda, who made a vow to give up her own career to be there for him but really longed for a life of leisure and the luxuries that came with being a surgeon's wife. He knew she was disappointed when he chose to become a general practitioner and even more disappointed when he took a job as an ER doctor, but he thought she would get over it and stand by him as she always professed she would. He never thought she would run off with his surgical mentor, leaving him with a wedding band and a honeymoon that had a no-cancelation policy.

Lindsay's smile turned into a frown. "I'm sorry for hurting you, baby. I was scared. I had cold feet, and I…" She faltered, and he knew it was a lie.

"You didn't have cold feet. You have a cold heart."

Rage flooded her eyes, and she stood abruptly, pulling the paper sheet off the table. "When did you become so cold yourself? I thought you loved me."

"I thought so, too," he replied, his tone even, his jaw still tight. "What ever happened to Dr. Miller?"

"I realized I didn't love him," she said. "But it doesn't matter. It was never about him."

"Then what was it about, Lindsay?"

"It was about you. You and your late hours and your study dates and your commitment to that hospital instead of me."

"Lindsay, I had a job, a demanding one, and boards to study for. I thought you understood that. I thought we were in it all together."

She laughed at him. "Together? When were we together? You became a stranger once you started working in the ER. I never saw you and didn't even know you anymore."

"No, Lindsay, you never knew me before. You had an image of me that wasn't real, an image of a life I never wanted. When I found my calling in the ER, you saw your perfect life with the mansion and the yacht spiraling down the drain."

"That's not true," she yelled at him.

Joe pictured the crowded waiting room and Melanie and Dotty outside the door. He took a deep breath and slowly exhaled.

"Lindsay, I'm working. Unless you're sick, get out. Go back to Houston and leave me alone."

On cue, her signature act began, the same act she had perfected in high school and continued to play throughout their time together. She blinked several times, and large tears bubbled from her eyes. She sniffed and tossed her blonde hair back as if she was trying to gain her composure.

"You don't mean that," she said quietly, her lip protruding in a pout as the tears ran. Her mascara remained perfect, and he knew she had planned for this event.

"Oh, I do. You need to leave."

"But I can't leave, baby."

A cold, hard reality hit him. She wouldn't have. Oh, but she would have. It would be just like her. "What do you mean you *can't*," he heard himself ask, already anticipating the answer.

"I live here now, Joey." She sniffed again before slowly smiling at him. "I read about this little town and thought to myself, this is just what I need. I can make a new start, and I can let Joey know that I still love him, and we can get back to where we left off."

Just as he thought. Joe put his iPad down on the counter and steeled himself. "Lindsay, I can't control where you live or what you think or how you feel, but I can assure you that we will not 'get back to where we left off.' Not now, not ever."

She stood and walked toward him, a contrite look on her face. "You don't mean that."

"I do." He met her gaze with a challenge.

"I won't give up," she warned.

"You will. It's what you do. Declare your love and then leave. It's what I've come to expect from you."

The slap was unexpected, but he didn't allow himself to waver.

She tried to sound demure, but he heard the acid in her voice. "I made one mistake, and you're going to hold it over me forever?"

He simply replied, "I'm not holding anything over you, Lindsay, and you no longer have any hold over me." He opened the door. "Goodbye."

Sitting at his desk now, he could still picture the look on her face as she walked out the door. He knew that look. She was not going to give up.

He glanced back down at the text.

Lunch? We need to talk.

Joe didn't reply. Instead, he scrolled to his photo app and tapped on it, He stared at the picture of Helena that he had saved. He wanted to reach out to her, to talk to her and hear her voice, but how could he do that now? How could he even think about Helena with Lindsay spinning her web right here in his corner of the world? Even halfway across the globe, Helena would know in a heartbeat if he and his ex-fiancé were seen having lunch together. He had to do something about Lindsay before Helena got home and before word got around that his ex was in town. But in a town as small as Buffalo Springs, how was he going to manage that?

***

Helena stood, mouth gaping open, eyes wide, and heart racing. The man in front of her was magnificent—tall, strong, handsome, perfect musculature, smooth complexion, and those hands! They were beautiful. The legs—oh, the definition! She could see every tendon and even from a distance, she felt as though she could see his blood pulsing and heart pumping. She had never felt so alive staring at a man, at any person for that matter. He was just so…so…perfect. His curly hair, his wide-set eyes, and—her eyes dropped to just below his waist—his beautifully chiseled...

Chiseled, she giggled to herself. *It's chiseled all right!*

She smiled broadly as she gawked at his nakedness, the slingshot flung across his left shoulder, the rock in his right hand, and his calm, cool expression. David stood seventeen feet tall, in bright white marble, a tribute to the giant-killer of Biblical fame.

Helena hadn't imagined there could be a single masterpiece by Michelangelo or any other artist that could come close to the magnificence of the Sistine Chapel, but here she stood, absolutely transfixed by this depiction of David. If only all men could be as perfect as the stone statue, she thought. Then again…She tilted her head to the side and assessed the gigantic male specimen. The real David wasn't so perfect. He lied, killed, had an affair, and wasn't exactly the portrait of faithfulness as far as women or God were concerned.

As she wandered away from the great hall where the statue stood, she thought about her experiences with men. None of them were perfect. Then again, neither was she. Perhaps she just needed to give Joe some time to figure out what he wanted, and perhaps she should do the same.

Helena looked at her watch and quickly finished exploring the Academia before hurrying to the Uffizi.

She had a scheduled time and didn't want to be late. She'd been imagining her stroll through the five-hundred-year-old building for the past ten years.

She took her time in the museum but stopped for a long time to gaze at the Roman goddess of love as seen through the eyes of Botticelli. She studied the beautiful woman standing inside the clam shell and marveled at the colors, details, and exquisiteness of the scene. These priceless works of art were what she dreamed of seeing as an undergrad. She was no artist herself, but that made her even more appreciative of the talent of others.

She stared at the supple belly of Venus, the curves of her breasts, and the serene look on her face. She embodied every type of love a woman could experience—sexual, ethereal, and maternal. Helena reached up and touched her own curls, a much lighter shade than the red-tinged color of the flowing, curly locks of the woman in the painting. Unlike Helena, Venus had a husband as well as many lovers, and the myths about her were all dreadful tales of deceit and loss.

Maybe being single isn't so bad after all.

Helena sighed and moved on with a deep longing in the pit of her stomach to experience all of the love that the goddess symbolized.

***

She was waiting for him when he left the clinic. He hastily turned the other way, but she pounced like a feral cat, her green eyes glowing in the evening light.

"You never answered my text."

Joe reflexively looked at his watch though he knew what time it was. "Have you been here all day?"

"No. Once it was too late for lunch, I decided to see if I could catch you for dinner."

He stopped beside his car. "Look, Lindsay, I'm not going to have dinner with you. I'm not going to engage in texting with you. I'm not going to have any type of relationship with you. If you really want to stay in town, that's your choice, but don't stay on my account."

She laid her hand on his arm, and he flinched. She let go and backed up a step.

"You're serious?" she accused.

"I'm serious," he confirmed. He opened the door and got inside the Lexus LX. Before he could close the door, Lindsay stepped in the way. She fixed a cold, hard stare on him.

"You're going to regret this," she said with animosity in her voice.

"I don't think I will." He reached to close the door, and she moved out of the way.

Joe started the car and backed out of the parking space but not before he saw the look she gave him—the determination in her eyes, the set of her jaw, and the heat that flooded her cheeks. She was angrier than a hornet, and he suppressed an icy chill as he wondered if he had just kicked the hornet's nest.

Eight

With a fresh, hot, krapfen in hand, Helena stood in line outside Il Duomo. She bit into the Italian doughnut and savored the sweet taste of the pastry. After the last bite, she licked the powdered sugar, cream, and chocolate from her fingers just as the guard opened the doors to the famed basilica. She downed the last drops of her latte and dropped the cup and paper wrapper into the trash can while her ticket was inspected. She followed the others into Giotto's Campanile and began the ascent up the 414 steps to the top of the bell tower. If nothing else, she decided, she was going to be in spectacular shape by the time she got home even with all the pasta, wine, pastries, and gelato she was consuming.

The view of Florence from the bell tower was awe-inspiring. She took several pictures of the landscape as well as the magnificent brick-topped, marble-paneled dome of the basilica. The bell tower stood at one end of the massive church and the dome at the other, but the dome was so large, Helena felt as if she could reach out and touch it from the tower. Puffy clouds and blue sky framed the gilt copper ball at the dome's pinnacle, and

Helena held her breath in anticipation of climbing to the outer terrace of the dome later that morning.

After having completed both climbs and taking dozens of photos, Helena, her legs trembling with fatigue, moved on to the Baptistry of St. John, an octagonal building where baptisms had been taking place for close to 900 years. The original Baptistry doors were cast in bronze and, like the replicas on the building today, depicted scenes from the life of St. John the Baptist and the eight virtues of hope, faith, charity, humility, fortitude, temperance, justice, and prudence. The doors only opened a few times a year, one being the feast day of the building's namesake.

Helena had perfectly timed her day to be at the doors when they opened. She was not disappointed as she arrived just in time to see the copies of the famed doors, dubbed by Michelangelo the *Doors of Paradise,* swing open and the Bishop of Florence lead the procession to the steps of the basilica. Helena had read that on the feast day of John the Baptist, all those who had been christened inside the Baptistry over the previous year gathered for a short ceremony inside and then processed through the heralded doors to the steps of the basilica for a photograph. She watched, tears streaming down her face, as people of all ages posed on the steps.

As soon as her ticket permitted, she slipped inside the building and marveled at the décor on the walls and ceiling. She then crossed the street and visited the Duomo Museum where the original bronze doors, restored to their glory, were on display. She stood in the museum for a long time and took a good, long look at the panels and studied their craftsmanship. The rest of the day was spent perusing the many shops, strolling across the famed Ponte Vecchio bridge, and pausing in the great piazzas to gaze at the statues and reliefs.

By the time night rolled around, Helena's entire body tingled with both excitement and muscle fatigue. Rather than climb another set of stairs, she took a taxi to Piazzale Michelangelo, a piazza on a hill high above the city, which she was told had the best sunset view of Florence. She watched as couples in wedding regalia posed by the wall that lined the hilltop, and crowds of people jammed together to enjoy the spectacular vista. The sky over Il Duomo changed from blue to purple to pink as the sun sank behind the city, each passing minute more beautiful than the last. Just after sunset, fireworks burst into the sky, and the spectators dropped to blankets or open stretches of grass to watch the light show dedicated to John the Baptist, the patron saint of Florence.

Reminded of the fireworks show she would be missing back home the following week, Helena watched with a bittersweet taste in her mouth. Her heart ached with longing for those she loved as she realized this would be her very first Fourth of July away from Buffalo Springs. It wasn't until she tasted the salty tears that slid through her parted lips that Helena realized she was crying.

***

Hoping to grab a quick lunch and a breath of fresh air Joe headed to the parking lot but stopped short just before he reached his car.

"What the…" He slowly approached the late model Lexus, expelling a string of profanities his brother would've been proud of. He reached into his pocket and made the call, barely taking his eyes off the front of the vehicle.

"Dale, it's Joe. Someone took a baseball bat to the windshield of my car…"

Hours later, Joe pushed away the paperwork in front of him and seethed at the thought of his car being vandalized. Though Lindsay had been questioned, there were no witnesses and no prints. She happily allowed the officers to search the apartment she was renting above the candy store, but they found no reason to press charges.

Dale assured Joe that they would find the culprit, but Joe knew they wouldn't. Lindsay was smart, very smart. He was the victim of her manipulations and calculations for years, and he was no stranger to the games she played. Sure, he'd missed them for all the time they were together, but once he was free of her machinations, he was able to see clearly how successfully she had fooled him many, many times over the years.

He should've known better than to make her angry, but he'd had no choice. He refused to let her think there was any chance of them getting back together.

"Knock, knock."

Joe looked up to see Andi in the doorway.

"I heard what happened. You okay? Dotty said you might have a few minutes to talk."

Joe snorted. "I'm fine. My car, not so much."

"A windshield can be easily fixed," she said entering the office and taking a seat in the chair in front of the desk. "Wade's pretty upset that this happened. Things like that don't happen here, except, of course, when the drug ring was trying to stop Wade and me from getting too close to their operation. But they're all long gone, and this isn't the norm for our town. I can't imagine who would do that to you or why."

"I've got a pretty good idea," he said with a scowl.

Andi raised her brow and beckoned for him to continue, but Joe wasn't sure he wanted to tell her about Lindsay. Would she go right out and contact Helena? Would it even matter? It had been a week since he'd contacted her, and she'd given up trying to reach him.

Andi must have gotten the message that he didn't want to share because she merely shrugged and looked away. "Nice office you've got here. I've heard a lot of good things about your practice. Melanie says you're hiring a partner."

"Not a partner exactly," he said, sitting back in his chair. "I've hired another doctor to work with me, but she won't have any stake in the business."

Andi's brow rose again. "She?"

"Dr. Amanda Pierce from Nashville. Like so many of us, she's looking to get out of the city and try life in a small town."

"When does she start?"

"Monday. She's staying at the hotel for the next few weeks and then moving into a house on Poplar Street."

"The Dashell house, I suppose," Andi said. "It's been for sale for a while now. Nice house."

"She seemed pleased with it."

Andi gazed at Joe for a moment before asking, "I heard from Helena this morning. She's absolutely in love."

Joe sat up and blinked. "In love?"

"With Florence, Italy. She's wanted to go there as long as I can remember. She studied Art History, you know."

"She told me. I'm glad she's enjoying herself." He settled back into his seat, but his heart still raced at the thought of Helena falling in love.

"Me, too. She's finally seeing all the works of art she drooled over for years."

"I know she studied art. Can she draw, too?"

Andi laughed out loud. "Draw? Helena? She can't draw stick figures." She shook her head and continued to chuckle. "But she loves art and all the history surrounding the famous paintings, sculptures, and buildings around the world. She wanted to be a museum curator for as long as I could remember, but that would've taken her away from Buffalo Springs, so she did what she thought was the next best thing—became a librarian."

"So she could read about all the famous paintings, sculptures, and buildings in the world."

"Yeah and teach others about them. She loves helping people do research and uncover the mysteries of the past."

Joe couldn't quell his curiosity. "Why did she stay? I mean, she told me it was her choice to save the library, or however you'd want to say it, but with all those dreams about art and travel and fancy museums, why do you think she stayed here in Buffalo Springs?"

"Why do I think she stayed?" Andi sniffed and cast her gaze to her lap. She cracked each knuckle then released a long sigh. "I think she stayed because of me."

"Because of you?"

"We're four years apart, you know. I left here at the age of eighteen to join the Navy and never looked back. I never had any intention of returning to Arkansas until it was time for me to be put in my grave." She brushed off a bit of flour on her black pants, the remnants of a day making pies and cakes in her bakery. "My parents were great, truly supportive and proud of me, one-hundred percent. But I think my being gone made Helena think that she had to stay, as if losing another daughter would be more than our parents could handle."

"From what I've seen, your parents are quite capable of handling just about anything that gets thrown their way."

Andi looked up at him and smiled, and not for the first time, Joe thought he saw what his brother had seen in her. "You're right, but you know Helena. She has the biggest heart of anyone I've ever known. She always puts everyone else's happiness before her own."

"Do you think she's content here? Living her whole life in Buffalo Springs, being the town librarian, never doing anything more with her life?"

Andi rolled her lips inward and lifted her gaze to the ceiling for a few moments before nodding her head. "Helena could be content anywhere. She has a knack for finding the good in every situation. She loves this town and her friends here. She absolutely loves her job. I think she just gets… lonely." She looked at Joe. "I think this whole trip was about satisfying her lifelong yearning to see the world, for sure, but also her way of remaining content with what she has."

"You don't think it will have the opposite effect? That she'll want to travel more and experience the world she's dreamed about for so long?"

"Oh, I think it will definitely do that, but I also think she'll always want to come back home." Andi leaned closer to the desk. "She's a catch, Joe. I mean that. She's brilliant, beautiful, caring, and has a great passion for life. She loves to help others and organize events and make things happen. But she also loves a good book, a quiet sunset, and the comforts of family life."

Joe cocked his head to the side and looked at Andi. "Are you trying to tell me something?"

Andi stood and placed her hands on her hips. "Just sharing some thoughts about my sister, that's all. I don't want to hold up your day, and I've got half a dozen orders to get to at the bakery before I can call it a day."

He watched her walk to the door but called to her. "Andi." She stopped and turned around. "Thanks. For checking on me, I mean. And for telling me… for sharing…"

"You're welcome, Joe."

After she closed the door, Joe turned to look out the window. How many times in the past few weeks had he gazed across the lawn and imagined Helena walking toward the clinic from the library? How often was she in his thoughts? He looked at his watch and frowned. He had a patient in three minutes. Later, he thought, he'd try to find the time to email Helena.

All thoughts of Lindsay and his car were pushed aside by thoughts of the curly-haired blonde with the sparkling blue eyes of a pixie.

***

Helena packed her treasures carefully among the dresses, slacks, blouses, and scarves she'd collected over the past few weeks. She fingered each piece before wrapping it and gently wedging it into the suitcase. There was the pottery bowl she bought for Andi and Wade with a blue, yellow, and green Tuscan design. There were wood and pottery salad tongs for her mother and a fine Italian leather belt for her father. She ran a finger along the smooth leather flap on the purse she bought for Allie before placing it next to the cute blouse she bought for her friend as well. She hesitated before picking up wallet she bought on an impulse for Joe. She turned it over in her hand, felt the soft leather, and lifted it to her nose to smell the masculine scent. Was it too personal? Should she give it to Jackson? Would he appreciate that more than the bottle of Ouzo she bought for him in Greece? She placed the wallet in the suitcase and decided she had time to think about it before she returned home.

It was 12:30 in the afternoon, and her train was pulling out of the station at three. Joe would still be asleep at this time. Did she have the time to email him? Should she even bother?

Helena sat on the bed and opened her iPad. There was a message from Andi telling her to call right away, but it was too early to call her. Though Andi enjoyed her early morning runs, she had begun sleeping in a little, the routine of military life fading into the past. Helena would wait and call later, perhaps from the train. She could describe the scenery to her sister as it rolled by.

Instead of calling, Helena tapped a reply telling her sister to check her email. She hastily threw together a mail message.

Hi Sis. How are things at home? Heading to Venice today. So excited! Have you seen Allie's puppy? She'll be so big by the time I get home. How are plans for the 4th? I'm sorry to miss it, but I saw the most spectacular fireworks show over the Arno last night. It made me think of home and all that I'm missing this summer, but I'm having a wonderful time. After Venice, I'm not sure where to go. North to Austria or west to Switzerland? Or farther west to France? What do you think?

She stopped and took a deep breath. Should she ask the real question on her mind? She plunged ahead.

How is everyone back home? Mom says she and Dad are fine and that Jackson is working a lot of hours. What about Wade? How's Dale holding up? And Joe? Are things well at the clinic? Sarah says things are great at the library. That's such a relief. Please fill me in on the rest.

Gotta go. Love you! -H

Did that sound casual enough? Would Andi think she was asking about everyone as a whole, or would she zero right in on Joe? Would she be able to read the homesickness in Helena's hastily typed words?

Helena sent the message with a shake of her head. Andi would know right away that Helena missed home and also what she was really asking—did Andi know why Joe kept getting hot and cold, and had he started seeing somebody else?

***

The patient in the hospital bed breathed steadily. He was hooked up to monitors, an IV, and an oxygen tube though that was just a precaution. Joe watched the man's chest rise and fall, grateful that the man's wife had trusted him but worried that her call to him rather than to 911 may have cost them precious time. Joe wanted the best for all his patients, but this one in particular needed to be okay.

Technicalities aside, he wasn't Joe's patient at all. Not until the call several hours prior, asking Joe to hurry to the house, had Joe ever treated him as a patient. The truth was, like most men, this patient probably never stepped foot into a doctor's office unless he absolutely had to. He'd certainly never been to the clinic; however, Joe had dined at the man's table, was friends with his children, and attended the same church. And, of course, there was—

The appearance of the neurologist in the doorway brought an abrupt halt to Joe's thoughts.

"Dr. Blake, isn't it? "

Joe stood and took the hand that was offered to him. "Good morning, Dr. Stearns. Please, call me Joe. "

"In that case, call me Bobby." The doctor let go of Joe's hand and cast his gaze toward the patient in the bed. "I assume we're sharing a patient?"

"Not exactly," Joe admitted. "I'm a friend of the family, and I did see him last night after his wife called me for help. I made the call to 911 and had them bring him here. I moved some things around on my morning schedule, so that I could come by and see how he's doing."

"Things looked pretty bad when they brought him in last night, but his vitals look good this morning. I was just about to do an exam and send him for another CAT."

Joe felt his heart plummet. Why hadn't she called 911? Why hadn't he as soon as she called and asked him to come to the house? Well, that answer was simple. She had made it sound like it was nothing to worry about, an upset stomach and a headache, nothing major, but would Joe mind taking a look anyway? At least she called and hadn't just sent her husband to bed.

"I'll wait outside," Joe said, moving toward the door.

"You saw him first, diagnosed him, and made sure he got here on time. I have no problem with you staying as his physician."

Joe wondered about the ethicality of his presence. "I appreciate that, Dr. Stearns, Bobby," he corrected himself. "It's just that…it's complicated. I mean, yes, his wife did call me, but my relationship to him is… Well I'm not sure what it is. I mean, his daughter and I…"

"Ah, so there's a woman involved?"

Joe sighed. "You could say that."

Dr. Stearns regarded Joe with interest but didn't seem to judge and didn't ask for more.

"Is the family on the way?"

"I believe so," Joe said.

"When they arrive, you can ask their permission to consult if you wish. Otherwise…"

Joe nodded. "Understood. Thank you. Take good care of him."

"I will," the doctor answered. "Mr. Nelson is in good hands."

***

Helena was just getting situated on the bench at the train station when her phone buzzed.

"Hey, there! I was going to call you from the train. I'm heading to Ven—"

"Helena, it's Daddy."

Helena's throat went dry, and a terrible ringing sounded in her ear. Her heart raced, and she blinked several times, trying to focus on where she was and what was happening. She felt like she was in a dark tunnel, no longer able to see anything.

"Helena? Are you there?"

She swallowed. "Andi? What's wrong with Daddy?"

"He had a stroke. At first, he just had an upset stomach, but when he started complaining of a severe headache and dizziness, Mama got worried and called Joe. By the time he arrived, Daddy couldn't speak. Joe called 911, but Daddy was unconscious when they got there."

"Andi, stop. Is he okay? Is Daddy okay?" She wiped away tears, oblivious to the curious glances of those around her.

"I don't know. He's at Washington Regional. He's still not awake."

Helena heard Andi's voice crack. She desperately looked around. What was the fastest way to the airport from here—by train or taxi? "I'm heading home. I don't know when I'll get there, but I'm on my way."

"No, your trip. I don't want—"

"Shush, Andi. You'd do the same. Even if you were on a mission in Afghanistan, you'd find a way to get home. I'll text you my flight info once I have it."

She didn't wait for Andi to say goodbye. She stood and looked for an information booth or anyone who could help her figure out how to get to the airport. By the time the taxi pulled up to the terminal, Helena had booked a flight. It was going to take her thirty-three hours, two stops, and almost three-thousand dollars, but she would soon be home.

***

Joe watched Andi pace back and forth in the room while he and her family sat and waited.

"Andi, sit down," Wade told her.

"I can't. What's taking so long?" She looked at Joe.

"I'm sure everything is fine. They need to establish the kind of stroke—ischemic or hemorrhagic. Then they're going to want to rule out persistent intracranial hemorrhage, identify the degree of injury caused by the stroke, and search for vascular lesions. There's a lot to be determined before they begin to factor in other causes as well as continued episodes, blood cell count, glucose, serum electrolytes, blood urea nitrogen, creatinine, troponin levels…" Joe stopped when he saw their faces. Andi's mouth was gaping open, Grace's hand covered her mouth and her eyes were wide, Jackson was pale, and Wade winced with every word Joe casually threw out. "Sorry. I know that all sounds scary, but it's routine stuff."

"Did you say he'll have continued episodes?" Grace asked.

Joe swallowed, feeling his Adam's Apple bob up and down. "No, that's not a guarantee. It happens in some patients." Where were his bedside manners? He was a better doctor than this.

At that moment, Joshua was wheeled down the hall. Grace jumped to her feet and went to the door.

"Well?" Grace anxiously asked.

"Sorry, Ma'am," the orderly replied. "I'm just the taxi driver. Somebody will let you know what's happening once the test results are in." They watched as he pushed the bed into Joshua's room, re-hooked the various wires, and hastily departed.

Joe watched Grace quietly go to Joshua's side. She whispered tender words of love and encouragement, and Joe felt like a voyeur. He turned away, locking eyes with Andi. She nodded and said, "Let's give Mom and Dad some time alone."

They all exited to the hallway. "Can we talk?" Andi asked.

Joe nodded and led the way back to the room where they all had been waiting for news.

"What can you tell us?"

Joe exhaled. "Not much. I've seen his charts and spoken with Dr. Stearns, but we don't really have any answers at this point. Most likely, it's hemorrhagic. That's what I'm seeing anyway. He had high blood pressure, was on blood thinners, and is overweight."

"How long until we know more?"

"There's no way to know, Andi. I'm sorry. It's a waiting game. The important thing is that we got him here within a crucial window of time. He was able to get the CT scan done right away, and they gave him medicine to counteract his blood thinners. Those are both vital interventions."

Andi took a deep breath and let it out. "So, now we just wait?"

"Unfortunately, we wait."

Andi looked down at her watch, and a look of relief spread across her face. "Helena is about to take off. She won't be here for another thirty-four hours or so, by the time she gets her luggage and hails a taxi, but she's on her way."

Joe wasn't sure if that made him feel better or worse.

***

Helena sat up in surprise when the cabin lights were switched on. She found it hard to believe that she had fallen asleep, but nearly three hours had passed since she closed her eyes. The first four hours of the flight were spent in a restless state, somewhere between terror and exhaustion. She prayed using the rosary she'd bought at the Vatican, but it didn't help quell her fears.

She did her best to stretch, wedged between a rather large man and an elderly woman. She excused herself and narrowly slid past the man when he stood to let her out.

Having used the bathroom and freshened up a bit, Helena returned to her seat. She checked her email with the internet connection she had paid heavily for and read Andi's update on their father. His stroke had been confirmed. There had been no follow-up episodes so far, and tests were still being run. Her family was at the hospital though they had gotten a hotel room for Grace the night before and were in the process of trying to convince her to go back and get some rest. Andi mentioned that Joe had called the clinic and cancelled all appointments so that he could be at the hospital as well, and the thought put Helena at east just a bit. She sent a short reply to let her sister know that she was still a little over three hours from touching down in Dallas/Fort Worth.

She thanked the flight attendant for the unidentified breakfast and slid open the window. She could see nothing but wispy clouds surrounded by the faint halo of the distantly rising sun. Longing for home, her European adventure already felt like a lifetime ago. She hadn't made it to Venice, and her only glimpse of the Eiffel Tower had been during the descent at Paris's Charles De Gaulle Airport. Still, she couldn't complain. She had traveled around the Greek isles, stood on top of the Acropolis, and visited St. Peter's and all the famed museums of Rome and Florence. Perhaps, someday, she would return; but if not, she had much to remember. All that mattered now was getting to her father as quickly as possible.

She ate very little but watched as the horizon glowed brighter with each passing minute. When the yellow rays of the morning sun began reflecting off the wing of the plane, she closed the window and began counting down the hours and minutes until she would be back on American soil.

***

The buzzing refused to abate, and Joe was tired of clicking the button on his phone to reject the calls. As annoyed as a fly trapped between the screen and the windowpane, he stood and walked into the hallway.

"What do you want?" he said angrily into the phone, trying to keep his voice low.

"You're not at work. The ditzy old lady said you called in sick. Can you do that?"

"First of all, Dotty is not ditzy, and she's not old. She's one of the best office managers I've ever known. Second, why are you at the clinic?"

Lindsay audibly sighed, and the sound grated on him. "Because I wanted to see you. Why do you think?"

"About what, Lindsay? I told you, I want nothing to do with you."

"Joey—"

"Stop calling me that." He looked around, embarrassed at his raised voice, but the Washington Regional Neuroscience Institute was a busy place, and nobody paid him any mind.

He walked further down the hall and lowered his voice. "Did you smash the windshield of my car?"

Lindsay gasped too loudly and with too much melodrama. "Joey, how could you think such a thing?"

He felt his blood pressure rise. "Why? Why would you do that?"

"Joey, I just don't know what you're talking about or why you would think I'd do something so horrible. Why, I think I might just sit down and cry over the thought of you accusing me—"

"Knock it off. I'm no longer a sucker for your pout or your act of contrition. I'm with a patient and his family. I don't have time for games."

"Oh," she said almost inaudibly. "I'm sorry. I didn't mean to interrupt."

"Yes, you did, and we both know it. I know Dotty told everyone who called or came in that I'm on an emergency call." He clenched his jaw and flexed his free hand. "Look, Lindsay, how long are you going to play this game? I'm not going to change my mind. You should go home. Back to Texas. There's nothing here for you."

"Oh, I don't know about that. You see, that's why I was calling. I met the nicest man yesterday. He was questioning me about your car, and I think he might be sweet on me."

The hair stood on the back of Joe's neck. The spider was setting her web to catch another fly, and he knew just who she meant to ensnare. "Lindsay, don't do this. He's in a bad place and doesn't need another broken heart."

"Joey, do I detect a hint of jealousy in your voice?"

"Lindsay, I'm warning you. Stay away from Dale."

"I'm sorry, Joey, I think we have a bad connection. Hello? Hello? Can you hear me?"

"Lindsay, I mean it. Don't—"

She was gone, and Joe's heart sank. He brought up Dale's number on his phone, but his call went straight to voicemail. Dale must be busy. Joe sent a quick text asking Dale to call him back.

He turned around and faced the room where Helena's family was waiting for a miracle. Wade. He needed to talk to Wade. Now.

Nine

Helena hurried through the terminal. It had taken forever to get through customs, and the security line to re-enter was even longer. She prayed she could make it to her connection on time. If she ever traveled again, she was going to spend the money to get one of those global cards so she could whisk through customs and skip the long security lines.

She stopped and looked at the directional signs. Which way to her gate? She took a left and sprinted down the moving walkway. She arrived at the gate just as the plane was boarding and said a quick prayer of thanksgiving that she had made it.

Once she was settled into her seat, she pulled out her phone—with the American SIM card back in place—for the first time since landing. She had texts from Allie offering prayers, Sara wishing her a safe flight, Joe letting her know he was there with her family, and Andi updating her on their father's condition. She read Andi's long text more than once.

Their father was still undergoing tests and was still heavily sedated. He had a brain bleed that was going to need surgery. Not until after they performed the surgery would they know his condition or his prognosis. Before she had a chance to respond, a flight attendant asked her to turn off her phone. Helena spent the entire two-hour, no internet flight fingering the rosary and reciting every prayer she had ever learned.

***

Joe watched silently as Wade held Andi. They sat on the couch in the waiting room, her mother and Jackson in chairs nearby. Half the town had either called or driven up to see them, and he knew they were exhausted. Joshua's surgery wouldn't end for at least an hour, and Joe hadn't been able to bring himself to tear Wade away from the family.

After Lindsay had ended their call, Joe marched right into the room to talk to Wade, but Dr. Stearns was there, informing the family that Joshua needed surgery to repair the bleeding blood vessel in his brain. Hemorrhagic, as Joe had suspected. There was no time to waste and no time to talk. Joe was thrust into action, answering what questions he could after Dr. Stearns left to scrub up for the operation. After answering to the best of his knowledge, Joe went down the hall to get coffee, but he didn't feel right asking Wade to leave Andi to go with him.

When he got back, he handed out the coffees to everyone. Andi took the cup without looking up from her phone. "Helena's landed. They just now touched down. She needs to get her bags and find a taxi."

"Tell her not to get a taxi," Joe said. "I'm on my way."

Andi looked up at him, her eyes exuding gratefulness. "Joe, thank you. For everything. I don't know what we'd do without you."

"You would've been fine, but I'm happy that I could be here."

"I feel bad taking you away from your clinic."

"Don't. That's what friends are for. Dr. Pierce starts tomorrow, so we'll be able to take care of the backup pretty quickly. Now, I'd better get going so Helena isn't standing on the corner waiting for me."

He rushed from the room in a hurry to get to the airport. He was anxious to see Helena, anxious to be the one to tell her that, so far, everything was okay, and anxious to see her before news of Lindsay's presence made its way around the town.

***

At the sight of Joe standing by the baggage carousel, Helena's heart caught in her throat, and she nearly burst into tears. She pushed her way through the crowd of people and allowed herself to be engulfed in his arms. For the first time since getting the call from Andi, she let herself drown in a torrent of tears.

Joe rubbed his hands up and down her back and made shushing sounds as she cried. Those around them must have thought this was a joyful reunion, and it might have been had she come home under different circumstances. She didn't care what onlookers thought; all that mattered was that she was home, and Joe was there to take her to Daddy.

She sniffed back more tears and pulled away, looking up into his face. He was scruffy, and he had dark circles under his eyes. Had he been at the hospital this whole time? The question gave way to other, more urgent ones.

"Daddy?"

"He's in surgery. They would've waited for you if they could have, but…"

"I understand," she said. "How much longer?"

Joe looked down at his watch. "Thirty minutes or so?"

"Let's get going then." She turned toward the carousel and pointed to her bags. "The turquoise one over there that matches my carry-on, and the leather bag behind it. I'll get that one if you can get the bigger one."

Joe walked past her and reached the turquoise bag as it turned the corner and pulled it from the belt. Before Helena could lift the leather bag she had purchased in Florence, Joe had taken the handle and pulled it over the shiny, metal frame of the conveyor to the floor.

"I've got all these. You just hold onto your backpack." He hoisted the leather bag on top of the larger suitcase and pulled those along with her carry-on behind him.

Helena nodded, hitched up her small, Italian leather backpack, and led the way out of the terminal.

The afternoon sun beamed down, and Helena welcomed the cooler temperatures that the mountains offered. Though June was just giving way to July, the air felt dry and comfortable, unlike the blazing heat she had left behind in Italy. She frowned as she followed Joe to his car. Had she really just been in Florence less than three days ago? It felt like a lifetime had passed.

Joe stopped and popped open the trunk of a Ford Fiesta.

"New car? It seems kind of small for you." *And inexpensive*, she thought.

"Not exactly," he said, not looking at her as he hefted her luggage into the trunk. "It's a rental."

"What happened to your car?"

She followed him to the passenger side where he opened the door for her and waited for her to get inside.

"Cracked windshield. Should be done by now," was all he said as he closed the door. By the look on his face, she suspected there was more to the story.

***

Once they were pulling onto the road, Helena turned to him. "Thank you for picking me up."

"You're welcome. I needed something to do. To help, I mean."

"I imagine you've been a big help. Andi says you've been helping them understand what's going on and how to maneuver through everything."

He quickly glanced her way and then looked back to the road ahead. "I'm doing what I can. I'm familiar with stroke presentation, the basic tests done for admittance, and what to look for, but beyond that, I'm a little rusty. It's been several years since I studied neurology in med school."

"Did everyone study neurology? I mean, I thought that would be a specialty or something."

He almost grimaced at the question but worked to quickly regain his composure. With Lindsay showing up in town, thoughts of his early days as an intern had become unpleasant memories.

"I studied to be a heart surgeon. There are a lot of correlations between the heart and the brain, so I learned a fair deal about strokes. I've been surprised by how much I retained."

"A heart surgeon? Really? You never told me that. Why are you running a clinic in Buffalo Springs?"

Dr. Amanda Pierce had asked him the same thing during her interview, and the answer had come as easily then as it did now. "I like the challenge, the unknown that each day brings, the chance to put so much of my medical school knowledge to work. I realized as soon as I finished my internship and began my residency that what I loved most from my rotations was the rush of the ER, all the different cases I was presented with, and the burst of adrenaline when the ambulances pulled up. It was much more exciting to me than the operating room."

"You must be bored to death at the clinic."

Joe laughed. "Just the opposite. It's like the ER only better. I'm on my own, nobody to look to for answers. I have to know immediately if it's a stomach bug or appendicitis because the hospital is too far away for guesswork. I get to diagnose and treat. And I can help underserved people who might not have sought out treatment at a hospital or large doctor's office. It's the best of both worlds. Most of the time." He thought of her father and how helpless he felt when he realized Joshua was having a stroke, and there wasn't anything he could do about it except call 911 and pray they got to the ER on time.

Helena was quiet for the last few minutes of the ride. He could see her pale as they pulled into the parking lot at Washington Regional. He could actually feel the fear filling the car as he parked.

They hurried inside and checked in at the front desk.

"It says your father has just come out of surgery," the volunteer told them as she handed Helena a badge. "The doctor might be with your family by the time you get up there."

After a quick thanks, Helena dashed for the elevator with Joe on her heels.

He watched as Helena hugged her mother, then Andi, then Jackson. Just as she gave Wade a quick, sisterly hug, Dr. Stearns appeared.

"Surgery went well. We were able to stop the bleed, and everything looks really good."

The family hugged and cried, overwhelmed by the news that surgery had gone well and that Helena had returned home safe and sound and in time to hear the news.

"We're going to let him sleep and try to wake him in the morning. Why don't you all go get something to eat, get a good night's rest, and come back tomorrow.

Joe saw the look on Helena's face and felt as though he could read her mind. The thought of not seeing her father pained her. She had only just arrived, and they were being told to leave. His heart ached for her.

"A night in our own beds would be nice, wouldn't it Mama?" Jackson asked.

"I don't know," Grace fretted. "Maybe I should stay."

"We'll take good care of him," Dr. Stearns assured her. "Really, I must insist you go and get some rest."

Joe watched Helena wipe away tears and put on a brave face for her mother. As though she felt his gaze on her, she turned and smiled. Joe smiled back, nodded, and leaned toward her.

"Can I get anything for you from the car?"

She shook her head. "I put my overnight stuff in here." She motioned to the backpack. "Just in case."

"Okay. I'll leave the rest of your stuff on your back porch. Will that work?"

Helena nodded and blinked, holding back the tears he knew she didn't dare shed in front of Grace. He gave her a half smile and turned to leave.

Halfway down the hall, he heard his name and turned back.

Relief emanated from Helena's beautiful face even as her eyes glistened with tears. "Thank you, Joe. Thank you for bringing me to my family."

"You're welcome, Helena. Let me know how he's doing when he wakes up tomorrow."

He left feeling lonelier than he'd ever felt in his life, lonelier than he felt when Lindsay left him, even lonelier than when they got word that Jeremy had died. Joshua was a lucky man. He had a wife and children who loved him and who loved each other. No matter what happened, they would all be there for each other.

Suddenly, he heard the echo of Darrin's words from a few weeks back, *It's not so bad, you know. That complicated life you're working so hard to avoid. There's something to be said for having someone to go home to at night.*

***

Helena thought she might break down and cry again, but she fought the urge as she followed Wade and Andi to Wade's car. She glanced to the other side of the lot, but Joe's car was long gone. She thought about how gentle he'd been with her, how caring and tender. She'd made a mess of his shirt with her blubbering, but he held her and let her cry. She wondered how he would act the next time she saw him.

There wasn't time to think about Joe on the way home. After Andi answered all Helena's questions about their father, the stroke, and the surgery, Andi had plenty of questions of her own. She kept Helena talking the whole ride, asking about her trip and marveling at Helena's descriptions of the cities, islands, churches, and museums. By the time they got to the house, Helena's body was reminding her that it was early in Arkansas but past midnight in Italy. With only a few hours of sleep in the past forty-eight hours, the mental and emotional exhaustion of worry, and the physical exhaustion of jetlag, all Helena could think about was sleep.

She drifted off during her prayers but not before thanking God for her safe trip home and begging for her father's speedy recovery.

***

The day was going to be hectic, but Joe was looking forward to showing the new doctor the ropes.

"It's so nice to see you again," Amanda Pierce said, her violet eyes sparkling. She was tall—almost matching Joe's six-foot height. Her long brown hair was pulled back into a ponytail. He knew from her employment papers that she was thirty-one, which he liked. It meant she had a few years of experience but could potentially stick around for a long time if things went well. She was attractive, with slight dimples that showed when she smiled, and she had an easy-going personality. She had an athletic build, and he remembered her asking in her interview about the local hiking and kayaking she'd read about on the internet. He liked that she interviewed him about the job and the area as much as he interviewed her about her credentials.

Though easy-going, she let him know when they met that she was a hard-worker and didn't like to waste time, so her next words didn't surprise him.

"I can't wait to start working. This is a new chapter for me, and I'm ready to hit the ground running."

Joe laughed. "You might be saying otherwise by the end of the day." He picked up his iPad and looked at the calendar. "I was out of the clinic yesterday dealing with a patient who's in the hospital in Fayetteville. We're pretty backed up."

"Like I said, I'm ready. What have we got?"

"Three kids with sore throats and fevers, one bad case of sun poisoning, a blood panel for a tick bite and a check for other symptoms, two pregnant moms here for monthly checkups, one routine diabetes check, four well checks, an athletic physical—"

"Stop! I'm overwhelmed already."

Joe laughed. "I warned you."

"Dr. Blake," Dotty stuck her head inside. "We've got a pretty bad cut out here from a filet knife."

"And the fun begins," Joe said. "Come with me. This is exactly the kind of injury we see a lot of around here."

A round of questions determined that Chester Harrington was cleaning "a mess of fish" he hauled in that morning when he heard the telltale sound of rattling behind him.

"I nearly sh—" He looked up at Dr. Pierce and blushed. "I nearly messed myself, and my right hand slipped, cutting into my left hand real good." He shook his head. "Ain't seen one of them things in years and thankful all I got is a slice on my hand and not a bite in my a—uh, some other part of my body."

Amanda lifted an eyebrow as she glanced at Joe, and Joe smiled.

"Well, Mr. Harrington, we are mighty glad of that, too. Now, I'm going to have Melanie come in and clean your hand and get it ready for stitches. We'll be back shortly. Uh, when was your last tetanus shot?"

Chester scrunched his eyes together and wrinkled his nose. "My last what?"

Joe shot Melanie a look, and she nodded, knowing to prepare the shot as well as the suture materials.

"Hey, Doc," Chester said quietly. "I aint' got no insurance or nothin'. But I got that nice mess of fish I was tellin' you 'bout. Any chance…" He raised his eyes to Joe as a red flush slid up his face.

"Why, Mr. Harrington, I would love a mess of fish for dinner tonight. You just settle that up with Dotty on your way out."

"Mighty obliged, Doc. Mighty obliged."

In the hallway, Amanda asked, "Is that normal? Bartering for care?"

Joe nodded, assessing the look on her face. "Around here, it is. Yesterday, I scored an amazing wood carving of a Celtic cross. I'm going to hang it in my house." He paused. "Will this way of doing business be a problem for you?" He thought he'd made it clear in the interview that billing was done differently in some cases, to put it mildly.

Amanda quickly shook her head, her lips pursed. "No, it's just that… How do you make ends meet? I mean, if there's not a steady flow of payments from patients or insurance?"

"Don't worry. You'll get paid every month, and in real dollars. I promise."

She shook her head. "It's not that. I'm okay with taking a barter now and then to help out. I'm just wondering how the clinic will be able to meet the high price of medical costs if we can't charge the patients the full rate."

"To be honest," he said in a low voice. "I'm still figuring that out. For now, I've got a lot of friends who are generous with their donations, both cash and equipment. If we can get the town's economy back on track, maybe these kind of problems will ease up." Not go away, he thought, but at least get better.

Amanda gave a curt nod. "I've got friends, too. Let me know what we need, and I'll see what I can do."

"I've got a short list, but it's really a minute by minute thing. Every day, I come across another need, another missing item, another case I can't help because I don't have the right meds or the right tools." Joe let out a long breath. "We just have to do what we can with what we've got."

Amanda tilted her head as though she was trying to get a better look at him. "You're a good man, Dr. Blake. A very good man."

***

"When… can I… go… home?"

They all laughed amidst the tears.

"Daddy," Andi said, "you just woke up. I think we need to give it some time."

Helena held her father's hand and stroked his knuckles, resisting the urge to cover the hand with kisses. She knew her father had a long road ahead of him. There hadn't been time yet to assess what he could or could not do but being able to talk was a good sign.

Joshua looked at Grace and with much effort, he asked, "Who's… going… take care… you… while I'm… working?"

Andi and Helena exchanged looks. Had her father meant to ask that? Was he confusing his words or confused about where he was?

"I can take care of myself, sweetheart. You just concentrate on getting better."

He took a breath and spoke again, dragging out his words. "I'm… thirsty. Can I… have… a… drive?"

"Daddy, do you mean you'd like a drink?" Andi asked.

"That's… what I… said," Joshua replied slowly, his brows furrowed.

"Andi," Wade said quietly. "Joe said this might happen, remember? Dad's brain and his mouth might have a hard time working together at first."

Helena listened to her brother-in-law and wrinkled her brow. *Since when did Wade start calling our Daddy, Dad?*

Andi nodded to acknowledge Wade's words but didn't say anything. The tightly bit lips and creased forehead said enough.

A nurse kindly pushed her way through to the bed. "I need to check some things, guys. How about y'all go get something to eat and come back in a bit? Mr. Nelson needs his rest. He's been awake for a while now, and you've all heard him talk. Believe it or not, just being awake and saying a few sentences can be exhausting for him. Just give him a couple hours to get some sleep." She looked toward the door. "Besides, I'm gonna be in a heap of trouble if Dr. Stearns finds all of you in here. After this, no more Miss Nice Nurse. It's two at a time until further notice."

Reluctantly, they said their goodbyes and went into the hall to discuss where to go for lunch.

***

Amanda's words stuck with Joe the rest of the day despite the frenzied atmosphere. Was he a good man? It hadn't always felt that way. He spent the past six plus years, after Lindsay's stunt on their wedding day, being anything but a good man. Jeremy's death had changed that. He wanted to help others in a more profound way, to make his life mean something the way his brother's life had, to return to church and not just follow Jesus the Divine Healer but follow him in all ways. That's what brought him here to this town that is so desperately in need and what had him putting out his own money to establish the clinic. The longer he was in this town, the more he saw families like the Nelsons, the better he got to know his new friends, and the stronger his longing to know Helena, the more he wanted to be a role model for others. He wanted to be a stand-up guy like Dale, a reformed man like Wade, and a loving partner like Darrin.

But with Lindsay in town, his past was coming back to haunt him. How long would it take before the good Dr. Blake was reduced to the former 'Dr. Casanova' or worse, the sinner and hypocrite he allowed himself to be over the past several years?

***

"It's going to be a long road," Dr. Stearns told them. "I'm not going to lie. The fact that your father can speak and is able to form sentences is a very, very good sign. His speech is labored, but it will get better, and in time, he will find the right words. He's having trouble swallowing which is normal but concerning. It means he can't eat or drink anything right away, and it can cause other complications, but we'll keep an eye on that."

Helena took notes as quickly as she could, marking things to ask about or look up. She circled the words, 'swallowing' and 'complications.'

"What kind of complications?" Andi asked.

"Pneumonia, among other things," Dr. Steans answered. "We're monitoring his bowels and bladder as well as his speech patterns and motor skills. It's much too soon to assess everything, and it will be a while before we can get him up to try to walk, so everyone needs to be patient." Dr. Stearns looked around at each of them. "He's going to need a lot of help. Not just from you but from doctors, nurses, physical and occupational therapists, maybe a speech therapist and maybe even a psychologist."

"A psychologist?" Helena asked. "Why?"

"Depression is a major outcome after a stroke. Many patients become easily frustrated when they can't do everything they did before or when their speech or writing doesn't match their thoughts. They often have feelings of anxiety and even anger. These can lead to depression."

"Will he be able to come home?" Grace asked, and the pain in her voice made Helena's heart ache.

"Not any time soon, I'm afraid." Dr. Stearns frowned, his eyes full of sympathy. "Your husband is going to need rest, round-the-clock care and observation, and more tests. Once we determine that he can leave, he'll need to go into a rehabilitation center."

"Where? For how long?" Grace's voice cracked, and Helena watched her mother's already pale fingers turn whiter as she clutched the arm of the chair. The blue veins rose to the surface, and she seemed so small, so vulnerable. Helena couldn't help but look away.

"How long depends upon his recovery, and that depends upon the severity of any complications as well as his own attitude and resolve. As far as where, there's an excellent rehabilitation hospital at Fort Smith."

"That's not far from Buffalo Springs," Wade said.

"Yes, and why I recommend it. And also because I'm there twice a week." Dr. Stearns spread his arms wide. "You are all a part of Joshua's medical team. He needs your support as much as he needs any doctor or therapist. I want him close to you so that you can visit and encourage him and also become familiar with his therapies. Our staff there will work with Joshua but also with all of you to get everyone to a place of comfort when it's time for Joshua to go home."

"But you can't predict when that will be?"

Dr. Stearns turned to face Helena. "No, I can't, and anyone who says he can is lying. There are many factors. Right now, the important thing is to stay positive. We're all going to work together to get your father to recover as fully as possible as soon as possible, but I'm not God. I can only do so much on my own."

Helena looked down at her notes. She still had so many questions and concerns, but she knew they could do this. They could work together to help her father recover. They were a strong, capable family ready to face any obstacle. Joshua Nelson had raised them that way.

Ten

The ride home from the hospital was quiet. The late afternoon sun was low in the sky, and Helena squinted as she navigated the transition from open highway to country roads. She glanced at her mother in the passenger seat.

"How're you holding up?"

Grace stared through the windshield, and for several moments, Helena didn't think her mother was going to respond.

With a heavy sigh, Grace answered, "I'm not sure. I think I'm doing okay, but…" She shook her head and took several breaths before answering. "I almost lost him." She choked back her cries. "We've been together since middle school. I never loved anyone else, never imagined being with anyone else. He was there for me when Daddy died when I was just fifteen. He and his family looked after me when Mama was bad off. On the days she couldn't make herself get out of bed, Joshua helped me with the farm. Selling it was the hardest thing I've ever had to do, but with Mama the way she was and it being just the two of us…Anyway, having Joshua there to lean on made everything okay."

Helena's grandfather was, she was told, the life of the party. He was larger than life, a man ahead of his time, or so they said, but Helena was never sure what he did that made them say that. When he dropped dead in the middle of his soybean field from a sudden heart attack, his wife—Grace's mother—spiraled into a deep depression from which she never recovered. Joshua, just a teenager himself, was Grace's rock then and had been ever since.

"I've never considered, even for a moment, that there would come a day when I would go home to an empty house. Of course, I know we'll both be called home someday, but I never actually stopped to think about what that meant, that one of us would leave the other… alone."

"Mama, you aren't alone. You have us kids. And Daddy's not gone. He's going to recover and come back home. You heard Dr. Stearns. He's sure Daddy will be able to recover." Though that wasn't exactly what he'd said, Helena knew her mother needed reassurance.

A chill ran down Helena's back as she thought about her grandparents. If they lost Daddy, would her mother succumb to the same disease Helena's grandmother endured? Would they have to eventually put her mother in a home for her own safety? No, they didn't do that anymore. Did they?

"Mama, I'm hungry," Helena said when her mother made no attempt to continue the conversation. Helena had no appetite, but that didn't mean she wasn't hungry. Her stomach was certainly letting her know that she needed to eat. "Let's go to Al Forna. I only went there once before I left, and I'd love to compare their dishes with what I had in Florence."

"I don't know," Grace hesitated. "I don't really feel like—"

"Mama, you have to eat. You're going to be doing a lot of traveling back and forth to the hospital and then to the rehab place. You know we'll take you as often as we can, but Jackson has work, Andi has the bakery, and I've got the library. You're going to need your strength if you want to go see Daddy regularly and keep up with your house, your gardens, and everything else you do. I'm buying, and you're eating."

Grace didn't respond, and Helena took her silence as acquiescence. She turned onto Main Street and parked in the town lot.

***

The restaurant was crowded, but Bianca, who immigrated to the United States as a young wife, welcomed them at the door with open arms and air kisses on each cheek. Bianca, an avid reader, was a regular at the library.

"Helena, you're home. Welcome back. Did you see everything I told you to see in Florence?"

"I tried to, Bianca. It was beautiful. Probably my favorite of all the places I went."

Bianca took hold of Helena's arms and held them out. "We are so sorry to hear of your papa. We have been praying for him."

"Thank you, Bianca. You know Mama, right?"

"Si, I know your Mamma. She does the beautiful flowers at church. Welcome, Mrs. Nelson."

"Thank you, Bianca. Please, call me Grace. Andi and Wade keep telling us that we should come here with them sometime, but I don't really know anything about Italian food other than spaghetti, lasagna, and pizza."

Bianca laughed, her dark eyes sparkling. "Grace, you are in for a treat. Tuscan food is a feast for the stomach and for the soul."

She led them to a table in the back, near the table where Helena and Joe…

Helena stopped short. Joe was at the same table they had shared. His back was to her, but she knew it was him. The broad shoulders, his height, and the slight curl of the hair above his collar gave him away. He was lifting a glass of wine while his dinner companion talked. She was beautiful, close to Helena's age, she thought, with long brown hair pulled back behind her head and the most beautiful rosy complexion. Or was that the blush of wine on her cheeks, or the blush of… Helena quickly looked away when the woman caught her eye and smiled.

Obviously catching his companion's glance and smile, Joe turned around, his eyes meeting Helena's.

She couldn't tell what he was thinking. His mouth turned up into a wide smile that faltered when she didn't return the cheerful look. He said something to the woman and stood, wiping his mouth with his napkin. He walked toward them both but went to Grace, laying his hand gently on her shoulder.

"Mrs. Nelson. It's so good to see you outside of the hospital. How are you doing? How's Joshua?"

"Dr. Blake, I've told you it's just Grace. Joshua's awake, trying to talk a little, but it's difficult. Dr. Stearns says he will be at Washington for a while and then can hopefully move to the rehab center in Fort Smith."

"I hear wonderful things about that place. And it's not far from here at all."

"Yes, Dr. Stearns said it would be ideal for Joshua." Grace blinked back a tear. "Dr. Blake—"

"Please, *Grace*, I've told you, it's Joe."

"Joe, thank you for everything. You saved his life, and I, I…"

"No, Grace, you did. You called me right away. It was your quick thinking and God's right hand that saved Joshua. All I did was check him out and call 911."

"And then you stayed with him at the hospital and helped us to understand what was going on. I don't know how to repay you."

"No, no. Don't think about that. I wanted to be there for you. For all of you." He looked at Helena, and her stomach flipped.

"We don't want to intrude. Please, go back to your dinner," Helena said. Her heart ached at the thought of him on a date.

"Come, let me introduce you," he said, reaching for her hand, but Helena backed away.

"Oh, no. We've taken you away long enough already. Mama needs to eat, and I've got to get back home. I'm going back to work tomorrow."

"So soon? Has Sarah already left?"

So, he was interested in Sarah, too. And she was only twenty-five. Helena knew he was cad.

"No, she's going to stay on. Wade convinced the town council that we really should have two librarians on staff. After all, we hope that the town will start attracting more people, and we have to have a modern, well-staffed library if we want to keep people coming in." She realized she was rambling. "It was nice seeing you, Joe. Thanks for all you did for my family. It's so good having friends and neighbors we can count on."

Joe looked like he was going to say something, but he simply nodded at her and turned toward Grace.

"If there is ever anything you need, Grace, anything at all, don't hesitate to call me."

"Thank you, Joe. You enjoy your dinner."

"Thank you. You do the same." He looked back at Helena and gave her a small, unreadable smile. "Have a good night, Helena."

Before she had a chance to respond, he turned and headed back to his date. The woman smiled warmly at him as he sat back down, and Helena silently complimented her for her patience.

They took their seats, Helena purposely taking the one facing away from Joe's table, and looked over the menu.

"Oh!" Helena gasped. "They have Sacchetti con Pera y Gorgonzola. Oh, Mama, you have to try it." She pointed it out to her mother.

Grace squinted as she read the menu and wrinkled her nose. "Pears and cheese in pasta purses? That sounds dreadful. What does it even mean?"

Helena laughed. "Bianca recommended a restaurant in Florence called Quatro Leoni, Four Lions. I went there, and the waiter suggested I try this. I had my doubts, too, but it was absolutely delicious. I don't remember seeing it when I was here with J… when I was here before. I wonder if it's a recent addition to the menu or if I ignored it and went for the more familiar items. I think I had the linguini."

"That's what I'm getting. I've heard of that."

"Well, you're going to try a bite of mine."

"Hmph," Grace retorted. "I don't think so."

The waitress approached and asked if they would like drinks. Grace asked for a Diet Coke, and Helena ordered a glass of Chianti and bread with olive oil. She was tempted to order calamari, but she knew she would never be able to convince her mother to try fried squid, and Helena didn't need the extra calories now that she wasn't on vacation and walking eight to ten miles a day.

Helena tried her best to give her full attention to her mother. She smiled but inwardly cringed when her mother went on and on about how wonderful Joe was.

She let her mother talk while she drank her wine and then asked for another, wishing she had just gotten the whole bottle. The dinner she was so excited to have went down without her even noticing the taste. She resented Joe for that even though she knew it was her own fault. She was behaving like a child, and she knew it.

"Ladies, have a nice evening," Joe said as he and his date walked by. "Helena, it's nice to have you home."

"Thanks," she muttered, noticing the way Joe stiffened at her lackluster response. He hesitated by her table, but she studied her plate as if she was going to have a quiz on the ingredients of the dish and was grateful when he moved on.

"Are you all right, dear?" Grace asked.

"I'm fine. More tired than I thought I was, I guess."

"Who was that woman?"

Helena pretended not to understand. "What woman?" she asked, looking around as if she didn't know.

"The woman with Joe. Pretty young thing, don't you think?"

"She was okay," Helena said snidely, knowing she was being unfair and unkind.

"Helena Sue Nelson. I know that voice and that look. I don't know what happened or didn't happen between you and Joe, but there is no need for you to be ugly to that woman. I raised you to be better than that."

Ashamed and penitent, Helena cast her gaze down and bit her bottom lip. "Yes, Ma'am. You're right, and I'm sorry."

"It's not me you should be apologizing to, but I'll let that go. Now, why don't you tell me what exactly transpired between you and the doctor."

Helena shook her head. "Absolutely nothing. We went on a few dates, and that was that. I could tell he was pulling away, but I don't know why. Maybe because I was leaving. Maybe because he decided he didn't like me." She shrugged and downed the rest of her wine. "Everything seemed great, and then, well, it didn't. And then you invited him to my going away dinner, and he was so nice, but when I got to Europe and tried to reach out to him, he acted distant again. So, I decided not to let him get to me. I set out to enjoy myself and not think about him or any other man. And then…" She thought back to the surprising email she had received while in the Greek islands. "He sent me a really nice email, and he said he missed me. I answered him back, and he answered, but then he didn't answer my next email. Almost a week went by, and then Daddy had his stroke, and I came home to Joe waiting for me at the airport, and even though I was upset and crying and worried about Daddy, everything seemed okay again. Until tonight."

She let out a long sigh and wiped her nose with the back of her hand. "I don't know what to think. I'm almost thirty years old, and I feel like I'm eleven all over again trying to figure out if Archie Lincoln liked me or just liked liked pulling my hair."

"Archie's a nice boy. I've always liked him."

"Mama, I don't care about Archie. I like Joe."

There, she'd said it. She hadn't admitted it to anyone other than Andi and not since before she went on her trip.

"Then, you have to tell him."

"Are you kidding? He was out on a date! I'm not gonna spill my guts to someone who goes on a date less than forty-eight hours after I get home."

"How do you know it was a date?"

"What else could it have been? We're at a nice restaurant, the same one he brought me to on a date by the way. They were dressed up and drinking wine. She was smiling and laughing, and he, he…"

"He only had eyes for you."

Helena's head snapped up. "What did you say?"

"The whole time he was eating dinner with her, he was turning around to look at you."

"No way. You're mistaken."

"Helena, I might be getting old, but I'm not blind. And I'm not stupid. Give your mother some credit."

By the time Helena dropped off her mother at home, she had thought about her mother's words and Joe's actions dozens of times. She knew her mother had good instincts, no, the best instincts. She may not have gotten much of an education, but she was smart, very smart. And she was a good judge of people and good at reading them. Could her mother be right? Did Joe only have eyes for her?

As she got ready for bed, she continued to think about it, but she kept going back to the same conclusion. Joe had every opportunity over the past few months to let her know if he had feelings for her. Every time it seemed he was close to admitting something, he pulled back. Either he was extremely confused, didn't want to let her down, or he had secrets he was working very hard to keep hidden.

***

"Bless me, Father, for I have sinned. It's been three months since my last confession."

"Welcome, my son. What's weighing on your soul this evening?"

Joe took a deep breath and shifted his knees on the hard, leather kneeler. "Father, I've lost my temper. I've cursed, and I came close to hurting somebody I used to love. I let pain and anger get the best of me. I've gotten jealous and had unkind thoughts of someone. No, that's not true. I actually wished someone would fall off a roof he was fixing when I drove by and saw him. I was immediately sorry, but still…" He sighed. "And I've been harboring resentment and feelings of, of…Hel- I mean, heck, I just want someone to go away. I don't wish her any harm. I just want her to go away."

"My, my. You have had a lot on your mind and your heart. Is there anything else?"

"I, I think I've hurt someone. Not physically, but I think I've caused her pain just the same. Or maybe I'm just being arrogant in thinking she had feelings for me to begin with. Either way, it's still a sin."

There was a long pause, and Joe could hear Father Michael's quiet breathing.

"Anything else?"

"Father? What if I can't forgive and forget? What if I can't stop the anger and can't stop dwelling on the hurt? Jesus said we need to forgive seventy times seven, but I can't forgive once. And it's having repercussions on every area of my life."

"Anger and bitterness can get the best of us, and they can eat away at our souls. Forgiveness does not come easily. It's a gift to be able to forgive someone who has hurt us. It's a gift to the forgiven and to the forgiver, and it's a gift that only comes to us through grace. Tell me, have you been attending Mass regularly?"

"I have."

"Very good. You receive graces there that you can't receive anywhere else. As well as here in this confessional. But you must go beyond simply going to Mass and confessing your sins. You must move past the hurt and the anger. You must forgive. That doesn't mean you have to forget. We can't let someone hurt us over and over or cause us to fail in other parts of life or in other relationships. I take it that's a big part of it, moving on to another relationship?"

"Yes. I just don't know if I can trust anyone else."

"My son, it's not the person who hurt you that cost you the ability to trust. You did that to yourself. Just because a person hurts you does not mean that others will do the same. And just because you may have chosen unwisely in the past does not mean you can't trust yourself to choose wisely in the present or future. You must forgive whoever hurt you, but you must also forgive yourself. C.S. Lewis—he was a closet Catholic you know—he once said, 'I think that if God forgives us we must forgive ourselves. Otherwise it is almost like setting up ourselves as a higher tribunal than Him.' So, my son, which is the worse sin—to allow someone else to hold power over you through your ability to not forgive them, or to make yourself greater than God through your ability to not forgive yourself?"

Joe was silent as he processed all that Father had said.

"Are you ready to say your Act of Contrition?"

Joe said the prayer that he had learned to recite in the second grade, but this time, more than ever, he meant it when he said the words, "I detest all my sins and all my empty promises because they offend you, my God."

When Father Michael prayed the Prayer of Absolution over him, Joe held back tears. He left the confessional and took a seat in one of the pews. He knelt down and said the prayers of penance as Father had instructed him, and he felt his shoulders become lighter without the burden of anger and resentment weighing him down.

***

"His ex-fiancé?" Helena nearly choked on the words.

"That's what she says," Wade told Helena and Andi over lunch on Sunday. "She says they broke up but are working things out." The three of them had driven to Fayetteville together, attended Mass there, and then gone to lunch. They would go to the hospital after they ate, and Jackson would be relieved of his vigil and take Grace home so she could rest. She had insisted on being at the hospital all day, every day, and her children were as concerned about her health as they were about their father's.

Helena thought back over every conversation she and Joe had ever had. She was certain he'd never mentioned having been engaged, not that it's something one casually brings up on a date. *Please pass the basket of bread, and oh, by the way, I was almost married once.*

"Why is she in town?" Andi asked before taking a bite of her sandwich.

"Apparently, she moved here to be near Joe. That's what she's telling everyone. She says they're back together and planning a wedding."

Helena's last bite of her BLT sat in the back of her throat. She tried to swallow, but her entire body was paralyzed. Together? Planning a wedding?

"Impossible," Andi said. "There's no way he's been seeing her with everything he has on his plate plus all the time he spent with Daddy. No way."

"We, we saw them. Mama and me. We saw them at Al Forno."

Wade and Andi both turned their gaze toward Helena. Her chest was tight, and she wanted to cry. "I took Mama to dinner there the other night, and Joe was there with a beautiful woman. They were eating and laughing. He tried to introduce us, but I cut him off. I told him we were interrupting and to have a good time."

Andi reached over and laid her hand on Helena's. "I'm so sorry, Sis."

"Mama said." She blinked and shook her head. "Mama said he only had eyes for me even while he was eating with her. I told Mama it was nonsense."

"Hold on," Wade said. "You haven't let me finish. This woman says they're together and getting married, but before Daddy's stroke, Joe started running with Dale and me. He all but admitted he has feelings for Helena. He said he hates the way Stan looks at you." He gestured toward his soon-to-be sister-in-law. "It was obvious he was jealous."

"That may be," Andi said, rushing to her sister's defense. "But it doesn't negate the fact that Helena saw them together."

"I don't know," Wade said. "I saw the look on his face when Helena's name came up. It wasn't the look of someone who's planning on marrying someone else."

"I told you," Helena said to her sister. "I said he was a cad."

"Don't you think it's a bit unfair to jump to conclusions about Joe just because you saw him with another woman?" Wade asked.

"Not if it's true," Helena said.

"Wade," Andi said. "You're the mayor. Can't you do some digging, ask around town, see if you can find out more about this woman?"

"Andi, I'm not going to use my position to dig up dirt on Joe's fiancé or girlfriend or whatever she is."

"And I don't want you to," Helena said, tossing her napkin over her half-eaten sandwich. "I don't care about Joe or who he sees. Now, if you'll excuse me, I'm going to use the ladies room."

Helena ignored their looks of pity as she stood and made her way to the restroom in the back of the deli. She couldn't care less about Joe Blake. He had no idea how to treat a woman and no idea how to be a real gentleman.

She stood against the door inside the stall and stifled her tears. Joe was not worth it. He was a selfish, uncaring cad, and she was through trying to decipher his cryptic ways. She slid the phone out of her back pocket and navigated to her texts. She opened the one from that very morning that she had been ignoring and sent a reply.

I would love to spend the Fourth of July with you. Thanks for asking, Stan. I'm looking forward to it.

Eleven

It's so good having friends and neighbors we can count on. The words rolled over and over in Joe's mind all weekend. Was that all he was to her? A friend and neighbor? What was going on with her?

He paced his office, trying to figure her out. She was the one who left the country, who went days without contacting him, who… who said he was missing from her. And he was the one who didn't write back once Lindsay came to town. He'd been doing his best to pray about Father Michael's advice, to find a way to forgive Lindsay, and to forgive himself for everything he'd done in his adult life.

"Joe? You have a minute?" Amanda stuck her head into the office.

"Sure, Amanda. What's up?"

"Your fiancé is here. She was on my list of patients, but she says—"

"My what?" He stomped across the room, threw open the door, and stormed past Amanda.

"Dotty, what is she doing here?" He yelled, not paying any attention to the people in the waiting room.

Dotty's face turned red. "I'm sorry. She said she was sick and needed a doctor. I knew you said not to let her in, but I thought maybe Dr. Pierce could see her."

Without a word, Joe turned on his heel and headed to the exam room. He pushed open the door and slammed it behind him.

"I told you not to come back here."

"I know you did, but I needed to see you. I've got this pain—"

"The only pain in here is you, Lindsay. I've had it with you. If you don't get out of here, I'm calling the police."

"I might be dying!"

"Good!" he shouted before leaving the room and slamming the door yet again.

He retreated to his office, but Amanda caught the door before he could slam it.

"Dr. Blake! I don't know what is going on here, but I signed on to work at a professional establishment. If you can't control yourself, and your fiancé, then I'm not sure this job is right for me."

Joe groaned and sunk into his chair, his face in his hands. "You're right. I'm sorry. I know better." He looked up at Amanda. "She's not my fiancé. She was, about seven years ago, and the breakup was her doing, not mine. She showed up in town a couple weeks ago, and I can't seem to get rid of her."

Amanda closed the door and sat in the chair across from his desk. "Well, that's a problem."

"You're telling me."

"Has she been showing up like this a lot?"

Joe nodded. "Here, in the parking lot, at my house, wherever she thinks she can run into me. I'm certain she smashed my windshield, but Dale—he's the chief of police—he says he can't prove it. I don't know what to do."

"Have you told her that you don't have feelings for her?"

"In no uncertain terms. More than once. She won't give up."

"Hmm. Is she a danger to you or herself?"

Joe didn't take a minute to think about it. "No. She's just persistent."

"Windshield aside?"

"She has anger issues, I admit it, but it seems she's bringing that out in me as well." He wiped his hand down the front of his face. "I'm at my wit's end."

Amanda closed her eyes and shook her head from side to side. "We need to tell Dotty that she isn't allowed inside. If she has an emergency, she needs to call 911 and be taken to the hospital. We can't let her interfere with what we do here, and we can't let her rattle the patients or the staff."

"I know, you're right. I'll tell Dotty that she needs to be very clear with Lindsay. She is not allowed on the premises."

Joe watched Amanda walk away. He was embarrassed, but he was also angry. He was doing his best to put Lindsay and the hurt she caused him behind him. Why did she have to show up now? Right when he was actually considering giving it a try with Helena?

***

Thank Heaven for Dotty, Paige, Sarah, and Dotty's recruit, Melanie. That was all Helena could think of as she looked around the town, fully decked out in red, white, and blue. It was as if she was Lorelei Gilmore looking out at the town square in Stars Hollow. Red, white, and blue banners hung from the eaves of every building, tri-colored flowers adorned pots along the sidewalk, and American Flags flew from every light post. It was like walking down the street in a Hallmark movie.

The town's planning committee had outdone themselves, but Helena, while proud of their accomplishment, found that she was a bit envious as well. She was always the one who planned things, who spearheaded committees, who organized events. When she left for Europe, she felt confident that she was leaving all those committees in good hands, and she was happy that they were doing such a good job. But she found herself at a loss. Sarah was handling the library beautifully, and Helena was happy for the extra set of hands and expertise, but the library had always been her purview. She was having a hard time delegating the things she had always done; and in her absence, Sarah had established her own way of doing things. While grateful that she could spend more time with her father and could take her mother to and from the hospital, she felt like her world was slipping away.

The aroma of freshly baked pies greeted her as she pushed open the door to the bakery. She inhaled deeply, eyes closed, and basked in the scents of flaky crusts, melting butter, and warm fruits. She stopped to look at the selection in the pie case—blueberry, lemon meringue, apple, Boston cream, and strawberry rhubarb. She frowned with the knowledge that the latter was the favorite of a certain doctor.

"Heading to the festival?" Andi's cheerful voice brought Helena out from her thoughts.

"I am. I told Stan I'd meet him by the merry go round."

Andi arched a brow. "Oh?"

"It's an easy meeting point. We're going to walk around and look at the booths for a bit, get a bite to eat, and watch the games and races."

"So, you're spending the afternoon with Stan?"

Helena shrugged. "Why not?"

Andi stopped and looked at her sister, her mouth twisted in annoyance. "Do you really think that's fair?"

"What do you mean?"

"To lead him on like that? Mama says he's been in love with you for years."

"I'm not leading him on. Stan and I are friends. There's no reason we can't hang out and have fun."

"Ignoring the part about him being in love with you, I see."

A small twinge of guilt tugged at Helena, but she brushed it aside. "Stan is not in love with me. We are friends. Period."

"And you're sure he's aware of that?"

"And what if he's not?" Helena snapped. "What if he is in love with me and wants to spend time with me? What's the harm in that? Do you want me to spend my entire life alone?"

"Of course not," Andi said with genuine concern in her voice. "You know I want you to be happy. I'm just not sure Stan's the one to bring you that happiness."

"Well, I don't see anyone else lining up for the job, do you?"

Andi and Helena stood starring at each other until Andi broke the silence. "This is because of the whole fiancé thing, isn't it?"

Helena plopped down into a chair at a nearby table. "Why didn't he tell me that he was getting back together with an old flame? Why wasn't he honest about the relationship?"

"I don't know." Andi joined her sister at the table. "When Wade and I first became friends…" She frowned. "I'm not sure we were even friends at the time. Anyway, I could tell he was holding back. He never talked about his past and never told me anything personal about himself. No matter how much I confided in him, he was a closed book. I had to wait until he was ready to open up, and it wasn't easy. I didn't trust him. I wasn't sure if he was one of the good guys or one of the bad guys. And in this town, that was a literal thing."

"So, what made him open up?"

"I opened up first. And I mean for real, not just confiding little things. I told him about Jeremy and the accident and how I blamed myself. He started talking about his sister—"

"Who got hit by a car and died when she was young, right?"

"Yeah. He told me how he blamed himself even though the accident had nothing to do with him. Then he told me about his girlfriend who died of cancer."

Helena gasped. "I had no idea."

"And neither did I. The point is, sometimes there are things in our past that are so painful, we aren't able to talk about them. We bottle them up, ignore them, pretend they never happened, and even block out the very people who can help us get past them."

"But this is different. Joe's ex didn't die. She's not only alive but back in his life."

"Are you sure about that?"

"I told you, I saw them together."

"Remember who you dated in high school?"

"Steve Warner? Of course. He teaches at the high school. I see him all the time."

"And do you get along?"

"Of course. Steve's a great guy. We've even gone out for a beer a few ti—"

"But you're not together, right?"

Helena bit her bottom lip. "No," she said slowly, dragging out the word.

"Then give Joe the benefit of the doubt. Maybe there's more to the story than he's willing to talk about just yet." A timer sounded from the kitchen, and Andi stood. "Look, Helena. I know you think Joe's untrustworthy, a real-life love 'em and leave 'em Dr. McDreamy, but I don't think that's true. When he first came to town, there was a real vulnerability about him. He was lost, just like I was, and he was searching for something, maybe somebody. He dug his heels in and right away started trying to help make things better for the town and for its citizens. He's not out for himself, and he's not on the prowl either. You're the one and only woman I've seen him with in the several months he's been here, and you and I both know that all the single women in town and half the married ones would latch onto him in a heartbeat. I think he's holding back because there's a part of his story that he's not ready to share. Maybe you're right, and he's getting back with his ex, or maybe she's hoping she can come back and fix whatever caused him to shut down to begin with. I don't know. But I think he's worth the patience and understanding to try to find out."

The timer buzzed again, and Andi hurried toward the kitchen door. "I'll see you at the festival."

Helena mulled over her sister's words. She was still committed to spending the day with Stan, but maybe she'd find a way to gently let him know they were just friends. And maybe she could also find a way to figure out just what was going on with Joe and this ex- or current fiancé of his.

***

Joe and Amanda closed up the clinic at noon. It had been a slow morning, and the EMTs were all set up at the festival beneath a large, red tent. Joe hoped there wouldn't be any need for treatment more advanced than bandaging a scraped knee or icing a twisted ankle.

He walked to his house to change his clothes and stiffened when he pushed open the unlocked door. He was certain he'd locked it that morning. In fact, there was no doubt. He'd lived in the city for too many years not to have made a habit of locking the doors. He took off his shoes and left them on the porch so he could slip silently into the foyer. He froze when he saw the smeared trail of blood on the wall.

A long-buried memory took him back in time to when he was a little boy, living on the base in Germany. He and Jeremy were friends with another boy on the Army base, and the boys spent a lot of time at each other's houses. One day, when the boys were just eight years old, they trudged through the snow after school to play at Charlie's house. As they neared the house, they began seeing drops of blood in the snow. They quietly opened the door, and Charlie called for his mom. Nobody answered, and the boys tentatively made their way inside only to be met with a metallic smell and a sense of foreboding. Upon seeing smears of blood on the walls, Joe felt, for the first time in his young life, true fear coursing through his veins. He clutched his brother's hand, and the two followed Charlie into the kitchen where they found Charlie's beloved dog lying in a pool of blood.

The image of the poor dog flashed through Joe's mind as he silently followed the trail of blood down his own hallway. He could almost hear Charlie's screams, his endless sobs, and his calls for his mother. Charlie's family left the base a few days later when his father was sent to a psychiatric facility back in the States. Joe never heard from or saw the boy again, and he never spoke of the incident to anyone except…

He stopped, his own blood running cold. What had she done?

He swallowed back the bile as it rushed into his mouth and edged his way around the corner into the kitchen. His knees buckled, and he stifled his own cry as he stared at the pile of fur and blood on the polished hardwood floor. He ran to the sink and wretched, shoulders heaving, tears running from his eyes and sweat from his brow. He ran water in the sink and splashed his face before realizing that the only thing he smelled was his own vomit. There was no metallic stench of blood, no tell-tale smell of death.

He eased his way around the island and forced himself to look down at the body. He felt his breath rush from his mouth followed by a series of heavy pants. He leaned down, hands on his knees, and breathed slowly, methodically, staunching the wave of dizziness that overcame him.

It was a stuffed toy. A stuffed dog covered with a substance the same color and consistency of blood. Thank the good… Joe jerked up, panic giving way to anger. She knew. She was the only one who knew, the only one with the knowledge to inflict that kind of horror, to bring back that haunting memory, to bring him to his knees.

He hadn't seen her in days, not since the scene with Amanda at the clinic, but he knew she was still in town. Word was beginning to get around, small snippets of rumor and gossip whispered by those who had heard her that day, and no doubt fueled by her own stories to others in town. He thought about Helena and the way she treated him at the restaurant that night, and it all fell into place. If only he'd reached out to her, tried to explain, but he'd been so busy at the clinic. With summer days came bicycle accidents and falls from trees and bloody toes and broken bones. Plus, Helena had her hands full with her own family woes.

Joe took out his phone and dialed Dale's number. He described the scene, not going into details about the connection to his childhood. That could wait until they were face-to-face. He retrieved his shoes from the front porch and went upstairs to change his clothes. Then he sat in the TV room and waited for Dale, his blood boiling, and his mind turning. What was that crazy woman going to do next?

***

Helena fell to the ground with a jolting thud. She couldn't remember the last time she had laughed so hard.

"Are you okay?" Stan asked.

"Perfectly," she said, still laughing. "Whose idea was it to have all these games and races?"

"Dr. Blake's." Stan talked while Helena busied herself with untying the bandana around their shins, careful not to let him see her expression. "He said his family used to vacation in some little town in Colorado that has a festival like this every Fourth. I'm told the committee patterned the afternoon of games after what that town does—the sack races, three-legged races, egg tosses, you know. We had some of this on Memorial Day, and it was a big hit, so they added more for today." He stood and reached for her, helping her off the ground.

"I like the way they organized it. I mean, breaking everyone up into multiple age groups."

"Yeah. I guess that was the doc's suggestion, too." Stan continued to hold her hand as they made their way to the food booths. "Ready for a snack? I could go for an ice cream cone."

"Sure," she said, feeling as though her hand were being held captive but not wanting to be rude and yank it away.

As they walked, Helena gazed at all the people who had gathered in the newly refurbished park, the fruits of the Memorial Day festivities. She recognized many of her friends and neighbors but was pleased to see just as many faces she didn't recognize.

They stopped and talked to friends here and there, and Helena smiled at all the activity and the line of booths filled with homemade treats and crafts. Many of the wares were the same ones that were at the weekly farmer's market, but she saw several others that must belong to out-of-towners. She made a mental note to stop by the stand that sold locally sourced honey. She was out and liked to add it to her tea. She also wanted to get some cherries and peaches, but those could wait until Saturday.

Stan let go of her hand when they reached the truck, and they chatted as they waited. The ice cream looked to be a big draw, and it took a while for them to get to the front of the line. She wondered where her family was and looked across the park for their familiar faces. After a few minutes of searching, she spotted Wade and Andi across the park. She started to raise her hand to wave, but before she could, Wade leaned down and gave Andi a kiss on the cheek before turning and leaving. They both had peculiar looks on their faces, and she wondered what was going on.

"Strawberry vanilla swirl," Stan said, handing her the cone.

"Thanks," she said, trying to act pleased. "I just saw Andi across the way. Can we go see what she and Wade are up to?"

"Sure. Lead the way."

Grateful that he hadn't tried to take her hand again, she began working her way around the crowded park, steering clear of the open space where the next wave of participants were lining up at the starting line. She licked the cone and lost sight of where she was going.

"I'm so sorry," she said when she bumped into someone and then made a small gasping sound when the attractive brunette turned around, a wide smile forming on her pretty face.

"No worries. You're Helena, right?"

Stunned speechless, Helena stared at the woman. Her first thought was, where's Joe? When the woman's smile faltered, Helena came to her senses.

"Yes, sorry. I'm Helena. I didn't mean to bump into you." She held up the cone. "I was paying more attention to my ice cream than to my surroundings." She blushed, feeling like an idiot.

The woman laughed. "I understand. That looks good. I might have to get myself one. I'm Amanda, by the way. Amanda Pierce."

"Nice to meet you, Amanda." Helena looked around. "Uh, where's Joe?"

Amanda shrugged. "No idea. We parted ways at the clinic. I think he was going home to change, but I haven't seen him since then."

"He's not meeting you here?"

Amanda shot a curious look at Helena before shaking her head. "No," she said though the word came out more as a question than a statement. "He said he was going to look for you…" She glanced at Stan then back at Helena. "I assumed he was spending the afternoon with you."

Helena felt her mouth drop open. Luckily, Stan jumped in.

"Amanda, you said? I'm Stan, Helena's…uh… friend."

"It's nice to meet you, Stan." Amanda looked from one to the other and gave them both a genuine smile. "Well, I may have misunderstood. I mean, Joe couldn't stop talking about you the other night at dinner, and then today he said…" She looked back at Stan. "Well, never mind. I'm new to town and not very good with names. I may have been confused. I'd better work on that so I don't mix up my patients." She laughed, and Helena forced herself to laugh as well.

"Patients?"

"Yes, at the clinic. I'm the new doctor Joe hired. Didn't he tell you that?"

Helena chewed at her lip and shook her head.

Amanda looked at Helena sympathetically. "I know you've had your hands full with your father. I guess you haven't had much time to talk to Joe lately."

Helena stammered out a quiet response. "No, we haven't had time to talk since I got back."

Amanda nodded. "Well, I'm going to go find that ice cream. You'd better finish yours before it melts. It was so nice finally meeting you, Helena. I'm praying for the best for your father. Stan, nice to meet you." She flashed them a smile before heading off in the direction from which they came.

The cold, sticky liquid slid over her fingers and Helena felt heat rush to her face. She hastily licked the melting ice cream from the back of her hand and murmured. "Sorry about that. Let's go find Andi."

"Helena." The tone of his voice halted her, and she turned to look at Stan. "It's okay. I know you like Dr. Blake. Everyone in town knows you like Dr. Blake. I just thought, with his fiancé back in the picture, maybe you could use a day with a friend."

Helena closed her mouth and bit her lip momentarily before looking up at Stan with a grateful smile. "You're a good guy, Stan. You know that?"

"I try," he said. "Come on. Let's find your sister."

"And some napkins," Helena said with a chuckle.

She followed Stan past a table covered in first, second, and third place ribbons and strained her neck, hoping to spot Andi again.

A sudden chill slid down her spine that had her looking back over her shoulder. She saw Amanda ordering her ice cream cone and continued to roll her gaze furtively among the faces in the crowd. She had the distinct feeling that she was being watched.

***

"And you're positive that this Lindsay person is responsible?" Wade asked Joe while Dale spoke to the officer taking pictures of the all-too realistic looking bloody dog.

"Yes, positive. Can I prove it? No."

Dale had called Wade after receiving the call from Joe, partly on account of Wade being the mayor and partly because the three had become good friends. Under different circumstances, Joe would've appreciated the gesture, but at the moment, he was too angry to be grateful for good friends.

"Dale's going to question her. Maybe he can get her to own up to it."

"He didn't have any luck getting her to admit to smashing in the windshield of my car."

"Is that what happened? I wondered, but honestly, with everything that happened with Andi's daddy, I didn't really have time to give it much thought."

"There's not much to think about. She did it but won't admit to it. Plain and simple."

"So, does that mean that you two are not back together?"

Joe nearly choked on his own breath. "Back together? Are you kidding me? She's a raging psycho!"

"You know, she's been telling everyone that you're getting married."

"Everyone? That's what she told Dotty, but seriously, everyone? She's that delusional?"

Joe clenched his fists several times and tried to get his anger under control.

"Hate to bring this up, man," Wade said. He gestured toward the stuffed dog on the floor. "But if you didn't already know she was delusional, you're not a very observant doctor."

Joe cut his eyes at Wade who held up his hands in protest.

"Hey, just sayin'."

Dale joined them. "We've got photos and the info on the tag for the stuffed animal. We can ask at the toy store, see if she purchased it there, but nowadays—"

"Amazon, Walmart, yeah, yeah. I know." Joe wanted to pull his hair out.

"Look, Joe, I can try to talk to her, but without any evidence, I'm going to be hard pressed to get her to say anything. You need to be careful. We don't know what she's capable of, and you could be in danger."

"I'm not in danger. She's crazy, but she won't hurt me."

Wade and Dale exchanged looks.

"What?"

Dale shrugged. "Some people surprise you. They can be more dangerous than you think they are."

Dale was right. Joe learned long ago that he didn't really know Lindsay, and this only confirmed that. For the first time, Joe was extremely grateful that he and Helena were not a couple, and he intended to keep it that way.

***

By mid-afternoon, with the hot sun blazing overhead, the booths shut down to allow the vendors to enjoy the day. Most of the shops closed, and the games came to an end. The streets were quiet, but the inside of the fire station was abuzz with anticipation. Paige and Allie, puppy in tow, joined Andi, Helena, and Stan for bingo where they vied for seats with nearly everyone else in town. Helena waved to Sarah across the room. The new librarian was sitting with Melanie and Trudy, Wade's cousin and secretary. It looked like nearly every person she'd ever known was taking their seats and readying their cards. Several businesses had donated gift certificates and other prizes, and Helena was pleased to see so many businesses, some newly opened and others that had struggled for years, embracing the town spirit. A quiet fell over the building as the caller began to call numbers.

Dabbing her cards, Helena nudged Andi with her elbow.

"What's going on?" she asked quietly.

"What are you talking about?"

"Don't try that with me. I know when you're hiding something. Where did Wade disappear to? What are you trying to keep from me? Is it about Joe?" She stole a quick glance at Stan, but he was furiously trying to keep up with the bingo caller, dabbing sloppy red splotches all over his handful of cards. *Amateur*, Helena thought with a smile.

"It's nothing, I'm sure."

Andi's tone and her refusal to look at Helena set off alarm bells. She held her dabber over B15 and felt her pulse quicken.

"What's nothing?" That same feeling of being watched came over her again, and she glanced around, noticing the queer look Allie was giving her.

"Some kind of trouble at Joe's. I don't know what. Dale asked Wade to head over there. I thought he'd have called or texted by now saying he was on the way back." She looked around as if she could conjure his presence but returned her gaze to her cards.

Helena swallowed and checked her own cards, sure that she missed the last number called. Once she had done a quick check of the numbers, she looked up and caught the eye of someone across the room. The woman, who stood alone in the open doorway of the firehouse bay, was blonde, very pretty, and dressed in what Helena was sure were clothes that did not come from the nearest Walmart. She held Helena's gaze before a slow smile slithered across her face in a way that made Helena shiver. Helena quickly glanced away, and when she looked back, the woman was gone.

Twelve

Nobody spoke as dark descended on the crowd. There was a chill in the air, the kind that made one shiver with discomfort. A knife had been discarded on the ground next to the blanket, and greasy fingers were coated, sticky and red.

"This was a good choice," Andi finally said, licking the spicy sauce from her fingertip. "But nothing is as good as Mama's fried chicken. I wish she and Daddy were here."

"I agree," Helena said, taking a bite of the still-hot, buttered corn on the cob. "Hopefully next year, they'll both be here with us, and we'll all be munching on her chicken." The new barbecue restaurant had opened just in time for the holiday, but the food held the bitter taste of the absence of the ones they loved.

"Hey, save us any?" Wade sat down next to Andi on the blanket she had laid out in the town park. Jackson was with him.

"We've got enough to feed the whole town," Allie said, pouring water into a portable dog bowl.

"You forget how much Jackson eats," Helena teased.

"Everything okay?" Andi looked at Wade with concern while Helena pretended to give her full attention to spooning out coleslaw for Jackson.

"Sure," Wade said. "Now that I'm back with you." He leaned in for a kiss.

Helena rolled her eyes, trying not to begrudge her sister's happiness.

"Mind if we join you?" Dale stood over them, picnic basket in hand. Jamie held a small cooler, and Suzy had her arms wrapped around a blue and white checkered blanket. Dale's brother, Cooper, held a plastic bag from the Shop-N-Save.

"Make yourselves at home," Helena said, gesturing to an empty patch of grass beside them.

Dale looked around at the group. "It's been a long time since the town was all together like this. What? Fifteen, twenty years?"

"Don't ask me," Jackson said. "I can hardly remember a time when the town wasn't struggling. I guess I was too young to hang out with all you old people back when times were good."

"Oh, poor little Jackson," Andi teased, reaching over to ruffle his hair. "Are you cranky? Is it past your bedtime?"

"Stop." He pushed his sister's hand away.

"I know how you feel," Cooper said, sitting on the blanket beside Suzy. "It's hard being the younger brother."

"Fourth of July in Buffalo Springs," Wade said, looking around. "I do remember what it was like back then. This used to be the biggest day of the year."

"Seems like you've all been pretty successful at achieving that again this year." Dale pointed to all the other blankets lining the park. "Good work, Nelson family. You've got a lot to be proud of."

"It wasn't just us," Andi reminded him. "This was the doing of the whole town."

"It's really great," Cooper commented. "Makes me happy that I moved back home. It finally feels like Buffalo Springs isn't the worst place in the world to live."

"Glad you approve, little brother," Dale said, swiping Cooper across the back of his head.

Allie held her bottle of water in the air. The park was an alcohol-free zone, but that didn't take away from the jocularity of the crowd. "Well, I'd like to propose a toast. To the best Fourth of July in many years and to everyone who had a hand in making it happen."

Bottles of water and cans of soda were raised, and Allie's sentiment was echoed by everyone in the group.

"Where's Joe?" Andi asked. "Y'all have been like the Three Musketeers lately."

Dale shot a quick glance at Wade before shaking his head. "Something came up today. He decided not to come out tonight."

"For the love of Pete," Helena said. "What is going on? I know something happened today. Why are y'all being so secretive about it."

Dale handed sandwiches to the kids and took a bite of his own. He chewed slowly, his eyes darting away from Helena's. He swallowed and washed it down with a long drink of Dr. Pepper. "Police business," he finally said, avoiding her gaze.

"What kind of police business?" Helena locked her jaw and gritted her teeth and bored her eyes into him.

"Ongoing investigation. I'm sorry, Helena. If you want to know more, you'll have to ask Joe."

She looked from Dale to Wade and then to Andi who just shrugged. She knew they were hiding something. She could tell by the way they avoided making full eye contact with her, and she felt it in the way Dale kept looking around as if on patrol, waiting for something to happen, like a sheriff in an old Spaghetti Western.

Always the good guy and peacemaker, Stan clapped his hands together. "Andi, I saw the boxes you brought with you. My guess is you've got some mighty tasty pies in there for dessert. Are you sharing?"

"Of course! Who's ready for dessert?" she asked.

Jamie and Suzy both raised their hands. With mouths full, they yelled, "Me!"

"After you finish your sandwiches and the rest of your dinner," Dale told them.

"Oh, Daddy," Andi said, putting on a pouting face. "It's July Fourth. Do they have to wait for dessert?"

"Please, Daddy." Suzy looked up at him, batting those big blue eyes.

Dale put his hand to his heart. "Girl, you kill me. You're so like your Mama."

Helena held her breath, sure that Dale's comment would add even more gloom to the evening. Instead, Suzy grinned widely. "You know what Mama always said."

The three of them chorused in unison, "Eat dessert first in honor of the ladies on the Titanic who never got theirs."

Dale sighed but continued smiling. "Go ahead, Andi. Cut all three of us slices of pie."

"Make that four," Cooper said.

They ate their desserts in silence, enjoying the delectable strawberry, lemon, and mixed berry pies. They watched the band set up for the street dance and contentedly lazed in the grass as evening fell.

Helena was glad to be home, happy to be with her brother and sister, and grateful that her father was slowly improving. She should feel content, basking in the company of her closest friends; however, despite the many blessings she could count from the past several weeks, she had an uneasy feeling in the pit of her stomach. Something was amiss, and she had a nagging sense of foreboding that she couldn't shake.

***

Joe sat on his balcony, watching the flashing lights in the sky. Yellow and orange streaks blossomed into blue and red flowery bursts and glittery white streams. The pops and bangs echoed through the air.

Somewhere, out there in the dark, Helena was sitting beneath her beloved moon, looking up at the same cascade of lights. And so was Lindsay.

Joe closed his eyes and let out a long breath. How many people in town knew that he and Helena had gone out before she left for Europe? How many would think it was meaningful? Would they spill everything to Lindsay if she questioned them with her alluring charm and manipulative smile? Not that there was anything to spill. He and Helena hadn't been seen together in town since she'd returned, and nobody outside of the family knew he'd picked her up at the airport. Lindsay had no reason to…

He shook his head. "Ridiculous," he said out loud.

Whether she knew about Helena or not, there was no reason to worry. He flat-out refused to believe that Lindsay was dangerous despite his earlier realization that he didn't know her as well as he once thought he did. Delusional and a tad deranged, maybe, but not dangerous.

Or was she?

He kept coming back to the fact that he really didn't know Lindsay. Not at all. After what she'd done today, maybe he was underestimating her. Maybe she was a danger to him or to…

He let his thoughts drift back to Helena, wondering who she was with—Stan?—and what she was doing. Was she safe? Did she know about the bloody dog, about Lindsay's antics? Was anyone looking after Helena? Was Stan in love with her? And was Helena beginning to return Stan's feelings for her? Did she feel anything for Joe, or had that ship sailed?

He slowly sipped his gin and watched as the finale lit up the sky with dozens of colored lights, sparkling and falling like rain. For the first time in years, Joe realized how much he hated being alone, how much he longed for the tender touch and gentle kiss of a woman, how nice it would be to hear the sound of little footsteps in the hall, and how it pained him to know that his best chance at happiness was probably lying on a blanket next to a nice, successful carpenter who only had eyes for her.

He'd wasted so much time, months, trying to deny his feelings, and now he was afraid to even speak to her in public. Once again, Lindsay had succeeded in ripping out his heart and tearing it to pieces, and he had a feeling she had only just begun.

***

"I guess this makes it official, doesn't it? I'm a real resident of Buffalo Springs." The woman held up the library card and gave Helena a bright smile.

"I'm not sure if it makes you a resident, but it does mean you're welcome to check out books and use the computers."

"Do ya have any suggestions?" She asked in her deep Texas drawl.

"Well," Helena said thoughtfully. "What do you like to read?"

"Romance." She sighed. "I'm a sucker for a good romance. How 'bout you?" The woman leaned closer, and her eyes sparkled as if the two of them were sharing a juicy secret.

"Yes, but I like other things as well. I'll read just about anything." Where had she seen this woman before? She looked back at the computer monitor. The name didn't ring a bell, but she was sure she'd met her, or at the very least, seen her. "How long have you been in town?"

"About a month now. I just love it. It's so quaint and friendly."

"Your accent…Texas?"

"Oh, honey pie, how did you know?"

An uneasy feeling crept into her bones. "I've known a few people from Texas." *One in particular.*

"I've heard that cute doctor is from Houston. What brought him here? Do you know?"

"Uh…" Helena studied the woman, Lindsay was her name. Something felt off about her. She seemed friendly, but too friendly. Her smile was wide, but she blinked too much, her eyes shifting toward the door with every other blink. Helena had never been cynical, but she was a good judge of character, notwithstanding her conflicting feelings about the aforementioned doctor, and she was wary of this woman.

"I believe Dr. Blake heard that we needed a doctor here in town. I'm not sure what else may have prompted his coming here." Helena held her eyes steady on the woman's face, careful not to give any sign that she was skirting the truth. "Romance, you said? How about the new Luanne Rice? I've got a copy right here that just came off the reserve list."

The narrowing of Lindsay's eyes was so quick, Helena almost missed it, but she was sure the woman was not happy with the change of subject.

"Sure," she said without much enthusiasm. "But if you don't mind, I think I'll peruse the shelves a bit before I check out."

"Of course," Helena said with a smile. "Help yourself. New releases are just around the corner to the right, children's books are arranged along the rest of the walls, nonfiction is in the middle, and fiction is up the spiral stairs. Let me know if you need help finding anything." She smiled sweetly then turned back to her computer as if she had pressing work to attend to.

Lindsay disappeared into the nonfiction stacks, and Helena did something she had never done. She slipped into her office behind the counter and tapped her mouse to awaken her computer. With glances back and forth between the monitor and the library, she brought up Facebook and searched for the name on Lindsay's library card. Nothing. Odd but not unheard of. She leaned up a bit and stretched her neck to get a better look of the outer room. Seeing nobody nearby, including the new card holder, she navigated to Google and typed the name. Millions of hits came up, everything from attorneys to doctors to B-list actresses. She closed her eyes for a moment, conjuring an image of the address that was on the driver's license. She typed in Katy, Texas.

Eyes bulging and heart beginning to race, Helena tapped on the link to the Katy Times from seven years prior. The photograph showed a glowing couple in their mid-twenties. The bride-to-be had her hand placed on the man's chest, displaying a diamond ring, sizeable but modest. His smile was wide, and his eyes sparkled as if he had just been laughing. Helena recognized the look. She'd seen it dozens of times over the past several months.

He was engaged to Lindsay Johnson, not Amanda Pierce. The resemblance and demeanor between the two weren't even close. The minute Amanda spoke, Helena could feel the genuineness, the caring persona, the friendliness. Not so with Lindsay. Helena felt on guard almost immediately. She knew something was not right. Lindsay was hunting for information, but was it truly about Joe or about Helena? Was she trying to figure out how much Helena knew about Joe or if she and Joe were an item?

"I'm ready," Lindsay's voice rang out from the circulation desk, causing Helena to jolt. She jumped from the desk and hurried to the counter.

"I'm sorry. A problem with a book order." She waved her hand in the air as if to dismiss the problem. "I'll worry about it later." She forced herself to smile and hoped Lindsay wouldn't notice.

As Helena scanned the books, she had to work to keep her feelings in check. Lindsay was checking out *The*

Knot Book of Wedding Lists, The Complete Wedding Planner for Brides, and the old standby, *Martha Stewart Weddings.*

"My sister is getting married this fall." Helena tried to keep her voice casual and gestured toward one of the books. "She said this one was a big help."

"Why, bless her heart," Lindsay gushed. "I'm planning on an earlier wedding, but we still need to work out a few of the details."

Helena kept her gaze on the monitor, fighting for control of her emotions. She tossed her short curls and flashed a killer smile. "Well, good luck to you and your groom. I hope you have a lifetime of happiness."

"Oh, we will, honey pie. I'm going to make sure of that."

A sudden chill ran down Helena's back at the tone of Lindsay's voice. She watched the new patron walk away, feeling the same sense of unease she had felt on the Fourth. She looked down at the counter and noticed the Luann Rice book, completely forgotten, and then, looked back toward the door. Again, she felt that something was just not right.

Helena absent-mindedly picked up the water bottle beside her. She raised it to her lips but abruptly stopped. She held out the bottle, inspecting it for a long moment. Her gaze drifted back toward the door through which Lindsay had left. Helena shuddered before casually walking into the office and pouring the liquid down the sink.

***

"Dr. Blake? Are you okay?"

Joe looked up to see Dotty standing in the doorway. He painted a smile on his face. "I'm fine, Dotty. What can I do for you?"

She walked in, closed the door behind her, and took a seat. "Nothing. It's you we're worried about, Melanie and me. We'd like to help."

Joe started to deny that there was something to worry about. He opened his mouth, but the look of concern on Dotty's face made him feel guilty.

"I'm fine, really. I've got a lot on my mind, but nothing either of you can help with. I do appreciate the offer though."

Dotty sized him up before shaking her head. "I may not have a medical degree, Dr. Blake, but I'm not stupid and I'm not blind. Everyone knows what that psycho is saying, and while you're putting up a good front, I know it has to be bothering you."

Joe snorted. "I've been trying to tune it out. I can only imagine what she's saying."

"I heard she was in the boutique yesterday asking how soon she could have a wedding dress in hand if she ordered it right away."

"Hmph." Joe sat back and entwined his fingers against his stomach. "Some nerve she's got. She terrorizes me, then four days later, she's ordering a wedding dress." He shook his head. "What did Nadine tell her?"

"That it takes at least eight weeks for a dress to come in, and then it has to be fitted and altered. Ms. Johnson wasn't happy about that. She said she could've had one made in Paris in less time."

Joe laughed out loud. "Oh, really? And when has she ever known anything about ordering clothes from Paris? She's all talk, you know?"

"Oh, I know, and so does everyone else. When she first came, people believed her about the two of you being engaged and all, but now…"

He sat up and placed his hands on the desk. "Now?"

"Now, after the outbursts she had here and the way she's carrying on about your 'relationship,' everyone just thinks she's crazy."

He let out a breath and sat back again, looking away. He stared into the corner of the room for a bit before turning back to Dotty. "What else are people saying?"

Dotty squirmed in the chair, glanced down at her hands, wringing them in her lap, then back up at Joe. "That you and Ms. Nelson broke up because she found out that you're engaged. They say that's why she left town."

Joe winced. "You know that's not true, right? I mean, we weren't an item to begin with, but her leaving town was something she'd wanted to do her whole life. It had nothing to do with me."

"Well, I know that's what she says, but…"

"But what?" Joe asked, trying to keep the anger from his voice. It wasn't Dotty's fault that people liked to gossip and spread rumors and inuendo.

"Well, her leaving was awful sudden, and you two were seen together on several occasions, having dinner, playing mini golf, strolling around town. Most of the town knows that you walked her home every night last winter before it started getting light in the evenings."

"Her family was in danger. Wade's house was nearly burned down, and Andi was attacked. Any gentleman would have made she sure she got home safely in the dark. And we work practically next door to each other." He felt as though he was protesting too much though all he said was true.

Dotty stared at him, her face pinched, her eyes squinting. "But you do have feelings for her, right? Helena, I mean."

Joe sighed. "Dotty, I realize we live in a small town where there few boundaries between work and personal lives, but I think this conversation has gone on long enough."

"I'm sorry, Dr. Blake. I was trying to help." She stood and headed toward the door.

"Dotty."

She turned back to him.

"Thank you. I do appreciate it. I'm…" He faltered. "Thank you."

She nodded and left, closing the door behind her.

Joe wasn't sure what he had been about to say. He'd never had anyone outside of his family or Darrin ask him if he was okay or how they could help him. This whole small-town thing was new to him, and he just wasn't sure how he felt about it. One thing he knew for certain, though, was that the talk about him and Lindsay had to stop.

***

Helena and Andi sat in wicker chairs on the back deck spooning fresh, hot peach pie slathered with ice cream into their mouths.

"Now this, this is what summer is all about," Helena said. "Where have you been for the past twelve years, and how did I not know you could make something so sinful?"

"You knew. You just forgot."

"I'm not sure I did." Helena licked the back of the spoon, refusing to miss a single taste of the pie. "I remember you baking pies sometimes, but I don't remember everyone going crazy about them like this. I mean, I know you won ribbons and all that, but this…" She scooped another bite, slowly sucked it off the spoon, and smacked her lips. "This is a bite of Heaven."

"I had a lot of practice while I was away."

"Well, I for one, am glad you're back."

"For my company or my pies?"

Helena wrinkled her nose and looked at her sister with one eye. "Do I have to answer that?"

"Hmm. I think I'd rather you didn't."

"How's Daddy?"

Andi took her time answering. "He's okay. He's still mixing up his words a lot. Dr. Stearns says he's going to do that for a while. He's anxious to come home, but he knows he needs to go to rehab first."

"And we're still moving him at the end of the week?"

"That's what they say."

Helena noticed the strain in her sister's voice. "You don't agree?"

"No, I do," Andi said, pulling her legs up under her. "It's just that… He has a long way to go before he can come home."

Helena nodded. "And he may not fully recover."

"Yeah. And I hate seeing him this way."

"I get it. It's hard watching someone you love struggling and not knowing how to help."

Andi squinted at Helena. "Are we still talking about Daddy?"

Helena bent down and dropped the empty plate to the floor, while considering a second piece, and mimicked her sister's pose, feet curled under her. "Of course. Who else?"

"Wade says Joe's fit to be tied. He doesn't know what to do about his ex."

"She came to the library this morning."

Andi's head snapped to attention. "What? Why?"

Helena shrugged. "She said she wanted something fun to read, but she checked out three books on wedding planning. There was something…off about her. That's the only word I can think of. She's all smiles and charm and *honey pie* this and that, but underneath it all, she just gives me the creeps."

"Wade says she's dangerous, Helena. I mean *Fatal Attraction* kind of dangerous."

"What does that mean?" Helena asked, feeling her blood run cold.

"I don't know. He says he can't tell me. Police business and all."

"Police business? Wade's not a cop."

"Mayoral privilege." Andi rolled her eyes. "Anyway, he and Dale have become pretty tight with Joe, so I guess Joe has confided some stuff to them. All I know is she did something on the Fourth that had all of them pretty spooked."

"And Dale didn't arrest her?"

"Not enough evidence."

"I'm not surprised. I'm telling you, An, she's super creepy."

"Just watch your back, okay?"

"Me? Why would I have to watch my back?" Even as she asked the question, she knew the answer.

"He's head over heels for you, Helena. Has been since the day you met. Anybody and everybody can see it except for you."

"And him apparently."

"I wouldn't be so sure. He was worried sick about you when Daddy had his stroke. He cares about Daddy, don't get me wrong, but he was worried about you. If you could've seen the relief on his face when you texted to tell me you'd landed, you'd have no doubt."

"Yeah, well, I do have doubts. Lots of them. And I doubt he's going to get away from Lindsay Johnson too easily."

"Helena." Andi's voice was low and serious. "I mean it. Be careful. I don't like that she showed up at the library. She could've been checking you out, eying up the competition. If she's as crazy as you think she is, you could be on her hit list."

"Andi! Don't say it like that! It's not like she's going around killing people."

"No, but there's a fine line between love and obsession, and she seems on the verge of crossing it if she hasn't already."

All thoughts of another piece of pie disappeared as Helena's stomach began forming tight knots. She recalled the feeling she got when she was about to take a drink of her water that had been sitting, unattended, on the circulation counter; and though she'd only seen her for a split second, she thought the woman who had been staring at her at bingo might have been Lindsay.

Was Andi right? Could she really be in danger? If so, what kind of danger did that mean Joe might be in?

Thirteen

The stairs to the second level of the candy store were new. The wood was freshly treated and still light in color, untouched by the sun or the rain or snow. There was no balcony or stilted deck, just steps that went straight from the small parking area to an exterior door twelve feet or so off the ground. Joe took the steps by twos, not feeling the least bit winded after his run over from the clinic. He had Wade and Dale to thank for that and felt a bit embarrassed that a lawyer/politician and a police chief were in better shape than the town doctor.

He hesitated at the door for only a moment before he pounded on it.

"Lindsay, open up. We need to talk." He didn't hear any movement on the other side of the door, so he pounded harder. "Lindsay, come on. Open the door."

He took a deep breath. Was she home? He turned around and leaned on the railing of the small landing, gripping it tightly, trying to remain calm and focused while he waited and looked in the small parking area beneath. Her car was there.

He turned back and raised his fist to try one more time when the door sprang opened. He almost stumbled inside but thankfully caught himself, shuddering at the thought of literally falling into her arms. "You're home."

Lindsay smiled. It was not the kind of smile that appeared at the sight of a new kitten but the kind that more likely would be worn by a lioness spotting her prey. "I'm home. Come in, Joe. I'm so happy you stopped by."

The apartment was tiny but carefully decorated. A pink couch sat in what passed for a living room. Behind the couch, plant-lined windows allowed the evening sun to stream into the room, casting a glow that made the apartment feel warm and cozy. A rug in shades of light blue covered the floor in front of the couch, and a large, leather upholstered ottoman served as both a footrest and a coffee table, holding a wooden tray with a magazine and television remote control. Across from the couch, next to the door where he was standing, a television, not too big or too small, hung on the wall. A small white counter separated the living area from a little kitchen. There was no table and chair set; there was no room for one. On the other side of the living room, Joe could see an open door that looked to lead to a bedroom.

The apartment was neat and tidy, and he couldn't help but think back to the Lindsay he knew in college who had clothes strewn everywhere, dirty dishes on every surface, and trash left wherever it fell. They had a running joke that their first purchase after the wedding would be a weekly service to keep their house clean.

From what he'd gathered from Wade, it was the only thing she and Helena had in common.

"I know it's small, but I like it. Less to clean," she said with a grin.

The thought that she could read his mind was too off-putting to consider, and Joe gave no indication that the notion had even come to mind. He made no pretenses as to why he was there. "We need to talk."

"That's what I've been waiting for. Please." She gestured to the couch. "Have a seat."

Joe eyed the couch, aware that it was the only seating choice. "I'll stand, thanks."

He saw the flash of irritation in her eye and the twitch of her jaw, but she hastily smiled and sat on the couch facing him. "Suit yourself."

"Lindsay," he began and then realized he should've thought this over. He needed to proceed delicately. "I need you to understand that what we had…" He hesitated, trying to find the right words. "It was good."

"It was the best. We were the best. I knew you'd come around."

He held up his hand at her movement to stand, and she eased back onto the cushion.

"It was good, but it ended. A long time ago. We've both moved on, grown up, and have separate lives."

"We don't have to have separate lives," she protested. "I know I was selfish. I always wanted things my way, but I've changed. Can't you see that? I came to you. I moved here. I'm ready to do things your way." She pouted, but he was unmoved.

"It's not a matter of doing things my way." He huffed in exasperation. "Lindsay, we aren't right for each other, probably never were. Time and space and maturity have only made that clear."

"Oh, but we are!" She clenched her fists. "You're the only man for me. I didn't see it back then when I, well, when I… Anyway, I know it now."

"Lindsay," he tried to keep his voice calm, tried to reason with her. "We were kids back then. We're adults now. We have different lives, different interests, diff—"

"How do you know? You haven't given us a chance."

"There is no us," he shouted. He wasn't making any headway, and he was tired of beating around the bush. "There will never again be an us."

Her eyes flashed with anger, and her hands clutched the cushion of the couch. From the fury he detected in those eyes, he thought she might rip the couch apart thread by thread.

She spoke through gritted teeth. "There will always be an us."

Joe shook his head. "No, Lindsay, there won't be." Even Joe noticed the sadness in his voice. Or was it weariness? Or wariness? "I'm sorry. I realize this isn't what you wanted to hear—"

She screamed and leaped over the table like the lioness she'd appeared to be earlier. Her nails clawed into his cheeks, and the surprise of her reaction had him so off guard that, for a moment, he felt like he really was being attacked by a lion. He grabbed at her flailing arms, but, unable to catch hold of her, raised his hands to protect his face. He backed away from her, but she was relentless. Daring to take a hand away from his face, he reached behind him and seized the door handle. With one swift motion, he swung open the door and dashed for the safety of the wooden staircase.

He practically jumped from the top step to the bottom, all the while hearing her screams and frantic cries as she followed him outside.

"You will pay, Joe Blake. You will pay for running out on me. Nobody walks away from me. Nobody!"

He ran all the way back to the clinic, his cheeks burning with both pain and rage. His only thought was, *You walked away from me you crazy woman. You walked away from me. And I thank Heaven you did.*

***

Helena held the 416-page Clive Cussler bestseller in her hand. The book, which had been in the overnight return bin, was the only copy the library owned, and Helena knew exactly who had checked it out. She frowned as she turned to look out the window in her office and stared at the backside of the clinic.

Joe must have slipped the book into the book depository sometime during the night or early that morning. He'd been a regular at the library since the first week he moved in, always checking to see if she had the latest Cussler or Grisham or Archer or similar legal thriller or action-adventure novel. She'd grown to know his tastes, often setting aside something she knew he would appreciate. He enjoyed Lee Childs but wasn't crazy about Diane Capri, who wrote companion books about Childs' alter ego, Jack Reacher. He liked nonfiction historical reads but shied away from political ones because, according to Joe, he liked knowing that government honesty and integrity existed at one time. He claimed to never read romance, but every now and then, a Nora Roberts made its way onto his library card, and they'd once had a quite enjoyable discussion about whether or not Robert Ludlum's *The Bourne Identity* was actually a romance. They both decided that it was.

Sighing, Helena checked the book back in, noted the name of the next patron on the hold list, and placed the book on the 'to be picked up' shelf. She busied herself with straightening the stacks, dusting the shelves, and making sure the library was tidy and ready for business.

Sarah had taken over the story time hour and was in the meeting room getting ready. Helena looked forward to seeing the chubby-faced toddlers swarm into the room just before ten. They had two age groups coming in this morning—two- and three-year-olds followed by four- and five-year-olds—and Helena's book club was meeting at two that afternoon. It was going to be a busy day, and Helena was glad to have the distractions.

As she suspected, the day went by quickly. The children were as enamored with Sarah as Helena was. Helena loved children and loved reading to them, but after a short two years of doing story time, she had grown bored with the books, the crafts, and the cleaning up of pretzel sticks smashed into the carpet and white grape juice pooling in sticky puddles on the tables. Sarah breathed a fresh new air into the tales of Beatrix Potter and *Mike Mulligan's Steam Shovel*. The mothers (and one father) raved about her story-telling skills and the new craft projects, and Helena enjoyed the stillness of the morning.

The afternoon book club was almost as lively as the toddler's story time. Harriet Lowe's suggestion of *The Guest List* was a triumphant choice, and the women raved about its similarity to Agatha Christie's classic whodunits. Helena wished her mother had been able to attend, knowing how much she was enjoying the piecemeal reading of the book as she spent long hours at the hospital, but Grace spent little time away from Joshua.

Late in the afternoon, the arrival of the UPS truck sent a thrill through Helena, and she hastily followed the nice-looking young man in his tight brown shorts as he wheeled the box into her office. A shipment of new releases always put the crumb topping on the French apple pie and made Helena feel like the proverbial kid on Christmas morning. There was nothing better, in Helena's opinion, than opening a box of books, smelling the ink and the freshly cut pages, running one's fingers along the still-perfect spines and the glossy dust jackets, and fanning the pages so that words ran together in long, straight lines like the images in an old-time flip book animation. Helena practically sighed as she slid the box cutter across the packing tape and peeled open the cardboard flaps.

"I meant to tell you..." Sarah said, dodging in from the circulation desk during a moment of calm. "I had the strangest request this afternoon while you were at book club."

Helena arched her brow, as she lifted the first book from the box. "Oh? What was that?"

"A new patron—she said you gave her a card the other day—came in with the oddest list of book requests I've ever seen. We had a couple, but the rest had to be ordered through inter-library loan."

Helena's mind went immediately to the only new patron she'd encountered that week, and her curiosity outweighed the delight of inspecting the new books. "What was on the list?"

Sarah's brown messy bun bounced as she quickly turned to see that they were still alone and then snapped her gaze back to Helena. "One was Sarah Schmidt's *See What I have Done* about Lizzie Borden. Another was *The Lady Macbeth of Mtsensk* by Nikolai...oh, darn. What's his last name? Anyway, Steinbeck's *East of Eden*, King's *Misery*, Flynn's *Gone Girl*—"

"Stop." Helena didn't want to hear any more titles. She shook off the shiver that gripped her shoulders. "They're all books about women who terrorize their loved ones or..." She swallowed the words.

"Or killed them." Sarah supplied. "I know. When I remarked that it was a collection of interesting reading, she said, 'research' and gave me a smile that sent goose flesh down my arms."

Helena was experiencing the same sensation at the moment. "Research?"

Sarah's head bobbed slowly up and down twice. "That's what she said, and I've got to tell you, it really rattled me. Then the O'Connor family came in, and, you know how that goes."

"Six kids and a friendly, talkative mom. It has a way of shaking any and all loose leaves from the branches of your mind."

Sarah laughed. "Is sure does. Anyway, I wanted to tell you about Lindsay. That's her name, right?"

"Yes, Lindsay from Texas." Helena bit her bottom lip. *Joe's Lindsay*, she thought, remembering Andi's warning from a couple days back, *there's a fine line between love and obsession, and she seems on the verge of crossing it.*

"Yeah, that's right. She has a thick accent. Anyway, I just thought of it. What kind of research do you think she's doing?"

A thud caused Helena to jump and stifle a scream. Her heart raced, and she took several deep breaths as Sarah ran to help the patron with a pile of overdue books he had dropped onto the counter. Helena ran her tongue along her sore lip and loosened the vice-like grip she had on the book in her hands, laying it down on her desk. She suddenly felt rather cold and walked uneasily to the thermostat to raise the temperature on the air conditioning.

"It's blowin' up a helluva storm out there," the man, a local famer, said to Sarah. "Best to batten down the hatches and head home if you can."

On cue, a crack of thunder shook the building, and Helena turned toward the door that led outside. She froze. Across the parking lot, hair blowing wildly in the gusty wind, stood Lindsay, looking every bit like the Medusa statue Helena had seen in the Piazza della Signoria with venomous snakes curling around the head and neck of the mythical Gorgon. Lindsay grinned at Helena as a flash of lightening streaked across the sky, casting an eerie glow around her pale white face and blonde hair, making her resemble the statue even more. Helena felt the Gorgon's power overcome her, and every nerve in her body turned as hard and cold as stone. She blinked, and the allegorical creature was gone as quickly as she had disappeared from the fire station on the Fourth.

"Helena, are you okay?" Sarah asked, seemingly from a different realm.

"I'm fine," she stammered. "My imagination was getting the best of me." She turned to Sarah and offered a feeble smile. "I think Henry's right. The sky is black as pitch. We'd better lock up and head home. It's almost closing time anyway."

Helena reached for the bolt and locked the door. Before she turned, she darted her eyes from right to left, taking in the lot and the expanse of grass between the library and the clinic. Nobody was there, yet Helena once again had the sensation of being watched, and she felt certain she knew whose eyes were upon her.

***

It took all her strength for Helena to close the door to her house. Papers flew off the kitchen counter as Andi slammed herself against the door next to her sister.

"It's bad," Andi said.

Helena nodded. "It's really bad. Did you see the sky? It was black when we started locking up, but now it's green." She swallowed. "You don't think…?"

"I haven't gotten any alerts."

At that moment, both of their phones emitted a series of long, ear-splitting beeps, and a siren sounded outside. Andi's eyes widened as she looked at her sister. "Holy mother of—"

"Come on," Helena yelled, grabbing her sister's arm. As soon as she turned the knob, the door flew open, nearly knocking them both down with its force. The vase of flowers on the foyer table toppled to the floor, but the shattering sound was unheard. The howling of the wind combined with the shrieking siren was so loud, Helena had to shout, "Follow me!"

They went onto the porch, and Helena watched Andi pull the door shut with all her might. Helena motioned to the side of the house, and Andi followed. Fighting the wind, Helena managed to throw open the door to the decades-old root cellar. They descended into the darkness and worked together to close and latch the door. The roar of the wind and wail of the siren were greatly diminished but still echoed in Helena's ears. It was blacker than coal in the musty smelling place, but she reached up and pulled a cord. A single bulb lit the cellar enough for them both to see. Helena pointed to a plastic tub in the corner where she kept a pile of blankets, safely stored away from mice and other varmints.

"I'd forgotten how suddenly it can come upon you," Andi said. "I thought Jackson was joking when he told me to download that app, but he wasn't kidding when he said those seconds could be the difference between making it to shelter and seeing the face of God."

"Not many tornadoes in the desert, I guess," Helena said, shaking out a blanket then making herself comfortable on the ground, kicking off her shoes in the process.

"Just dust storms. But let me tell you, they blind you more than any driving rain I've ever experienced."

Helena was quiet, listening to the sounds from above, praying that their family was safe. Joe's face came to mind, and she said a prayer that he, too, had heeded the warning of the siren or app. An image of Lindsay standing against the blackened sky came to mind, and Helena squeezed her eyes tightly, forcing the picture away.

"You okay?" Andi asked.

"Fine," she answered hastily.

Something crashed against the cellar door, and four eyes shifted toward the only thing protecting them from the elements. They could hear pelting sounds against the door. The single bulb flickered above them but thankfully stayed lit.

"Sounds like rain," Andi said.

Helena nodded. "I think you're right. Not hail, so that's good."

"Could still be coming," Andi reminded her. "First the rain, then the hail with…"

"The updraft," Helena finished the sentence. "The center of the twister."

Andi reached for her sister's hands and clutched them tightly. "I didn't miss this."

"You think Mama and Daddy are okay?"

"I'm sure they are."

Though Andi knew no more about her parents' safety than Helena did, it comforted Helena to hear her older sister say the words. She grasped for something to talk about, something that would take her mind off the storm if that was possible. She thought of the odd list of books Lindsay requested but shook it away, opting for a happier topic.

"How are the wedding plans coming?"

"They're coming."

Helena felt Andi's smile rather than saw it as she was staring off into the blackness on the other side of the room.

"The invitations have been sent, but we haven't had many replies. Of course, it's still early." They both jumped at a rattling at the cellar door then breathed sighs of relief when it calmed and the rain continued. Andi spoke in a low, soothing voice. "It's funny. I've never had to sit down and compile a list of my 'friends' before. It was…hard."

Helena knew what she meant. Andi's closest friends had all been killed in a helicopter crash almost a year before. It was still difficult for her to talk about without tears coming to the surface.

"Surely, you invited Monica and some of the, uh, wives…" She felt Andi nod and looked at her sister. There were no tears there now, only a small smile and a faraway look in her eyes.

"I did. Monica and I have been close since the Academy. The wives…that was a harder decision. We were all close, but it wasn't the same between me and them as it was between me and their husbands. We were a team, and I always worried that their wives didn't understand that. But after the…well, they were so kind, so caring. I realized that they were part of the team, too, just in a different way."

"Do you think they'll come?" The rain was letting up a bit, and Helena prayed the storm was passing. The alternative was the updraft, and she didn't want to think about what that meant.

"I…I think so. Some of them anyway. It'll be hard for Maddie. She has a little one, almost one now." Andi let out a long, sad breath. "I thought Cindy might come. She was engaged to Evan, but her mother just passed, so I'm not so sure."

"Is Mamma still planning on doing the flowers?" Helena asked, changing the subject from the questionable guest list to cheerier details.

"She insists on it. Won't they be beautiful?"

"They will be."

Andi stiffened, and Helena gulped in a sharp intake of breath. "What was that?"

"Not hail," Helena said. She strained her ears and listened for another sound. "It sounds like footsteps. Someone's in the house."

"They sound awfully muffled. Are you sure?"

"The cellar was reinforced years ago, so it's almost soundproof, but I'm sure." She jolted at another sound. "Did you hear that? It's a voice." She could barely make it out, but she was sure someone was calling her name.

"Do you think it's safe to go out?" Andi asked.

"I don't hear anything." She tiptoed toward the door and cautiously undid the latch. No wind fought her efforts to lift the door, and the only water that fell on her face was the rainwater that dripped from the edges of the door. A pale sliver of moonlight pierced through the leaves on the tree next to the house.

"Helena!" She heard the frantic call and hurried from the underground haven.

"Joe? We're here!" She rushed toward the porch as he bounded from inside and practically flew down the steps, sweeping her into his arms.

Helena felt the rapid beating of his heart as he clutched her to him, his chest cradling her like a saddle on a horse, his arms harnessed around her back.

"Oh, thank you, God. I was trapped in the clinic, and I watched it. I watched it go by, heading in this direction. I called, but you didn't answer."

She gently pushed back and reached into her pocket for her phone. Ten missed calls. One from Jackson, two from her mother, seven from Joe.

"We were in the cellar. It's reinforced, so I guess there was no signal. Or maybe the storm caused cell interference." As she spoke, she came to the realization that he wasn't just concerned. He was desperately worried. About her. Another realization hit her as his words combined with the memory of the rattling of the cellar door. "You said you watched it. Do you mean…?" She looked around, suddenly aware of the rain gutter dangling from her roof, swaying in the lingering gusts of wind. Her screened door was standing against the railing on the far side of the porch looking like she had purposely removed it and propped it there.

A large sycamore not far down the street had been uprooted and narrowly missed a house. Shingles, branches, and other bits of debris littered yards, and some windows were broken. Mailboxes had been lifted from the ground and thrown about as if Godzilla had torn through the town, picking up the mailboxes like toys and discarding them when he was finished playing. All in all, the damage was minimal.

"It doesn't look bad. Probably an EF-0, a 1 at most," she remarked. "Thank Heaven. The town is just starting to get back on its feet."

She looked up at him and saw him staring at her, his face awash with emotion, but she couldn't read what it meant. "Are you okay?"

He met her eyes with his. "I am now."

A warm thrill swept through her. "Joe, I—" She broke off, unable to find the words.

***

Without thinking, he grabbed her, pulled her back into his embrace, and pressed his lips against hers. He felt the resistance for only a second before she flung her arms around his neck and kissed him back. He moved his mouth from her lips to her cheek, to the hollow beneath her ear, then to her throat, desperate to shower her with affection, to show her how worried he was. She kneaded her fingers into his neck, and he felt his pulse quicken.

The clearing of a throat brought him to his senses, and he quickly let go and had to reach out to steady her. She had a dazed look on her face.

"You might want to take that inside." Andi's voice from behind Helena was low but clear, and he looked over to her and nodded.

"I'm sorry. I didn't mean to…" He looked at Helena. "I'm so sorry. I was just relieved that you're okay."

A look of disappointment crossed her face, and he hastened to correct himself, almost pleading with her. "I mean, I prayed that you were okay, that nothing had happened to you. I needed to see, to feel…" He stopped, feeling awkward at this rush of emotion, but she smiled at him, and he saw the warm glow in her eyes.

"I like the way you checked on me, Dr. Blake. It's not a procedure I've experienced before when having a doctor check my vitals or my well-being."

He grinned despite his embarrassment and shook his head. "It's not the way I usually check on my patients, Ms. Nelson."

He watched as she raked her bottom lip through her teeth and, knowing her, was certain she blushed behind the cloak of night when she said, "I think I'd like to make a follow-up appointment sometime."

He heard Andi snicker. "I've had enough excitement for one night. I'm gonna head inside and call Mama and Wade. I'll let them know that you're both okay."

Joe waited until Andi was inside the house before he reached for Helena's hands. He held them both and gazed into her eyes. He saw her stiffen, and she reached up and touched the deep scratch on his cheek. He involuntarily winced.

"Did something hit you? A branch maybe? Do you want me to clean it up?"

The irony of her question made him smile, but the memory of the nails digging into his flesh had him frowning.

"No, that was…something else." He took a deep breath. "I'm sorry I haven't been around much. Things are…complicated."

"Lindsay?" she asked, and he felt the jagged edge of a knife in his heart.

"You've heard."

"I've heard all kinds of things, Joe. Maybe you could clear them up for me."

"Maybe it's time I did just that." He swung their arms gently and looked up toward the moon. "Do you think we're in the clear now? As far as storms, I mean."

He looked her up and down as her gaze wandered around. Her curls were matted down in the back, and he thought she must have been leaning back against the back of a chair or perhaps the wall of the cellar. She was still wearing her work clothes, but her feet were bare, and he wondered if she had kicked off her shoes in the house before retreating to the cellar, or if the shoes were lying on the dirt floor underground. He could tell, even in the shadows, that her toes were painted, and he wondered what color they were.

"I think we're good for now. I hope so anyway." She looked up at him, and he had a great desire to scoop her up, carry her inside, and tuck her in bed. That's all. Just tuck her in, kiss her goodnight, watch her fall asleep, and guard her through the night. It occurred to him that it was the most intimate thought he'd ever had about a woman.

"We need to talk, but it's been quite a night." He heard voices and looked down the street where neighbors had gathered to assess the damage. "We were lucky. All of us."

She nodded. "I think you're right, and yes, it has been." She stifled a yawn and suddenly looked tired, as if she has was just feeling the toll of what had taken place in the past hour. "You'll call?" she asked.

"Can I make you supper? Tomorrow night?"

Helena squeezed his hands. "I'd like that, but we're moving Daddy tomorrow. I'm not sure what time we'll be back."

"Call me. I'll have dinner ready for you whatever time that might be."

She stood on her toes and kissed him gently on the cheek. She let go of his hands and turned to go. "Thank you, Joe. I'll see you tomorrow, then," she called as she climbed the porch steps.

"Good night, Helena." He watched her go and silently prayed for the right words and the right manner to tell her all that he had to say. When he turned to head home, he saw the moon hanging low in the sky, a silent reminder that Helena was depending upon him, and he needed to be the reflection she and God wanted him to be.

***

"A confirmed EF-1," Andi, mitts on her hands, told Helena as she reached into the commercial oven and retrieved a pie. The scents of butter, flour, and peaches clung to the air.

"I can't believe how lucky we were. If the wind speeds had been just a little but faster, well, I don't even want to think about it."

Andi took off the mitts and laid them on the counter next to the cooling rack from which the tantalizing double-crusted pie was calling Helena's name.

"Lucky is an understatement," Andi said, shaking her head. "I'm just glad that Jackson and Mama were home and not on the road. Remember that time we were on our way back from Little Rock? Was it from a wedding reception? Anyway, Daddy pulled over when the hail started, and Mama dug out her Rosary and started praying. I was sure our lives were going to end that night. I can still see that twister tearing through the trees just ahead of us."

"What I remember is how the car lifted, just a bit, but enough for us to feel it hovering back and forth above the ground like Doc Brown's car in *Back to the Future*."

"Speaking of doctors…" Andi said, her eyes twinkling. "This is yours." She gestured toward the freshly baked pie.

"It is? Andi, you didn't have to do that. I would've been happy with one from case."

"I know, but I wanted to do this. I've been a mess ever since Dr. Steans called to say we needed to wait another day before moving Daddy. This helped put my nerves to rest."

"I'm just so relieved that Mama and Daddy weren't at the rehab center when it got hit by the twister. And I'm so grateful that the damage was minimal."

"Me, too." Andi pushed the pie toward Helena. "This will have cooled down just enough for you to enjoy it with a scoop of ice cream after your supper. I'm sorry that strawberries and rhubarb aren't still in season. I could've still gotten them, but the peaches are at their peak right now. I guarantee this will knock his socks off."

Helena laughed. "Anything you bake would someone's socks off, but I appreciate the effort." She reached across the metal prep table and grabbed her sister's hand. "Thank you. I mean it. It means the world to me that you'd bake a pie for us."

"Helena, I'd do anything for you. You're my maid of honor." Andi winked at her sister.

"And you're not getting any details out of me about the bridesmaids' party. I told you, it's all a secret."

"Why, Helena Sue." Andi batted her eyes and spoke with the thickest Southern drawl she could muster as she boxed up the pie. "I do declare you are as ornery as a rattlesnake."

Helena took the pie and turned to leave, calling back to her sister. "Bless your little ol' heart." She smiled as she left the bakery. Nobody knew how to politely insult each other better than Southern sisters.

Fourteen

Joe opened the door, his grin widening. "You've been by the bakery, I see."

"Why Dr. Blake, what makes you think I didn't rush home and bake this all by myself?"

"I am so sorry," he said, bowing to her. "Please, I beg forgiveness."

An image of Rhett Butler greeting Scarlett O'Hara at Twelve Oaks filled her mind, and Helena laughed. "Scandalous, just scandalous," she said. "Truth be told, I can't tell the difference between sugar and baking soda. But give me a catfish or a mess of okra, and I'll have your mouth-watering before they're out of the fryer." She followed him through the living room to the kitchen.

"And my arteries clogged before I get up from the table."

Helena laughed. "You may be right about that." She put the pie on the counter and looked around the room, deeply inhaling the tantalizing scents of garlic and balsamic vinegar wafting from the stove. "Andi would think she'd died and gone to hog heaven with a kitchen like this." She ran her hand along the marble counter on the island.

Maple cabinets and drawers lined the walls, nestling a beautiful farmhouse sink in front of a glorious three-windowed view of the backyard where an impressive garden boasted all sorts of vegetables. Pots of herbs lined a deep windowsill behind the tall, arched faucet. Tan, brown, and sand-colored brickwork filled the space between the upper cabinets and lower drawers. A double oven and gas stovetop sat between deep drawers on the right-hand wall, while a huge refrigerator, encased by wall-to-ceiling pantries, sat to the left of the sink, a couple cabinets in between. The island had cabinets on one side and what looked to be a microwave and bread warmer alongside more cabinets and above lower drawers on the other. Recessed lights, between the wooden beams in the ceiling, lit up the room. In the middle of the table stood the vase that Jess Swanson had made. It was filled with Black-Eyed Susans, and the sight of it made Helena smile.

"Was this kitchen like this when you bought the house?" She never thought of the older couple who sold him the house as gourmet cooks.

"Well, I guess that's my first confession of the evening."

She turned toward Joe and arched her brow. "Oh?"

"I'm a bit obsessed with cooking."

"Does that mean that you designed this kitchen?" She looked around with a whole new appreciation for the room and the man standing in it.

"I did. It was the first thing I did when I bought the house."

She eyed the stonework and the Tuscan tile accents. "You really do love Italy."

"And I can't wait for you to tell me all about your Italian experiences over supper."

Helena went to the stove where a saucepan was on simmer. She inhaled the aroma of the glistening black sauce. "What is this? It's intoxicating."

Joe laughed. "A balsamic reduction." He picked up a wooden spoon and gave the viscous sauce a quick stir before glancing at a timer counting down on the stove. "This is almost done. Are you ready to eat? It will only be about five more minutes."

"Are you kidding? My stomach did a somersault as soon as you opened the front door. It smells amazing in here."

He picked up a bottle of wine and held it out for her to see the label.

"Belle Uve? Is that the vineyard you toured?"

"It is. I thought you might like to taste the wine that so…entranced me." The way he said the word, *entranced*, and the look in his eyes took her breath away. She nodded, unable to speak.

Joe picked up two glasses from the table and filled them both, handing one to her. She followed his lead, smelling the wine and then gently swirling the liquid around the glass. She felt butterflies swirl in her stomach. She mirrored his action, bringing the glass to her mouth and tilting it so that the wine ran through her lips, over her tongue, and then smoothly flowed down her throat. Her eyes didn't move from his, held captive by his gaze. She never realized how sensual wine tasting could be.

A smile slowly spread across his face. "The wine has entranced you as well."

"Something like that," she breathed.

Helena jumped at the sound of a timer, and Joe blinked, the moment broken.

"The bread is ready." He took the bread from the oven and turned it onto a cutting board which he placed on the table. "Please, have a seat."

He opened a second oven and removed two perfectly cooked cuts of filet mignon flanked by asparagus and roasted potatoes. "I just added the filets to the veggies to keep everything warm."

She watched as he gently transferred the food to white dinner plates and then drizzled the balsamic reduction over the steaks. Her mouth was watering as he carried them to the distressed farm table on the other side of the island and laid them on pretty blue, yellow, and green patterned placemats.

"This looks as amazing as it smells," she said, watching him move the vase with the flowers to the counter and take the seat across from her. The table was long enough for a large family, but they sat in the center of it facing each other.

"I knew you had to cut your time in Italy short, so I decided to make a recipe my Tuscan grandmother used to make."

"A Tuscan grandmother. That explains all of it—the love of Italy, the taste for Italian wine, and the cooking obsession."

He smiled. "Guilty of all of the above. Would you like to say grace before we eat?"

He never ceased in surprising her. "I would. Thank you."

They bowed their heads and prayed in unison. After she crossed herself, she looked up and found him looking at her with an intensity that made her toes curl. She felt the impulse to rake her teeth across her bottom lip and hastily smiled, trying to hide her nervousness. Joe raised his glass.

"A toast?"

She nodded and raised hers.

"To twisters."

Helena snorted. "To *what*?"

His self-assured demeanor faltered, replaced with a look of gravity. "If not for the twister last night, I'm not sure we would be here tonight. I wanted to reach out to you, but…" He blinked. "I didn't know what to say. And then when I thought something might've happened to you." He shook his head. "All I could think of was getting to you, making sure you were okay, and…well, you know what happened next."

Helena felt that somersault in her stomach again, but this time, it wasn't because of the aroma of the food. "To twisters," she said quietly, holding his gaze.

They watched each other over the dancing flames of the taper candles as they each took a drink of wine, and

Helena could feel her blood pumping through her veins. He was one sexy man, and the kitchen, the meal, the wine, and the knowledge that he cared about her only made him sexier.

It was then that she realized, Joe was a true Southern gentleman. Why had it taken her so long to see the truth?

"Maybe we should eat before it gets cold," Joe said, severing their eye contact with a quick glance at his plate.

Helena blushed as she looked down at her own plate and reached for her knife and fork. She closed her eyes as she tasted the filet and enjoyed the tanginess of the balsamic reduction against the juicy char-broiled flavor of the steak. "This is to die for," she said. "Simply the best thing I've taste since I've been home."

"Then my cooking was a success." Joe smiled at her, and her heart flipped.

Helena tried to concentrate on her meal, but her body was reacting to Joe's presence in ways that would make a harlot blush.

"Tell me about your cooking. What brought on that obsession? Besides your grandmother, I mean. Something must have made you want to learn to make meals like this."

"It was a way to center myself after work. In the ER, I saw so many horrific things. Going home to an empty house just made those images fester in my mind. I needed structure, direction, something I could control but didn't have to think about. The family recipe book that my mother made for Lindsay as a wedding present became my saving grace."

Helena didn't know if he was trying to get a reaction from her, but she continued to eat, waiting to see if he would say more about Lindsay or their now confirmed once upon a time engagement.

Joe refilled their wine. "Speaking of Lindsay and the wedding, I'd like to clear the air, if that's okay with you."

She laid down her fork and gave him her full attention, unsure of what he would say and too nervous to keep eating.

"I'm sure you've heard Lindsay's name batted about town."

"I've heard the name and met the namesake," she said, reaching for her wine. His eyes widened.

"Oh?"

"She's visited the library a couple times." She held off on saying more, waiting to hear what he had to say about the woman who claimed to still be his fiancé.

"And did she happen to say anything about, well, about me?" His look was one of concern, his mouth tight and his eyes blinking.

"She acted like she didn't know you but was clearly fishing for information about where you came from and what I might know about your past."

"What did you tell her?"

"Nothing. I acted like we barely knew each other." Learning about Lindsay, seeing his kitchen, and eating this scrumptious meal, she realized it was true. Every time they were together, she glimpsed more of his true character, but in many ways, he was still an enigma to her.

"And she didn't tell you anything?"

"Joe, let's not beat around the bush. If there's something I should know, just tell me."

He shook his head. "Absolutely nothing. Lindsay and I were high school sweethearts. We somehow made it through college still attached, and I asked her to marry me much to the chagrin of my family who never cared for her but respected my decision. Turns out they were right. She left me at the altar."

"Joe, I'm so sorry. That must have been terrible."

He inhaled through his nose and released a long sigh. "It was, but it didn't take long for me to realize it was the best thing that ever happened to me. I moved on, eventually. I'm not going to lie. She threw me for a loop. I spent the past several years avoiding commitment."

Helena wasn't sure what to say and merely nodded.

"I'm ready to commit now, Helena. I've changed. I'm not the man who was with her, and I'm not the man who spent years trying to get over her in ways I'm not proud of."

"Perhaps you've grown into the man God intended you to be. Maybe that's why she wants you back."

"I don't think that's it. Honestly, I don't know why she's trying to get me back, but I'm not sure Lindsay is…" He searched for the word. "Stable."

"I'm sure you're right."

His forehead rose, and his eyes widened. "Why do you say that?"

Helena told him of their short conversation and shared the list of books Lindsay requested from Sarah.

She knew she was violating a sacred rule by telling him what Lindsay checked out—the American Library Association would have a fit about that—but she felt that his safety was more important than Lindsay's right to privacy.

"And a couple times, including just before the storm, I caught her staring at me."

"What do you mean? What happened just before the storm?"

Helena frowned as she pictured Lindsay's exemplification of Medusa just before the fury of the storm whipped through town. "I was locking up, or about to, when I saw her across the parking lot. She was just standing there, and then she smiled. I mean, I guess you would call it a smile, but it was more than that. It was…oh, I don't know. It sounds silly."

Joe watched her, his eyes ablaze. "Just say it," he said calmly but with an edge in his voice.

"Her smile was almost sinister. Goading or even threatening in some way. And it wasn't the first time she'd looked at me like that. I saw her on the Fourth, across the fire station during bingo. She looked at me with the same, same…sinister smile. I really don't know how else to describe it."

Joe's chin lurched up a bit. "When on the Fourth?"

"Some time in the afternoon. It was after…" She tore a piece of bread and looked around. "After Wade left to see whatever it was that happened here."

She saw Joe's eyes dart to a place on the wood floor next to the island, and she followed his gaze, seeing nothing. She looked back at him, but he was still staring at the floor, distress written on his face, obviously seeing something that wasn't there.

"Joe? Are you all right?"

He shook his head and slowly moved his gaze back to her. "She knows," was all he said.

"She knows?" A chill ran down her spine.

"She knows how I feel…" His Adam's apple bobbed as he swallowed. "About you."

***

The room began to dim as he closed his eyes, anxious that the evening was going to take a turn in the wrong direction. He pulled a long breath through his flaring nostrils and slowly let it out before opening his eyes and focusing on Helena. Her mouth hung open a bit, and he could see the mix of emotions in her eyes.

"I'm sorry. I didn't want it to come out like this."

She nodded slowly as though she couldn't quite comprehend his words, and he realized, she probably couldn't.

"What I mean is, I missed you terribly when you were gone. Before you left, I was…conflicted. I didn't know what I wanted. No, that's not right. I knew, but I didn't want to admit it. Darrin knew, Wade knew, Dale knew. Heck, I think even Andi knew."

"Darrin?"

"He's my best friend. He and Jeremy and I were inseparable growing up. He's almost as much a brother to me as Jeremy was."

"And what did they know?" she asked quietly.

"They knew that I was falling for you, but I wasn't ready to admit it." He tilted his head back and sighed. "Like I said, she threw me for a loop when she left me at the altar, and I didn't want to feel that pain again." He looked at her, imploring for understanding and not pity. The look in her eyes only showed an engaged interest and prompted him to go on. "She ran off with my surgical mentor, broke up his marriage, and broke my heart. I turned the pain into anger and swore off all serious relationships."

"I'm so sorry, Joe."

Her apology caught him off guard, but he nodded slowly. "Anyway, that's how I lived my life. Until I met you. I walked you home all those nights out of an obligation to your sister. Jeremy cared about her deeply, and she was gracious enough to let me come here and try to help out. I felt I owed it to them both to take care of you. Then we went out a few times, and I knew I was in trouble. Just before you left, I tried to slow things down, cut them off really, but I just couldn't do it."

"You did a pretty good job. When I left, I knew you had decided to let me down easy." She wrinkled her brow. "But then you emailed me…"

"I missed you. I wanted so badly to reach out, and Darrin told me I should. He knew I'd regret it if I didn't, but then Lindsay showed up."

"And then Daddy had his stroke, and I came home. If I hadn't come home, would you and Lindsay…?" The flame of one of the candles flickered as if the rest of the sentence puffed through the air like a draught.

"Gotten back together?" He scoffed. "Hardly. I realized right away that Darrin and Jeremy had been right about her all along. She was a charmer, but not in the good sense of the word. She's a manipulator and a schemer. She doesn't have an honest bone in her body, and she has no idea what it really means to care about someone. She did me a favor by showing her true colors before it was too late."

Helena bit her lip in that adorable way she did when she was nervous or deep in thought, but his desire to kiss her right where her top teeth rested was absent. He was keenly aware that something he had said was bothering her.

"Penny for your thoughts?" He repeated the words he'd said on their date that now seemed like a lifetime ago.

Helena released her lip from the grasp of her incisor and smiled. "The price has gone up, Dr. Blake." She tried to tease, but he saw the look in her eyes as she attempted to cover her feelings.

Joe leaned toward her, clasping his hands in front of him on the table. He became vaguely aware that their dinner had long since grown cold. "Talk to me, Helena. What's on your mind? I can see some worry nagging at you."

"It's your tone and the way you look when you talk about her. I can't help but wonder if there's still something there between the two of you."

"You'd think less of me if I admitted the way I feel about her."

He saw disappointment flash in her eyes.

"It's not what you think," he assured her. "I actually went to confession because of how I feel about her. I don't love her." He leveled his gaze at Helena. "I hate her." He watched her gaze falter and knew he'd been right. "I told you, you'd think less of me."

Helena shook her head. "No, it's not that." She reached up and tucked a loose curl behind her ear. "I'm sorry she makes you feel that way. Hate is so strong an emotion. They say there's a fine line between love and hate, but I think there's a very solid line there for you. I see it in your eyes, hear it in your voice. I wasn't lying when I said there's emotion in the way you talk about her. I just needed to be clear on what that emotion was." She tilted her head, and her expression softened. "But Joe, hate is a double-edged sword. It can eat you up inside, destroy you, cause you even greater pain. Hate is the opposite of how we were created. God made us for love, to love, and out of love. In the end, He wants us to feel only that, for when all else is done and gone, 'faith, hope, and love remain…but the greatest of these is love.' It's all that matters, Joe. Everything else is trivial, including pain, regret, sorrow, and especially hate. In fact, hate is more than trivial. It blocks love, keeps it away, and twists it into something else. Hate makes love impossible."

Her voice was soft and low, soothing and caring, admonishing but gentle, and his heart opened in a way it never had before.

Joe stood and walked around the table. He reached for her, and she placed her hands in his so that he could pull her to standing. He looked into her eyes, those beautiful blue eyes of a pixie.

"Is this love?" he asked in a whisper.

"I hope so," she whispered back.

When his lips met hers, he thought his heart would explode. He knew he would never be able to get enough of her, never tire of her, never feel whole again without her in his life, at his side, in his bed and at his table, laughing, crying, sighing, and loving. She had become the very breath he breathed, the blood in his veins, and the marrow in his bones.

***

His blood coursed through him like flowing lava, burning, boiling, seething with an indescribable passion. His arms tightened around her until he heard her gasp, and he loosened his hold, aware that he was crushing her against him. Sweat ran down his face and back from the intensity of the heat and the powerful feelings that swelled within him. The flickering flames illuminated the darkness of the night.

"I'm afraid it's a total loss," Chief Rollins said. The fire blazed behind him, and Joe felt as though his heart had been wrenched from his chest as he watched the clinic, engulfed in flames.

"Thank you, Archie," Joe managed to say, fighting back the urge to scream, kick, or cry. He bent his head until his forehead rested on the top of Helena's soft curls. She turned herself in his arms so that she was facing him and pulled him tightly to herself.

"Oh, Joe," she whispered. "I'm so sorry. I'm so sorry."

"Joe, can I have a minute?" Dale's voice rang with concern, but Joe suspected their chat would be all business. Joe relinquished his hold on Helena and faced Dale.

"I'm sorry, Joe," was the first thing Dale said. "I imagine this must be devastating for you."

"To say the least." He looked up at the blaze and then back to Dale. "Any clues as to how this happened?"

"Not yet. We're going to have to wait for it to cool down, and then the county fire inspector will have to come down and take a look. Do you have any thoughts about what might've happened?"

"You know damn well that I have thoughts about how this happened."

"Joe." Helena gripped his arm. "You don't think…?"

"Of course that's what I think," he spat. "I want you to find out where she was, who she was with, and what she was doing. Smell her—" He broke off before the curse spilled out and cast a quick glance at Helena. "Smell her clothes if you have to. Run some kind of test on her hair. I don't care what you have to do. Just find whatever evidence you need to put her here at the time that fire started."

"You know I'll do whatever I can, Joe. But first," he said, looking pained. "I have to ask where you were."

"Are you kidding me?" Joe exploded.

"Joe, I'm sorry. I have to. It has to go in the report."

"He was home, having dinner with me." Helena held firmly onto his arm. "It's all still there—an unfinished meal for two, half empty glasses of wine, candles with the flames blown out. You can see for yourself."

They might have had two fires that night if Helena hadn't thought to blow out the candles before they ran from the house. Their kiss had been interrupted as abruptly as their meal had been, but she'd managed to stay calm as their attention shifted from one type of fire to another.

Dale looked at his friend with interest. "Joe? Can you confirm that?"

"Yes, we were having dinner at my place," he answered testily. "I've got a surveillance camera facing the front porch. You can see Helena arrive around six and us leave right after you called." He clenched his jaw as he looked at the flaming and smoldering remains of the clinic. "A lot of good security cameras did here. Anything they caught is long gone."

"Did the feed go anywhere? Into the cloud? Onto a server at your house? Anywhere?"

Joe shook his head. "I never thought I had a need for that. I figured the worst that would happen was somebody breaking in to steals meds. I never imagined this. It's not like I had anything flammable."

"Are you sure?" Chief Rollins asked as he approached them. "No anesthesia or oxygen tanks?"

"No. I only have the need for nitrous oxide, laughing gas, but that's noncombustible." He shook his head. "Maybe some cleaners and disinfectants, but I don't see how they could start a fire on their own."

"No equipment that uses an open flame?"

"Absolutely not. It's a medical clinic, not a chemistry lab."

"Just trying to cover all bases," Rollins said in his slow, baritone drawl which, along with his mustache, made him a dead ringer for movie star, Sam Elliott. "We've got it under control. Should have it out completely within the hour. Won't be safe to go near until tomorrow though. I'll call the county inspector and see how soon he can get here."

"Thanks, Archie. Appreciate that," Dale said. "Joe, go home. Get a good night's rest. I'll call you tomorrow."

"Are you going over there now?"

"I am. You go home."

"I'm going with you."

"Joe," Dale and Helena both said at the same time.

"Don't tell me no," he yelled.

"Anything I can do to help?" Wade asked, stepping out from the shadow of a tall oak tree.

"Take him home," Dale said firmly. "And make sure he stays there."

"No. I'm going with you, Dale. Don't try to stop me."

Wade grabbed Joe's forearm. "Let's go, Joe. Don't do anything stupid. Dale's got an official investigation on his hands, and I'm sure you don't want to jeopardize it." Wade's voice was as hard as steel, and his eyes bore into Joe like a titanium drill.

"It was her, Wade. I know it. You know it. He knows it." He jerked his head toward Dale's retreating back.

"If it was her, Dale will find out."

"How?" Joe yelled, out of patience and seething with rage. "She's already gotten away with the other stuff."

"This is different, Joe. It's hard to cover up arson. She's overstepped this time."

Joe yanked his arm away from Wade. "I hope you're right. She's stalking Helena, you know." By the look on his face, Wade did not know. "She may have been following her. This could have been retaliation for us having dinner together tonight. Think of what else she might do." He instantly regretted his words when he heard Helena gasp. He turned to her and curled his hands around her biceps. "I'm sorry. I didn't mean to scare or upset you."

"It's…all right," she stammered, and his fury vanished. All that was left was the desire to protect her.

He pulled her to him and pressed his cheek to her forehead. "I'm sorry. Let me take you home. I'll go home after that. I promise."

"Let me take you both home," Wade said. "Your car is fine until tomorrow.

With one last glance at the diminishing flames, Joe followed Wade to his car. He held his arm protectively around Helena and silently vowed that he would keep her safe at all costs.

***

Andi's face and voice were full of concern. "You don't have to go, you know. Jackson and I will be there. We can help Daddy get settled."

Helena twirled her spoon around the bowl of Special K and spoke without looking up at Andi. "I know, but I want to go. It will help get my mind off things."

"I hear Joe was madder than a nest of hornets."

Helena smiled wryly. "To say the least."

"Other than that, Mrs. Lincoln, how was the play?"

"Dinner was nice." Helena felt heat rising to her cheeks. "More than nice." She raised her eyes to look at Andi through her lashes.

"Oh. My. Gosh. Spill."

"Did you know he's practically a gourmet cook?"

"Really?"

"With a kitchen to back it up. You would die."

"What did he make?"

"Filet mignon with balsamic reduction, asparagus, and… um. There was something else." She scrunched up her nose as she tried to remember what else was on her plate. Her lack of recollection wasn't lost on her sister.

"Didn't do much eating, I suppose?" Andi nudged Helena with her elbow.

"Well, we were interrupted…" Helena left it at that, following the rule that a true lady would never kiss and tell.

"Oh. Of course," Andi said. "Poor Joe. I hope they chew her up and spit her out."

"Me, too." Helena thought about her conversation with Joe. If he didn't hate Lindsay enough already, he sure did now.

"Hey, you okay?" Andi asked with concern. "I mean, I know it was a shock and all, but is there something else bothering you?"

"For someone who was gone all of my adult life, you sure know me well."

"What's wrong?"

Helena's phone vibrated, and she picked it up and read the message. "Jackson says they're waiting for us."

"Okay. Can't keep Mama waiting. But this conversation isn't over."

"Don't worry about me. It's Joe I'm worried about. He's fit to be tied, and I'm just concerned about what he might be fixin' to do."

"Don't worry. Wade's keeping an eye on him."

***

Joe yanked the door open and blinked. “What do you want?”

“Good morning to you, too,” Wade said, pushing past Joe and walking into the house.

“Don’t you have somewhere to be? Like at work?”

“Man, there’s a snake in your boot this morning.” Wade took a seat on the couch and propped the ankle of his cowboy boot across his knee.

“What do you want, Wade?” Joe was at the end of his rope and had no desire to play games. He stood in the open doorway, his arms folded across his chest.

“I’m just here to check on you. Figured you might need something to keep you busy today since you don’t have anywhere to go.”

“Is that supposed to make me feel better?” He shifted his weight and waited for Wade to answer.

“Look, Joe, I get it. Nothing is going to make you feel better right now. I’ve been there, remember? Callahan nearly burned down my house with my mother inside it last fall.”

Joe winced. Wade was right. Though Miss Blanche was safe, and the fire those drug runners set to his cherry trees never reached the house, Wade knew quite well how Joe was feeling. He closed the door and dropped into a nearby chair.

“I’m so angry I could chew nails and spit out a barbed wire fence.”

“I get it. I really do. If I hadn’t trusted Dale to do his job and didn’t have Andi to lean on, I’m not sure what I would’ve done.”

"Do you think he can make a case?"

"If she left any trace of evidence, they'll find it. The fire inspector is trained to look for the smallest clues."

Joe sighed. "I sure hope you're right."

"I know I'm right," Wade said confidently. "I'm also right that today is a perfect day for fishing."

Joe grinned. "Oh, really? Is that your expertise as a small-town mayor talking?"

"No, it's my expertise as Arkansan talking. Have you been fishing since you came to town?"

"A couple times. In the national park."

"Well, then, let's get this show on the road, Dr. Blake. I've got some beautiful fishing holes to share with you that only the locals know about."

Joe shook his head as he stood. "This is the last thing I want to do, you know."

"I know, and that's exactly why I'm gonna insist you do it."

Fifteen

"I want… to go… home." The words were a bit slurred and took effort to produce, but they were clear as a bell to everyone in the room.

"Daddy." Andi knelt down in front of her father's wheelchair and took his hand. "We want you to come home, too. This is just a temporary layover."

Helena held back tears as she watched the exchange. Without the need of verbal communication, they had all agreed to let Andi do the talking. Despite the many years she was away serving her country, she would always be Joshua's little girl. Some sisters might be resentful of that, but Helena appreciated it. She knew that her relationship with her mother was much different from Andi's, and Jackson, being the baby and only son, enjoyed an altogether different bond with both parents.

"You've made such great progress, Daddy," Andi continued. "Now, you're going to learn to walk and dress yourself and feed yourself and work your way back to caring for yourself. You know you want that. You don't want Mama doing all the work, do you?"

And that was the deciding factor, Helena knew. Joshua looked up at Grace with tears in his eyes, heaved a long sigh, and looked back at Andi. "Ooookay," he managed.

They got him settled in his room and began the task of making it feel like home. Allie had sent a beautiful bouquet of gerbera daisies in bright, festive colors, and the girls surrounded it with framed photos of their family. Joshua's favorite shirts, many depicting bald eagles and American flags, were laid in the dresser drawers along with several pairs of sweatpants which he would hate but would be more comfortable in than the blue jeans he usually wore.

The staff at the rehab center was friendly and welcoming, and Joshua's personal nurse, a spirited black woman with a smile like an angel, acted as if they were old friends. By the time they left, everyone felt good about Dr. Stearns' choice for Joshua's rehabilitation. It wasn't until they were nearing Buffalo Springs that Helena found herself feeling like a bundle of nerves.

"Have you heard from your friend, Joe, today?" Grace asked.

Helena looked across the back seat to her mother. She noticed Andi turning her head in Helena's direction from the front seat and Jackson peering at her in the rearview mirror.

"He texted early this morning to wish us luck with Daddy and said he was going to be tied up most of the day with the investigators and the insurance company." Helena swallowed down the lump in her throat. "He worked so hard to renovate that clinic, to acquire donations of supplies and equipment and money, and to get people to trust him. He put so much of his own money into helping the people of our town and to becoming one of us. Why?" She heard the anguish in her own voice. "Why did she have to do this? Why destroy the clinic, a lifeline for so many people, in order to get to Joe?"

"You really think it was her?" Jackson asked.

"Who?" Grace inquired.

"Joe was once engaged to someone, a real witch if you ask me. And I'm not just being ugly because of my feelings for Joe," she said, looking at her mother. "She's nuttier than one of Andi's pecan pies."

"What's she done that makes her nutty?" Jackson asked.

Helena thought about the wedding books and the odd book requests. That wasn't something she could share with anyone who asked, including her family. She recalled the two times she felt that Lindsay was watching her and wondered if retelling the stories would make Helena sound like the crazy one. She knew something had happened at Joe's on the Fourth, but she still didn't know what that was.

"Um…" She hemmed and hawed, raking her lip through her teeth until it was raw.

"I don't think we know all the details," Andi supplied from the front seat. "Wade told me that this Lindsay person is being investigated for a couple incidents, including the fire at the clinic, but he's not allowed to share details. From what I can gather, Wade and Dale both believe she's a danger to others and possibly herself."

Grace clutched Helena's hands. "What about you? Is she a danger to you?"

"I don't think so, Mama." Helena tried to sound confident, but she was as worried as her mother about her own safety.

"You have nothing to worry about, Mama. Joe isn't going to let anything happen to Helena."

"And neither will we," Jackson said as he pulled into Helena and Andi's driveway. Joe and Wade sat on the porch, and Helena's stomach lurched at the site of the men waiting for them.

"Are you good, Mama? Do you need anything?"

"I don't need a thing other than your Daddy home and for you girls to be safe."

Helena leaned over and kissed her mother on the cheek. "I think we all feel that way, Mama. I love you."

"I love you to the moon and back, Sugar."

As Andi and Helena watched their mother and brother drive away, Helena said a silent prayer that their family was safe and could all be together again soon, at home where they belonged.

"Good day or rough day?" Joe asked, coming behind her and leaning in to kiss her on the cheek.

"Good day, all things considered." She turned to face him. "And a rough day, all things considered."

"Let's go inside," Wade told them. "We have some things to discuss."

Joe took Helena's hand, and they followed Wade and Andi into the house. She looked up at him, trying to read his expression, but he gave nothing away, and Helena wondered what more this day could have in store.

***

"Here's what we know," Wade began. "A window in the back of the clinic was broken. There was minimal damage in that room other than the window, and it was clearly, according to Dale, broken from the outside and opened enough for someone to climb into the building."

"Someone small?" Andi asked.

"Small enough," Wade said. "Smoke patterns as well as melting patterns in the glass and plastic containers indicate that the point of origin was the medical supply closet."

"Was there anything in there that was flammable?" Helena looked at Joe.

He shrugged. "Just about everything. Bandages, tape, gauze, exam table paper, paper gowns, alcohol."

"Alcohol," Wade interjected. "I don't know how he knows, but the inspector suspects alcohol was the accelerant, and he's the expert, so I'd go with that."

"Well, there was certainly a lot of that. We buy it in bulk online."

"It's a good place to start a fire," Andi said. "With alcohol as the accelerant and all the fibrous materials, it would light up like a match."

"And it did," Wade told them. "The fire was fast and furious. Once it started, it had all the ammunition it needed to get real hot, real fast. The door to the closet was open—"

"Which would never have been done on purpose," Joe told them.

Wade nodded. "It was open, and the flames spread quickly to the other rooms. It was an old house, and pretty much all the building components were solid wood and not flame retardant."

"How much was lost?" Helena asked.

"Pretty much everything," Joe said. "What wasn't burned was ruined by smoke or water. Like Dale said last night, it was a total loss."

"What about the room at the back that had minimal damage?" Helena asked. "Can you salvage anything?"

Joe shook his head. "Nothing that could be used in a sterile environment."

"And Lindsay?" Leave it to Andi to not duck around the elephant in the room.

Wade answered. "No alibi. Says she was home asleep. Dale got a warrant, but he didn't find anything. No clothes that smelled like smoke or shoes with alcohol splashed on them. A load of clothes was in the wash which she claimed she'd put in earlier that day and forgotten about."

"Can it be tested?" Helena asked hopefully.

"Unfortunately, not, according to Archie. Clothing items washed right away with liquid detergent don't retain the smell of smoke."

A hush fell over the group. After a few minutes, Helena spoke. "She's gonna get away with it, isn't she?"

Wade stood and began pacing. "I don't know. Dale is questioning everyone who might've seen anything. He's looking at any security footage from the buildings near the clinic as well as the candy store."

"The candy store?" Andi asked, brows raised.

"That's where Lindsay's been living. She rents an apartment above the store." Joe stood and went to the back door. He stared out onto the deck for several moments before turning around. "There's got to be some way to tie her to this. She's smart, but I hardly think she's got a criminal history as an arsonist."

"Hmph," Andi snorted. "I wouldn't be so sure."

Wade stopped pacing and looked at her. "Wait a minute. You might be onto something."

"You think she has a history of arson?" Helena asked.

"Maybe, maybe not, but what are the chances Joe is the only man she's ever fixated on?"

Joe looked at Wade. "What are you thinking?"

"It's been years since she left you. There had to have been others in between then and now. Maybe she's left a trail. Maybe she's turned psycho on other men, or even other women, people who didn't bend to her will. Maybe yours isn't the first car she's damaged or the first house she's broken into or the first place she's burned down."

"I have to ask," Helena said. "What exactly happened at your house on the Fourth?"

Wade and Joe exchanged looks. "Have you got any gin? If I'm going to tell you what happened, I'm going to have to start at the beginning."

Andi stood. "No gin, but I've got whiskey. Who else wants a glass?"

Everyone answered in the affirmative, and once it was poured, Joe told them about his childhood friend, the nightmares he had as a kid, the haunting effect that day had on him for years, and the fake dog Lindsay allegedly left in his kitchen.

Helena threw back what was left in her glass, hoping to quell the queasiness she felt at picturing the bloody stuffed dog in Joe's beautiful kitchen.

"She's more deranged than I thought," Andi said.

Remembering the titles of the books Lindsay requested for her 'research,' Helena reached for the bottle and refilled her glass.

"Uh, Helena, how many times have you had whiskey?" Andi asked.

"Let me think. Other than this? None." She took a long sip then winced as the whiskey hit the back of her throat.

"Maybe you'd better slow down, little sister."

Helena bit her lip. "Remember what I told you, Joe? About the books?"

He nodded.

"Maybe we ought to do a little research and find out exactly what the characters did in them. I've read some of them but not all."

Joe looked startled for a second before sitting back down in the nearby chair.

"What's she talking about?" Wade asked.

"I can't tell you," Helena said. "Not without a warrant, but I might be able to look into some things." A chill ran through her as she thought of the grim task. "I just hope I can find the answers quickly enough."

***

"That was the scariest film I've ever seen," Joe said as the credits to the 2014 film, *Gone Girl* scrolled down the screen.

"Scary in a what-kind-person-does-that kind of way." Helena snuggled closer to him on his couch. "It more than gives me the creeps to think that she checked out the book. How will you be able to sleep after watching that?"

With Helena's warm body spooned against his, Joe thought of a few ways that would help him sleep better that night, but he pushed the thoughts aside. He was a changed man. This time, he was doing things differently, the right way. Besides, Helena was firm in her faith, and he wasn't going to even suggest they do anything they would regret.

He tightened his arm around her waist and breathed in the smell of her hair. He would be content to stay like this all night. No nightmares would beckon as long as he was holding her in his arms. The thought vanished as she pushed herself up to a sitting position.

"Do you think she checked out the book because she really wanted to replicate some of the creepy things Amy did, or do you think she just wanted to send me a message?"

Joe sat up beside her. "Hard to tell. I thought I knew her once, but now… I just don't know."

"Well, she hasn't started going around telling everyone she's pregnant like in the movie, so that's a good sign."

The very thought made him sick to his stomach. "And she hasn't put on a disappearing act."

"Or framed you for a crime you didn't commit."

A sudden thought struck him. "What if the fire wasn't meant to look like an arson but like insurance fraud? That would destroy me both financially and professionally."

"But would she do that? If she really thinks you'll come around and marry her, what would that gain?"

He ran his hand through his hair. "You're right. That makes no sense."

Helena looked down at her watch. "It's late. I'd better get home. I don't like Andi being there alone, and I have to work tomorrow."

"Where's Wade tonight?"

"His Mama took a turn for the worse today. He went up to the nursing home to be with her, and he thought he might stay at a hotel tonight in case he needed to be close by."

"I'm sorry to hear that. I don't know Mrs. Montgomery well, but she seems like a special woman."

"Andi adores her. This is going to break her heart almost as much as Wade's."

"At least she and her husband had a long, happy life together. Look at Dale."

"I know. He's such a good guy."

A realization hit Joe. "Helena, I don't want to waste any time." He turned and took her hands in his. "Jeremy died before he and Andi had a chance. Dale lost Ruth less than twelve years into their marriage. Life is too short to wait."

"Joe." Helena looked stricken. "What are you thinking?"

"Let's go to Houston. Get out of here for a few days. Let the police do their work without either of us being in any danger. I want you to meet my family."

Relief washed across her face. "Oh! Okay, um, maybe I could work that out."

"Sarah will cover the library, won't she? I'm at a standstill until I get all the necessary permissions and insurance money to level and rebuild the clinic. It's the perfect time to go."

"What about Andi? I don't want to leave her alone."

Joe waved his hand dismissively. "Andy will be fine. She's a former SEAL for heaven's sake."

Helena took a deep breath, and Joe was afraid she was going to decline, but she breathed in deeply and gave him a wide grin. "Okay, then. I'll talk to Sarah."

Joe couldn't remember the last time he was this happy. Lindsay had already robbed him of his happiness once, and he refused to let her do it again. He stood and pulled Helena up with him. He wrapped his arms around her and planted a kiss on her that was sure to straighten her curls. He was taking her home to meet his parents and Darrin and his sister, Serena. If only Jeremy could've been there, too.

***

Helena arrived at the library early despite the late night out. It had been four days since the fire, and nobody had seen hide nor hair of Lindsay. Was she still in town? Helena wondered as she unlocked the door and stepped inside. Though the library was already bright with the morning sun, she flipped on the lights as she made her way toward the office. She put her lunch of salad, a bag of cherries, and some Pretzel Crisps—her latest food obsession—in the fridge and slipped her purse in the bottom drawer of her desk.

The book drop was overflowing with books, so she set right to the task of emptying it. She pulled three books out and placed them on the cart to be checked in but stopped when she spied the box nestled among the books.

Helena frowned. *Now, how did that get in here?*

She reached for the familiar pink box tied with a ribbon that said, 'The Sweet Shoppe.' A note was attached, the handwriting—For Helena—unfamiliar. The box was warm, and the tell-tale scent of pie arose as she lifted the box from the book drop. Andi was an early riser, but she would never have baked a pie and left it in the book drop, and she was in the shower when Helena left, having just returned from a run.

Helena sat the box on her desk and slowly opened it, inhaling the scent but unable to identify it. Purple filling oozed from one of the vent holes in the top crust, and Helena thought for a moment it might be blueberry, but it didn't smell like blueberry. She tapped her finger on the gooey filling and raised it to her nose to be sure. Her tongue poked through her lips, but just as it was about to touch her finger, she drew her hand back. A memory from many years ago abruptly came to her mind.

Helena had been about eight years old and was camping with her Girl Scout troop. The girls were on a hike, and it was getting close to lunchtime. Paige spied a bush nearby and exclaimed wildly about the ripe, juicy blueberries. The girls were so hungry! Just as Paige pulled a cluster of berries from the bush, Allie's mom—their troop leader—yelled for Paige to drop the berries immediately. Mrs. Michaels produced a bottle of hand sanitizer and proceeded to pour it over Paige's hand amidst the girl's protests. As she cleaned her hand, Mrs. Michaels explained to the girls that these were not blueberries, but a highly toxic plant called pokeweed. The pokeberries, if ingested, were highly fatal, and even the juice, when absorbed through the skin, could cause sickness and death.

With that memory in mind, Helena hastily ran to the sink and washed the sticky filling from her finger. Just to be safe, she grabbed a paper towel, doused it with soap and hot water, and rubbed it on her nose. Her heart raced as she washed her hand a second time, and she nearly leapt out of her pants when Sarah called to her from the outer room.

"Holy Mother of Mercy," Helena said when Sarah entered the room.

"What's wrong?"

"You nearly gave me a heart attack, but that's not the problem."

Sarah moved closer to the desk. "That's still warm. Andi must've been at work really early this morning."

"It's not from Andi," Helena said, reaching for her phone.

"It's not? Then who?" Sarah reached toward the pie, and Helena swatted her hand away.

"Don't touch it!" She held up her hand. "Dale, it's Helena. I need you at the library." She heard Suzy's voice and realized she'd gotten him at home.

"Is everything okay?"

"Yes, everything's all right, but I had a box left in the book drop that you might want to take a look at. I'm sorry to call so early. I just thought—"

"No need to apologize. What's in the box?"

"It's a pie but not one of Andi's, I guarantee it. I think it's from Lindsay"

"Lindsay? Why would she send you a pie?"

"I'll explain when you get here."

"Okay. I'll be there soon."

Helena disconnected the call and looked at Sarah, whose eyes were wide with shock.

"From Lindsay?"

"Yes, and I think it's poisonous."

Sarah plopped down in her chair at her own desk. "Are you serious?"

"Well, I don't know for sure." Helena looked down at the pie and frowned. She raised her eyes to Sarah's. "Do you think I'm being paranoid? Maybe it's not from her. Maybe somebody else sent it using a box they already had from Andi's shop."

"Helena, how often do patrons drop off pies in the book drop?" Sarah leaned closer. "Especially ones who check out books like she did. She's crazy, Helena. I wouldn't put anything past her."

"I was hoping she'd left town. I haven't seen her in a few days."

"I have. I ran into her in the bakery the other day when you all were getting your father settled. Noreen was just ringing her up when I ran in to pick up some cookies. I was dying for something chocolate!"

"Was she buying a pie?"

Sarah's gaze shifted to the box on the desk. "She sure was. I bet that's the box the pie was in."

"I'd wager you're right."

Helena saw movement outside the window and glanced out to see Dale's cruiser pulling into the lot.

"Is the door unlocked?"

"Not yet." Sarah looked at the clock and stood. "It's just about nine. Should I go ahead and leave it open once I let Dale in?"

"Yes, please. I'm gonna close the door while he and I chat. Can you man the front?"

"Of course." Sarah left the office to open the door, and Helena sent a quick text to Joe. She wanted him to know that everything was okay. In a small town, the chief's car showing up at the library before opening would be the talk of the gossip mongers, especially in light of the clinic fire.

"Helena." She looked up at the sound of Dale's voice.

"Hi, Dale. Why don't you close the door?" She waited for him to shut the door to the main room and gestured for him to take a seat in the chair Sarah had abandoned.

"What's going on?"

Helena briefly filled him in on the discovery of the pie. "I know it sounds crazy, but do you think it could be pokeberry?"

Dale arched a brow. "Hmm." He pulled a pair of gloves from his pocket, slipped them on, and lifted the pie to his nose. He sniffed several times. "I can't say I'd recognize the smell of it baked in a pie. I reckon maybe we could have it tested though."

"Then, can we do that?" Helena urged.

Dale's mouth twisted in thought.

"What?" she asked.

"We can, and we will, but it won't prove anything. Even if it's poisonous, we can't tie it to Lindsay. Unless you have a camera aimed at the box." He motioned toward the drop box.

Helena sighed. "Never needed one before. But you can bet I'll have one installed after this." She thought for a moment. "But Dale, Lindsay bought a pie just a couple days ago. This could be the box that pie was in. Couldn't we go at it from that angle?"

"Helena, how many pies do you think your sister's shop sells in a day?"

She furrowed her brow. "I don't know. On a good day, a dozen or so? On a normal weekday, maybe a few." She heaved a sigh. "Which means anyone could have had one of her boxes."

"Yep. No judge or jury is going to convict on that."

"There must be some way to tie her to this." She looked at the gloved hand that held the pie. "What about fingerprints? She could've left prints on the box or the pie tin."

Dale inspected the tin and looked down at the box. "She could've worn gloves when she touched the tin, but the box… She most likely would not have worn gloves when she bought the pie. That would've drawn attention."

"Hold on," Helena said, picking up her phone. "Hey, An, it's me. Can I talk to Noreen?" She nodded at Dale and waited for Noreen to pick up the phone. "Hey, Noreen. How are you?"

"I'm great, Helena. How about yourself?"

"Great, thanks. I have a question for you." She glanced at Dale. "Do you remember selling a pie to a blonde the other evening when Andi and I were moving Daddy? It would've been just before closing time."

"I do. She and Sarah came in at almost the same time."

Helena nodded, both in agreement with Noreen and to signal Joe. "Yes, that would've been her."

"She's Joe's ex, isn't she?" Helena could heard the clinking of utensils in the background.

"She is. Strange question for you. Did you put the box into a bag or hand it right to her?"

"Um, let me think…"

Helena began tapping her foot and mentally prodded Noreen to hurry up with the information.

"She was in a hurry, especially when Sarah walked in. I was going to put it in a bag, but she just slid the money across the counter and grabbed the box from my hands. She practically flew out of the shop."

Like a witch on a broomstick.

"Thanks so much, Noreen. That's all I needed to know." She said goodbye and hung up. She felt almost giddy when she gave the news to Dale. "She grabbed the box herself."

"Helena, that's good, but don't get your hopes up. You touched the box, too, and so did Noreen, and probably Andi. The prints might be good, but they might not."

Helena reached into a drawer and pulled out a small, clear, plastic trash bag. She opened the bag and held it out for Dale. "I know, but it's better than nothing."

Dale nodded. "You're right. I'll send it to the state lab."

The door to the office flew open, shifting their attention to the man standing in the doorway.

"Helena, is everything all right?" Joe moved his gaze from her to Dale and back to Helena.

"Everything is fine. I'll explain in a minute." She looked at Dale. "What else do you need from me?"

Dale looked over his notes. "I think I got everything. Let me know if anything else out of the ordinary happens, and I'll ask around, see if anyone was at work early next door at town hall or at the barbecue joint across the road. Maybe they saw something. And I'll send both the pie and the box to the lab with requests for prints and testing."

"Thanks, Dale."

"You're welcome. I'm just glad you didn't eat any of the pie. Most people I know would dive right into a pie they thought Andi had made."

"Lucky for me, I live with Andi. I knew there was no way that came from her."

Dale said goodbye to both Helena and Joe and left the room. Joe closed the door behind him and rushed to Helena. "What the heck was that about?"

Helena recapped the story once again, watching Joe's face go from surprise to concern to anger to downright distress.

"Helena, we need to leave. Tonight. I won't have you in danger."

"Joe, I haven't even had a chance to talk to Sarah."

"There's no time like the present."

She held up her hand, picked up her phone, and tapped the screen. She could hear a mixer running in the background when Andi answered.

"Hey. I know you're busy, but I have to tell you something. Joe and I are going to Houston for a few days to see his parents. We're leaving tonight if Sarah is agreeable."

The only sound coming across the line was the whirring of the mixer.

"Andi, did you hear me?"

"I heard you. Isn't this a little sudden?"

Helena locked her eyes on Joe's. "It is, but something happened this morning."

The whirring stopped. "Helena, what's going on, and does this have something to do with Lindsay buying that pie?" Andi had lowered her voice, and Helena could tell that she was on the move.

"It's a long story, and one that I promise to tell you, but right now, I have to call Mama and talk to Sarah."

"Are you okay?"

"I am. I'll fill you in later."

Again, Andi was silent.

"Andi, I'm okay. I promise I'll call back."

"Okay. Just take care of yourself."

Helena said she would and disconnected. She called her mother and told her she was heading to Houston but didn't elaborate. She gazed out the window, almost surprised when she didn't see Lindsay lurking nearby.

"What about the library?" Grace asked.

"Sarah will cover," Helena said, hoping it was true.

"Well, all right then. I guess I'll see you when you get back. When will that be?"

Helena looked at Joe. "When will we be back?"

"Whenever Dale says it's safe."

"Um, Mama, I'm not sure. We haven't really decided yet. But soon, I promise."

"Helena, is there something you're not telling me?"

"No, Mama, of course not. You know my travel was cut short this summer, and with the fire and all, Joe needs to go back to Houston to get more supplies. He wants me to go with him and meet his parents."

She could hear Grace slowly inhale. "Does this have anything to do with that woman who's after Dr. Blake?"

Helena opened her mouth but closed it, unsure as to how to answer. "In a way. Joe thinks it would be best if he were to leave town for a bit, maybe give her a chance to rethink coming here."

"Helena Sue Nelson, I'm no fool, and you know that. I don't know what's going on, and I'm not going to press the matter. Just know that I'm going to find out whatever it is you're not telling me."

"Mama—"

"Just go. Have a good time and be careful. We'll talk when you get back."

"Thank you, Mama. I love you."

She hung up and let her head drop backwards, taking a deep breath before looking back at Joe. "I guess I'd better talk to Sarah."

"I'm going to call Mama and then buy the tickets." He went to her and took her in his arms. "I'll do whatever I have to do to keep you safe."

His goodbye kiss told her that he meant it.

Sixteen

"Hey, Dale. Any news?" Joe answered the phone while throwing clothes into a suitcase at a furious rate, not paying much attention to what he was packing. His only focus was on getting Helena out of town as quickly as possible.

"Joe, I heard from Wade that you and Helena are leaving town."

"We are. I've got tickets booked for later this afternoon."

"Joe, I need you to know that's not a good idea right now."

"Why not? You know what happened this morning. Helena isn't safe."

The voices in the background faded with the distinct click of a closing door.

"Joe, I've got to ask you a question. Did you take out an insurance policy on the clinic?"

He stopped tossing clothes and stood still. "Of course, I did. That's standard. Why?"

"When did you secure the policy?"

"When did I get the insurance? A day or so after I signed the settlement papers. I took out a policy on the clinic and a malpractice policy for myself."

"You didn't take out a second policy on the building and its contents on the thirtieth of June?"

Joe sat on the bed. "No, I didn't take out a policy in June. What are you talking about?"

"Joe, I need to advise you to get an attorney."

"What for? What's going on?" Joe's head was swimming. He understood what Dale was saying, but he didn't understand why there was this mix up. "Look, when I get to Houston, I'll call my insurance company and straighten this out."

"Joe, I'm not sure you're getting it. I just got off the phone with the insurance adjustor. You, or someone claiming to be you, took out a second policy for two million dollars on June thirtieth. That's just three weeks before the fire. They're fixing to press charges against you for arson and insurance fraud."

Joe's mouth went dry. "Arson? Insurance fraud? Dale, you gotta believe me. I never took out that policy. You know how much the clinic means to me, what I've put into it. Why would I throw it all away?" But as he asked the question, he knew exactly what had happened. His instinct had been correct, and his off-the-hand question to Helena the night before played in his mind. Lindsay hadn't just set him up as an arsonist; she had gone a step further and taken out a policy in his name.

"The adjustor is saying you spent a lot of your own money, more money than you're worth, and that you're in over your head. That's all I can say. For your own sake, you need to call an attorney. Now. If they press charges, this is out of my hands."

After the line went dead, Joe sat staring at the phone, unable to fully comprehend what was happening. He opened the call app and tapped a few buttons.

"Wade, I think I'm in trouble. I need a good attorney. Can you help?"

***

A steady rain fell outside, lending to the gloom inside Helena's kitchen. Joe, Helena, Andi, and Wade sat around the table. Helena's head was swimming with information, or drowning, to be more accurate. She felt like she could hardly breathe. Even the sound of the rain on the roof, normally a comforting pitter patter that lulled her to sleep, offered no consolation. She tried to concentrate on what Wade was saying, but the urge to crawl into bed and cry like a small child was becoming hard to fight.

"Joe, look, the first thing I did when I moved back home was to seek reciprocity, so technically, I can practice here, but the real issue is that I can't be legally unbiased."

"Wade, I don't understand," Helena said. "The clinic isn't owned by the town. Where is the bias?"

"Helena, as mayor, I represent the town. If I was to be Joe's attorney, I'd be seen as using my power to help someone get away with a crime. It wouldn't help Joe at all, and I'd be putting his interests before that of the town."

"This is in the interest of the town." Helena felt desperate and needed Wade to understand. "Joe is innocent, and somebody robbed the town of a medical clinic. How can representing Joe be anything but looking after the interests of the town?"

Wade huffed and shook his head. "It's just not that simple."

"You believe Joe is innocent, right? I mean, we were together when the fire started. You know that. "

Joe put his hand over hers. "That doesn't really matter at this point, Helena. I could've hired somebody to do the dirty work. Just because I didn't light the match doesn't mean I'm innocent."

Helena looked from Joe to Wade and then back to Joe. "But you are innocent."

Andi stepped in. "Helena, we know Joe didn't have anything to do with the clinic fire. We all know that the most likely culprit is Lindsay, but we don't have any evidence, and there is the second insurance policy. That's awfully damaging to his credibility."

She looked at Joe. "So, what do we do?" It bothered her that he'd been so quiet other than to reiterate how he *could* have been responsible for the fire.

"The first thing we need to do is find Joe an attorney," Wade said. "The next thing is to get our hands on those insurance papers. If Joe didn't sign them, someone else did."

"And I have a pretty good idea who," Helena said. "But how?"

"I've been thinking about that," Joe said. "Lindsay wasn't exactly the model student back in school. She constantly skipped class but always had a note."

Wade nodded. "Sounds like most of the spoiled kids I knew in high school. They always got away with everything, and Mama and Daddy were usually right there backing them up."

Helena didn't bring up the fact that Wade himself was the proverbial spoiled rich kid, except his father would've tanned his hide had he tried to use his family's money or influence to get himself out of trouble. She supposed that was not unlike his position now.

Joe continued. "Yeah, but it wasn't her mother or father writing the notes. Lindsay had a knack for forgery. She could copy anyone's signature and make it look more authentic than her own."

"Nice girl you dated," Helena muttered.

Joe sighed. "It was part of the attraction, to be honest. She was always out for having fun but never the kind of fun that would hurt anyone. At least, not in her eyes. It's one of the reasons Jeremy never liked her. He was a big believer that any dishonest action was harmful to someone in some way."

"That was Jeremy," Andi agreed. "He was as strait-laced as they came."

"He was." A moment of silence passed between them before Wade spoke.

"So, you think she forged your signature?"

"How hard could it be? She could've called, pretending to be Dotty, and set everything up, then picked up the paperwork herself, again acting as Dotty, and then sent them back, signed and notarized by Ms. Lindsay Johnson."

"She's a notary?" Wade asked.

"Yep. She started working at her Daddy's bank right after college when I was in med school. She worked mainly in the mortgage department and had to get her notary certification in order to effectively do the job."

"She would never have notarized it herself." Andi said.

Joe frowned. "You're right, but I bet she could find someone to do it. Few people at the bank could tell her no. She'd be crying in Daddy's office faster than they could blink. And she has a way of finding the dirt on everyone."

"She apparently knew that we were together before we did," Helena said dryly.

"Okay, first things first," Wade said. "Let's get that attorney lined up. I went to law school with a criminal defense attorney in Little Rock, Opal Richardson. She's as smart as a whip and does a lot of white-collar crime."

"There's a lot of white-collar crime in Little Rock?" Helena asked.

"Helena, there's white-collar crime everywhere," Wade replied. He looked at Joe. "You need to stay in town. I'm sorry about that. It won't look good if you leave. In fact, I would just go on with business as normal. Figure out what you need to replace at the clinic, talk to someone about clearing out and rebuilding. Try not to let this phase you. The more normal you act, the less guilty you look."

"What if Dale shows up with a warrant?"

"You go with him, calmly and quietly, and then you call your attorney."

"Then let's get that attorney. The sooner we get this over with, the better."

"In the meantime," Andi said. "What do we do about Lindsay?"

"I want to talk to Opal about that, but my suggestion is that we hire a PI. We need someone to question the other notaries at Lindsay's father's bank as well as whoever set up that policy with the insurance company. She'll also look into past complaints about Lindsay. Opal will probably have someone on retainer for stuff like this. I know I did."

"You had a PI on retainer?" Andi asked, looking impressed.

"Mergers and Acquisitions can get dirty. I had to know what I was dealing with and whom. I investigated every CEO, CFO, and stockholder, not to mention the company's holdings, prior business deals, and political connections."

"Wow, quite the Richard Gere, weren't you?" Andi said.

"When I had to be," Wade admitted. "It's a ruthless business."

"Lucky for me your Julia Roberts never came along."

"Okay, stick a fork in me. I'm done." Helena looked at Wade. "Call that attorney. You two can do your kinky role playing later. At *your* place." She looked pointedly at Wade.

"Chill, little sister. Nobody is going to be doing any role playing. We've got work to do. Joe," Andi turned toward him. "We've got your back. And Helena's. We'll get to the bottom of this. Don't worry."

"I hope so," Helena said. "The sooner we've got Lindsay out of our lives, the better."

***

Joe wasn't surprised when he opened the door and found Dale standing on his porch. He had been going over his spreadsheet of donors to the clinic when the doorbell rang.

"I take it this isn't a social call."

"I wish it was."

"Will you call Helena and ask her to come over and lock up for me?"

"You can take the time to do whatever you need to do."

"Thank you," Joe told his friend.

Dale followed Joe into the kitchen and looked around. Joe wondered if Dale was purposely averting his eyes from watching his friend tend to the mundane tasks that shouldn't symbolize anything monumental but felt like they did. He closed his laptop and switched off the kitchen light. "Would you mind checking on things for me, while I'm…?"

"Sure."

He saw the tightness in Dale's expression and heard the sadness in his voice. "I'm not holding this against you," Joe assured him. Dale nodded and shifted his gaze, unable to look Joe in the eye.

Joe walked back toward the front door and lifted a set of keys from the hook on the wall beneath a photograph of him and Jeremy on the beach in Galveston. He handed the keys to Dale.

"Let's get this over with." Joe turned around, hands behind his back, and waited.

"I'm not gonna cuff you, Joe," Dale told him.

Joe turned back around. "I suppose that should make this a tad less humiliating."

He watched Dale swallow and take a deep breath before the chief of police, one of his only friends in town, began reading him his rights.

***

"This isn't how I thought we'd conduct our first in-person meeting," Joe said sardonically.

Opal brushed him off. "Happens all the time. Let me fill you in on what I've found so far."

She was attractive with dark brown skin and short black hair. She wore pearls around her neck and small gold hoops in her ears. She wore two rings, stones modest in size, but no wedding band. Her cranberry-colored suit was expensive as was her briefcase. Opal apparently did well for herself. He hoped that was a good sign.

"The insurance policy was bought online through a reputable company."

"How did that company know about the fire? I only called the agent I personally worked with."

"According to the documentation, your receptionist called, a Ms. Dorothy Olsen."

"That's my receptionist, but was it really her calling?"

"Ms. Olsen swears it was not."

"She won't be arrested, too, will she?"

"Not at this time."

That didn't feel reassuring to Joe. "Okay, what else?"

"The address given as yours is a post office box in Harrison. That was where any potential insurance payoff would've been sent."

"And the company didn't bother to check it out to see if it was actually my PO box?"

"There is a box in your name."

"My goodness. She is the woman from the movie."

"Excuse me?"

"She thought of everything. She left no lose ends. She's set me up perfectly. How in the world am I going to get out of this?"

"Joe, do you recognize the name, Wilton Gardner?"

He shook his head. "Never heard of him."

"About two years ago, he took out a restraining order against Lindsay Johnson."

Joe widened his eyes. "What did she do to him?"

Opal looked down at her notes. "Seems the two were having an affair. When he ended things, she allegedly picked up his son from school, claiming that there was a family emergency. The boy was just five-years-old."

Joe's stomach twisted. "What did she do to him?"

"Nothing. She took him to the zoo, bought him ice cream, and made herself out to be a good friend of Daddy's. Then, when she dropped him off a block from his home, she left him with a present for his mother, a milkshake from his mother's favorite ice cream shop, where she and the little boy had gone after visiting the zoo."

"I'm afraid to ask. What was in the milkshake?"

"Cyanide."

Joe tasted the bile in the back of his throat. "Did she…?"

"No. By that time, the police had been called. They confiscated the milkshake and sent it to the lab immediately."

"She would've died almost instantly, or the little boy could have drunk it on his way home."

Opal nodded.

Joe leaned forward, aware that he was being watched through the mirror. "Why in the name of Pete is Lindsay still on the street?"

Opal shrugged. "They couldn't prove she was the woman who took the kid."

"What do you mean, they couldn't prove it was her?"

"She wore a wig, thick glasses, talked without the trace of an accent, according to the kid and the few who were interviewed—the school secretary, the ticket taker at the zoo, the teenager in the ice cream shop. There was nothing distinctive about her."

"And nobody got her license plate number or tracked her cell phone location?"

Opal shook her head. "Nobody saw the car, and the kid was too young to identify it. Her cell phone never left her house all day, where she claimed she was home sick and hadn't left."

"And the neighbors didn't see her come or go? Didn't notice the car gone?"

"No. It's a busy neighborhood where nobody pays much attention to each other. Not unlike most neighborhoods today."

Except in Buffalo Springs where everyone knows everybody else's business. "But the guy is sure it was her?"

"He claims it couldn't have been anyone else, but he had no case. Any defense attorney worth his or her salt would have gotten her off."

"Anything else?"

"That's all I've got so far. I've got a guy on it. If there's more, he'll find it."

"She tried to poison my, er, Helena Nelson, a friend."

"We're looking into that, Joe. And into the damage to your car and the incident at your house. If she's made even the slightest mistake, we're going to find it."

Joe nodded and stood, and the door to the hall opened. A guard walked in and stood beside him.

"Thanks, Ms. Richardson. I appreciate your help."

"I told you, Joe, call me Opal. We're going to be spending a lot of time together. Your bail is being arranged. You should be out soon." She thanked the guard and left.

Joe was taken back to his cell to await his release. He supposed the insurance company could contest his discharge. He had money, a passport, and a purchased airline ticket, but he trusted Dale and Opal to assure the judge that he was not a flight risk. He just hoped that while they were watching out for him, someone was watching out for Helena.

***

Helena, Andi, Allie, Paige, and Sarah huddled around a table in a dark corner at Rick's. Helena's phone sat on the table next to her tall glass of spiked lemonade. Her eyes darted toward the door nonstop.

"Helena, stop," Allie ordered her. "Relax. Everything is going to be okay."

"Okay? You really think everything is going to be okay? Joe was arrested, I was almost poisoned, the clinic was burned down, and that woman is still out there somewhere."

"And as soon as they can tie her to those things, Joe will be out, and she'll be the one sitting in jail," Andi assured her. "Until then, we've got your back."

"You're not going to spend one second alone," Allie said, placing her hand on top of Helena's. "We're all gonna make sure of that."

"And we've got our own insurance policy right here," Andi said, patting the bulge at her waist.

"Great," Helena said. "I just have to sit here until the shootout starts."

"I, for one, think it's cool that your sister is a former SEAL and is watching out for you," Sarah said. "I'd never be able to shoot someone."

Helena looked at Andi and wondered if she'd ever shot anyone. Helena had never thought to ask. Andi had shot *at* the drug dealers, but Helena didn't think that was the same as shooting to kill.

From the corner of her eye, she saw the door open, and Joe walked into the bar. Relief washed over her as she stood and went to him on shaky legs, grabbing each chair as she went by to keep herself upright and moving. She collapsed in his arms.

"You're out." She looked up into his worried face. Tiny lines were etched around his mouth, and the hollows beneath his eyes were dark. He needed a shave, and his hair was mussed, but Helena didn't care. She was just grateful that he was out of jail.

"For now. Can we t—"

"Come on." She squeezed his hand and led him to the table. She saw Andi motion to Arlene to bring Joe a drink.

"Hey, Joe. Welcome to the Comfort and Aid Society," Allie said. "We're inducting Sarah as a new member."

Joe looked around the group. "The what?"

Allie laughed. "It's what we started calling ourselves when we all moved back home after college. I work for an abuse shelter in Harrison. Paige is a graphic designer and marketing genius who seems to be on every committee in town, and Helena, also a consummate volunteer, is a librarian. We realized one day that we all help people in one way or another. Hence, the name."

"She's lying," Paige said. "It's because the first drink we ever made ourselves was Southern Comfort lemonade, when we were sixteen, and Allie's parents were out of town. It's what we still drink when we get together."

"Really, Paige? You give out our sorority's biggest secret to the first man who sits at our table?" Allie scolded.

Helena knew they were trying to get her and Joe to relax, maybe even laugh, but she wasn't in the mood. She guzzled the rest of her sweet and smooth-as-hard-candy drink. She grabbed Joe's hand. "Let's get out of here."

"Helena, where are you going?" Andi called.

Someone said something she couldn't make out, and the whole table burst into laughter. Helena ignored them and pulled Joe toward the door.

"How did you find me?" she asked once they were outside.

"Wade told me where to look. Where are we going?"

"My house, where we can be alone, and you can fill me in. It's closer than your place, and Andi's going out with Wade tonight. Allie and Josie were on watch, but she and her so-called guard dog can have the night off now that you're out."

She looked both ways before crossing the street and headed toward her house, but Joe stopped her when they reached the sidewalk.

"Helena, we need to talk."

"I know, and we will. As soon as we get to the house."

"Helena, stop."

She stopped in front of the tourist center and looked at him. "What?"

"I can't go to your house, and you can't go to mine."

"What are you talking about?" She crossed her arms in front of her chest and cocked her head.

"We can't see each other. That's why I went looking for you. It's over."

"What's over?" A sinking feeling went through her.

"We are. Whatever you think we had, it's over. I've told you that I'm not into commitments, and it's time you accept it."

Passersby were beginning to slow down and ogle at them. Helena took a step closer to Joe. "What is going on?" She glanced from left to right, self-conscious yet desperate to know why he was doing this.

Helena's lifelong nemesis, Carlene Pogue, waltzed by, nose in the air and a smug smile on her face. "Gee, Helena, I sure hope your day gets better."

Helena resisted the urge to trip her as she passed. Instead, she sucked a long stream of air through her nose and narrowed her eyes at Joe. "Joe, why are you saying these things?"

He tightened his face and exhaled, giving her a look that conveyed frustration mingled with disgust. "Helena, enough. It's over. I told you I'm not a man who likes to commit. I don't know what made you think you would be different. I don't do relationships. I'm sorry if that hurts, but it's the way it is. I suggest you find someone else to cling to."

Helena watched as Joe turned, hastened around the corner and walked away as if he was responding to an emergency call. Helena thought she would die right there. As if the pain wasn't enough, the humiliation was devastating. Several people hurried past, unwilling to be pulled into her drama. She glanced across the street and saw her friends standing, agog, in front of Rick's. Rather than cross back to them, Helena started walking toward her house before picking up the pace and making a run for the shelter of home.

***

Joe sat in his living room, a glass of gin in his hand. He watched through the curtains as twilight turned into night. The best thing he could do right now was to sell the house, pack his bags, and head back to Houston. Of course, that was impossible. He'd been given a direct order not to leave town.

He tossed back the gin and reached for the bottle that sat on the floor beside his chair. How many glasses had he had? He held the bottle up and saw the small amount of liquid left. Too many. He put the bottle down and set the glass on the antique candlestick table next to the chair. It had belonged to his grandmother and was one of the few pieces of furniture in the house that meant something to him.

He felt his phone vibrate in his pocket and reached down to pull it out. He declined Wade's call and placed the phone next to the empty glass. He propped his elbow on the arm of the chair and cradled his head in his hand. What a mistake he'd made coming to this dead-end, hole-in-the-wall town. He thought he'd find healing here, but all he'd found was heartache. If this was what Darrin and Helena considered God's plan, he and the man upstairs had some reckoning to do.

***

"Of course, he's not answering." Helena blew her nose for the tenth time—at least that, but she'd lost count—and tossed the tissue onto the sofa cushion. She scowled at Andi, perched on the arm of the chair. "I told you he was a scoundrel who couldn't be trusted." She turned her glare toward Wade who was leaning forward in the armchair, elbows on knees. "And you! How dare you lead me to believe he had feelings for me."

"Helena, everyone can see he has feelings for you. Maybe he's afraid he'll go to jail and doesn't want you to get dragged into that," Andi told her.

"I'm telling you, he was very serious when he said he does not do commitments or relationships and that whatever *I* thought we had is over."

"Helena, I'm sure there's an explanation," Andi tried to reason.

"There is! He's a scoundrel, a scallywag, a rogue!" The more she thought about it, the less sad she was. She was working herself up into a fury.

Wade looked helplessly at Andi. "Want me to go over there and see what's going on?"

"No!" Both women shouted at once.

"Leave it alone for now," Andi told him.

"Forever," Helena confirmed. She stood, picked up the tissues and threw them away, then began pulling pots and pans from the cabinets.

"What are you doing?" Andi asked.

"Making dinner. We left Rick's before we ordered. I'm starving."

"Are you sure you—"

"Yes, I'm sure, darn it." Helena slammed a pot down on the stove.

"Um," Andi looked at Wade. "Maybe you'd better go."

Helena noticed that Wade wasted no time giving Andi a quick kiss and hightailing it out the door.

"What are you making? Can I help?"

"No. Just get out of my way."

Helena went to the fridge and rummaged through the shelves and drawers. She slammed the door and opened the freezer. She pulled out an unopened quart of Betty Jean's homemade blackberry ice cream and held it up.

"Work for you?"

Andi smiled. "Perfect."

Helena grabbed two bowls and spoons and emptied the entire container into the bowls. "Let's go out on the deck. I think we need some air."

The night was pleasant, and Helena sucked in the scents from her garden. Not the masterpieces that her mother's gardens were, but they still filled the air with fragrance—blue sage, coneflower, poppy mallow, and verbena populated the landscape. She let the aroma and the evening breeze, along with the ice cream, calm her.

"Here's the thing," she finally said, licking the last of the ice cream from her spoon. "I really thought we had something. I mean, he even said the L word."

"Joe told you he loved you?" Andi sat up in her chair.

"No, but he said he thought it was love, hoped so, something along those lines." Their words and their kiss just before that fateful phone call replayed in her mind. "I don't know what changed."

"I guess Lindsay is what changed. I mean, I guess her actions made him change his mind. Maybe all her antics made him remember why he swore off relationships to begin with."

Helena rested her head on the back of the chair and watched as the stars slowly lit the night sky one by one.

"I guess so. I mean, if I had dated someone like that, I'd probably run the other way every time I thought about getting serious with someone."

"Maybe by morning, Joe will have had some time to think things over."

"Maybe," Helena said. "But Andi, I saw the look on his face. He wasn't sad to walk away. He was relieved. He didn't want me in his life, and he felt better once he told me so." She started to tear up again and sniffed several times to hold them off.

"I'm so sorry, Helena," Andi said quietly. She reached across and patted her sister's knee.

"It's not your fault." Helena kept looking at the sky. "It's getting late, and it's been one heckuva day. Go to bed. I'll be all right."

"Are you sure?"

Helena nodded. "I'm sure. I just want to be alone for a few minutes."

She sensed Andi's hesitation, but after a moment, her sister gathered the bowls and spoons and went inside. Helena couldn't help but smile. Her sister was a neat freak who knew that Helena would most likely go to bed without giving the bowl a thought. "Goodnight, Helena," Andi said from the doorway. "Love you."

"Love you, too, Sis," she replied without taking her eyes from Cygnus the Swan. She remembered many nights as a child, she and Andi watching for the first star to come out, making a wish, and then continuing to watch until they could see the entire swan in flight from her beak to her tail, the wide wings opening across the sky. How many wishes had she made over the years, and how long ago had she stopped believing they would come true? Why had Joe made her think that her wishes were finally being granted only to squelch them, turning any hope she had from a shining, promising star into an endless black hole?

Seventeen

Joe didn't think the morning sunlight on his back was the reason for the sweat that gathered under his shirt collar. He was furious, and the pounding of his fists on the door had become his mode of venting. He knew he had to get out his aggression in the safest way possible.

The door swung open and Lindsay stood, one hand on her hip and the other on the knob, with a sickeningly sweet smile on her face.

"It's over," Joe said to her. "You've won.

"Is that so? What's over? And exactly what have I won?"

He wanted to wipe that self-assured smirk off her face but kept his bruised, throbbing hands fisted at his side.

"This little game you're playing. You got your way. I've got nothing left here. I hope you're happy."

"You're right. You've got nothing left here. Nobody in this town will ever trust you again, not after you've committed insurance fraud or the way you broke that poor girl's heart in the middle of the downtown. Everybody's talking about it, you know. They're calling you all kinds of names. Your reputation in this town is ruined."

"I guess word travels fast in a small town, but you already knew it would, didn't you?"

"I don't know what you're talking about," she said, the smirk on her face widening. "It seems to me that you brought all your troubles on all by yourself. I don't understand how you ever thought you could find happiness in a place like this. You belong back in the city, performing surgery, living in a grand house with a devoted wife by your side. You would never be happy here in this small town or running that clinic that was costing you your entire life savings. And you would never have been happy with her, some low class, backwards, little girl." She took hold of the front of his shirt and began pulling him inside the apartment as he fought the urge to slap her. "Let me show you what a real woman can do for you."

With her free hand, she pushed the door closed and then wrapped both her arms around his neck and pressed her lips to his.

It's amazing how some memories never fade. He remembered the taste of her lips and the way she took control of his body and his senses. He recalled, all too well, the familiarity of her kiss, but Joe found no pleasure in her embrace. Without gentleness, he extricated himself from her hold and took a step back. He noticed the look of dismay on her face and found some pleasure in it.

"I told you it was over. Not just your game but everything. You've managed to take from me everything that had become important. After my brother died, I had to find a way to go on. I realized that losing you had never been a hardship. Losing someone you truly love and trust is the real hardship. Coming here, making friends, feeling like I was actually making a difference in people's lives, those are the things that matter. You've taken all of that. Those are things I might never get back. And you stand there acting like I ought to be grateful, like I owe you my thanks, like you aren't the reason that my life has fallen apart once again. How could you ever think that I could even entertain the possibility of taking you back?"

Her fury was palpable, her green cat-like eyes burning through him, and she lashed out, nails extended like claws on a tigress. He caught her wrist and squeezed it, the sudden realization coming to him that there was no end to what she would do to get what she wanted. For a moment, the face of the woman from the movie came to mind, and he actually found himself afraid. He shook it off and let go of her hand, vehemently pushing her away.

"How can you say these things to me? I've shown you the truth. These people…" She gestured wildly as though the whole town stood right behind him. "They turned on you the minute things went bad. They were never your friends. Even that librarian, who you seem to think you're in love with, isn't fighting to keep you the way I have. Everybody in this town sees you as an outsider, someone who doesn't belong. You and I both know the truth, Joseph Samuel Blake. You spent your entire life trying to be somebody you're not. You want to be the hero, the one who saves people, the one who puts others' needs before his own. Well, I've got news for you. You will never be your brother."

If she had been a man, he would have punched her. No, he would've done more than that. He would've left the apartment without her still standing, and she would have been lucky if she ever stood again. Hippocratic oath be damned. As it was, he turned around, opened the door, and walked out of her life. She was right. He wasn't Jeremy, and he would never save the world; but he was finally a good man in good standing with God, even if not with everyone else, and that was one thing she could not take away from him.

***

Helena felt like the world's worst sister and an even worst maid of honor. She sat in the meeting room at the closed library, a smile plastered on her face, and pretended to be enjoying the silly game they were playing. When Noreen, Andi's employee and cake decorating extraordinaire, showed up at the library and pulled her aside the day after her and Joe's 'break-up,' or whatever it was, and asked if Helena had found the time to send out shower invitations, Helena wanted to be sick.

"Oh, Noreen. I'm the worst. I didn't even realize how close it was getting. Not only have I not sent invitations, I haven't planned a thing."

Noreen gave her a sympathetic smile. "I thought that might be the case. Look, why don't I take over? I know you and Paige are the volunteer queens in town, but I've got five older sisters. I've been to more than my share of bridal showers."

"Oh, Noreen, I couldn't ask you to do that." She really couldn't, but suddenly Helena, expert volunteer, planning princess, most organized person in town, wanted desperately for Noreen to take over.

"You didn't ask. I offered. You have a lot going on right now, and I'm happy to step in."

Helena pulled at her lip with her teeth, knowing she should say no but without the energy to do so. "Oh, thank you. You have no idea what this means to me."

Noreen waved her off. "Don't worry about it at all. It will be our secret."

Now, surrounded by her friends, her mother, and other businesswomen in town, Helena wanted to crawl into a hole every time Noreen said, "Helena and I came up with this great game" or "menu" or any number of things that Helena had no hand in at all. Bless her heart, though, Noreen was doing everything in her power to protect their secret. Helena had never felt so guilty.

"Helena, our movie buff, thought of this fun game. Keep your papers face side down. When I say go, you have sixty seconds to fill in as many of the correct movie titles as possible. On your mark, get set, go!"

Helena smiled as she watched the guests, faces scrunched in concentration, try to solve the riddles. Giggles ensued along with cries of "don't look at my answers" and "that's my favorite movie." Andi, who hated to be the center of attention, seemed to be having a great time, and for that, Helena was most grateful whether she'd truly had a hand in it or not.

The afternoon flew by, and when Helena and Andi returned home, stomachs stuffed with cake and arms overflowing with gifts, Helena realized she had spent most of the afternoon not thinking about Joe. She was both relieved and saddened by the realization, wanting nothing more than what Andi and Wade had. She'd gone through most of her twenties without wanting that, accepting that she would never meet the man of her dreams in Buffalo Springs, and content to be the spinster librarian, and it bothered her that she fell so easily back into that mindset. Just because things hadn't worked with Joe, that didn't mean that she was destined to be alone forever. Did it?

"Whatcha thinkin'?" Andi asked, as she sorted the gifts into piles on the couch.

Helena dropped into the chair. "Just wondering if I'm destined to be Mary Hatch instead of Mary Bailey."

Andi frowned at her sister. "What in the Sam Hill are you talking about?"

"You know, George Bailey's wife. She's all happy and pretty and has a great life until there is no George Bailey. And then she's the shy, frightened, faint of heart spinster librarian. It's not a pretty transition and one my library school classmates and I laughed at, but now I'm wondering if that's my future."

It must have taken a second for Andi to understand what Helena was talking about, but her look of confusion morphed into understanding and then into concern. She knelt down on floor in front of her sister.

"Helena, you do know that's an unwarranted stereotype made even more popular by Frank Capra in his exaggeration of the alternate world George entered, right? I mean, *It's a Wonderful Life* is a *movie*. You're not a character and certainly not a caricature used to demonstrate what happens when one loses her soulma…" Andi clamped her mouth shut.

"See? It may be a stereotype, but there must be a reason people think it's true. Sure, not all single librarians become lonely old maids, but what about the ones who lose their soulmates? What happens to them?"

"They move on," Andi said quietly. "They find a way to live, to find happiness, to even forgive themselves if necessary."

Helena took a sharp intake of breath and wrapped her hands around her sister's. "Oh, Andi, I'm so sorry. Of course, they do."

Andi squeezed Helena's hands. "And you know what else? They often find that the person they thought was their soulmate wasn't the right one after all. Helena, look at you. You're only twenty-nine. You're smart, you're beautiful, you're—"

"Okay, okay. I'm all that, and I even offer a little extra to hold onto." She grinned and fanned her hands in front of her seated figure. She still thought about those extra ten pounds from time to time, but she was amazed by how much her mindset had changed this summer. After seeing all the women, naked as jaybirds, on the beaches in Greece, not confined by societal rules or encumbered by feelings of inadequacy, she saw herself in a different light.

"I'm serious," Andi said. "You look great. In fact, I think you look better than ever. Have you looked in a mirror lately?"

"To see the dark circles under my red puffy eyes?"

"No. To see the beautiful woman you've grown into. I mean, you were always the pretty one, but my goodness, Helena, you're actually drop-dead beautiful."

Helena pushed her sister away. "Oh, stop it." While no longer so self-conscious about her body, she wasn't willing to go as far as 'drop-dead beautiful.'

"I mean it. Going to Europe, seeing some of the world, being strong for me and for Mama, facing all this mess head-on changed you. It's like you've grown into the woman you're meant to be."

Helena thought about that. Ever since she got home from her trip, she had felt more worldly, and it was more than a new love of her body. Though she felt insecure around Joe before she left, seeing herself as the veritable country bumpkin, she had come to look at herself the way Joe did, or the way he had. Either way, she was actually beginning to feel like an adult and not an older version of her teenaged self. An adult who liked herself and all that she had to offer.

"Maybe you're right about that," Helena said. "I do feel more…mature, I guess, than I did before I left."

"And it shows. Men will be lining up to take you out."

She wasn't sure that was what she wanted, but it was a nice thought. At that moment, another thought struck her. Joe might not be interested in her any longer, but that didn't mean she had to abandon all that she was when she was with him. She had become a better version of herself, and that was whom she wanted to be with or without him.

***

"I wondered when you'd show up," Joe said, opening the door for Amanda to enter the house.

"I would have come sooner, but you seemed to have a lot on your plate, so to speak."

He led her to the kitchen and gestured toward the table. "Have a seat. Can I get you a drink?"

"Sweet tea?" She pulled out the chair and sat down, moving her gaze around the room. "This is an awesome kitchen. My brother would be so jealous."

"Does he cook?" Joe slid the glass across the table as he took a seat.

"Does he cook?" She laughed. "He's a CIA graduate, top of his class."

Joe tilted his head, and the puzzlement must have shown on his face because she quickly swallowed her tea and laughed.

"Culinary Institute of America."

"Oh! Not a spy who loves to cook then."

"Hardly. Though he could bring even the most sinister of men to his knees with his Boeuf bourguignon." She closed her eyes and took a deep inhale as though she could smell it cooking. Joe let her enjoy her memory before cutting to the chase.

"Speaking of sinister men…"

Amanda faced him with a stern look. "If you're referring to yourself, I would hardly call you sinister."

"So, you're not in agreement with the rest of town on the assumption of my guilt?"

She laughed, a deep, guttural laugh. "Are you kidding? Of course, not. And neither are Melanie and Dotty." She reached across and laid her hand on his, and he felt a moment's unease before she said, "We've got your back, Joe. I may not know you very well personally, but I've seen you work, watched you with your patients, and listened to the way you interact with everyone, including your colleagues and employees." She pulled her hand back. "Besides, I saw on my first day here what a piece of work your ex is."

"Don't get me started," he groaned.

"We've talked to your attorney, you know. Dotty, Mel, and me." He noticed her use of the familiar and wondered if the women had become friends outside of the office. "We've told her that we're all willing to testify to your character and work ethic."

He felt a warm glow spread over him. "I appreciate that, Amanda. I really do."

"In fact, Joe." She leaned toward him. "There are a whole lot of people in this town who are willing to vouch for you. You may think that they've already determined your guilt and handed down your sentence, but that couldn't be further from the truth."

He raised his brow. "Oh, really?"

"Yes, really." She picked up the glass of iced tea and guzzled the rest of it. "Boy, this stuff is good." She put the glass down and looked at Joe. "Now, about that clinic of ours. What do we need to do to get it back up and running?"

***

"The Lord is telling us that He has our backs. He's looking out for us, and we shouldn't give in to fear or worry or anxiety. 'Do not be anxious about your life, what you will eat or what you will drink, nor about your body, or what you will put on.' Those are trivial things in the grand scheme of life." Father Michael's homily held Helena's attention as if he were speaking directly to her. For so many years, she'd thought about everything she ate and wondered how much each morsel was adding to her waist and her thighs; but this summer, that had changed. Why had she spent so much time worrying about such things? She loved to eat, and she loved the enjoyment of a good meal as much as she loved the companionship of those with whom she shared it, and that's all that really matters. And besides, there were so many other things to worry about.

She turned her head slightly toward the opposite side of the church. Joe sat in rapt attention, his eyes glued to the priest. He was alone as usual, and Helena found herself feeling sorry for him. His reluctance to commit to a relationship was heartbreaking for her, but what about for him? Did he really want to spend the rest of his life alone? She sighed quietly and turned her attention back to the altar.

"Have I ever told you that I love musicals?"

The congregation laughed. Father Michael found a way to weave a plot, a character, or even a song—often sung by himself—into most of his homilies.

"There's a very popular musical among little girls, and I bet most of you have heard of it. The story of *Little Orphan Annie* is a great exemplification of Jesus's words. Annie sings a song that some of you may know." His smile and twinkling eyes revealed that he knew very well that they were all familiar with the tune, and the many nodding heads affirmed it. "Annie always tells everyone, 'the sun'll come out tomorrow.' She teaches us all that on a day that's grey and lonely, we should just stick out our chins and grin, and remind ourselves that the sun will come out tomorrow." He looked around at his congregates, and Helena had the distinct impression that he paused, for just a moment, when his eyes met hers.

"Jesus is essentially telling us the same thing in this Gospel. He's telling us that no matter how bleak things look, no matter how grey or lonely or sad, there will be a tomorrow. He is in control and will see us through. He will bring the sun back into our lives. All we have to do is trust him and have the faith to allow God to lead us into the light."

Helena smiled. How amazing was it that Father always knew exactly what it was she needed to hear?

***

Joe listened intently.

"Jesus asks, 'which of you, by being anxious, can add a single hour to his span of life?' He doesn't want you to worry about things beyond your control. Like the sparrows that 'neither sow or reap nor gather into barns,' your Father in Heaven will take care of you. He knows what you need, what you long for, and how to meet those needs and those desires. Trust Him. He will lead you from the dark night into the bright sunlight of tomorrow." Father Michael folded his notes and slipped them into a hidden pocket beneath his flowing chasuble.

Was that meant for me? The priest's words replayed in Joe's mind as they stood for the recitation of the Creed.

As if by instinct, Joe turned his head slightly to see the people seated across the aisle. Nestled between Grace and Andi, sat Helena. They stood, shoulder to shoulder, reciting the Creed, and Joe thought, *Those are three of the strongest women I've ever known.*

He felt a sharp stabbing pain in his gut at the thought that he had disappointed them, that he had hurt them, that he had hurt her. But did he have a choice? He had to do something. He had to make sure she was safe.

…no matter how grey or lonely or sad, there will be a tomorrow. He is in control and will see us through. He will bring the sun back into our lives. All we have to do is trust him and have the faith to allow God to lead us into the light.

Had Joe been doing that? Had he been allowing God to be in control, or had he been trying to be in control, handling the situation through panic and fear rather than with the faith that everything would be okay?

Joe was a beat behind when the rest of the congregation sat for the offertory. He'd been lost in his thoughts about control and faith, God and Lindsay, and Helena. He glanced her way once more and felt a longing, a desire for her to glance his way. He needed to tell her, to let her know that he had faith, that he trusted that God would see them through, and that he trusted their love for each other. But she never looked his way. Turning back to the altar, he prayed that she could find a way to have faith in him once again.

***

The night was warm, but Helena felt cold inside. Her heart was breaking, no matter how much she tried to tell herself that Joe was not the one. She sat on the back deck and stared into the trees that formed the border between her backyard and the one that belonged to the house where Dale grew up and where his parents still lived. With all the changes the town had seen over the years, some things always seemed to stay the same. In some small way, that brought a sense of comfort to Helena.

There was a slight shift in the air around her, and the hair on the back of her neck raised, causing a shiver across the top of her back, but her fear vanished instantly. It was not Lindsay. She sensed Joe before she heard him, and she fought the urge to close her eyes and inhale his scent, his presence. Was he truly there, or was he a figment of her imagination, a magic trick conjured by the breeze that drifted through the star-filled night?

"Can we talk?" His voice wasn't more than a whisper, and she wondered again if she was imagining him standing behind her in the shadows.

Her throat felt constricted, and she wasn't sure she could speak. She nodded slowly and waited for him to join her on the dimly lighted deck, but he stayed beneath the willow tree.

"Can you…" He hesitated and quietly cleared his throat, apparently suffering from the same affliction of constriction. "Can you turn off the light?"

It was an odd request, but she found herself rising and carefully sliding open the screen door. She felt for the switch and plunged the deck into darkness, the moon hidden behind the big tree. She tiptoed back to her chair and waited for him to show himself.

Joe waited several seconds before making his way up the two steps and onto the deck. He sat in the chair that Helena had begun to think of as 'Andi's chair' and clasped his hands in front of him, his head hanging low. After what felt like days, he lifted his head and met her eyes with his.

"Thank you."

His words confused her, and she blinked several times before asking, "For what?"

"For agreeing to talk."

She swallowed and nodded. "Go ahead," she gently prodded. "Talk."

He ran a hand through his hair, and she realized he needed a haircut. It was the first time she'd seen his hair unkempt, even more so than when he'd been released from custody. He scratched at his chin, and she wondered if he was still unshaven as well. She squinted in the darkness and tried to make out his appearance. He wore shorts, a polo shirt, and running shoes. They looked clean, but it was dark. She wasn't even sure if his shirt was red or blue. His eyes, though, were clear and determined.

"Faith."

"Excuse me?"

"Faith. It's what I'd forgotten. Faith in God, faith in you, faith in…us."

"I…" She faltered. "I'm not sure I understand."

"I was thinking like a man, a stupid earthbound man, and not like a child of God. I felt like I needed to be in control rather than letting God be in control. I thought my plan was the right plan."

"And your plan was…?"

"Hurting you, pushing you away, making you believe that I wanted out."

A small piece of her heart took a cautious step. "And?" she asked hesitantly, feeling her pulse quicken just a bit.

"And I was wrong. I wanted you to believe I could live without you because I had to believe it myself. More importantly, I needed Lindsay to believe it."

"Joe…" She found herself leaning toward him, expectant, hoping, praying…

Joe leaned toward her and reached for her hands. "I was afraid for you. I'm still afraid for you. But I can't do this alone. I need you. I need us. I think the only way to face this, to fight this, is together." He took a deep breath. "But for now, she can't know. She can't know that we're together." He squeezed her hands, and she thought she felt her hands tremble. "Can we be? Together, I mean."

Helena looked down at their hands, his large, strong protective, caring, healing hands wrapped around her trembling hands. She was afraid to respond, afraid to let her feelings show, afraid to trust.

Trust.

All we have to do is trust him and have the faith to allow God to lead us into the light.

She looked up into his eyes, and she saw it. She saw the faith, the trust, and the love. She smiled, biting her bottom lip, and looked into those eyes, hoping her eyes reflected the same sentiments. She slowly nodded.

Neither spoke, but Helena heard the words, felt them in her heart as he pulled her slowly to her feet. He slid his hands along her arms and onto her back, and she reached up to loop her arms around his neck. She smiled as she felt the growth of a short beard against her cheek and then her lips and chin. Under the faint light of the waning moon, she lost herself in his kiss, and she knew without a doubt that tomorrow, there would be sun.

***

Helena quietly made her way through the dark house toward her bedroom.

"Mind telling me what's going on?"

She stopped and peered through the darkness. Andi was leaning against the doorjamb to her room. Her dark hair was invisible in the dim moonlight, but her white pajamas gave her an eerie, supernatural look.

"Just heading to bed," Helena said lightly, not meeting the blue eyes that shone in the dark.

"What did Joe want?"

Helena froze just inches from her own bedroom door. "Joe?" She asked.

"Come on, Helena," Andi said gently. "Look who you're talking to. Did you think that I wouldn't pick up on voices out back or Joe sneaking off into the trees?"

Sometimes Helena hated living with a former SEAL intelligence commander. "Please, Andi, just go to bed."

"How long have you two been sneaking around?"

"We're not sneaking around. It's nothing. Just go to bed."

Andi made no attempt to move. Helena debated ignoring her and just going to bed herself, but she'd never kept anything important from her sister even all the years Andi was away. She tried to figure out what to say, but Andi spoke first.

"You're playing a dangerous game, little sister. The least you could do is have backup."

"This isn't combat, Andi, and it's not a game." She wasn't sure if her growing anger was meant to be directed at Andi, Lindsay, or Joe. "It's my life, and I'm not going to let some crazy person take it over."

"What are you planning on doing? Hiding in the dark every night until she goes away?"

"Something like that," Helena murmured. "Look, I don't know what I'm planning on doing. I just know that, when I'm not with Joe, I'm not complete. That might sound old-fashioned and silly and even sexist, but it's true." She felt tears welling up and fought to control them.

Andi took the two steps toward her sister that allowed Helena to fall into her arms. "It's not silly, and it's not sexist. It's human, and it's understandable."

Helena sniffed but didn't let herself cry.

"I hate to see you hurting, and I hate to see you having to play hide and seek in the dark just to see the man you love. I promise, things will get better?"

"How?" Helena looked at her sister, seeing her more clearly as the moon shifted and shone brightly through the sliding glass doors behind her.

"Dale is doing everything he can to pin all this on Lindsay, and Wade says Opal is the very best. They're going to find answers. And if they can't, I know people who can. We're going to beat her, Helena."

Helena nodded, pressing her lips together. "I pray you're right." She gave Andi another hug. "Thank you. I'm going to go to bed. Maybe I'll actually sleep tonight."

Helena felt Andi's gaze on her as she slipped into her room and closed the door. Her emotions swirled around her mind and heart no differently than the twister had swirled through their town causing fear and uncertainty, creating chaos with its intensity.

Eighteen

For three nights, Helena waited in the dark, but Joe didn't show up, or at least, didn't make his presence known. She couldn't hear his footsteps, smell his soap, or feel his breath on the back of her neck. She tried reading, her iPad set to night mode, the porch light turned off, but her mind couldn't take in the words. She tried playing games but became bored with the monotony of the colored shapes and exploding candies. For the most part, she just sat, praying things would get better, and imagining the life they could have if only…

On the morning after the third night, Sarah looked at Helena with pity. "Are you sleeping at all?"

Sarah had become more than a co-worker. She had blended right into their little group and become a friend. Helena wished she could tell Sarah, all her friends, about Joe showing up at her house, but she had promised him she wouldn't. Only Andi knew, and she knew no more than what she witnessed—Joe's presence on the porch and their kiss. If she had listened in to what was said, she hadn't said so to Helena. Perhaps she had told Wade. Yes, she most certainly had told Wade. Helena knew they held no secrets from each other, not anymore. Had Wade said something to Joe? Was that why he was staying away? The unknown was killing her.

Even Dale had called to ask if Helena had seen Joe. She felt terrible lying to him, but she promised Joe that nobody would know about them. She told Dale the truth—she hadn't seen Joe in a day or two and, as far as she knew, he was home, staying out of the public eye.

She gave Sarah a half-hearted smile. "It's hard to sleep with one eye open." Helena meant it as a joke, but the truth of it encircled them like the smoke from her grandfather's pipe.

"Any news?"

"Not that I know of." And that was the truth. Dale hadn't given her any information when he'd called, and she couldn't exactly ask. Andi and Wade knew nothing, or weren't saying, and Joe was MIA. She hadn't even seen him in town. Had he left town? Was that night meant to be a goodbye? She shook her head. No, he would have told her so instead of giving her hope that everything would be okay.

Sarah evidently took the shaking of her head as a sign that Helena didn't want to talk about Joe. Her already piteous look became even more so. "Let's get the girls together after work. It's going to be a busy weekend, judging from the increase in tourists the last two weekends. Let's get together and unwind before the madness begins."

The past two weekends had been busy even in the library. With the growing number of visitors in town, the shops, restaurants, and little tourist center were filled almost to capacity. Helena heard that some of the older residents were retiring to Florida or Texas and listing their homes on Airbnb. A developer had bought the Warren farm, and a new hotel was being planned that would include a swimming pool, tennis courts, and even a conference center. Nobody would have believed any of that was possible just six months ago.

"I think that's a good idea," Helena told Sarah. "I could use a night out with the Comfort and Aid Society."

Sarah laughed. "I'm even starting to like that drink." She looked over at the door and smiled at the O'Connor family bustling into the room. "Duty calls."

"I'll send a text in the group chat," Helena promised.

She watched Sarah greet the harried mother of six and smiled. What a find she'd been, the perfect complement to Helena's boisterous, flirtatious, often overzealous personality. Sarah was friendly but soft-spoken, approachable but knew when to keep her distance, and a magician when it came to kids. Helena often wondered who the lucky man would be to sweep her off her feet, but Sarah seemed to be interested only in work, hanging with the girls, and getting to know the town. She never mentioned going on dates, and she never talked about any ex-boyfriends. In fact, Sarah never talked about her past at all, a fact Helena had never realized until now. She continued to watch the younger woman with the kids and wondered about the real reason Sarah had taken the job in Buffalo Springs…

Helena, deep in thought, reached up and scrunched the blonde curls at the back of her head, still damp from her morning shower. She turned at the sound of the back door opening and froze when Lindsay walked in. Her smile caused Helena's blood to run cold. She saw Sarah turn, her eyes going wide at the site of the other woman.

Helena wanted to run into the office, slam the door, and hide until she was gone, but she couldn't. Whether it was fear coursing through her veins or anger, she honestly didn't know. This was the woman who had ruined her life, yet she pranced into the library like she owned it. She marched right up to the counter and dropped the stack of books down in front of Helena.

"I'm returning these," she said casually, that sly smile still on her face.

Helena looked down, surprised to see the wedding planning books. She looked at Lindsay, brow raised, but remained silent.

"I don't need them anymore. The groom's going to jail. Pity. I never pegged him for a crook." Her voice was steady, no trace of irony or even triumph. Helena refused to engage though she felt her ire in the tight clenching of her jaw. She took the top book from the pile and scanned the barcode, refusing to acknowledge Lindsay's lingering presence. As Helena reached for the next book, she froze. The sinister shadow of Annie Wilkes loomed over writer, Paul Sheldon, and the red, blood-scrawled title, Misery, danced across the cover.

Lindsay leaned over the counter. Her breath was tainted with the stench of stale coffee. Her lowered voice was as hard and cold as the old ice fishing pond on a January day.

"He's lying, you know. About the fire, the insurance, the dog, and me. Whatever he's said, he's even lying about his feelings for you. All he does is lie, but that's all about to end. He never should have started telling lies about me or trying to lie about who he is. He's going to regret lying to me about wanting to be a surgeon. Then he'll be sure never to lie again."

Before Helena's gasp fully escaped from her lips, Lindsay was gone.

"Helena, what is it? What did she say?"

"Call Dale," Helena whispered. "Call him now. Ask him if he's seen Joe."

Helena didn't remember fleeing to her office, but that's where she was when she found her trembling fingers frantically tapping buttons on her phone. It rang and rang, going to voice mail over and over. "Come on, Joe. Pick up." After three tries, she left a message. "Lindsay was here. She's planning something, Joe. Where are you? Why aren't you answering?"

"Dale said Joe hasn't been seen by anyone for a couple days. There's a warrant out for his arrest, issued this morning when he was declared missing." Sarah stood in the doorway. "Is everything okay? What can I do?"

"I don't know," Helena said, unsure as to exactly which question she was responding. "I've got to go. Can you handle things here?"

Sarah nodded. "I can, but Helena, I don't think you should go anywhere. She could be setting you up."

"I think Joe's in trouble." She frantically turned things over on her desk. Where had she put her keys?

"Then let Dale take care of it." Sarah rushed inside and slammed her hands down on Helena's desk, getting Helena's attention. "Helena, listen to me." Her voice was shrill. "That woman is deranged, out of her mind, as loony as they come. You can't go after her. When someone's crazy like that, you can't provoke them. You just have to bide your time, wait for the chance to get away—"

"I'm not trying to get away from anyone. I'm going to look for Joe."

"And what if you find him? What if she has him tied up somewhere like in one of those books she requested? What are you going to do then? At least wait for Dale to get here. He can go with you."

"He's not going to allow that. You and I both know it." She spied her keys on the floor under the desk and quickly bent and retrieved them.

"And what are you going to accomplish on your own?" Helena looked at Sarah and could see that she was becoming hysterical. Looking beyond her friend and co-worker, she saw Mrs. O'Connor in the doorway, eyes wide, tightly holding her youngest, a little girl with long, stringy hair, her arms clasped around her mother's leg.

"Is there something I can do to help?"

Helena looked from the mother and child to Sarah. "Please, Sarah," she implored. "I've got to find him."

As Helena ran from the room, she realized that her plea wasn't as much for Sarah's understanding as it was a prayer. *Please, God, let me find him, and let him be okay.*

***

Joe's head ached so badly his teeth felt like the vibrating tuning fork his piano teacher used when she visited his house to tune their old Steinway. He pressed his hands to each side of his head to stop the pain and dizziness. What had happened? He could remember nothing past leaving his house the previous night after dark to see Helena. The first time had been easy, so he took the same route, heading to Dale's childhood home where the tall trees provided the cover he needed to get to the fence line up that led to Helena's back deck. He had just turned the corner near the Mackenzie house when everything went black.

He forced his eyes open, but he still couldn't see. Was it still night? Where was he?

He tried to stand, but his head felt like it was being held under water. Concussion. But how? Had he tripped? Been hit by a car? Why couldn't he remember, and where was he now? If something had happened or someone had found him, wouldn't they have taken him… Taken him where? He was the only doctor in town, and other than to his own house, where would they have gone? This was certainly no hospital.

Joe lifted his hand to the back of his head where it pulsed and throbbed. He felt dried blood. A lot of it. The collar of his shirt was stiff but dry. Instinctively, he held his fingers up in front of his eyes, but it was too dark to see if there was any tell-tale red on them. They felt dry, no sticky, congealing blood. He'd been here for a while.

Taking slow, easy breaths, Joe managed to get to his feet. He waited several seconds, hands on the cold, wet wall behind him, until he felt somewhat steady. He reached out in front of him, feeling his way in the pitch blackness of wherever he was.

It smelled dank with the faint odor of mildew, and it was cold despite being late July. He could hear absolutely nothing, as if he was miles from everything or in some kind of soundproof booth or cave.

Cave. The word took on a new meaning when his hands hit solid rock on the other side, only about five feet from where he woke up. He followed the rock wall to the left until he hit wood. Feeling across, his came to what felt like a door. He moved his hands along it until he found a latch, but it wouldn't budge. Where the heck was he?

He kept moving his hands along the wall, his eyes slowly adjusting to the darkness but never enough to actually make anything out. He stumbled over something and reached down, feeling his way across the object. It was a shovel, new by the feel of it, no rust or chips. He felt around and identified a metal bucket, a sledgehammer, and an axe. It was a strange assortment of tools, and he felt confused by the oddity of the building and its few contents.

Feeling around again, Joe located and picked up the shovel and then put it down, searching for the sledgehammer. He found his way back to the door and raised the tool over his head. He aimed for the door, a vague, shadowy thing, slightly lighter in color than the walls, if the surrounding darkness could even be described in terms of color. He swung and missed, feeling the dizzying effect of the heavy tool, the swinging motion, and the pressure in his head. He stumbled but caught himself and forced himself to stand upright and focus on the door. He swung again, missing the door as it swung open. He was so blinded by the light that he dropped the sledgehammer and covered his eyes, his head thundering with pain. He dropped to the ground.

"What the…? Give me that!"

Before he could think or react, he felt the sledgehammer being yanked up off the cold, hard ground. He tried to look up, to see the face of the person who entered the room, but it was too bright. He couldn't see her, but he could hear her, and the room suddenly felt even colder despite the open door and the sunlight that poured in.

"What are you doing awake so soon?"

"Lindsay," he gasped. "Where am I?" His head felt as if it was spinning like the gyroscope he had when he was younger, bought on a visit to NASA, that spun on its axis while perched on a thin metal base.

"Don't worry about where you are. It's what we're going to do that matters." She closed the door, pitching them into blackness again, and he actually found himself grateful for the soothing darkness.

"What we're going to do?" he repeated, groping for a wall to stabilize himself so he could stand.

"You wasted your hands, those beautiful, gifted hands. You were supposed to use them to perform life-saving surgeries. They were our tickets to the life we were meant to have. But it was a lie. All if it. You were never going to be any kind of surgeon, and you never wanted the life we were meant to have. Well, if you aren't going to use your hands for surgery, then what need do you have of them?"

His stomach twisted, and bile rose in his throat. What did she mean? What was she thinking?

"You know, that librarian you seem to think you're in love with? She and her friend have been quite helpful." He could make out her form in the darkness. She was holding something. He gasped at the sudden flash of light, and watched the small, flickering flame grow a bit larger. He could clearly make out a lantern, an old-fashioned one with oil and a wick. She hung the lantern from a hook on the wall. "They got some books for me. Some very interesting books."

"Lindsay, I feel…" he said through ragged breaths. "What did you give me?"

She ignored him. In the dim light, he watched as she turned the bucket upside down. She turned and looked at him, pulling several rope cords out from somewhere. Did she have a bag of some sort? He wasn't sure. She dropped the cords and took out a thermos.

"One of the books was about a woman who poisons her father-in-law. She sprinkled poison on mushrooms, but that was so boring. I thought a pie would be much more fun. It was tricky, doing it without touching those awful berries, but I did it. Of course, that girlfriend of yours figured it out and gave the pie to that good-looking police officer." She reached out suddenly, holding his hair in one hand and yanking back his head. She poured the contents of the thermos down his throat as he struggled to breathe and tried to expel the liquid. "Lucky for us, there are all kinds of ways to poison somebody." Within seconds, the room was black again.

***

Helena banged on the door to Joe's house, but there was no answer. When she heard the approaching car, she turned to see Dale's cruiser pulling into the driveway. He threw open the door and stood, calling to her, "What do you think you're doing?"

"The same thing I hope you're doing."

"Helena, you're interfering with an official investigation. Come over here."

"Are you looking for him, Dale? He hasn't been seen in days. He's a missing person. Do you have a BOLO out, or whatever it is you do?"

"Helena, every man in my department is looking for Joe. The judge issued a warrant for his arrest. He's a fugitive. Now, come here."

Reluctantly, she walked toward his car. "He's not a fugitive, and you know it. Can't you break in? What if he's in there? What if he's hurt?"

Dale shook his head. "Helena, look, the truth is, I don't really know anything about Joe. None of us do. I believed him, but now, his disappearance just makes him look more guilty."

Helena told Dale what Lindsay said at the library when she returned the books.

"I'm telling you, Dale, she has him. If he's not here, she's taken him somewhere. She's crazy."

Dale's eyes widened. "Okay. I'll check out the house, but you stay here." She turned as he made his way toward the house. "Helena, I mean it. Do not follow me inside."

She raked her lip with her teeth as he knocked on the door, called for Joe, searched the porch—presumably for a key—then took out his gun and used the butt of it to break the window. He reached inside and unlocked the door. Before going inside, he looked back at her.

"Don't even think about it."

She watched him disappear inside.

After several grueling minutes, he appeared on the porch, phone pressed to his ear. He made his way toward her as he spoke. "Eric, get someone over to Dr. Blake's house… Full forensics. See if you can find anything… No, nothing, but his wallet is on the counter, and his car is in the driveway. There's still a dirty plate in the sink. I don't think he planned to leave." He made a face and looked at Helena. "Where?"

She held her breath.

"By my fence? Who found them?" He motioned for her to get in his car, but she was frozen in place. "Yeah, come try them out. See if they fit the house and the car."

"What was found?" She felt her heartbeat go faster and was surprised it wasn't pumping itself right out of her chest.

Dale waved for her to be quiet. "That's right. Wade saw him Tuesday morning, so yeah, two days. Send Pete to question Wade. See if he has any idea what Joe's plans were, where he might be, why his keys would be in my yard…Yeah, I'm calling them now. Thanks." He disconnected the call and motioned again for her to get inside the car.

"Do you know how to reach his parents?" he asked, closing the driver's side door.

Helena shook her head. "I was supposed to meet them before…" She blinked. "Before he was arrested. What's going on?"

"Do you know their names?" She nodded. Dale tapped the Google app on his phone and handed it to her. "Help me find them."

***

When Joe awoke, his hands and feet were tied with the cords. His head throbbed, and the feeling of being held under water had returned. He was sitting against the rock wall, and she was watching him from across the room. His eyes adjusted quickly to the faint glow of the lantern, and he could see the bucket, still overturned in the middle of the room, with both the axe and sledgehammer beside it. He looked back at her, seeing her eyes on him, that bone-chilling smile playing on her lips.

"Welcome back. Did you have a nice nap?"

He stared at her, unwilling to play along with this game. He tightened his jaw, at the same time clenching his fists, the rope pulling and digging as his hands moved. His vision blurred in and out of focus. He was so sleepy. It was all he could do to keep his eyes open.

"I didn't get a chance to finish telling you about my summer reading. There was another book, *East of Eden.* Have you read it?" She didn't wait for a reply. "I never did. Never saw the movie either, but I devoured it after checking it out from the li-brar-y." She elongated the word and smiled, tormenting him with the fact that she had been so close to Helena. It worked, and he felt the additional pain of worry and despair. Was Helena okay? Was Lindsay working her way up to telling him that she had done something to her? He couldn't bear the thought.

"There's this woman, Cathy, crazy as a loon but smart as a whip. She burned down her family home with her parents still inside." She chuckled as if that was funny, and Joe felt his insides go soft. He was afraid he would vomit but refused to give her the satisfaction. "Lucky for you, I chose the clinic instead. I thought about the house, knowing the two of you were inside, having your cozy little dinner, toasting each other with wine and smiling in the candlelight." She made a gagging sound, and bile rose in his throat. She had been watching them. "I decided I'd rather stick with plan A. That came from another book. I think you know the movie. I saw you watching it together. You know, the one where the wife frames the husband for her death and then convinces him to take her back when she mysteriously turns up alive." Even in the pale light, he could see the smile spreading across her face. "Only I didn't want to pretend to be dead, so I thought of another way to frame you instead."

"Why are you doing this?" He finally asked. He thought he saw the rise and fall of her shoulders, a faint shrug or a heaving breath, he couldn't tell.

"Why not? I mean, it's fun. Exciting even. Thinking of ways to hurt you, to humiliate you, to make you suffer."

"What did I ever do to you?"

"You disappointed me." The matter-of-fact reply, the even tone of her voice, and the steel in her eyes told him that she had no real reason. She had done it because she wanted to. She felt that she had been lied to, had suffered, though it was through no fault of his, and she wanted to inflict pain and suffering on him.

"So, now what?" he asked, trying through the haze to match her matter-of-fact tone. He attempted to focus, mentally and visually, wishing his head would stop rotating like that blasted gyroscope.

Her smile widened, and it sent chills down his spine. "Now, we get to my favorite book of the summer. It's a tale by Stephen King about a writer and his biggest fan. How apropos, don't you think? You're in love with a book lover, and Annie was in love Paul, a writer."

Joe recalled the book, one he read many years before the theatrical release. He'd also seen that movie.

His eyes flickered to the tools on the ground—a sledgehammer and an axe. Terror flooded him, and he felt the warm flow of urine saturate his pants. He felt helpless, like the nine-year-old staring at the bloody body of his friend's dog.

"You're familiar with it, I see. Did you read the book or just see the film? You know they're different right? In the film, Annie hobbles Paul with a sledgehammer, but in the book..." Her eyes went to the tools and then shifted back to Joe. "In the book, she simply cuts off his feet with an axe." She took a deep breath and exhaled, shaking her head. "I've been sitting here trying to decide. Would you be more miserable with severely mangled, decrepit, useless hands or with no hands at all?"

***

"Dale here, go ahead. What've you found out?"

They'd already called his parents as well as Dotty, Melanie, and Opal. Nobody had seen or heard from Joe in the past twenty-four hours. He had talked to his parents the previous morning, but he'd given them no reason to worry, at least, not any more than they already were about his predicament.

Helena watched as Dale nodded, his eyes focused on the road ahead. "Gotcha. I'm on that side of town. I'll check it out. Send Pete over, too, with that dog of his. I don't know what I'll find and may need backup. In fact, dispatch an ambulance, and call my brother. Tell him to come with his rescue gear." He cast a sidelong glance at Helena. "Just in case."

"What?" Helena asked when he disconnected the call, fear gripping her.

"First, the keys the kid's dog found were Joe's. They fit his car and his house. Second, Stan Higgins saw Lindsay's car turning into the national park late last night. He was on his way back from Harrison, and she turned in front of him. He had to slam on the brakes so he didn't hit her, and she was driving so fast, her tires squealed as she made the turn. He didn't see anyone else with her, but it might be worth taking a look."

Helena tried to remain calm, but her heart was racing like a thoroughbred. The park was massive with forests and caves and a rushing river; and Dale was calling in a bloodhound, an ambulance, and his brother, an Arkansas Search and Rescue Patrol. Helena wasn't sure which of those terrified her more. The scenarios ran wild in her mind. "She was going to the park after dark? Lindsay doesn't strike me as the camping type."

"Me neither." Dale turned on the lights and sirens and peeled out of town.

***

"Enough talk." Lindsay stood and clapped her hands together a few times, scattering dust and dirt into the air. "Let's get this over with."

Barely able to hold his head up, Joe tried to summon the strength to fight her. "What did you give me?"

"Don't worry. Nothing that will kill you." She stopped and looked at the cave ceiling. "Not yet anyway. I made sure the doses were small enough to keep you alive. Of course, it does build up in your system…"

She put her hands on her hips and gave him the same menacing smile he'd seen too many times that day. "I want you alive for this and as alert as you can be without being able to fight me off. Whatever happens after that is in the hands of that supreme being you've become so fond of lately."

"Rohypnol? Ketamine?"

"Wouldn't you like to know, Dr. Blake?"

She grabbed the front of his polo shirt and dragged him the few feet to the bucket. "Can you sit up?"

"Probably not," he said honestly.

"Hmph. Well, that won't do."

He didn't know where she found the strength—she'd always been tiny and certainly never showed any desire to lift or carry anything on her own—but she managed to get him propped up on the overturned bucket, his hands on the flat bottom. He slumped over, unable to sit up even he wanted to, which he did not. He might be powerless to stop her, but he wasn't going to help her either.

"I guess we'll have to try something else."

She dragged him back to the wall, leaning him against the rock. She reeked with the stench of perspiration, and he wondered when she had last showered. Or was he smelling himself? She spread his legs as far apart she could.

"What did you do to yourself?" She made a tisking sound and shook her head. "Did little Joey have an accident?"

She laughed as she retrieved the bucket and put it between his legs, placing his tied hands back on top.

"Now, what shall it be? Mangled or missing?" She paced the small space, clucking her tongue, shaking her head, and tapping her lips with her finger as though trying to solve the riddle of the Sphinx. "I know." She turned to look at Joe. His heavy eyes slowly blinked twice as he tried to focus on her. "How about you decide. Which would you rather have? Hands that will probably never work again? Or no hands at all?" She shook her head. "No, no, that won't do. You could always get those prosthetic things." She smiled like she'd won the lottery and held a finger up in the air. "Mangled it is. Good choice, Doc."

He began to heave and turned away, his stomach clenching and convulsing, but he didn't even have the strength to wretch. When he turned back, Lindsay had the sledgehammer in her hand and was moving her head to this angle and that, assessing which way to swing the hammer.

Nineteen

"Here!" Dale yelled. "I've got fresh footprints."

Helena followed closely behind Dale, Pete, Cooper, and a park ranger, fiercely defying Dale's orders to stay inside the locked car.

Pete released Daisy, his pet bloodhound, and commanded her to follow the tracks. The dog sniffed several times then took off down the trail, her tail standing straight up as she went.

When they caught up with Daisy, she was sniffing around the old mine shaft. Dale looked at Pete. "What do you think?"

"It's unlocked." He nodded toward the door where the lock dangled, the shackle hanging open.

"And it's not the right lock," the ranger said, his voice low. "Someone replaced it."

Guns drawn, the two officers stood on either side of the door. "Lindsay Johnson, this is Chief Dale Mackenzie. If you're in there, open up."

"Stay back, Ma'am," the ranger said, holding his arm out to bar Helena from approaching.

Helena kept her eyes on the door and strained to hear something. Anything. A howl of pain pierced the air, and Helena sucked in a breath, thrusting herself toward the door. The ranger caught her and held his arms around her waist as she kicked and elbowed him. "Let me go!"

Dale nodded to Pete who nodded back and then to Cooper. Without another word, Cooper kicked in the door, and Dale and Pete stood, guns pointed inside the shaft.

"Freeze?" Dale yelled.

Helena stopped fighting the ranger and peered through the crack between the two men. She blinked several times, trying to make sense of what she saw.

Lindsay stood over Joe, a sledgehammer in her hands. She turned toward the door, her eyes ablaze with fury. Before Helena could register what was happening, Lindsay charged at the men, the hammer coming down in a forceful arc.

The sound was sharp, fast, and deafening. Helena watched as Lindsay's body pitched back and then fell forward, the heavy sledgehammer making a loud thud as it fell to the ground, and her head making a gruesome sound as it hit the head of the hammer.

The ranger let her go, and Helena pushed her way through the men and into the shaft, scrambling over Lindsay's body to get to Joe.

"Joe! Joe!" she screamed, pushing his hair off his face as she pulled him to her, collapsing onto the dirt floor and cradling his limp body in her lap.

***

"All charges have been dropped," Opal told Wade, Andi, and Helena. They sat in the waiting room at the same hospital where they sat those many weeks prior when Joshua was brought in after his stroke. Helena wore fresh clothes, thanks to Andi, but she thought she could still smell Joe's blood and body fluids on her skin.

"Lindsay meticulously detailed every phase of her plan in a journal, right down to notes she took while reading the books she checked out from the library. Joe's insurance company is going to write him a check, and I've been contacted by many friends and colleagues throughout the south asking how they can help get him get up and running again." She looked at the small group, and a wave of sympathy flowed across her features. "Do we know if he'll be able to…?"

The question hung between them. It had been hours since Joe had been taken into surgery and then taken to a room. None of them were family or emergency contacts, so they had been given little information. Still, Helena refused to the leave the hospital, at least not until she was allowed to see Joe.

"Dr. Stearns and Dr. Barton were hopeful, but we really don't know," Helena told her. "The doctors couldn't share much with us, of course. Plus, Joe's heavily sedated and might be out for some time. We probably won't know how much he can use the hand until after he wakes up."

Opal nodded. "Keep me posted, okay?" She stood, and the rest of the group stood as well.

Wade reached out his hand. "Thanks, Opal, for everything. I appreciate your help."

"It was nice representing a good guy for a change." She smiled, taking his hand.

They said goodbye and sat back down, waiting to hear more. Helena was exhausted, physically and mentally, after the ordeal and the long hours of surgery, but she refused to leave. Wade and Andi wouldn't let her wait alone.

They had no idea what had taken place inside that dark, dirty, mine shaft, but what they could piece together was straight from a horror movie. Joe's left hand and fingers were shattered, and from the looks of things when the men pushed open the door, his right hand was next. Joe was right-handed, and Helena thanked God for small miracles.

Joe was severely dehydrated, drugged with an as-of-yet unidentified narcotic, and sitting in his own waste, most likely a by-product of fear, pain, and the proximity of death. With the knowledge of the books Lindsay had checked out from the library, and her own fascination with film, Helena knew instantly what Lindsay intended. If they had been thirty seconds later…

Helena swallowed hard. She didn't want to think about that. Joe was safe. He would need many surgeries to repair his left hand, and it still might never be the same, but he was alive. They could tell his parents that much when they arrived.

She lifted a bottle of water to her lips just as Dr. Stearns walked into the waiting room. She rose, anxious to hear anything he could tell them.

"Joe's still not awake, but I'm told that his hand looks good. Dr. Barton is an excellent orthopedic surgeon, and with Dr. Ortega in the OR with him, they feel confident they were able to set the bones and save the nerves. Time will tell."

"When will he wake up?"

"Helena, I wish I could answer that. He was given some potent stuff, and he was in shock. Even without the hand injury, he might not have survived much longer if you all hadn't found him." He looked up as Dale entered the room.

"Sorry I took so long. Lots of paperwork."

"No problem, Dale," Helena said. "Thanks for coming."

"Of course," he said, turning toward Dr. Stearns. "What's the news?"

Dr. Stearns pressed his lips together without responding.

Helena looped her arm through Dale's. "It's okay. Dale's the one who saved him."

"I know you," Dr. Stearns said slowly.

"I was here a lot in the last couple years. My wife, she uh, she was a patient here. Dr. Cook's patient."

Understanding dawned on him, and Dr. Stearns closed his eyes. "I'm so sorry."

"Thank you." Dale cleared his throat. "What about Joe?"

"I'm afraid I can't tell you much more. His father is his emergency contact, but he gave us permission to share some information with Helena. She can fill you in, and Dr. Barton will update Mr. Blake when he arrives. Do you know when they will be here?"

Helena looked at her watch. "They should be here any minute."

"Okay, then. If you all need anything, let me know."

They thanked him, then Helena sat back down, turning her gaze toward Dale. "Opal was here. She told us that all charges were dropped."

"They were. Eric said he'll have nightmares every night for the rest of his life after reading some of the entries in the journal he found when his forensics team went through Lindsay's apartment. I know how he feels."

Dale visibly shivered, and Helena cringed. She didn't want to imagine the nightmares that Joe was going to have.

They made small talk while they waited for Emily and Donald Blake. As soon as Helena spotted the distinguished looking couple, she knew exactly who they were.

Donald was tall with the same striking blue eyes as his sons, and he exuded a military presence that made him seem even taller. Emily was the picture of sophistication in her white cotton pants, striped blouse, and Jack Rogers sandals. Her perfectly fixed hair and natural makeup gave no indication that she had just spent what was undoubtedly a grueling ninety minutes on an airplane. But it was her eyes that gave away her pain and worry. Behind the couple was a beautiful dark-haired woman with Joe's eyes and chin. She must be Serena.

Helena stood and tentatively walked toward the family. When her eyes met Emily's, the woman's facade broke, tears welled in her eyes, and she rushed to Helena with her arms open wide. They held each other, both sniffling and heaving, as Donald, Wade, Dale, and Andi made introductions.

"How is he?" Emily asked, searching Helena's eyes for any sign that there was good news.

"He's out of surgery. We don't know much else. She…" Helena faltered. "She did terrible things." The crying began again, and Dale took over, telling them as gently as he could all that had transpired over the past thirty-six hours.

When they finished, Emily and Donald clung to each other on the waiting room couch and, with their daughter beside them, wept in each other's arms.

***

"Joseph, son, can you hear me? Can you open your eyes?"

That voice. That commanding, sometimes demanding, always loving voice came from beyond the dream, no, the nightmare. Maybe if he followed the sound, he might be able to escape. If it was a nightmare. What if it was real? What if…?

"Joe, sweetie, please wake up."

Another voice, pleading, coaxing, gentle, and loving. It was the voice that soothed his tears, made the monsters go away, and reminded him, always, of how much he was loved.

"Mama," he whispered.

"He's talking! I heard him!"

The voice sounded urgent, joyful, and…relieved.

It took great effort, but after several attempts, Joe slowly forced his eyes open. He blinked sluggishly, tentatively, wincing at the bright lights and white walls. He remembered everything as being so dark—pitch black actually—cold, and musty smelling. Now, he was weighed down with blankets, and he smelled antiseptic, lots of it, mingled with the lingering smells of blood and sweat.

"Joseph, can you hear me?"

He slowly moved his eyes up to see the face of his father, then shifted them to see his mother. They looked worried though they smiled down at him.

"Where am I?" His voice was hoarse, and his parched throat seemed to be coated with glass.

"Washington Regional Medical Center, Fayetteville, Arkansas."

Joe tried to swallow, but his throat was too dry. "Water," he croaked.

His mother grabbed a paper cup from a bedside table and held it to his mouth. He sipped and ran his tongue over his chapped lips. From the corner of his eye, he saw a nurse checking his vitals.

"Do you remember what happened, Joe?" a man in a white coat—a doctor—asked.

"It was dark, a cave? Someone—" He gasped. "Lindsay!" He started to sit up, but a wave of nausea hit him, and he collapsed onto the bed.

"She's…" his father hesitated. "She's dead, Joe. Lindsay's dead."

Joe felt his eyes go wide in surprise. Or was it disbelief? Relief? All of the above. He breathed heavily. He closed his eyes, but a sudden memory flooded his mind—the sound of screaming. His eyes flew open.

"Helena!"

"She's in the waiting room with Serena," his mother told him. She smiled. "She's a lovely girl. You've been out for quite some time, and we've had several nice, long talks. We tried to get her to go home and rest, but she refused to leave."

"She's okay?" He felt his breathing slow. Thank heaven she was okay.

"She's just fine. Anxious to see you."

He felt an itch on his left leg, tried to scratch it but couldn't move his hand, or the whole lower part of his arm. He realized his arm hung in the air, supported by a raised sling, and he felt the heavy cast against his flesh. A wave of recollection threatened to drown him. "My hand?" he asked frantically.

"You had surgery," the doctor told him, his face floating above as if painted on a cloud.

"How bad?"

He saw his parents exchange a look, and his gut wrenched. He waited, looking from one to the other.

"Dr. Barton can answer that," his father said. "There was a lot of medical jargon."

After overseeing a medical base for ten years, Joe knew that his father understood medical jargon just fine. He closed his eyes and sighed. "How bad?" he asked through clenched teeth, then opened his eyes and looked up at the doctor.

The face, still hovering above, spoke. "You'll get use of it back, maybe ninety percent if it went as well as it seemed, but it will take time."

Ninety percent wasn't bad, he told himself. It could have been much worse. At least he wasn't a surgeon. The thought almost made him laugh. The one thing she'd always wanted him to be was what she set out to take away.

"We won't know a whole lot until the cast comes off. That's going to be three weeks. We'll remove the stitches then and do some assessing. Another three to four weeks for the second cast, and then the real work begins."

Joe nodded and thought through the recovery process. He'd need physical therapy, probably have to relearn how to use his hand, maybe have limited movement in some or all of his fingers. He'd have to work back up to some things, but he could do just about everything he needed to do with his right hand.

"Helena," he whispered, knowing he didn't have much time. He felt himself fading. Just thinking about

Lindsay and about his recovery was taxing, and he knew he needed rest.

"I'll get her," a nurse said. "Hang in there, Dr. Blake. She'll be right in."

"We're going to go get something to eat," his father said. "Your sister will want to see you, but we'll try to hold her off until morning."

Joe barely had the strength to nod. His eyes were so heavy. His hand was beginning to throb, and he realized his head was splitting. He vaguely remembered thinking, at some point during the ordeal, that he had a concussion. "She… can… come in. Even if I'm…asleep."

He thought he heard them say goodbye and maybe an 'I love you' from them both. The darkness was returning, sucking him down…

"Joe," her voice pulled him back, and he easily opened his eyes, even offered her a smile.

Helena took his free hand in hers and squeezed it. "Oh, Joe. I was so worried."

He saw the tears and longed to reach up, to wipe them away, but even his good hand felt too heavy to lift, and her grip was comforting.

"I'm… here, Helena," he whispered. "Not going… anywhere…"

He heard her weeping but couldn't console her. How he ached to hold her, run his fingers through her curls, and spread kisses across her freckled face. The darkness was swallowing him again, but this time, a Cornish pixie took his hand, led him to a place of slumber, and cast a sleeping spell over him. It was the best sleep he'd had in weeks.

Epilogue

September 26

The sun was settling low over the mountains as the wedding party posed for pictures outside the rented barn on Davy and Betty Jean's farm. The bride and groom were the picture of happiness, but it was the maid of honor and a handsome groomsman who looked past the rest of the party, talking to each other with their eyes.

Helena couldn't remember the last time she'd been this happy. Had she ever been this happy? She bit her lip as the answer came to her in an instant. The evening Joe made her dinner and asked, *Is this love?* The night he snuck onto her back porch and took her in his arms. The day he came home from the hospital. All of those were truly happy moments, but this…this was the highest level of happiness she'd ever reached.

Her sister was married. Her father was home, not fully recovered, but home. Her mother was back in her garden and in her kitchen, doing the things she loved. Joe and Amanda, with the help of friends around the world, were working with the architect and builders to make the Jeremy Blake Medical Clinic the biggest, most advanced clinic in the Ozarks. And Helena was in love. One hundred percent, pie in the sky, happier than a pig in mud in love.

When the picture-taking ended, she stood in the grass, her bare feet cool against the blades—leave it to Andi to shock them all and tell the girls to remove their shoes for the last photo—and gazed at the man approaching her. With one hand, he reached around her back and pulled her to him. She responded, meeting his lips with hers.

"Time for the fun to begin," Joe said, his piercing blue eyes sparkling as he looked at her.

"Let's get this party started," she said, tossing her bridesmaid bouquet into the air and pulling him to her for a longer kiss.

***

They made their way toward the barn where champagne flowed, and music filled the air. Helena followed Joe straight to the dance floor. His left hand was in a sling, but his right hand fit perfectly into the small of her back, and he pulled her close to him. Her curls tickled his chin, and he inhaled the scents he'd come to know collectively as hers. The aroma of lavender in her hair mingled with her light rose-scented perfume and her honey-scented soap. He closed his eyes and swayed to the music.

When the song ended, he took her hand and walked her to the edge of the field. The stars were beginning to poke through the fabric of the sky, and a crescent moon hung above the Ozark peaks.

"A penny for your thoughts," Helena said, and he heard the smile in her voice before he even looked down at her face.

He extended his free hand and pointed to the sky. "See that moon, the way it's shaped, as if it's waiting for something to lasso it?"

"I see it," she said.

"I want to give you that moon."

"Joe Blake lassos moon," she said, paraphrasing George Bailey's promise to Mary Hatch.

Joe chuckled. "I mean it. Some people say they'd like to give someone everything on earth, but that's not enough for me. I want to give you all of that and more."

"You know, Joe, I have everything I need right here." She reached for his hand and turned him toward her.

As he gazed into her eyes, he had no doubts, no fears, no uncertainty or misgivings. Despite Helena's doubts, Joe's destructive choices, and Lindsay's mad tactics to thwart God's divine plan, his plan was, as always, perfect. Joe would never again try to circumvent the journey God laid in front of him, for it was along that strange and sometimes heart-breaking path that God led Joe to the woman in front of him with the bright blue eyes, sun-bleached hair, and smattering of freckles.

Helena Nelson was a magical creature, a fairy tale pixie come to life, and she had weaved a magical spell over him the first day he ever saw her. He wanted to spend the rest of his life following God's path, living and working in these mountains under that big white moon, and discovering all the magic that their future holds—together.

The End…

Until we return to Buffalo Springs in *Sapphires in Snow*, coming in 2023.

Read the story of the vineyard, Belle Uve, and all its secrets in *Whispering Vines*, and prepare to be entranced by its sequel, *The Good Wine*, available now.

Acknowledgements

When I was writing the book, *Desert Fire, Mountain Rain*, I envisioned not just a couple but a town, a town that had a life of its own and was destined to grow much larger than the confines of a page. In this town, I discovered people, not just Andi and Wade, but Helena and Joe, Jackson, Melanie, Dale, and countless others, all with stories to be told. I knew, without a doubt, that I had stumbled onto something I never thought I'd find – a series.

Throughout the time that I was writing *Under the Summer Moon*, the entire world was trapped in a surreal existence that reminded me of a snow globe. It was if we were confined to a small space with a small group of people and allowed to do only a small handful of things. Outside, fear, doubt, uncertainty, and misgivings swirled around like falling snow. Since I couldn't go outside to escape what was happening in the real world, I closed myself inside. Inside my house, inside my office, inside my mind, I found another world. It wasn't perfect. There was still fear and uncertainty, lack of trust and absence of faith. However, love and faith prevailed, as they always do.

I could not do what I do without the love, help, and support of my dear friends and loving family. Thank you, Tammi Warren, for igniting the inspiration for the town of Buffalo Springs. Thank you, Anne Novey, for spending so much time on this book with me, for being my beta reader, critic, editor, and friend.

Always there for me, always rooting for me, always ready to play a game or watch a movie when I need a break, always willing to order pizza on those days Mom has been too busy typing to think about dinner, and always happy to listen to my plots and characterizations, my husband and daughters keep me going. They, along with my parents, are my cheerleaders and coaches. They are, with my God and Savior, my inspiration and my foundation. Judy and Richard MacWilliams, Ken, Rebecca, Katie Ann, and Morgan, I love you all.

About the Author

Amy began writing as a child and never stopped. She wrote articles for magazines and newspapers before writing children's books and adult fiction. A graduate of the University of Maryland with a Master of Library and Information Science, Amy worked as a librarian for fifteen years and, in 2010, began writing full time.

Amy Schisler writes inspirational women's fiction for people of all ages. She has published two children's books and numerous novels, including the award-winning Picture Me, Whispering Vines, and the Chincoteague Island Trilogy. A former librarian, Amy enjoys a busy life on the Eastern Shore of Maryland.

The recipient of numerous national literary awards, including the Illumination Award, LYRA award, Independent Publisher Book Award, International Digital Award, and the Golden Quill Award as well as honors from the Catholic Press Association and the Eric Hoffer Book Award, Amy's writing has been hailed "a verbal masterpiece of art" (author Alexa Jacobs) and "Everything you want in a book" (Amazon reviewer). Amy's books are available internationally, wherever books are sold, in print and eBook formats.

Follow Amy at:
http://amyschislerauthor.com
http://facebook.com/amyschislerauthor
https://twitter.com/AmySchislerAuth
https://www.goodreads.com/amyschisler

Book Club Discussion Questions

1. Helena is a grown woman still living in her small hometown. She longs to see the world. Did you ever feel that way, or do you still? Where would you go if you could go anywhere in the world? Do you have advice for those who wish to explore?

2. Helena did go off on a grand adventure, and she went alone. Have you ever traveled alone? Did it change you? How? If you have never travelled alone, would you? Helena's experience changed her and made her love and accept herself more. How do you think you might benefit from a solo travel experience?

3. When Helena returns to Buffalo Springs, she hears about Joe's fiancé, sees him with Amanda, and automatically assumes the worst. She is quick to doubt Joe's feelings for her and believes only the bad things that she hears rather than looking for any signs that things are not what they seem. Are you quick to jump to the wrong conclusion or not believe the best about people? Do you think this is the norm for most people? How can we change our way of thinking to see the good in people rather than the bad? Should we?

4. Joe spent years trying to prove to everyone, especially himself, that he did not need or want love. Have you ever felt that way? Did you fight the natural tendency we

as humans have to love and be loved? Did love find you anyway?

5. Joe's friend, Darrin, encourages him to follow God's plan for him. Grace encouraged her daughter, Helena, to do the same. Have you ever thought about God's plan for your life? Have you and God been at crossed purposes at times? How was that situation resolved?

6. Joe returns to his faith when he moves to Buffalo Springs and decides to live a better life. At any point in your life did you fall away from your faith? Did you return? What prompted that return?

7. Amanda is surprised to learn that Joe accepts nonmonetary payment for his medical services. Have you ever encountered a medical practice that still does this? What are your thoughts or feelings about it? How would you suggest that the needs of the uninsured are met?

8. Often, those who attend church services will leave feeling that the priest or preacher was speaking directly to them personally. Joe and Helena both felt that way, and it led them to reconciling. Have you ever experienced this at church or in any other setting? Did it prompt you to do or change something in your life?

9. I hear so many adult women say that they don't feel a true kinship with the other women in their circle. Andi

and Helena are both blessed with being part of a tight-knit group of women who lift, encourage, and look out for one another. What can women do to lift each other up and support each other rather than tear each other down? Do you think that tendency in our world will ever change?

10. Helena finds herself dealing with a moral dilemma when she realizes that Lindsay may have checked out library books to learn how to hurt people. Should she have told Joe about Lindsay's library loans? Should she have gone further and told Dale? How do you think she should have handled this situation knowing that librarians are guardians of the privacy of their patrons?

Bonus: *Under the Summer Moon* is book two in the Buffalo Springs series. Book three will begin with Jackson's college graduation and return to Buffalo Springs where he will have several major life decisions to make. Who would you like to see featured as the next main character or characters in the series?

Lightning Source UK Ltd.
Milton Keynes UK
UKHW010053100122
396757UK00010B/252